MOONSTORM

MOONSTORM

BOOK ONE IN THE MOONSTORM TRILOGY

YOON HA LEE

DELACORTE PRESS

Text copyright © 2024 by Yoon Ha Lee
Jacket art copyright © 2024 by Priscilla Kim
Map illustration copyright © 2024 by Daniel-Andre Sorensen

All rights reserved. Published in the United States by Delacorte Press,
an imprint of Random House Children's Books,
a division of Penguin Random House LLC, New York.

Delacorte Press is a registered trademark and the colophon
is a trademark of Penguin Random House LLC.

Visit us on the Web! GetUnderlined.com

Educators and librarians, for a variety of teaching tools,
visit us at RHTeachersLibrarians.com

Library of Congress Cataloging-in-Publication Data is available upon request.
ISBN 978-0-593-48833-1 (hardcover)—ISBN 978-0-593-48834-8 (lib. bdg.)—
ISBN 978-0-593-48835-5 (ebook)—ISBN 978-0-593-80925-9 (int'l ed.)

The text of this book is set in 11-point font.
Editor: Hannah Hill
Cover Designer: Liz Dresner
Interior Designer: Jen Valero
Copy Editor: Colleen Fellingham
Managing Editor: Tamar Schwartz
Production Manager: Tim Terhune

Printed in the United States of America
10 9 8 7 6 5 4 3 2 1
First Edition

Dedicated to Helen Keeble, my favorite writer, friend extraordinaire. Thank you for showing me the BUTTER.

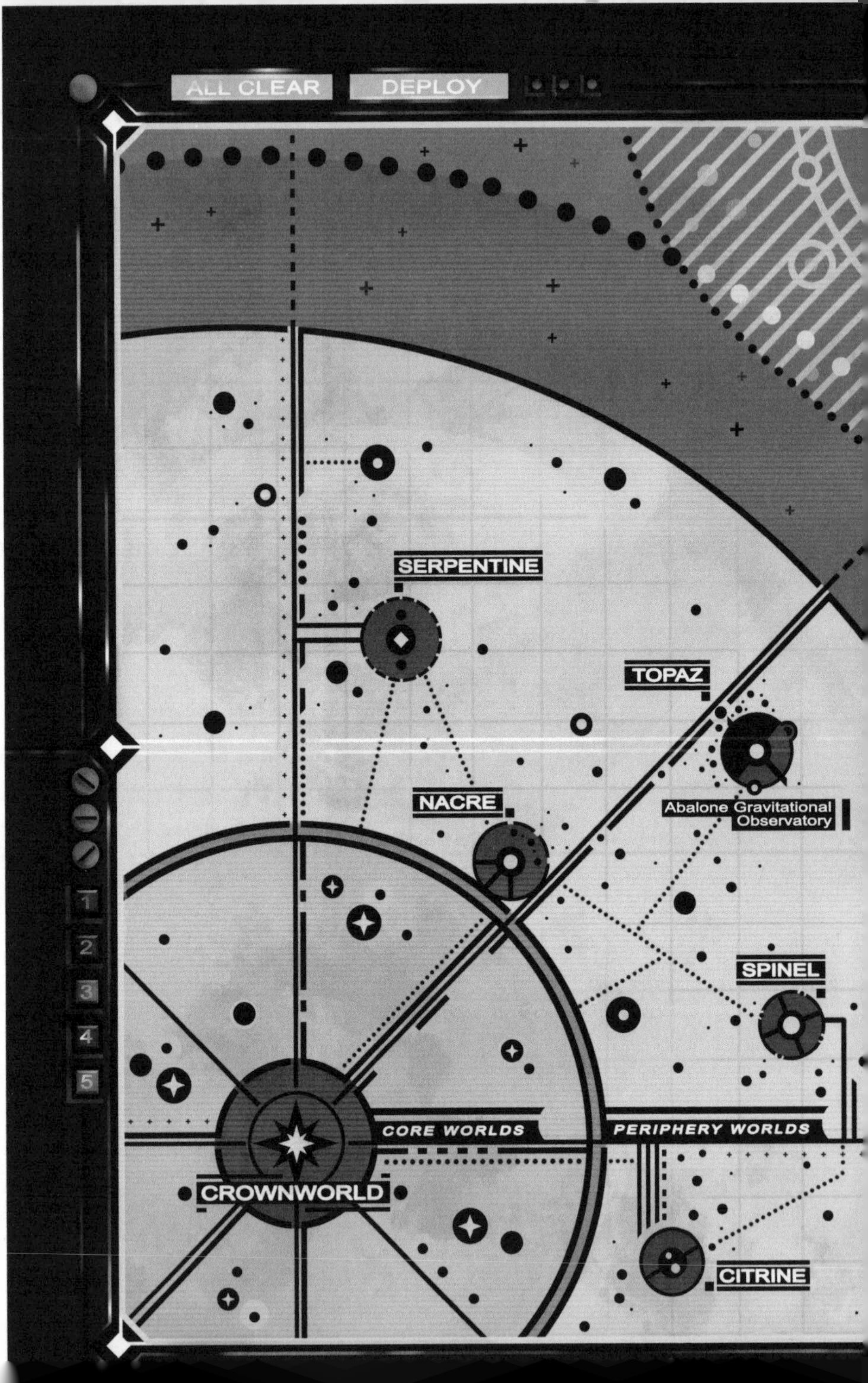
ALL CLEAR
DEPLOY
SERPENTINE
TOPAZ
Abalone Gravitational Observatory
NACRE
SPINEL
CORE WORLDS
PERIPHERY WORLDS
CROWNWORLD
CITRINE
1
2
3
4
5

THE MOONSTORM

CARNELIAN

THE EMPIRE OF NEW JOSEON

MOONSTORM

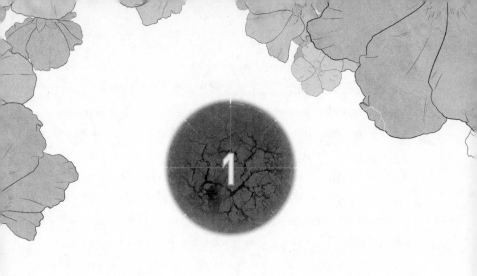

Hwa Young, then called Hwajin, was ten years old when her world, quite literally, fell apart.

It wasn't a world, technically, but a clanner moon called Carnelian for the red hue of its soil. Like all the moons and moonlets in the Moonstorm, it had an erratic orbit. Unfortunately, this month its path had taken it close to the border of the Empire of New Joseon, which left the adults of Hwajin's household arguing over whether they needed to evacuate and shelter from Imperial attackers.

Mother Aera glowered at Eldest Paik, who stood blocking the door. "You're wasting time," she said. "The sooner we get out of here, the safer we'll be. I was just on the comms with the lookout tower. The Imperials are sending a real fleet for once, not a detachment of raiders."

"It's just another false alarm," Eldest Paik said. Zie had unusual light eyes, almost amber, which shone against zir tawny

1

skin and black hair, shared by most clanners. The oldest of the household's five adults, Paik was adamantly against taking shelter. Zie sounded so reasonable that Hwajin almost believed zir, even if the other four adults and older children looked skeptical. "There hasn't been a full-scale assault since I was a little. The Imperials will harass us for a bit, then go away, like they always do when a moon swings too close to their territory."

Hwajin watched in silence, fidgeting with a toy she had outgrown half a year ago, a long stick carved to resemble a blaster rifle. She had begun practicing with the real thing when she turned ten. Unlike a kinetic rifle, which fired bullets instead of energy bursts, there was no recoil to worry about. All the clanners, including Carnelian's settlers, understood the importance of training young, training early, not only to hunt moon-rabbits for the stewpot but to defend themselves from bandits—or Imperial marauders.

The clanners and their intricate networks of families had settled the Moonstorm in centuries long past. Most of them were descended from explorers and adventurers, miners and scientists, who had preferred their freewheeling communities to the Empire's stricter, centralized rule. At first the Empire had left them alone. But that had changed before Hwajin was born, and so she had always known the Empire as a threat.

According to her family, the Imperials worshiped their Empress and carried out strange, twisted rituals—too strange and twisted to be described in detail to a ten-year-old, which of course made them much more interesting. The Imperials' rituals summoned gravity, just like theirs did, but their gravity and the clanners' couldn't coexist, like oil refusing to mix with water.

The Imperials had been fighting for generations to replace the clanners' rituals with their own, so they could take control of the entire Moonstorm.

Ordinarily, in a situation like this, Hwajin would have just accepted Eldest Paik's lead. But Hwajin was Mother Aera's heart-daughter—what the Imperials called a *clone,* as if the relationship could be reduced to mere genetics. When Hwajin grew up she would have the same angular face, the same long-lashed dark eyes, the same rangy hunter's build and reflexes. Hwajin couldn't help but feel closest to Mother Aera, and she hated disagreeing with her. The three other adults—bearlike Manshik, graceful Minu, Yura who cooked so well—were nice enough to her and her siblings and cousins. But Hwajin herself was Mother Aera's only heart-child, and she was quietly proud of the fact, even at a time like this.

Still, she wished the household's adults would come to a formal decision one way or another, signaling their vote on a course of action by displaying their knives: blade outward for yes, hilt outward for no.

"At least wait for the sirens," Eldest Paik added, a small concession.

"By the time we hear the sirens it'll be too late," Mother Aera shot back.

A headache pounded against Hwajin's temples, although she didn't dare interrupt to ask for willow tea. Ever since she was small, the adults had drilled into her the importance of united action. The clanners had a motto: *Do as others do. Stay where others are. Unity is survival.*

A queasy sensation began to spread through her stomach.

When she looked down at her feet, automatically seeking the reassurance that *down* was where it ought to be, the queasiness grew worse.

For a moment, as Eldest Paik and Mother Aera continued to argue, Hwajin felt like she was so light that she would float away and fly into the air. Out of habit, she put the toy rifle in her lap and grabbed the edges of her chair. That didn't help. The chair wobbled slightly as one of its legs, unbidden, rose a centimeter into the air. She bit back a yelp.

At first Hwajin thought the household's failure to unite had triggered a failure in local gravity. Surely one argument couldn't affect it this badly? Maybe the neighboring households were also arguing. That might cause it.

"Eldest," said Uncle Manshik, "we have to come to a consensus." He pointed at Hwajin's chair. "We're losing our gravity."

It wasn't the only object that was floating. Hwajin's toy rifle hovered in the air for a few seconds before touching down again. A cushion shifted; a table rose off the floor and rotated by a few degrees.

Hwajin slid off the chair and landed on the floor—which wasn't something she could take for granted anymore.

The settlement's horn went off, long loud blasts. As a small child, Hwajin had thought it sounded like a hunting horn. She'd enjoyed scampering amid the grasses and pretending she was a hunter, driving off the moon-beasts in search of her own prey. By the time one of her older siblings, Sejin, explained what the siren meant, Imperial raiders had wiped out an outpost on one of Carnelian's sister moons.

Hwajin loved her home. She loved the hilly region of Carnelian where they lived. She loved the starblooms that blanketed the hills' slopes, glimmering softly in the dark of night. She loved braiding garlands of the flowers to drape over their pillows so they could breathe the tickling-sweet fragrance as they slept.

She didn't want to leave the walls of rust-colored stone, the windows of rutilated quartz. She didn't want to wait in the boring shelter. While it had been three years since they had last been forced to take shelter, she remembered the stifling air, how uncomfortably she'd huddled with her siblings while playing card games. Sejin cheated, anyway, and bossy Najin sided with him when she complained.

In particular, she didn't want to come back to find the walls defaced, the doors smashed open, the starbloom garlands torn apart in a search for some treasure she didn't own.

"Time to decide," Mother Aera said. She produced her knife like a stab, blade out. "We're leaving."

One by one the other adults displayed their blades, everyone except Eldest Paik.

Hwajin was ashamed of Eldest Paik. Zie was outnumbered. The least zie could do was show zir knife, even if it had to be hilt first, and complete the ritual.

Without waiting for the stubborn Eldest, Mother Aera hefted the bag she'd prepared, which rested against the wall of the common room. One by one everyone picked up their bag. Everyone but Paik and the littlest one, the two-year-old who was too young for a name. Hwajin winced as the straps dug into her shoulders, but she was selfishly glad Mother Aera had prevailed.

The sense of vertigo that had plagued Hwajin ebbed away. Maybe the ritual was good enough to fix things, despite Eldest Paik's stubbornness. Maybe she didn't have to worry about the gravity after all. They would be safe in the shelter, and after a bunch of boring card games they would come back home and everything would be all right.

Eldest Paik stood to the side, scowling. Hwajin had never noticed before how stooped zir shoulders were, how rheumy zir eyes, the strands of gray in zir black hair. She'd always thought of zir as being tall and unbowed, the bravest one. Surely zie would acknowledge the household's will, come along, and lend them zir wisdom.

Hwajin never found out whether Eldest Paik would have abandoned the family. Years later, she'd dream of Eldest Paik's furrowed brow, zir outstretched hand as zie reached toward them—

To stop them? To join them?

She would always wonder.

The attack came all at once, while Aunt Yura stood in the doorway, struggling to get her bag clear. Except Aunt Yura wasn't there anymore. The last impression of her that Hwajin received was her long hair curling outward in all directions.

The downward hand of gravity had vanished.

Hwajin heard shrieks. One of them was her own. For several moments, she saw the world as through a kaleidoscope. Fissures opened in the house's floor, walls, windows. A lamp with an expensive paper shade exploded into a fine mist of light and sparks.

From the time she could understand words, before she could speak, Hwajin had been drilled in what to do in case of gravity failure. But the drills only accounted for minor failures. What use was it to grasp for hand- and footholds if the walls had shuddered apart? When her whole family had been pulled away from her?

She reached out for the flailing hands of her brother, Sejin, who had been standing behind her as they grabbed their bags. At a time like this it didn't matter if he was the one who made fun of the way she braided her long hair—she needed her brother, needed the solid comfort of his grasp. But as she tried to clutch him, a chunk of wall crashed into her. It knocked her in a direction she didn't recognize as up, down, or sideways, anything but *away*. She stifled a scream as a bigger chunk smashed into Sejin. She didn't recognize him in the spray of blood and grotesque jigsaw of flesh and bone that was left.

"Sejin?" Hwajin whispered, eyes stinging from the particulates swirling chaotically around her, dust knocked loose when the house crumbled into dangerous hunks of rock. The nook by the window that she'd loved so much, the embroidered cushions, the scribbles she and Sejin had made on the wall to "decorate" it for Mother Aera's birthday—all gone.

Tears floated free, forming gleaming spheres in the reduced gravity. They mingled with the globules of her brother's blood. Bile choked her for a moment. She couldn't reconcile the butcher's meat and its stink with *her brother.*

Hwajin looked around wildly for Mother Aera. Surely she would know what to do? The suddenness of Hwajin's motion caused her to tumble in the near free fall, and her stomach lurched.

Just then, a knife floated by, its handle carved with the character for *heart*.

Mother Aera's knife.

Hwajin snatched it out of the air and jammed it into her belt, resisting the urge to burst into tears—knowing, in that moment, her heart-mother was gone, too. And she would never get a chance to say goodbye.

Hwajin was swimming in the air, could feel herself breathing too fast and too shallowly. Without gravity to maintain the atmosphere, the air and its life-giving oxygen were bleeding off, slowly replaced by the aether that permeated space. She could breathe aether for a time, but the delirium it caused would make it harder for her to survive.

The thought caused Hwajin to hyperventilate more, until a shard of quartz from a shattered window pierced her side.

Hwajin hissed in pain and looked around wildly for someone, anyone. She saw nothing but the ruins of the house, floating clumps of dirt already disintegrating into a haze of ruddy particles, bruised moonblossom petals. Maybe her family only existed now as ghosts in the halls of her memory.

Do as others do. Stay where others are. Unity is survival.

Then she spotted Uncle Manshik clinging to the remnants of a wall, which floated above the ground. His face was bleeding, and beyond him Hwajin saw unmoored stones, uprooted bushes, a terrifying storm of detritus that was sucking everything around it into its gaping maw. "Here!" he called. "Come to me!"

If she had obeyed the motto she'd chanted all her life, Hwajin would have died, too.

But she didn't. An instinct she could scarcely name told her that going to Uncle Manshik would get her killed—that he was too close to the storm, exactly where she didn't want to be.

"Uncle, look behind you!" she cried. But she didn't have time to wait; instead, she took advantage of a nearby chair, miraculously intact, and kicked off in the opposite direction, away from the miniature storm.

Moments afterward, she craned her head to find Uncle Manshik—but he was already gone, swallowed by the storm's chaotic, lethal swirl of debris and roaring winds. She choked back a sob, then cried out as more debris drove into her skin. As much as she wanted to collapse into a heap of grief and shock, she needed to find shelter. One-handed, she fumbled with her bag, which she'd cinched to her waist, something Mother Aera used to remind her to do. Tears started up again. Uselessly, she told them to stop. She could mourn later.

She reached in and grabbed the first thing she touched: spare boots, dyed a wretched yellow. What good were spare boots going to do her?

Hwajin twisted around, trying desperately to orient herself. The Moonstorm didn't have fixed constellations, although the Empire was supposed to, and all she saw as she gazed at the rapidly splintering space around her was a dim drift of stars that flowed slowly from one pattern to another.

There was one large chunk of moon floating some distance away, an amputated, reed-haired hill trailing broken roots. She set her sights on it, sucking in a breath that made the shard in her side throb fiercely. After choking down an involuntary sob, she pointed herself in the direction of the floating moon-island and threw her boots in the opposite direction.

Her stomach was still knotted up with nausea and tension. If she'd eaten anything recently, she would have thrown up. Instead, she dry-heaved as she floated toward the moon-island, a belated adrenaline reaction.

After her body had finished its inconvenient rebellion, Hwajin startled, realizing suddenly that she was off-course. Practicing aim was one thing when she did it as a game with her siblings and cousins, another in the midst of an attack. She scrabbled in the bag again for another projectile, found a canteen of water, put it back. Who knew when she'd see a source of water again?

There was the knife she'd snatched from the air and shoved in her belt. She couldn't give up the last memento she had of Mother Aera, even if she hadn't earned the right to an adult's voting knife.

She ended up grabbing a book that she'd packed to pass the time in the shelter. She knew from the texture of the cover and the heft of the book which one it was: a collection of fables about the heroes who'd fought the Imperials and driven them back from the border of the Moonstorm. Absurd as it was, she'd thrilled to the idea of clanners with their more primitive weapons prevailing against the Imperial armies, especially Imperial lancers.

But the stories of night-archers and aether-riders hacking up fleets of Imperial starships and their lancers seemed far away and childish now. Scowling, Hwajin flung the book from her as hard as she could. She hated herself for giving it up so readily, when paper was so scarce on Carnelian. Or, what remained of Carnelian, even if she could scarcely wrap her mind around the enormity of what was happening. She was shocked when tears flooded her eyes again. As she blinked them away, they drifted off like star-jewels of regret.

I don't care, Hwajin told herself fiercely. All that mattered was reaching the moon-island. She threw a second book. Kept herself from crying more.

At last, the island came within reach. Hwajin grabbed hold of the reeds on the second try, her hands clumsy and numb. The aether was already affecting her coordination. She prayed to the heart-lineages that the reeds wouldn't break off in her hands, and for once, her luck held. Slowly, carefully, she pulled herself to safety on the hill's slope.

"Safety" didn't last long. Hwajin was in the middle of pulling out the shard in her side—another thing she shouldn't have done, they told her later—when she heard a concussive not-sound, felt the heat of a shock wave crest over her. The island shuddered, and she flattened herself against its surface.

After the shock wave passed, Hwajin looked toward its source. It would have been more sensible to stay huddled so the Imperials wouldn't spot her—but she was delirious with fear and exhaustion, and curiosity overcame pragmatism.

In the luminous-dark swirls of aether, Hwajin saw a platoon of Imperial lancers for the first time. There were six of them, bipedal humanoid figures that were three stories tall, taller than any buildings the clanners had ever built. They resembled armored warriors from the days of Old Joseon, their cockpits glowing balefully like eyes from peaked helmets atop massive shoulders. Finely polished lamellae plates protected the torsos, and articulations around the all-important joints gave the lancers their mobility. Each lamella was engraved with Imperial symbols of courage and bold fortune. Two were orange and gold, two silver-blue, one green and gold, one a dazzling red and blue. Awestruck, Hwajin registered only that they wielded different weapons depending on their colors, from massive versions of the rifles she'd trained with to rocket launchers and even a bladed polearm that could have sliced a starship in two.

Hwajin stared, too entranced by their martial beauty to be properly terrified, even if they had destroyed her home. Her household had passed around stories about the lancers, some disparaging, some fearful. Nobody had mentioned the sheer imperious glory of their presence. A sick yearning started up in her heart.

I want to pilot one of those.

The lancers propelled themselves through the aether by means of levitator engines mounted on their backs, coming closer and closer to the moon-island where she was huddled. In response to some signal she couldn't hear, three of them fired cannon, rifle, missiles in unison at a target far in the distance—at other *clanners*, Hwajin reminded herself. She squinted against the assault of blue light, which blotted out the few nearby moons and their faint glow.

At first she thought they would pass her by. Then the lancer squad approached *her* island, and fear gripped her heart. She flattened herself against the ground again, hoping against hope that they wouldn't stomp on her.

The ground vibrated as one of the lancers landed next to her. After a moment, she peered out through her fingers. It was the red-and-blue one.

The cockpit's glow brightened as it opened and a radiant figure, also wearing red and blue, emerged. To her astonishment, the pilot was a person like herself, except an adult, and taller than any clanner she had met. She'd known intellectually that lancers had pilots, but she had vaguely expected them to be monstrously different from regular people, with antennae or goblin horns or lizard tongues.

Well—the pilot appeared mostly human. One of their eyes

glowed red, the other blue. Hwajin was convinced that she had fainted and passed into the realm of dream.

"Hey there," the pilot said, crouching so as not to tower over her. With exquisite gentleness, they brushed the dirt from Hwajin's hands and face, then produced a candy out of the air, like a magician's trick. "You don't have to be afraid. The Empress keeps all her children safe. You are one of her children now."

She's not my *Empress,* Hwajin almost said. Still, her mouth watered at the fruity smell of the candy. Suddenly she was ravenous, and it took all her self-control to keep from snatching the treat from the pilot.

The pilot grinned conspiratorially, which surprised her. Nothing Hwajin's family had told her about Imperials had suggested that they might be *likable.* "Not hungry? More for me, then."

Nettled, Hwajin sat up, grabbed the candy, and stuffed it into her mouth. The sweet-sour flavor of hawthorn berries exploded against her tongue.

The pilot held out their hand. "This place won't last much longer. Let's get you out of here." Indeed, dirt crumbled from the island, and clumps of reeds drifted off into the aether.

Hwajin wasn't looking at the pilot. Instead, she gazed up at the glowing cockpit, imagining herself inside one. She wanted her own lancer, wanted the beauty of their flight in formation, those coordinated strikes. Wanted to be the strong one, rather than the victim huddled in the reeds hoping for an unlikely rescue.

She would do anything for that kind of power.

2

Six years later

On the last day of the boarding school's military readiness class, Hwa Young of the Empire of New Joseon rose half an hour before reveille to clear her mind of nightmares. She did this every morning. If the other students found out that she dreamed about moons flying apart, especially her nemesis, Bae, they'd have questions she didn't dare answer.

Hwa Young sat cross-legged in the middle of her temporary bunk at the campgrounds outside the city where they trained most weekends. She was supposed to be sinking into her morning meditations right about now, but her mind was elsewhere—namely on what she was going to get her best friend, Geum, for New Year's.

The New Year's Festival, which celebrated the Empress's birthday, was only a couple months away. Everyone would grow a year older. Hwa Young, like her classmates—too much to call them *friends*, except for Geum—would turn sixteen. Almost old enough to fight as a soldier.

Two more years before she was old enough to apply to be a lancer pilot candidate.

Back on Carnelian, the clanners had counted age differently, by marking individuals' birthdays. Hwa Young still remembered her own birthday, on the twelfth of Mirrormonth by the clanners' calendar, although she knew better than to mention it. On her sixteenth birthday, she would have received her knife from the household elders, a ritual she would never undergo now—although she had her own memento, which would have to do.

Instead, in New Joseon, the day was given over to festivities honoring the antler-crowned Empress and her All-Wisdom. Households tuned into recitations of praise poetry and performances of song and dance reenacting how New Joseon's founder, the first of the Imperial line, had conquered what was now the crownworld and united the first noble houses, which became the trusted, prosperous core worlds. Hwa Young loved the dancers with their tassels and embroidered costumes, the upbeat music with electric zither and fast beats and catchy vocals, and tried not to feel like a traitor because of it. After all, New Joseon was her home now.

It was tradition to exchange gifts on New Year's, and Hwa Young and Geum had never missed a year of gift exchanges in their six years of friendship. As soon as they returned to Forsythia City, on the peripheral world of Serpentine, where their boarding school was located—where she, unlike her schoolmates who had families in the city, lived as a ward of the state—Hwa Young needed to do some last-minute shopping for Geum. With any luck, she might be able to snag one of the fancy starship models that Geum coveted if the vendors were still offering special deals.

With that decided, Hwa Young launched into her calming meditation, the one she had done every morning for the past six years. She closed her eyes and built up an image of herself sitting in the cockpit of a lancer, its control panels brightening at her touch. It would be white tinged with silver and blue, the wintry colors that were her favorites. She imagined herself perfectly cradled by its seat, her hands resting on the joysticks that gave her power to make it walk, or fly, or fire its weapons.

Hwa Young tilted her head back, lips curving upward as she envisioned herself in the heat of battle, with laser fire narrowly missing her as she dodged every shot, guiding her lancer toward the enemy. In these meditations, she always fought faceless enemies, usually starfighters that zipped and soared and blew up in satisfying explosions whenever she raked them with her lancer's weapons. Someday she'd be the Empire's best lancer pilot, unmatched in combat.

She had gotten only ten minutes into the visualization before she heard a shriek. The visualization evaporated. *Oh no,* she thought, *are we under attack?*

No one else in the class would have suspected such a thing. Violent crime was rare in New Joseon, even on the less wealthy periphery worlds like Serpentine. The Empress's space patrols kept bandits and raiders at bay. Still, Hwa Young hadn't survived this long without a healthy dose of caution.

Hwa Young grabbed the knife she kept under her pillow, the

sole reminder of her heart-mother and her former life as a clanner, then crept to the door of her room to listen.

"You know those are contraband! I'll have to confiscate them for your own good."

It was Bae. What did she mean, "contraband"? Hwa Young shoved the knife in a pocket, then sighed and opened the door, reassured it wasn't a *real* crisis. She poked her head out into the hallway that ran down the center of the barracks where they'd been staying and saw Bae standing not far away from her.

Bae was the tallest of all the girls, an infuriating half head taller than Hwa Young herself, with what the poets called a willow-tree figure. As if that weren't enough, she had classically beautiful features in a flawless oval face, porcelain-perfect skin, and large, dark eyes, the kind of elegance that highborn families like Bae's bred for. The first time Hwa Young had seen her, she'd wished that someone so perfect, with that natural air of command, could be her friend. She'd given up on *that* quickly enough. *And* Bae was first in every class—all but one.

The unfairness of Bae's gilded perfection struck Hwa Young all over again. Bae benefited from the finest tutors that money could buy, thanks to her family's wealth and connections. Hwa Young came in second every time, studying alone and working hard in her efforts to defeat Bae.

Now, however, something else caught Hwa Young's attention. Bae's hair, normally a riverfall of glossy black tresses, was shorn in a bob. She must have gotten one of the other girls to cut her hair. Hwa Young's hand went involuntarily to her own head, although her hair only went down to midback. Her heart sank.

"You can't just *take* them!" protested floppy-haired Seong Su. "That was two months of my allowance!"

Hwa Young's gaze moved down from Bae's face to her hands. Bae was holding a handful of cards. Hwa Young tried to get a closer look.

"What are *you* staring at?" Bae demanded, shifting her glare to Hwa Young. "You're not his supplier, are you?"

"Are playing cards forbidden now?" Hwa Young shot back.

Bae fanned out the cards toward her, close enough that Hwa Young could get a good look. They were holographic trading cards depicting the elite lancers of First Fleet, which guarded the crownworld where the Empress made her home. One showed the famous red-and-blue unit *Paradox,* piloted by Ga Ram, captain of the Royal Guard, one of the Empress's own children.

Hwa Young was transported back to the night when she'd lost her clanner family—and traded it for a new home. Captain Ga Ram and zir squad had found her cowering in the reeds. She'd expected them to shoot her. Instead, the captain zirself had descended from *Paradox* and raised her from the dirt, smoothed the grit from her hair and hands, offered her a sweet-tart hawthorn candy.

The Empress keeps all her children safe, zie said to her. *You are one of her children now.*

Hwa Young repeated that promise to herself every night, even now.

Bae was still talking to her, and Hwa Young wrenched her attention back to the present. "These cards contain classified information," Bae declared. "They were declared contraband."

If she said so, it must be true. Bae always knew about new

Imperial declarations before anyone else. Her mother, the advisor to the planetary governor, kept her informed.

"I'm going to have to turn them in to the instructor," Bae added.

Seong Su took the opportunity to sidle back to his room and shut the door. For her part, Hwa Young regretted her involvement. It was always a mistake to quarrel with Bae. Everyone, including the instructors, took her side. They were afraid of offending her powerful mother.

From her very first day at the boarding school, Hwa Young had made the mistake of challenging Bae's dominance, by showing her up on a math problem, of all things. Hwa Young had blurted out a correction when Bae had made a rare mistake answering the teacher. As if anyone but the teachers cared about the quadratic equation. Bae had had it in for her ever since.

"By the way, your hair is out of mode," Bae added with that haughty offhandedness that she had mastered. "You'd better cut it before people start asking questions."

Today? Hwa Young wanted to ask. She hated the prospect of cutting her hair. She'd resisted doing so during her six years as a ward of the state. Clanner women never cut their hair except in mourning, and she was loath to give up the tradition, or the way her long hair made her look increasingly like her deceased heart-mother, disloyal as the sentiment was. In the past she'd finessed the matter by pinning up her hair. But no one defied the crownworld's conventions, especially in matters of fashion. And Bae meant business if she'd cut her *own*.

By this time, Instructor Kim, who slept down the hall, had heard the racket and emerged from her own room. "Bae, Hwa

Young," she said, as stern as ever. "You shouldn't be quarreling in the hallway."

She'd cut her hair, too.

"Your hair, Hwa Young," the instructor added. "Since you're up early, you can take care of it."

Hwa Young swallowed her reflexive protest. A good Imperial citizen didn't contradict authority. She resisted the urge to look at her feet, as though her reluctance would cause her to float off the floor and reveal her rebellious streak. At school they always talked about how New Joseon's gravity depended on its citizens falling into line and adhering to the traditions and rituals of the Empire. This gravitational center formed the foundation of its large, densely populated worlds and the way they orbited stars in an orderly fashion, as opposed to the much smaller, meandering moons of the clanners.

Besides—the truth she clasped close to her heart—only the best Imperial citizens became lancer pilots.

"Yes, Instructor," Hwa Young murmured.

It was time to let go of her heritage. It didn't matter that clanner women wore their hair long, just as clanner men cut theirs short and the nonbinary eijen favored asymmetrical styles. She wasn't a clanner anymore. If it took cutting her hair to fit in and become a suitable pilot candidate, she would do it.

Hwa Young had given herself haircuts before, mostly to trim ragged ends, and knew from experience that the results were untidy. *Don't be stubborn*, she told herself. She needed help.

She didn't dare trust the other girls, who spent their time

kissing up to Bae. Bae's best friend, Ha Yoon, would undoubtedly agree to do it only to make the process as torturous as possible. She could ask a boy, but most of them resented her for outperforming them in combat readiness. In their previous training sessions, Hwa Young had risen to the top of their class, beating out the boys who prized their physical prowess—even beating out *Bae*, for once. Not that it would last once they returned to their regular boarding school classes.

That left her one friend, Geum. With a sigh, Hwa Young gathered up her courage and walked three doors down the left side of the hall to Geum's room. *It's just a haircut. No big deal.*

It didn't *feel* like it was no big deal. It felt as though she was about to amputate the biggest thing that made her different from the others with their wealthy families and tutors. Imperial girls usually kept their hair shoulder length. The school uniforms in Imperial blue were supposed to promote unity, and Empress forbid that the students be prevented from showing off their family's status by wearing fancy jewelry or clothes at the cutting edge of fashion at the after-school dances.

Steeling herself, Hwa Young knocked on Geum's door: three rapid taps followed by a pause, then three more. Not a particularly *secret* signal, but people generally didn't want to be mistaken for either of them, so it did the trick.

"One sec!" Geum's voice called out.

Hwa Young stifled another sigh. Geum was a great friend—her *only* friend—but zie had a lackadaisical sense of time. The longer she had to linger out here, the more likely it was that—

Sure enough, Ha Yoon strutted up to Hwa Young, who wanted to groan. Bae's best friend already had *her* hair shorn in the new style, plus two artful curls neatly framing her face.

"Behind the times again, I see," she said with mock concern, her gaze going pointedly to Hwa Young's hair.

Don't let her see that she's getting to you. Hwa Young shrugged as nonchalantly as she could manage, trying not to stare. Sometimes she wondered if Bae had chosen her second-in-command purely on the basis of her appearance. Ha Yoon was almost as pretty as Bae herself, and she had a fuller figure that she liked to show off anytime she wasn't in school uniform. Hwa Young hated to admit it, but short hair suited the other girl.

Ha Yoon tossed her head and smirked at Hwa Young. "I could do yours, if you like. Make you look good for a change." She mimed scissors with her right hand.

To Hwa Young's relief, Geum opened the door just then. "Sorry, am I interrupting something?" zie asked, arching an eyebrow.

Geum had the looks that could have gotten zir in with the cool kids, if zie had wanted to: skin that never suffered from acne, an elegant visage, hair that looked artfully mussed over zir large eyes. Zie also possessed the smarts to impress the teachers, especially in the science and technology classes. Instead, zie had given up a status of "lovable eccentric who likes to collect action figures and hack video games" in exchange for Hwa Young's friendship, which was of dubious value as far as the other students were concerned, and a reputation for being That Person who had the worst taste in relationships.

"Give it a thought," Ha Yoon urged, as though Geum weren't standing *right there.*

"Sorry," Hwa Young lied. She swept into Geum's room and firmly shut Ha Yoon out, wondering, as she always did, if Ha Yoon's offer was genuine after all. If deferring to Ha Yoon would help her get in with the good graces of Bae and the others . . . She banished the thought from her mind; they would never accept a lowly ward of the state.

"She hassling you again?" Geum asked.

Hwa Young shook her head. "Just the usual." She didn't want to admit how fragile she felt, even to her one friend. It would mean revealing too much.

"It's the haircut thing, isn't it?" Geum said, zir voice lowering sympathetically. "I just heard, like, ten minutes before you knocked."

Hwa Young forced herself to smile. "Yeah. If you could . . . ?" She waved a hand next to her head.

"Sure, sure. Let me find my clippers."

Geum had befriended Hwa Young on her first day at boarding school, during their lunch hour. Not knowing any better, Hwa Young had sat in the pleasant spot in the schoolyard beneath the maple tree that Bae and Ha Yoon had claimed as their own. The two girls had lost no time in making sure Hwa Young understood her mistake. Hwa Young still remembered how Bae towered over her even at ten years old, her face haughty and cold: *You don't even come from a good family. You'll never amount to anything.*

Hwa Young had shuffled off, crying because she couldn't make herself *stop,* only to find someone taking her hand: Geum. At that age, Geum had been short, with round cheeks. *You can sit with me,* zie said, loudly enough to be heard by the everyone in the schoolyard. Zie did the same every day thereafter.

Hwa Young had once asked Geum *why.* Why befriend the newcomer, instead of making nice with the queen of their class? Geum only dimpled and said, *My dads told me not to make friends with mean kids.* Which was something that only *another* wealthy, prestigious family, one that didn't have to fear the retribution of Bae's mom, could say. Sometimes Hwa Young wondered if Geum appreciated how lucky zie really was.

Lucky or not, Geum always had time for her . . . as long as zie wasn't hacking into video games so zie could cheat on the boss fights, or chatting with one of zir herd of cousins. Most important, zie had time for her *today*, when she needed this haircut.

To her horror, Hwa Young discovered that tears were trickling down her face—just as Geum returned with the clippers in hand.

If Geum had fussed or made a big deal of it, Hwa Young would have burst into tears in earnest. Instead, Geum pointed to the chair at zir desk, brisk and matter-of-fact. "Sit. I'll take care of it."

Hwa Young gulped and nodded, hating herself for revealing weakness, any weakness. *Why does this matter so much to me?* she asked herself. Mother Aera was long gone. New Joseon had taken her in and given her a new home, a new identity. She was Hwa Young, one of the Empress's children, citizen of New Joseon, future lancer pilot.

It was just *hair.*

I have to be as true as ice. Cold and perfect and flawless.

But she was a long way from that ideal, and she knew it.

The clippers buzzed against her head, so close to her scalp that Hwa Young had to keep herself from flinching. For a moment she almost mistook the strange new lightness of her head for a gravity fluctuation, a sign that her faith was wavering—but no. It was the more mundane fact that she no longer had hair all the way down to midback.

My heart is true, Hwa Young told herself, making herself believe it. Hair was a small sacrifice in exchange for fitting in, for keeping the playing field as level as possible with Bae. And soon enough she'd find a way to surpass Bae in all their classes together, and become one of the school's nominees for the lancer pilot candidacy program.

"Almost done," Geum said, still brisk. "A whole new you!"

Yes, Hwa Young thought, her tears now dry. *A whole new me.*

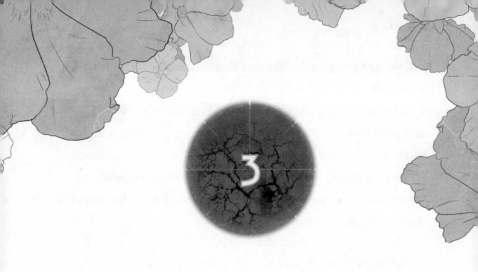

3

An hour later, her hair freshly cut, Hwa Young lifted her kinetic rifle to her shoulder at the outdoor firing range and peered through the sight at the target. She breathed calmly, in and out, knowing that she'd accounted for everything. Earlier this training session, she'd zeroed her rifle so its aim was true in local gravity on the world of Serpentine. The Empire claimed it had standardized gravity within its territory, but everyone knew that the values fluctuated from place to place, time to time.

Most of her classmates zeroed their rifles only when Instructor Kim reminded them. Hwa Young took the training more seriously because of her ambitions. The rest of them could coast on their family connections. She didn't have that option.

In a way, Hwa Young regretted that the readiness class, the one place where she was number one, would end today. She enjoyed being outdoors, learning how to distinguish poisonous mushrooms from safe ones, or the nighttime sessions when they navigated by the local constellations. Regular boarding school classes, on the other hand, promised the drudgery of memorizing poetry and mathematical formulas while being stuck inside.

"Fire on three," Instructor Kim said to the row of twelve students. All of them wore pale blue student uniforms consisting of crisp button-down shirts and slacks. The instructor herself stood out due to her black jacket. "One, two . . . three."

Hwa Young inhaled once and pulled the trigger at the top of her breath. She did it the same way every time, the best way to ensure consistent aim. The bullet flew true, leaving a neat black hole in the center of the target.

Instructor Kim walked from one end of the line to the other, critiquing as she went, as though the placement of the bullet holes weren't chastisement enough. Hwa Young was the only one who had hit the bull's-eye dead center, although Bae had come close. *One area where I can beat you,* Hwa Young thought.

The instructor paused next to Hwa Young and inspected her stance. "Acceptable." That was all she ever said to Hwa Young. At least it wasn't animosity. Some of the other instructors were openly hostile, assigning her to clean up the classroom after hours or run errands.

Everyone in the boarding school knew Hwa Young's status as a ward of the state. Hard not to, when she'd shown up in a shirt that had the orphanage's name embroidered on it. They might as well have branded her.

She'd worked hard to keep her identity as a former clanner a secret, at least. Thanks to the orphanage director's lax computer security and chaotic recordkeeping—a great way to line his pockets with extra money intended for the orphans—Hwa Young had foxed her own file to make it look like she came from an Imperial family near the border that had run afoul of raiders.

At least she'd had those months at the orphanage to learn Imperial customs and get used to her new name. *Hwa Young* meant "beautiful flower," although she knew herself to share Mother Aera's raptor features. She would never be a rival for Bae in *that* department.

A few of the others shot Hwa Young annoyed glances, while absent-minded Seong Su merely whistled and stared off into the violet-tinged sky. She told herself it wasn't important what the others did. They might consider the class a mere formality, but she knew better than most how much it mattered.

"Turn in your rifles at the depot," Instructor Kim said. "Hae Sun, watch where you're pointing that." She addressed the rest of her remarks to the whole class. "Remember, always treat your piece as if it's loaded. And march in cadence. It will be good practice."

Seong Su, who on top of everything had *terrible* muzzle discipline, nodded overemphatically. Hwa Young flinched when, for a moment, he had his muzzle pointed at his own chin.

The instructor noticed too. "It doesn't matter whether the safety is on or off," she said, unsmiling. "Never point your piece at anything you don't want to kill."

"Sorry, Instructor," Seong Su said, and this time managed to get it right.

The instructor oversaw their efforts to get into rhythm as they began marching, but there was only so much even she could do. Most of the students had dreams other than the military. Ha Yoon, for instance, spoke openly of hoping for a cushy posting with the planetary government one day, while Hae Sun planned on working at the Transportation Ministry like his father.

A career in the military promised Hwa Young a chance to win prestige on her own merits. It was a place where even the lowliest recruit could rise to glory. After all, the second-highest-ranking lancer pilot in the Empire, glamorous, amber-eyed Mi Cha, had come from humble origins. Her parent had been a sewage worker.

The military's legendary willingness to offer anyone a chance turned off Hwa Young's classmates . . . except Bae. Just her luck that her archrival, too, wanted to become a lancer pilot, and made no secret of it. Hwa Young was willing to do anything to come out ahead.

As they headed toward the depot, Hwa Young lost herself in the natural beauty that her classmates took for granted. The Empire's geomancers and gardeners had a tyrannical idea of what a standard Imperial planet should look like. The instructors were at pains to tell them that every world in New Joseon featured the same pine trees, the same mountains, the same raucous flocks of magpies and cranes. At least it was an *aesthetic* tyranny.

At this time of year, the forsythias for which the city was named were still bright yellow, with newly budding leaves. The magnolias bloomed white and succulent, and the winds out of the north brought with them the promise of a fragrant spring. Hwa Young thought of Carnelian and its carpets of starblooms, absent here. She sometimes caught herself doodling their five-petaled flowers in the margins of her notes, and always scribbled over them. After all, no one knew the secrets of her past, not even Geum.

Hwa Young turned in her rifle to the unsmiling clerk and joined the others on the way to the hover-shuttle that would convey them back to the city proper. She'd always found it amusing that New Joseon was so averse to admitting that its citizens might ever be in danger that even military training courses like this one took place at training grounds outside the city limits—out of sight, out of mind. But even as a ten-year-old, when she'd first been placed with the orphanage, Hwa Young had rapidly picked up on the fact that, at least on a periphery world that hadn't yet attained core world status, the Imperials weren't as united as they liked to boast. Citizens observed the daily prayers to the Empress and meditated on statuettes depicting her upon the Chrysanthemum Throne, and as a result, up stayed up and down stayed down. That didn't mean they never disagreed, or that political quarrels ceased to exist.

Bae had lingered at the depot so that Hwa Young had to pass her to get to the shuttle. She caught Hwa Young's eye, smiled too sweetly at her, and whispered, "*Acceptable.* You're catching up!"

Hwa Young stiffened. No matter how many times she hardened herself against the insults, they pierced her every time. She looked straight ahead, pretending she hadn't heard. Pretending the coolness of the air on the back of her neck, formerly covered by the long hair she'd clung to for so long, didn't sting so badly.

Still, heat rushed to her face. From behind her, she heard Bae's sniff. Hwa Young knew she wasn't fooling anyone, however much she wished she had a visage like ice, cold and impenetrable.

During her first days on Serpentine, at the orphanage, she'd gotten into trouble by flying into rages and fighting with the other children. The orphanage's director had lectured her on thinking before she acted. Telling her that she needed to fit in, even if the others didn't accept her as one of them.

Eventually the message got through. Hwa Young learned to suppress her anger, transforming it into determination. She prayed to the Empress for guidance, and guidance came. *Remember the lancers,* she thought every night, visualizing her idol Mi Cha and her green-and-gold lancer *Summer Thorn. I will be a lancer pilot.* She was one of the Empress's children—not literally, but in the way that every citizen was—and deserved the Empress's protection.

If she proved herself, the Empress would reward her hard work. She was counting on it.

Hwa Young shook off her thoughts and clambered into the shuttle. Geum had saved a seat for her. Zir elegant face was framed by careful asymmetric curls today. "Hey," zie said, smiling. "You did great."

Hwa Young flushed guiltily. She hadn't been paying attention to Geum's performance because she'd been fixated on Bae. "Thanks," she said. "Did you hit the target?"

"Two rings out," Geum admitted. "I never get any closer. Up, down, sideways—anywhere but the bull's-eye."

"Try to pull the trigger either at the top or bottom of your breath. Pick one and stick to it. Doing it differently each time is why your aim is inconsistent."

"There goes Hwa Young again," Bae remarked from the back of the shuttle. "Can't even stop criticizing her only friend."

Hwa Young flushed again. "I didn't mean it like—"

Geum patted her hand. "It's all right." Still, zie didn't look directly at her—a sign zir feelings were hurt.

Hwa Young swallowed and squeezed Geum's hand back. "I'm sorry," she murmured. One of these days she'd learn to hold her tongue.

The instructor powered up the shuttle. Its blank gray control surface lit up as it connected to her neural implant. Everyone in New Joseon was fitted with one when they turned fourteen. The shuttle's controls morphed into an interface customized to the instructor's preferences, white rectangular panels and buttons with all the personality of a shipping crate.

The hour-long ride back to the city always felt as though it dragged on much longer. Hwa Young dreaded going back to the boarding school's campus as much as she enjoyed the weekend excursions—and the chance to defeat Bae.

Hwa Young had tuned out the gossip of Bae and her cronies, which concerned the latest gifts—bribes, really—Bae's mom had sent to the crownworld. Instead, Hwa Young racked her brain for the best places to sniff out a New Year's gift for Geum. She looked over at Geum, who had pulled out zir phone and was, to all appearances, in the process of hacking into Ha Yoon's phone to draw fox ears on her user portrait.

Suddenly, Geum dropped the phone in zir lap and grabbed Hwa Young's arm, fingers gouging her painfully. Zie was staring out the front window.

Hwa Young hissed in pain, then said, "What—"

"They wouldn't start New Year's fireworks a couple months early, would they?" Geum asked in a voice that trembled slightly.

Hwa Young's gaze was dragged upward toward the red flash

that effloresced across the horizon, the red stars that sped toward Forsythia City's protective dome. Her heart jackhammered.

Missiles.

The shuttle screeched to a halt, jolting its passengers. The seatbelt dug into Hwa Young's shoulder. Bae let out an undignified squawk.

"Quiet," Instructor Kim barked from the driver's seat, the first time she'd spoken since the drive began. A tinny voice crackled from the comm unit, only to dissolve into static.

Hwa Young tried, and failed, to suppress a flare of alarm. Maybe she was wrong; maybe someone had just messed up the fireworks, though it didn't make any sense. But Hwa Young knew what missiles looked like, could recall the signs of attack from that day six years ago.

Surely not on Serpentine, which had known peace during the six years she'd lived here.

Maybe it's a drill?

But what kind of drill would knock out communications as well?

Moments later, they heard the boom, felt it through the shuttle's walls and floor. Geum's grip on her arm tightened. At this rate Hwa Young was going to lose circulation in that arm. A petty concern when something much bigger was happening.

We're under attack. We're really under attack.

Violet-blue afterimages from the red falling stars—*missiles*—flared before her eyes. Only practice from a childhood she'd left behind kept her taking deep, steady breaths, rather than hyperventilating in panic. As much as she disliked most of her twelve classmates, she was suddenly glad to be with them, rather than facing this alone.

"The city," Bae said, small and stunned, in the brief stillness that followed. "What if my family . . ."

It was the first indication Hwa Young had ever gotten that Bae cared about anything but being number one.

Hwa Young flashed back to the day when she'd lost her own family, felt the weight of Mother Aera's knife. She didn't want that for anyone else, not even Bae. "Your folks will be fine," she said quietly.

Bae shot Hwa Young a startled glance. Ha Yoon had her arm around Bae's shoulders and was saying something in a comforting undertone. For once Ha Yoon's expression was gentle instead of snotty.

They'll take care of each other. Hwa Young wondered why she had bothered to say anything. A cold snake of dread coiled around her heart.

She didn't have parents to worry about, not anymore, but what about Geum's family, who had shown her such kindness? Geum brought her home with zir on holidays. Zir fathers always asked about her favorite foods and made sure to include them at the family table. One of Geum's little cousins gave her a lucky coin pendant, which she still had. And the care packages the family sent included sesame cookies for her, because they knew she loved them. *They have to be safe,* she told herself. *The Empress will keep them safe.*

But here, on a planet far from the crownworld, the words felt hollow.

Hwa Young had memorized the location of every one of Forsythia City's bomb shelters, a precaution that even Geum had teased her about. The memory of Carnelian's destruction drove her to prepare like this, although even she had thought it was unlikely that the knowledge would ever come in useful. She would have preferred to have memorized useless trivia than to live through another bombardment. But it didn't matter anyway; Hwa Young didn't know where to find shelter outside the city.

Another shock wave caused the shuttle to tremble. Instructor Kim hit the brakes hard, then U-turned the vehicle, which emitted a high-pitched shriek.

"What are you doing?" Ha Yoon asked in a shrill voice. The other students were white-faced, unable even to speak.

"New plan," the instructor said crisply. "We're getting to shelter. Anyone who didn't buckle up earlier, now's the time."

Bae cried, "But the city's the other way!" She pressed her hands to the window as if she could drag the receding city back into reach.

"Exactly," the instructor snapped. "And the city's under attack. Now quiet."

Bae spat a curse, her face twisting in mixed fury and despair.

Similar emotions churned in Hwa Young's gut. But she knew the credo. On Carnelian it had been *Do as others do. Stay where others are. Unity is survival.* New Joseon used different words: *Trust the Empress. Move at her will. Act as her hands.* Still, the intent was similar.

A hush fell over the group at first. Then one of the boys started sniffling, and set off his seatmate. Their sobs were unnaturally loud in the confined space of the shuttle. One kid recited the Imperial credo under zir breath in a rapid, pinched monotone. Hwa Young shut the noise out. It wasn't as if they'd accept comfort from her, anyway.

"Clanners," Geum muttered. "It's got to be clanners."

Hwa Young flinched, and hoped zie misread the reason for her reaction. "What makes you say that?"

Geum looked at her strangely. "Who else could it be?" Reluctantly, zie added, "I guess it could be bandits, but what kind of bandits would be that well-organized?"

Empress, please let it be bandits, Hwa Young thought. She didn't want the ugly ghosts of her past to rear up in real life.

Instructor Kim paid no attention to the students as she drove off the road, headed for—where? Hwa Young knew better than to voice her misgivings. The shuttle's levitators operated best over level ground or slight inclines, not heavy terrain. Still, what choice did they have? They could hide from the attackers more readily away from civilization.

The others already had their phones out. Geum had retrieved zirs. Hwa Young didn't have anyone to check in with, so she peered at Geum's.

Zie messaged zir fathers: *Saw the attack. Are you okay?*

NO CONNECTION, zir phone said.

Geum squeezed zir eyes shut. "This can't be happening this can't be happening this can't be happening."

I have to be the calm one, Hwa Young thought, because if she fell apart, Geum would *really* lose it, and then where would they be?

"I bet the attackers knocked out the communication towers and satellites first thing," she said, her voice trembling even though she willed it to be steady. "That would explain why the instructor hasn't been able to contact anyone, either. I bet your dads are fine."

Still, Geum continued jabbing at zir phone as if zie could make the *NO CONNECTION* message go away by sheer force of will. Luckily, Hwa Young had downloaded a local map on her phone, just in case, which she pulled up now. She had never forgotten the terror of drifting in the starry aether, not knowing where she was in a world fallen to kaleidoscope pieces.

The shuttle accelerated suddenly, smashing Hwa Young back against her seat. She looked up from her phone and out the window, trying to get her bearings. They were in the hills well outside the city. Early spring blossoms freckled the tall grasses; leaves swirled in the shuttle's wake. In the distance, Hwa Young saw the rising mountains and their dark cloak of pine trees— sacred grounds that were sculpted and maintained to bring prosperity and good fortune to the city in the south.

Hwa Young raised her voice: "Instructor! We can't go there. They'll bomb geomantic sites next." Any attackers would know they could gain an advantage by disrupting the flow of good fortune, with consequences like vehicles breaking down unexpectedly or missed communications.

"That's already understood," Instructor Kim said, her voice revealing no more emotion than ever. Hwa Young glimpsed the side of her face like a crescent moon, blade-keen and dangerous. "There's a bunker—"

"Watch out!" Geum shouted.

A deer bounded out from the grasses. It was a massive buck with antlers worthy of any crown. Hwa Young would have sworn it came out of nowhere. It careened into the side of the shuttle, then fell, bellowing.

In the city or on a road, this would have been survivable.

But the shuttle hadn't been designed for off-road travel, and they had reached rockier ground. The shuttle jolted against an outcropping and flipped.

Hwa Young's stomach churned, as the shuttle landed upside down with a heart-stopping thump. The impact reverberated through the vehicle, vibrating through her teeth. The seat harness dug punishingly into her shoulder and torso.

Several people screamed. Geum's fingernails were going to leave permanent bruises in Hwa Young's arm.

Hwa Young blinked, dizzy from the rush of blood to her head, the coppery taste in her mouth. What now?

A student in the front gasped. It was Dong Hyun, the one who'd started sobbing earlier. "The instructor," he said shakily. "Is she—is she okay?"

Hwa Young refocused on the front seat.

Instructor Kim did not remotely look okay. Blood dripped from a cut in her scalp. Her head hung from her neck at an angle that made Hwa Young's stomach roil. Worst of all, her seat belt dangled uselessly: a safety failure at the worst possible time.

"Check the instructor's pulse," Hwa Young said, although she knew. She knew.

Dong Hyun gaped. "What—?" The word was swallowed by his useless snuffling.

The first priority was to see if there was any hope of saving the instructor. *The Empress wants us to respect authority.* Hard to do that if the authority figure was dead. Then they needed to make sure all the students were okay.

Someone had to take charge—especially if the instructor was dead—and that was going to be her, apparently, because everyone else was too frozen with shock to *do* anything useful.

Before Geum could protest, Hwa Young braced herself against the shuttle's side and unbuckled herself. She landed in an ungainly heap, but managed to untangle her limbs and scramble right side up. Then she shoved past Geum and Dong Hyun to press her fingers against Instructor Kim's neck, silently apologizing for the liberty.

Empress, please—

No such luck. "No pulse," Hwa Young said flatly.

Someone shrieked. After a moment's shocked silence, the other students began to babble in panic.

"What now?" Bae asked, raising her voice.

On any other day, Hwa Young would have shot back a chilly retort. Today, their rivalry seemed petty and far away. "We have to right the shuttle and get to that bunker. First that means we need to exit the shuttle, and then one of us will need to drive."

"I can drive," Bae said. "But it's not like either of us knows where the bunker is."

Hwa Young tapped her phone and checked the map for directions. But the bunker wasn't on it. She kicked herself inwardly for downloading a map available to the general public, which was apparently missing some details.

Feeling like a ghoul, Hwa Young leaned over Instructor Kim's body. The shuttle's navigation system had reverted back to its dull, featureless gray when the instructor died and the connection to her neural implant snapped. "Nav might still be working. You'll have to connect to it to find out. I'll take shotgun and keep an eye out for any more deer." She didn't mention that deer weren't the only creatures who lived out here.

"Everyone okay?" Hwa Young called out. "Roll call."

One by one, everyone called out their names, even Bae, in the accustomed order. The classroom ritual seemed to steady the others, despite the fact that they were still upside down, buckled into a vehicle that had turned turtle.

"Out," Hwa Young said. For a moment she wasn't sure they would listen to her.

Bae glanced at her, then nodded. "Do what she says."

The students clumsily piled out of the shuttle, yelping as people elbowed or kicked one another in their haste to get out.

The deer was still thrashing beneath the vehicle by the time everyone had emerged. It seemed to have broken a leg. "Stay clear," Bae said, high and sharp. "One kick and it'll shatter your skull."

The vehicle was light for its size, but it took their combined strength to push it away from the deer, even with the aid of levitators in emergency mode, then roll it right side up. The deer screamed in panic, attempting futilely to stand up and bolt.

Thankfully, two of the students—Seong Su and Min Kyung—were large and strong, even if Hwa Young had to glare at Seong Su to keep him from cracking inappropriate jokes about roadkill.

"Where . . . what do we do with the instructor?" Geum asked. Zie opened the door and swept zir fingers over her face to close her staring eyes.

In normal times, there would be special rites, and the body would be given some dignity. There was no time for either. Hwa Young peered back the way they'd come. While the city was no longer visible, red light glowed from the horizon. Fire, or things worse than fire.

First things first. Hwa Young muttered an apology once more as she relieved the instructor of her sidearm, a pistol.

"Seong Su, Min Kyung, move the body into the trunk," Hwa Young said. She stood looking at the deer, wishing there were some way to save it. While she'd hunted small game back on Carnelian, she had made sure none of her prey suffered more than necessary.

"What are you going to do?" Geum asked.

"The necessary thing." Hwa Young approached the deer as closely as she dared, then thumbed off the safety and fired.

None of us asked for this, she thought, unsure whether she was addressing herself, the other students, the deer, or the luckless Instructor Kim.

After Seong Su and Min Kyung relocated the instructor's body, the students reentered the shuttle one by one. Bae took the driver's seat without flinching from the splash of blood. Hwa Young claimed shotgun next to her, determined that they wouldn't have a second accident. She didn't trust Bae, but she didn't wish the other girl dead, either.

Hwa Young glanced back at the horizon. The red glow had brightened. That couldn't be good news.

Bae started the shuttle. The interface flowered awake for her, the buttons and display panels decorated with subtle filigree and barbs. There was a sharp beauty to it that fit Bae's personality perfectly.

Bae drove more slowly than the instructor had. Hwa Young scanned the rocky landscape and its shrubbery, looking for more hazards. She could hear Instructor Kim's body thumping in the back as it rolled or slid each time Bae made a course correction, and Hwa Young had to suppress a shudder.

Her heartbeat had slowed down for the first time since the attack began when a shadow engulfed the shuttle, too big, too sudden, to be a cloud crossing the sun. Beside her, Bae cursed violently.

Hwa Young's breath seized in her throat.

Someone had found them.

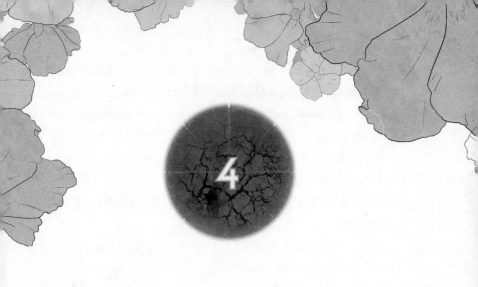

4

"**G**et us to cover," Hwa Young said to Bae. She could see the shadow's source now, an aircraft or starship. Its long, triangular silhouette, spiky rather than smoothly curved, told her it wasn't Imperial.

Bae laughed harshly. "What cover? If we drive into the trees at this speed, we're going to crash into something."

She wasn't wrong—the edge of the forest rapidly gave way to dense stands of pine—but Hwa Young didn't want to give up that easily. "If we're beneath the trees, that aircraft won't spot us. We need to detour through the edge of the woods until we reach the bunker."

Bae sneered at Hwa Young but did as she asked. "If we die out here," she said as she steered the shuttle toward the fringe of woods, "my ghost will bring bad luck to all your descendants."

Hwa Young wondered if the shadow above them would grow and grow until it swallowed the world. More likely Bae would lose control of the vehicle, just as Instructor Kim had, and they'd smash into a tree. The trees out here weren't young, either. With trunks that thick and sturdy, the shuttle would lose in any collision.

The drive devolved into a tense quiet, interrupted by the occasional moan, gasp, or sob. For all her griping, Bae was a competent driver, with good reflexes. Hwa Young had to admire her sangfroid.

With the canopy overhead, Hwa Young could no longer tell whether the aircraft was tracking them. She hoped not. She heard hysterical laughter from the back, then recognized the voice of Ha Yoon as she calmed the panicking student.

"Here we are," Bae said.

Hwa Young spotted the bunker through the trees, a gray, ugly concrete block unlike the more graceful buildings she was used to in the city with their peaked roofs and painted roof tiles. "That looks like a good spot," Hwa Young said, pointing out the lee of a great boulder at the edge of the wood. The boulder would conceal the vehicle from any observers in the bunker, just in case. "We just might fit."

"Good luck ever backing out of that parking job," Bae muttered.

"Please, Bae," Hwa Young said, even though it galled her to defer to Bae and her superior status. "If anyone could do it, you could."

"Fine." Bae decelerated smoothly and parked, only jolting the shuttle's passengers once when it scraped against the side of the boulder. Bae left it in standby mode rather than powering down. It was a smart idea, Hwa Young admitted to herself.

"Will the soldiers in the bunker let us in?" Geum asked.

Say one thing about the Empress's edicts: everyone knew that soldiers were stationed at the bunkers set at strategic intervals throughout the periphery worlds despite the fact that no one had expected an attack. Hwa Young wondered if the guards were prepared for the emergency that had overtaken them, or if the cushy posting had made them soft.

Geum sounded rattled, and Hwa Young couldn't blame zir. She wished she could squeeze zir hand comfortingly. Instead, she twisted around in her seat to smile at zir, doing her best to project calm.

But Ha Yoon wasn't having any of it. "What if they tracked us?" she asked in a quavering voice. "We should scatter."

Don't infect the others with your fear, Hwa Young thought, annoyed with the other girl.

"We have to stick together," Bae said imperiously. "Everyone, say the words with me."

Reluctantly, they all recited the credo: *"Trust the Empress. Move at her will. Act as her hands."* They repeated it until they achieved something resembling unison and Bae nodded in satisfaction.

"I don't see why you're listening to *her,*" Ha Yoon said sulkily, jerking her chin toward Hwa Young.

Hwa Young choked down a laugh. She didn't like deferring to Bae of all people, but if that was what it took to get this group pointed in the right direction . . .

"Wait," Hwa Young said. As she'd glanced toward the building, she thought she'd spotted something, an anomaly in front of the shelter. "We can't leave the shuttle yet."

Now that she was studying the ground, not the structure, the details came clear. Two sprawling bodies in front of the door. She didn't think they were taking a nap.

The attackers had gotten here first.

"What's the issue?" Bae demanded. Then: "Oh."

"Maybe they're taking a break," Seong Su chimed in, although he didn't sound convinced. "Or they're . . . oh."

Up until this point, Hwa Young hadn't permitted herself to think about what it meant that they were under attack—probably by clanners. The people she'd once belonged to. That she came from the *other side*.

The bodies made it all too real. If the clanners came across her now, they'd only see another Imperial girl. An enemy. They wouldn't hesitate to shoot her, just like they'd shot the guards. She of all people knew how much clanners hated and distrusted Imperials—and she'd made her choice to embrace New Joseon six long years ago.

The Empress keeps all her children safe, Hwa Young chanted to herself, just as the captain of the Guard had promised her all those years ago . . . but the Empress was on another world far away.

They were on their own.

"Do you have any ideas?" Hwa Young asked Bae, who stiffened. Hwa Young hadn't meant to sound so challenging. The words had come out that way out of sheer habit.

But Bae only said, "We need to keep an eye out in case anyone approaches us. Be ready to resist."

"We shouldn't have turned in those rifles," Geum muttered.

Yeah, because that would have been great, Hwa Young thought sarcastically, although she didn't say it out loud. She didn't want to hurt Geum's feelings. But if they still had guns, they'd probably have lost half the class to friendly fire, or rifles going off and bullets ricocheting within the shuttle's confines.

Another boom juddered through the woods. The trees shivered; leaves and pine needles rained down, pattering against the shuttle's roof. The sky flushed red-orange, backlighting the bunker. An explosion. Under other circumstances, Hwa Young would have admired its beauty. Now, all she could think was *If they come back and find us, we're doomed.*

At least she'd claimed the instructor's pistol, although she'd already used one bullet. She'd make the other five count, if it came to that.

Yet another boom. This one was louder. Closer. Brighter.

Hwa Young had an unwelcome vision of the woods roaring with flame, with themselves trapped in the inferno. Helpless.

But they weren't weaponless, even if a mere handgun wouldn't dent an attacking vehicle. They had another resource—their shuttle. The question was, could they use what they had without getting killed in the process?

While Hwa Young's mind raced through the possibilities, Geum said, "We better turn our phones off. Power down the nav system, too."

"Why?" Hwa Young asked.

"I don't know what's going on out there," Geum said in a tight, unhappy whisper, "but think about it. Our transmissions are encrypted, but even if the enemy can't figure out *what* we're saying, they can probably track us. They may have killed whoever was guarding that bunker, but they might think we're reinforcements and backtrack to clean up."

"We have to abandon the shuttle," Bae concluded. "Everyone,

turn off your phones." Only now did the other students obey, since Bae had given the order. "Otherwise the next missile or whatever it is will blow us up."

"I was playing a game," Seong Su complained.

Bae gave him the evil eye. "Do it."

He sighed dramatically and flicked the power off.

"If we troop into the woods without supplies, we're going to get lost and die," Seong Su added dryly.

Are you trying to make everyone give up? Hwa Young thought, resisting the urge to clench her hands in frustration. Pointing it out would only make matters worse. "I have a plan," she said. "Our biggest asset is the shuttle. I'm guessing the raiders are attacking high-priority targets first. It's what I would do. Sooner or later they're going to wonder what we're doing out here, and they'll come after us."

Bae slitted her eyes at Hwa Young. "I'm listening," she said unpromisingly.

Hwa Young needed them to understand her idea. How could she best get it across? "What is a bullet?"

"You're the only one with a gun," Geum remarked. "I don't think that's going to dent a starship."

"No, think about it," Hwa Young said, frustrated at the bewildered looks on the others' faces . . . frustrated with herself for struggling to find a good explanation. She hesitated, then blurted out, "There's nothing magic about a bullet. It's just a projectile mass with some gunpowder to speed it toward its target. We have a projectile mass. A big one. It isn't powered by explosives, but it *will* go fast, and if we disable the safety protocols, we can program it to go anywhere we want."

"The shuttle," Geum breathed.

Bae was nodding, however reluctantly.

"We cannibalize the shuttle for anything we can, since it's not safe to approach the bunker," Hwa Young went on. "There should be a first aid kit in there. Maybe emergency supplies." Which probably had Instructor Kim's blood all over them, but she could have hysterics over that when they were no longer in a crisis. "Then we program it to speed right toward our attackers and crash into them."

"It's just one shuttle," Bae said. Her sneer had returned. "Besides, how are you going to aim it? It's not a rifle, in case you haven't noticed."

"I can get it to do that," Geum interrupted. "Normally the collision detection system makes it *avoid* crashing into other vehicles. If I set it to do the opposite . . ."

After a considering pause, Bae sighed. "Okay, I'm in. While the shuttle does its thing, we can hike away to safety. We'll be harder to spot farther into the forest."

Everyone here had known Bae since childhood, and they were used to seeking her approval. *Someday I'll be the one in charge,* Hwa Young thought resentfully. But today wasn't that day.

"One thing," Geum said. "I'll have to turn the shuttle on fully. That means the enemy will be able to track the power signature, if they're paying attention."

"Do it," Hwa Young said, "and be fast."

Geum nodded without waiting for Bae's approval and got to work.

"Everyone else get out," Bae said. Her mouth twisted. "We should remove the instructor's body from the trunk."

Shame flooded through Hwa Young. She'd been thinking of the instructor's corpse as an inconvenience, as though the woman had ceased to be a person because she'd died. Never mind that Hwa Young endeavored to think about her clanner family, all dead, as little as possible.

"Seong Su, help me with the body," Hwa Young said. Not much of a penance, but Seong Su was big and strong and amiable. "Bae, Ha Yoon, will you strip the shuttle of supplies?"

While Geum poked at the shuttle's control panels, everyone else clambered out of the shuttle, shivering. The wind had picked up. Temperatures would drop further once nighttime came.

Hwa Young and Seong Su worked together to remove Instructor Kim's corpse, somewhat the worse for wear, from the trunk. It struck Hwa Young as incongruous that the instructor looked smaller and more fragile in death, yet her body was heavy and clumsy to maneuver.

"Carrying the body will slow us down," Hwa Young said, hating herself for pointing it out.

Bae's lip curled. "You're saying we should ditch the instructor?"

Hwa Young bit back a retort. Beneath the challenging words, she could hear Bae's fear and uncertainty. "We don't have time to dig a grave." A solution occurred to her, however inadequate, and she nodded at the emergency kit. "There should be some thermal blankets in there. We could cover her in one and weight it down with stones beneath the trees. It's better than nothing."

Bae scowled. "She's not *meat*."

Hwa Young almost liked the other girl. Bae hadn't exactly cared for the instructor—who had?—but she respected authority, and she had a strong sense of propriety. Hwa Young nodded. "Okay, you're right. We bring her with us and hope we can give her a proper burial later."

Hwa Young directed Seong Su and Min Kyung to carry the corpse. When the latter opened zir mouth to complain, she glared zir into submission. This was a rotten day for everyone. Zie needed to shut up and do zir part.

"It's done!" Geum gasped from the front of the shuttle. "I've rejiggered the collision detection system so it'll still avoid trees and stuff, but it'll accelerate *toward* other vehicles rather than avoiding them."

"You're a genius," Hwa Young said, meaning it. "Send it off *now*, before—"

A boom punctuated her words. Hwa Young wished she had binoculars so she could see what was going on, but with all the trees and hills in the way, she wouldn't have had a clear view of the city anyway. She didn't finish her sentence. Didn't need to. If they delayed, the attackers would root them out and destroy them.

Geum's family, Hwa Young thought, trying to ignore the cold lump at the bottom of her stomach. Geum hadn't said a word about them, but she knew zie was worried sick. Who knew whether anyone's families in Forsythia City had survived?

Geum punched the interface a few more times, then closed the door and backed off. "It's going!" zie said unnecessarily.

"Let's get away," Hwa Young said. Seong Su and Min Kyung heaved sighs but had the wisdom not to push her patience further.

The shuttle accelerated much more quickly than Hwa Young had ever seen one go before, arrowing out from between the trees toward the source of the earlier explosion. She suddenly respected the engineers who had programmed its safety protocols to make sure that the fragile, all-too-human passengers who would ordinarily be inside wouldn't be smeared into paste. It rose a full meter off the ground once it had cleared the forest, its levitators whining almost inaudibly.

Hwa Young and Bae led the way, always keeping the edge of the woods in sight. Disturbingly, Hwa Young glimpsed the shuttle circling as though it couldn't decide where to go.

Seong Su jogged up to walk alongside Hwa Young and Bae. Hwa Young glanced back, startled: someone else had taken over his job as corpse-bearer. She didn't want to waste time arguing about it, as long as the task was getting done.

"You guys are crazy prepared," Seong Su said. "I never . . . I never thought anything like this would happen. Not on Serpentine."

"The Empress likes us to be prepared," Hwa Young said to Seong Su, because he was still keeping pace with them and the silence was getting awkward. It was the blandest, most unhelpful platitude she could think of. Anything to make him go away so she could concentrate on keeping everyone alive.

Seong Su didn't get the hint. "I kinda wish I'd been a better student," he said, kicking annoyingly at the ground as he walked. "I mean, I never thought any of it *mattered.*"

Oh no. He was getting *confessional,* and she wasn't here to be his counselor. Could she trust him with a meaningless task? "Seong Su," she said. She held out a survival knife she'd taken from the first aid kit. "Start marking our trail. Carve an X into every five trees as we go."

"I, wha . . ." Seong Su deflated as she stared at him, willing him to take the knife and leave her alone. "Sure, uh, I guess I can do that."

Hwa Young hoped he didn't cut himself with it. Surely he couldn't be that much of a klutz.

Bae caught her eye and arched an eyebrow, as if to say *Not bad, even for you.*

Hwa Young gritted her teeth and smiled back, just the tiniest upward twitch of the corners of her mouth.

The woods breathed leaf-song around them as they trudged onward, rustling and whispering in the wind. Hwa Young imagined hostile ghosts hiding behind every tree, haunting every ridge. *They'll hear us,* she thought, listening to the trampling of feet on grass and stone, but there was nothing she could do about that.

For the rest of her life, Hwa Young suspected she'd hear that irregular concussion of explosions drawing ever closer, like a malevolent drum corps. She spotted orange-red flashes washing past the leaves and branches, which left actinic blue afterimages dancing in front of her eyes. Ha Yoon kept glancing back as though she expected demons to erupt from the rocks and ferns, although they were well into the woods and the trees blocked their view of any details.

"Where *are* we going?" Bae asked under her breath. "And what's up with that stupid shuttle? It should be long gone and I can still hear it. It's going to lead the enemy right to us."

Geum stiffened and muttered something inaudible.

Hwa Young appreciated that Bae wasn't broadcasting her doubts for the whole group to hear, even if Bae's innate hostility radiated off her like a sullen wind. "I took a look at the topographical maps earlier," she replied quietly. "We can keep going downhill until we hit a creek and—"

The shuttle's whine crescendoed as it headed back toward them.

"Geum," Bae said in irritation, "it shouldn't be doing that.

You messed this up." Her tone implied *of course you did*, which made Hwa Young bristle.

"I don't know why—" Geum began, ready to argue with zir least favorite person.

Hwa Young's heart contracted when she glimpsed a flash of light on metal through a break in the woods: the shuttle veering off at a sudden angle. What was it doing?

Just then, Hwa Young heard a whistling noise.

"A missile!" Geum cried.

Hwa Young didn't waste time asking questions. Geum wasn't the only one who watched the (probably censored) news bulletins of war at the Empire's borders. Anyone who played video games had heard some version of that high-pitched screech.

"Everyone take cover!" Hwa Young yelled.

She had barely ducked behind a fallen log when a furious orange light burst over the tops of the trees. Strangely, it didn't penetrate beyond that, as though an unseen force had shielded them from the attack. Hwa Young choked down a scream, her nostrils abruptly full of the pungent smells of moss and dank fungus and decaying wood. A bug scuttled along the back of her neck, just above the collar.

A shower of branches and leaves rained down. The students scattered. Hwa Young burrowed closer to the log, praying it would offer her shelter. She winced as a splinter drove into the flesh of her forearm.

At least the forest wasn't burning around her, and no one was floating. The gravity seemed stable—even if the reason for their unity was shared fear.

When the light faded, leaving disorienting blue-green afterimages across her field of vision, Hwa Young peered up through her fingers. The treetops had been sheared off, leaving the sky visible through a haze of metallic smoke.

Why aren't we dead? she wondered. Something—or someone—had shielded them from the attack.

Then she saw it: an angular Imperial lancer towering above the shorn trees, clad in scale armor of orange and gold. Its massive shoulders featured missile mounts, and its force shield blazed inferno-red. Someone had come to their rescue after all.

The shuttle accelerated back toward them, its engine screaming.

Hwa Young watched in horror as the shuttle, following its programming—the programming *she'd* instructed Geum to give it—collided into the lancer and exploded.

5

Five minutes later, the orange-and-gold lancer thundered to a halt, blackened by the explosion—but intact. It dwarfed the shorn trees. The cockpit in the head popped open, and a pissed-off fellow Imperial in a navy blue uniform, his face red and his sleeves singed, emerged. "You down there! Who's your representative?"

Hwa Young flinched at the lancer pilot's obvious anger. But she had to take responsibility for this mess. Especially since she could hear Geum moaning amid the others' gibbering and crying. When Hwa Young looked back at her friend, she realized that some of the shrapnel from the exploding shuttle had hit zir in the head. Blood streaked zir face and zir eyes were glassy. Hwa Young's heart seized, and she swung back toward the pilot. He was her best hope of getting Geum—and the others—medical attention.

She stood up, then tilted her head back in a futile attempt to meet the pilot's gaze. "That's me," she shouted back.

A clever if precarious-looking lift system, formerly hidden, unfolded itself from the body of the lancer and lowered the pilot to the ground. Up close, he looked no less intimidating, even though he couldn't be much older than eighteen or nineteen, with a face that was all angles and glowering brows, and a jagged scar down the right side of his face. His broad, stocky build included a fair bit of muscle. She wouldn't have wanted to confront him in a fight.

"Your name, citizen," the pilot snapped.

Were his eyes *orange*? No, they had to be a lighter shade of the usual Imperial brown. Her mind must be playing tricks on her.

"I'm Hwa Young," she said, using an extra-polite formality level just in case. Hangeul, the language common to New Joseon and the clanners, marked courtesy not just with special pronoun forms but also as part of the verb conjugation. She didn't have a family name, unlike her classmates, and she wondered if he would pick up on that.

"Good for you," the pilot said with a scowl. "I'm Eun." He, too, failed to give a family affiliation, but Hwa Young knew it was for a different reason. Pilots owed allegiance to the Empire as a whole—to the Empress herself—and not their blood-kin. They dropped their family names as soon as they passed training.

Bae approached the two of them, brushing twigs and leaves from her hair. Hwa Young had almost forgotten about the other girl's existence, focused as she was on securing medical assistance for Geum and the others. "I'm Chang Bae," she said peremptorily, "daughter of Chang Ae Ri, advisor to the planetary governor. Some of the students here are injured."

Of course she'd make sure the pilot knows about her mom, Hwa Young thought sourly.

"I've called for backup transport," Eun said impatiently. "The fighter ships have taken out the hostiles. Medics will tend to your wounded." He stared down his nose at Hwa Young. "*You* were the one behind the rogue attack shuttle?"

Hwa Young's guilt transformed into dislike at Eun's gruff tone. "Yes," she said, her voice icy. Bae would rat her out if she didn't confess, anyway. She debated explaining the situation, but there was no point. He wouldn't care.

Eun harrumphed. "Zie is going to *love* you."

Zie who? Hwa Young wondered. But she didn't want to waste time asking questions she wouldn't get the answers to.

"Congratulations, Menace Girl. Since *you're* the asshole troublemaker who shuttle-bombed my lancer, I'm keeping an eye on you so you don't implement any more bright ideas. You're riding with me. The rest of you, hang tight until backup arrives."

Hwa Young had the dubious satisfaction of seeing Bae gape at them both, as though this were an *honor* instead of some sort of backhanded punishment—although it *did* feel like a prize to Hwa Young. Scarcely daring to hope this was real, she left the others behind, sparing Geum another worried look over her shoulder, and came over to the lift.

She was going to ride in a lancer, the dream she'd harbored all these years. The dream she nurtured like a seedling every time she meditated. She was about to find out whether her imagined version was anything like the real thing.

Eun's lancer was a magnificent specimen. Those missile racks looked like they could take down a dreadnought-class starship all by themselves. Even standing still like a vigilant soldier, light gleaming on the scales of its fire-colored armor, the lancer exuded power.

This wasn't how she'd envisioned getting up close to a lancer. What surprised her more was that the lancer felt *wrong*. Its very presence grated against the edges of her mind. She wanted a lancer, all right—but she didn't want *this* one.

She hoped this wasn't a sign she wouldn't be a suitable pilot.

"Oh, and your gun. Hand it over." Eun stared imperiously at Hwa Young.

She suppressed her scowl and gave him the instructor's pistol. Not like she had much choice. He shoved it into his belt after conscientiously checking it over, which only made her feel a little better.

I'm sorry, Geum, she thought, torn between wishing she could stay with zir and her yearning for the lancer, even the wrong lancer. *What kind of friend am I?*

Sure, Eun had as good as given her an order . . . but Hwa Young knew in her heart of hearts that she would have been tempted to go with him anyway. She didn't like finding this out about herself. As she gazed back at Geum's crumpled form, she promised that she would do everything in her power to make sure Geum received all the help zie needed.

The lift barely accommodated two people, but the cockpit seated two as well. Hwa Young squeezed past Eun into what was either a copilot's or passenger's seat, although there was no copilot in evidence.

She stared in fascination at the angular readouts and control panels, momentarily letting go of her aggravation toward the pilot and her worry about Geum. It looked so *different* from what she had imagined, all fiery colors and jagged lines. Everything about the cockpit made her edgy, and she didn't like that either. She'd hoped to feel immediately at home, as she had imagined in all her meditations.

"Who's your copilot?" Hwa Young asked, watching intently as Eun's hands danced over the panels, casting shadows over them without actually touching them.

Eun glanced sideways at her, his scowl faltering. "We're dealing with unusual circumstances. It's classified."

That's odd. Was the lancer unit understrength? A full unit should include at least a dozen pilots *and* their copilots. "Isn't that an uncomfortable way to work?" she asked, changing the subject and nodding at the panels. "How do you control it?"

He laughed scornfully. "What, you expected a joystick or something? A direct link is much more efficient."

Hwa Young fell silent. She hadn't known that, but she should have guessed. It was the same principle that customized interfaces for simpler vehicles like shuttles or cars, but much more advanced.

Maybe the reason this lancer felt *wrong* was that it was customized for Eun, and not her. The thought cheered her.

Eun spoiled the moment by adding, "Redo that strap. You don't want to fall out of your seat once we're airborne."

The lancer leapt into the air with surprisingly smooth acceleration. Hwa Young was pressed back against her cushioned seat. She gazed out the cockpit window in awe as the lancer flew in defiance of aerodynamics, using larger versions of the levitators the ill-fated shuttle had possessed—antigravity, but of a type mastered by the Empire's technology.

A hundred more questions rushed into her head on how piloting worked, but she settled for observing silently, her heart alight. She didn't want to distract Eun when their lives might depend on his piloting . . . and she was savoring the moment in the private sanctum of her heart, so that she could return to it over and over in her meditations.

Serpentine's blue-violet sky, with its shrouds of smoke and clouds and the occasional hell-flash of explosions, gave way to heart-stopping blackness and the glittering eyes of the local constellations. Hwa Young remained silent. Eun's hands shook, but that didn't seem to impede his piloting. She thought of the morning at the firing range, which felt like it had happened during another lifetime, and longed for a weapon of her own.

Who am I kidding? Hwa Young thought over the rapid beating of her heart as the lancer sped onward. She'd yearned to pilot a lancer since the first time she saw one, the terrible secret she kept embedded in her heart like an icicle. Lancers had destroyed Carnelian, yet they represented power. The ability to make a difference.

If Carnelian had possessed lancers of its own—if the clanners had been able to *unite* enough to build up their industrial base and master the gravitic technologies that enabled lancers to fly and fire their deadliest weapons, singularity lances—maybe they wouldn't have fallen so easily to New Joseon.

I'm a citizen of New Joseon now, Hwa Young reminded herself. One of the Empress's children. The clanners' failings were no longer her concern.

Besides, she couldn't afford to lose herself in memories of her unwanted past when she was *in* an Imperial lancer. While a passing thought wouldn't affect their flight, she didn't want to screw up and slip into some clanner habit or ritual that would give her away, or contradict the Imperial rituals that reinforced the lancer's functioning.

A tiny elongated figure came into view, shaped almost like a carp, if carp gleamed silver and blue. It couldn't be one of Serpentine's moons. As it loomed larger, Hwa Young realized that it wasn't, in fact, small. In space, as opposed to on a planet or a moon, she had nothing to compare distant objects to in order to determine their scale.

The figure was a starship, its sinuous curves interrupted by the protrusions and hatches of gun turrets and missile racks and sensory arrays. Hwa Young wished she'd paid more attention to Geum's chatter about the Imperial space fleet. She'd always been fixated on the lancers rather than the starships that took them from battle to battle.

Geum. I hope zie's all right.

Eun broke the silence. "That's the Eleventh Fleet," he said proudly. "We were assigned to protect this section of the border. We're going to the flagship, the *Maehwa*." *Plum blossom.*

A bell tone sounded. Eun's fingers twitched. "*Maehwa*, this is Hellion. I have one passenger, a refugee from the former city of Forsythia. Request clearance for landing."

Former city. Hwa Young's guts knotted up as the implications sank in. The population of Forsythia was over seventy thousand. Surely she and her class couldn't be the only survivors.

She should open her mouth. Ask. But Eun might answer, and that would make it real. And then she'd fall apart, and she couldn't afford that, not until she'd made sure her classmates and Geum were safe.

"*Maehwa* to Hellion," said a brisk voice. "Cleared for landing in docking bay six."

Eun wasn't paying attention to Hwa Young or her inner turmoil. Hwa Young kept her face as still as a mirror, not wanting to reveal more to him than she had to.

The *Maehwa* grew larger and larger, resolving into fractal vistas of antennae, closed gunports, the blue-silver shine of armor plating. Then all Hwa Young could see was the docking bay, a mechanized maw opening to admit the lancer. Eun's hands continued shaking, but the maneuver went smoothly. The lancer flew in headfirst, then jackknifed neatly to land on its feet. Hwa Young stifled a sigh of relief as she felt it making contact with the deck, and then the reverberation of the bay door closing.

"Not bad," Eun said grudgingly.

Hwa Young blinked at him, wondering what he meant.

"Almost couldn't tell it was your first time in space."

Long practice kept Hwa Young from shooting back, *It wasn't.* She knew better than to hint at her secrets.

Eun shrugged. "Have it your way."

The cockpit opened, letting in a rush of chilly air. Hwa Young sneezed at the onslaught of unfamiliar smells. Even the city—former city—had smelled of leaves and earth from the small gardens that the city planners and geomancers had planted on every street. You couldn't walk down a block without chancing across some intimate vista consisting of miniature pine trees or cosmos or ponds arranged so cleverly that they looked as though they had occurred naturally, if nature admitted such perfection.

Here there were no plants, no flowers, no tang of earth, but rather metal and fire and something it took her a moment to place as . . . meat? Her brain caught up with her a moment later, and she gagged silently. Not *food*, but burnt flesh.

"Stop gawking," Eun growled. "Let's disembark."

Moving carefully so she didn't trip and fall to her death, she joined Eun on the lift.

Hwa Young took the opportunity to study her surroundings. Ten other lancers occupied the docking bay. Powered down, they were a featureless dull gray, humanoid and as large as ever, but without armor or weapons or any hint of personality. She glanced back at Eun's and saw it, too, morph back into its resting state until it was indistinguishable from the others except for a stylized painting of a flame on its chest and the singe marks.

On the side of the nearest one she glimpsed a painting of an upside-down golden antler crown, decorated with comma-shaped jades in green. She puzzled over its significance. The Empress wore an antler crown, a tradition from New Joseon's founding. Surely it was treasonous to mock her symbol like this? She'd expected some ferocious predator instead, like a tiger, or a warrior out of the histories, or even something resembling the sharp-thorned rose like the one painted on Mi Cha's lancer *Summer Thorn*.

The bay's metal walls showed a greenish patina, and different sections had been painted with cryptic symbols in blue. The deck displayed gouges and scorch marks, some of them crisscrossing the patterned lane markings. One of the gouges, deep and black, was surrounded by a temporary barrier of yellow cones and tape so no one would trip over it and injure themselves.

Hwa Young fought against a pang of disappointment. While some people wore navy uniforms like Eun's, everyone looked rumpled. The ones bearing welding tools or swarming around strange machinery were dressed in practical gray fatigues; those must be the technicians and mechanics. Others, bearing weapons, strutted about in green; those would be the marines. She'd expected sailors and marines in dress uniform, lined up as though for inspection, or maybe marching smartly. She *definitely* hadn't expected the miasma of sweat and anxiety.

One of the mechanics in gray stormed up to Eun and Hwa Young. A streak of black grease marred his blocky, squarish face. "What is it with you and explosions, Senior Warrant Officer?" he demanded.

Eun rolled his eyes. "Long story." He slanted an annoyed look in Hwa Young's direction, then gestured toward his singed lancer. "Fix her up, will you?"

The mechanic didn't get the hint, even though a tall young person in navy blue was walking up to them, making no effort to soften zir footsteps. Granted, it wouldn't be hard to miss them amid the dismaying tumult of the docking bay. "Your lancer is a complete mess!" the mechanic went on. "One of these days you're going to end up like—"

"Like what?" the newcomer interrupted from behind him.

Hwa Young assessed the stranger with instinctive wariness. Despite the apparent friendliness of zir tone, zie carried zirself like someone used to wielding authority. Zie had tucked a slate under zir right arm. The left hung limply from the shoulder, ending in a withered, clawlike hand. Trying not to stare, Hwa Young bowed in greeting, noting how Eun and the mechanic snapped to and saluted.

Aha—she surreptitiously examined the insignia over zir chest while Eun gave his report. A commander. A quick glance confirmed that both zie and Eun wore the sun-and-lance symbol that signified the lancer units.

Hwa Young sized zir up further while zie spoke in jargon to Eun. Zie had an oval face with a strong jaw and smiling dark eyes beneath asymmetrical short-cropped hair. She'd been fooled by zir height—zie topped her by almost a head, with a deceptive leanness despite the way zie radiated strength, but zie was only in zir early twenties.

In fact, no one in the docking bay appeared to be much north of twenty except the mechanics. Many of the spacers and marines looked sixteen, seventeen, eighteen. Occasionally younger. Hwa Young hadn't known there were people this young in active service. She'd always understood that she would have to wait until she turned eighteen to apply to be a lancer pilot.

The commander turned to Hwa Young. "You must be Eun's guest," zie said genially. "One of the survivors of that terrible attack. I salute you."

"'Guest,'" Eun muttered under his breath.

She bowed again. "I'm Hwa Young," she said, using the most polite verb forms.

"I'm Commander Ye Jun," zie said. Despite the way zir eyes crinkled in a friendly fashion, there was a certain artificiality to zir manner. "Welcome to the Eleventh Fleet. I'm the handler for the fleet's lancer unit."

"All *one* of us," Eun said, this time loudly enough that both Ye Jun and Hwa Young could hear him.

Hwa Young's eyebrows shot up. "For the flagship?" That

couldn't be right. There should be a company of twelve lancers embedded in any single fleet, each crewed by a pilot and copilot, plus a thirteenth command-and-control lancer unit to serve as handler. She had assumed that the other lancers all had pilots busy with other duties.

Hastily, Hwa Young scanned the docking bay again. She hadn't miscounted.

Only two of them, including the one she'd arrived in, had pilots. The two with the painted emblems, presumably.

No wonder Eun hadn't wanted to talk about his nonexistent copilot.

A great time to change the topic. "Commander," Hwa Young said, remembering her original mission, "I have friends planet-side. One of them has a head injury. Are they—are we all being evacuated?"

"The Empire is cutting its losses in this sector," Commander Ye Jun said.

At first she couldn't make sense of zir words. Wasn't it the Empire's job to defend its worlds?

Zie kept speaking. "To be frank, Hwa Young, Imperial HQ has decided that we can't afford to hold Serpentine because it's too close to the Moonstorm border, and we're needed for a major offensive elsewhere. What we *are* doing is evacuating as much of the population as we can accommodate."

Hwa Young stared in shock, unable to speak.

Eun couldn't resist opening his mouth. "You mean we're drafting anyone with two legs and a working pair of hands."

Commander Ye Jun shifted zir gaze to Eun. "Hellion, am I conducting this briefing, or are you?"

Eun's brow knitted. "Listen, Commander, maybe you want to give it to this earthworm with honey words and a ribbon, but she's going to learn the truth eventually. Especially when you assign her a specialty and tell her to shape up."

"Hellion—"

"And especially when this is the fourth border world we've abandoned! I don't care how much the newscasters spin encouraging propaganda about how we have the clanners on the run and the periphery worlds have nothing to worry about while the core worlds turtle in on themselves and leave the rest of us to—"

"*Hellion.*"

To die. Hwa Young, left reeling as though each of Eun's words had struck her like a kick to the stomach, could finish his sentence for herself.

This can't be true. The Empress protects her children.

Some children more than others, apparently.

Commander Ye Jun stared at Eun until he lowered his eyes, his face reddening.

"Sorry," Eun muttered sullenly. He didn't sound sorry in the least. "But she deserves to know the truth."

"It's all true, as far as that goes," Commander Ye Jun said, turning back to Hwa Young. "But there are good and bad ways to present information. As some of us need to learn."

This time Eun had the sense to stay silent.

"Let me guess," Hwa Young said, her mouth dry. "You're recruiting us."

"We're going to be *assessing* you and your friends," the commander said. "Then we'll draft those of you with skills we need." Zir voice was not unkind. "It's part of the war effort, citizen. The Empress's will."

Hwa Young smiled bitterly. *"Trust the Empress. Move at her will. Act as her hands."*

Commander Ye Jun returned her smile. "Quite so."

She'd always wanted to be a lancer pilot. It beat being assigned some dull duty like checking for mold in hydroponics.

At the same time, this was hardly the triumph that she'd imagined. The Eleventh Fleet in disarray. Serpentine abandoned because of some strategic calculation. The revelation that *other* Imperial worlds had already been surrendered to clanner attacks—and she'd never heard about it.

It'll be different once I become a pilot, she told herself desperately.

But first— "I really need to know what happened to my classmates."

If Geum's condition had worsened and she hadn't been there, she would never forgive herself.

Hwa Young could *see* the abacus calculations happening behind Commander Ye Jun's eyes. She revised her estimation of zir upward. Despite the amiable exterior, zie must hold the position of lancer handler for a reason.

The mechanic cleared his throat. "Sir, begging your pardon, I should get a start on *Hellion*'s repairs. They're liable to take a while."

"Go ahead," the commander said, and the mechanic stomped toward the docked, featureless lancer, swearing as he looked it up and down. "You too," zie added to Eun. "I want an after-action report from you. A real one, no copying and pasting manhwa dialogue as filler, you hear? Some of us actually read those things."

"You're no fun, *sir,*" Eun grumbled, and headed off after a parting salute.

Hwa Young looked back at the commander, willing zir to respond to her question.

"Our medical facilities are state-of-the-art. You needn't fear for your friend. What was their name?"

"Zir name is Geum of the An family," Hwa Young said. "Zie would have been with the rest of my class." Quickly, she rattled off everyone's names, even Bae's and Ha Yoon's, then added, "Our instructor was a casualty. I—we didn't have any way to perform the funeral rites for her."

Commander Ye Jun tapped a query into the slate. It didn't escape Hwa Young's attention that zie angled it so she couldn't read the screen. Zie looked up after a moment, zir expression inscrutable. "Your classmates are being transported to the fleet. Your friend will be admitted to sick bay."

"Is zie—"

"They'll treat zir there." The commander smiled sympathetically. "I know you're worried, but we'll take care of zir, promise."

Hwa Young couldn't help wondering if the commander really cared about a stranger's fate, or if zie had accessed Geum's school records and identified some useful skill or talent. "I want to see zir once zie arrives."

"The medics won't like that. Let them do their job, and we'll do ours. You'll have a chance to see your friend again after zie's been released from sick bay and given a role in the fleet."

" 'Ours'?"

Commander Ye Jun's smile became lopsided. "You're going to make an *excellent* recruit, citizen."

Recruit. A painful flare of hope started up in her chest. "I'm not eighteen yet—"

"There's been a policy change. We take people at sixteen and up."

Hwa Young stared unseeing at the commander. She'd never expected her heart's desire to be right around the corner—yet here it was.

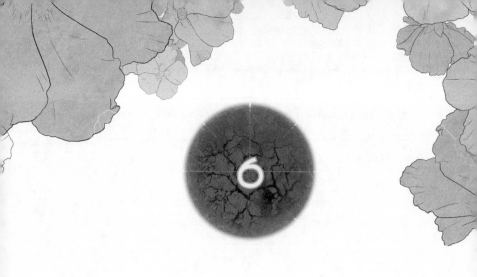

6

After Hwa Young received the news about the policy change, Commander Ye Jun fobbed her off on another soldier. The grumpy, scarred person herded her to a temporary holding area in one of the storage bays along with other frightened civilians while they awaited processing. She went limp with relief at the sight of ordinary people, evidence that she and her classmates weren't the only survivors of the attack.

While the sergeant in charge doled out water in recyclable containers and dismal prepackaged meals, Hwa Young looked around for people she recognized. She spotted Seong Su hunched in a corner, his usual cheer deflated.

"Seong Su!" She strode up to him.

His face brightened. "Hwa Young! Good to see you."

"Where's everyone else?"

"Dunno, they separated us. Took some of the injured to sick

bay and so on." He hesitated, then added, "They told us Geum will be okay."

She nodded, too overwhelmed by gratitude to speak.

He pointed out two other students, Ha Yoon and useless Dong Hyun. No sign of Bae, thank goodness.

Seong Su scooted over to make space for her in the crowd. Hwa Young murmured her thanks. She ate, drank, and used the facilities, such as they were. She hated the reek of her sweat; hated that it made her no different than anyone here, ragged and weary.

The New Year is only a couple months away, Hwa Young thought with a sense of unreality. *The Empress's birthday. I never got a gift for Geum.* All because she'd waited for a last-minute bargain that never materialized.

Seong Su, for his part, was inclined to chatter. He pointed out other refugees from Serpentine, including some girls who hadn't yet conformed to the new haircut, and the teens in a corner playing a game of hwatu flower cards, and hwatu strategy, and the taste of the rations, and . . .

Hwa Young tuned him out and focused on the others. Some of the refugees looked a few years older. None much younger. No babies, no small children, few old folks. That bothered her. How selective had the Eleventh Fleet been with their rescues— and who had done the selecting?

She knew what they said about lancer pilots, that eighteen years old was the ideal time for a pilot to begin training. They'd never specified why, though, and her efforts to find out more details had met with reminders that she shouldn't be digging into classified materials. Afraid of scuppering her chances, she hadn't pressed further.

In the ordinary course of events, she would have faced two more years of school, two more years of military readiness classes. Then a series of tests focusing not only on her physical fitness but her aptitude in mathematics, physics, tactics. She'd studied assiduously.

It was infuriating to think that the attack might rob her of her chance.

Hwa Young paced a tight circle around Seong Su, who directed a stream of witless prattle in her direction. The holding area was demarcated by a temporary barrier that wouldn't have stopped a toddler. She estimated that it contained a hundred people and noted the exits. The obvious ones, anyway. If Seong Su was right, the other refugees were elsewhere.

"Did you get any chance to talk to Bae before they took her away?" Hwa Young finally asked him.

He shook his head. "Nah, the moment the soldiers showed up with their shuttles she was all sweetness and honey. You know how she sucks up to whoever's in charge."

She did know. "Aren't you tired at all?"

"I couldn't sleep even if I wanted to."

Soldiers showed up an indeterminate time later to distribute sleeping mats. People babbled and protested as the soldiers herded them roughly so the mats could be organized in a sensible grid, with space between them to form makeshift corridors. As much as Hwa Young resented the crowded quarters, she had to appreciate the soldiers' unsentimental efficiency. She and Seong Su ended up right at the edge closest to the exit.

"You'd think they could give us a proper place to sleep," Seong Su complained once he'd flopped down on his mat.

Hwa Young shrugged. "It's probably easier to wait to assign us permanent quarters based on our new roles."

In the storage bay, she had no sense of time passing except the excruciating clock of her own exhaustion. Still, she might as well take the opportunity to get some rest. She was so tired that she didn't care how uncomfortable the mat was. Seong Su was already snoring. She curled up on her side and let sleep sweep her away.

Hwa Young woke an indeterminate amount of time later to Seong Su nudging her shoulder. He was holding out a packaged meal featuring a cartoon picture of a smiling chicken. Heat radiated from the box. "Hey," he said shyly. "I was gonna let you sleep, since you looked like you needed it, but they were passing out lunch and I thought you'd like yours while it was still warm."

She sat upright, blinking the grime out of her eyes. For a moment words failed her at the unexpected kindness. "Thank you," she said awkwardly.

According to ship's time it was a little past noon. The food wasn't much to speak of, chicken and rice porridge with a single banchan side of gimchi, but it filled the void in Hwa Young's stomach. As she ate, she eavesdropped on the others' conversations, especially those of the soldiers who oversaw the refugees, presumably to keep them in line. They were worried about whether they would get reinforcements as promised; apparently Eighteenth Fleet was supposed to have rendezvoused with them weeks ago, bringing more soldiers, supplies, and . . . lancers?

More time passed. Hwa Young was considering napping again when a new person arrived: a stooped older woman wearing glasses and a uniform with unfamiliar insignia. Hwa Young sat up straight. She marked the insignia to look up later: a flower with an eye at its heart.

The sergeant escorted the woman to the edge of the holding area, right in front of Hwa Young. "You," the sergeant said, pointing at Hwa Young. He counted off nine more people, including Seong Su. "Go with Dr. Jin."

The other refugees were good Imperial citizens. They queued up as though they were waiting for a bus or a train. As though they weren't trapped inside a starship headed to the front lines of the war against the clanners.

But Hwa Young stepped into place in front of Seong Su, determined not to be hidden by his bulk. She raised her voice: "Excuse me, where are you taking us?"

The sergeant growled under his breath, but a look from the woman quelled him. "We all have a part to play," she said in a hoarse whisper, as though her voice had been damaged. "My job is to determine what your shipboard assignments will be."

You could have said "tests," Hwa Young thought cynically. *Just like school.* "Thank you, Doctor," she said, adjusting the formality of her speech accordingly. No sense antagonizing the person who'd decide whether she'd spend this journey cleaning toilets or doing something more meaningful . . . like training to be a lancer pilot.

Dr. Jin led them to a waiting room that accommodated ten people. A hatch at the other end had no nameplate, only a plaque displaying the same ominous flower with an eye at its heart. A faint fragrance suffused the air but couldn't over-power the stench of sweaty, anxious people, including Hwa Young herself.

The others sat obediently.

Hwa Young remained standing. Nerves plucked at her, but she ignored them and stood straighter. "I'll go first, Doctor."

Dr. Jin's eyebrows flew up, but she nodded. "Very well. Come with me."

Hwa Young followed her into the office. It featured an ex-pansive desk of metal, with magnetic brackets holding a slate in place. There was another door behind the desk, and she won-dered where it led.

Half the desk was occupied by a baduk board with a game in progress, its black and white stones forming zones of influence on the nineteen-by-nineteen grid. A large box of milky green jade, its surface carved with symbols for good luck, rested to the side. It was almost as large as the board itself. Hwa Young couldn't imagine how much high-quality jade that size was worth.

The doctor gestured for her to sit in the single chair across from the desk, so she did. "Your name."

"I'm Hwa Young." When the doctor waited, she added, "I'm a ward of the state. I have no family." It stung every time she said that, but she locked away the pain. She couldn't afford to be distracted by uncertainty now of all times.

Dr. Jin's expression flickered. "Ah, yes. Commander Ye Jun thought you might make a suitable lancer candidate. I, how-ever, have yet to be convinced. We *prefer* for lancer candidates to come from well-established families."

Hwa Young clung to the story of Mi Cha, who had risen

from the humblest of origins. Perhaps it would be better if she didn't bring up Mi Cha, however. "Are you personally processing every refugee, Doctor?"

Dr. Jin regarded her with hooded eyes. "That's not your concern. Tell me, *ward of the state*, do you play baduk?" Her voice dripped skepticism.

What, because she didn't have parents, she was supposed to be some uncivilized savage?

Like a clanner, a defiant voice whispered in the back of her head. Only long habit kept her from glancing down at her feet to check if she was floating.

Hwa Young swept her gaze over the board. "White and black are evenly matched."

Dr. Jin's breath huffed out as if she hadn't expected an immediate answer. "If you were playing black, how would you prevail?"

In answer, Hwa Young grabbed the jade box, ignoring the doctor's gasp, and plunked it down on top of the baduk board, scattering the white and black stones in all directions.

"Why bother with these small, insignificant stones," Hwa Young grated, "when I could use a *real* weapon. One that can make a *real* difference. Like a lancer."

Dr. Jin rose, her face twisting. "If I have any say in it, you'll *never*—"

The door behind her whisked open. The doorway framed Commander Ye Jun.

"Excuse me," zie said, zir voice cold—but the coldness was not directed toward Hwa Young. "I've seen enough. She's in."

The doctor sneered. "You have terrible taste in pilot candidates, as always."

"I want her. You'll sign the papers."

"What, so you can get her killed like the others at Spinel? She won't thank you for your *brilliant leadership*, Commander."

What? Hwa Young wanted to interject. *What happened at Spinel?*

She'd expected lancers to be feted and respected. She'd expected them to be *heroes*, like the captain of the Guard with *Paradox*. Like zir lieutenant Mi Cha. She had never contemplated the possibility that her leadership wouldn't be competent.

There must be a misunderstanding. Maybe Dr. Jin has it in for the commander for some personal reason.

But the words rang hollow.

Commander Ye Jun was unmoved by the doctor's spite. "That's my problem. Sign the papers."

Dr. Jin turned her sneer on Hwa Young. "It's highly irregular for a *ward of the state* to—"

Hwa Young choked down a hysterical laugh. *Ward of the state? How about former clanner?* She certainly wasn't going to blurt out the truth now. Not when she was so close to her goal.

"There are a lot of things that are irregular in the Eleventh Fleet," Ye Jun remarked.

Dr. Jin remained obdurate. "I'm not issuing a badge to a girl without a *family*."

Great. Hwa Young had repeated the story of Mi Cha's meteoric rise to herself since childhood, confident that she, too, would be chosen despite her lowly origins. She hadn't counted on running into resistance from some random bureaucrat.

"Good thing for you I came prepared." Commander Ye Jun retrieved a blank gray disc from zir pocket. Zie nodded at Hwa Young, zir expression warming subtly, and tapped a syncopated rhythm on the disc. It reshaped itself into the silver sun-and-lance badge of a pilot candidate. "This is your ID. It's also authorized to give you directions within the flagship. You'll be bunking with the other lancers at 16-ja. I'll give you further instructions after you've settled in."

Hwa Young accepted the badge. She felt as though she were glowing like a supernova. "Thank you . . . sir."

Commander Ye Jun's expression turned grim. "Don't thank me yet. The doctor isn't all wrong."

What the hell was that about? Hwa Young thought as she walked briskly through the *Maehwa*'s corridors. On the one hand, she had almost made it. She was a pilot candidate. All she had to do was make it through training and join the ranks of the pilots to claim her own lancer.

On the other hand, Commander Ye Jun had intervened on her behalf—and zie had at least one enemy among the shipboard authorities. What if there were others?

She had envisioned a celebration of some sort, with lanterns and flowers, the awe and congratulations of her peers. Imagined being able to fling her success in Bae's face, show everyone who had treated her with such scorn that she could triumph in spite of them.

Instead, no one had marked the occasion. Here she was, striding through the *Maehwa*'s corridors, completely alone. She'd passed some of the crew already, but none of them had given her a second glance. As far as they were concerned, she was still nobody, and that stung.

It will be different once I have a lancer of my own, Hwa Young promised herself again.

And what had happened at Spinel—another periphery world, she remembered vaguely from her classes—that had gone so badly for the commander?

It didn't take Hwa Young long to figure out how to pair the badge with her own neural implant. The badge projected a holographic map with the route to the quartermaster marked in blue. She imagined the map was the kind of thing that got you sniped if you used it in the field—*Here I am, come shoot me!*

Hwa Young considered detouring for sick bay to look for Geum, then reluctantly decided against it. Perhaps she could use her new status to push someone to give her information on zir. Which meant dressing the part, which meant visiting the quartermaster and getting her pilot candidate uniform like Commander Ye Jun had told her to.

She wondered if she should be saluting the officers yet, but none of them gave her more than the occasional askance look. Fair enough: she didn't look like a pilot candidate yet, so best not to confuse the issue. She hoped at some point she could get a shower so she didn't stink of mud, moss, and exhaustion.

When she finally arrived, the quartermaster, a bearded man whose name tag was so badly defaced that Hwa Young decided not to risk guessing, eyed her with distaste. "Do they ever send new recruits who *don't* stink?" he grumbled. "No offense, whatever-your-name-is, I can always smell an earthworm from the other side of the ship."

Hwa Young couldn't blame him. Besides, he didn't sound entirely unfriendly, more like someone who complained out of habit.

"I'll shower first thing, sir," she said with what she hoped was the right combination of deference and humor. If she had to find allies on the ship, this wasn't a bad place to start.

He snorted. "Of course you will. Let me see your badge so I don't accidentally fit you out as an admiral." He guffawed at his own joke, then sobered when he read the assignment out of the badge. "Pilot candidate, huh? Good luck with *that*."

"What do you mean, sir?"

"Not for me to say," the quartermaster demurred, to Hwa Young's intense frustration.

Geum would have been able to charm the information out of him . . . but Geum was injured. Bae would have *wrung* the answer from him. Hwa Young herself didn't want to push too far and get a reputation as a troublemaker. Especially when it concerned the person who could give her a change of clothes.

"Stand up straight," he said, bringing out a body scanner.

She did, and blinked as it traced the contours of her form so he could use the matter printer to produce a uniform that fit. Its initial bland gray gradually turned blue to match his garb. He folded the resulting bundle with surprising care and handed it to her along with a pair of boots she could already tell were a half size too big. "Don't mess it up, Candidate," he told her. "Resupply's dicey when you're always on the run."

"Dr. Jin mentioned a sidearm," Hwa Young lied when he made no move to give her anything else.

The quartermaster lifted an eyebrow. "You're a sharp one, aren't you?" He disappeared into the back, then reemerged with a sleek handgun. "This is a—"

"Mark 25 flare pistol," Hwa Young finished. "I assume you don't issue kinetic weapons to people shipboard so they don't puncture the hull." The aether wasn't friendly to people who prefer to breathe oxygen.

He whistled. "Okay, you're not just any recruit. You want a spare battery pack for it, too?"

What would he have done if she hadn't identified it correctly? Denied her the spare? Hwa Young limited herself to a "Yes, please," and wondered how many people went undersupplied because they'd pissed him off.

She made it to the bunkroom without further incident. The hatch had been spray-painted "16-ja," which she had worked out meant sixteenth room in the ja corridor. Waving the badge in front of the electronic lock caused it to disengage, and the hatch whooshed open.

Inside were Eun . . . and Seong Su, his hair damp. Hwa Young stared at him in vexation. How was *he* such a hot prospect that they'd shooed him in like this? She didn't think she'd spent *that* long with the quartermaster. Maybe they'd had more than one person processing candidates.

Eun and Seong Su played a board game at a cramped table that barely accommodated the latter's oxlike bulk. Beyond them, four bunks dominated the room. The top and bottom bunks on the left already had bags on them, while the ones on the right hadn't yet been claimed. Seong Su caught sight of her and waved sheepishly, as if to say *Life is weird*. Eun, preoccupied with the game, hadn't seen her yet.

Four bunks . . . well, that made sense. Commander Ye Jun must have a cabin of zir own. She hoped there were more pilot candidates in other bunkrooms of their own, enough for all the lancers.

Eun growled, "I don't care if you're Admiral Chin or you're

an ace pilot from the Eighteenth Fleet, you stink like a swamp pig."

"Excuse me," Hwa Young said as civilly as she could, filing the fleet admiral's name in her memory in case it came in useful later. "Could you let me know where to wash up?" She'd already started off on the wrong foot with Eun. She didn't want to irritate him further. Not when they'd be comrades.

Eun finally looked up. His eyes widened. "*You?* Menace Girl?"

"I've been accepted as a pilot candidate."

"I should have left you on that worthless planet."

Hwa Young stiffened, but before she could make a retort, Seong Su waved his hand in front of Eun's face. "Eun, she saved my life. Everyone's lives, down on Serpentine."

Great. Her ally was the class clown, who had somehow qualified too. Had Commander Ye Jun picked him for . . . for what? It wasn't like Seong Su's size and physical strength meant anything inside a cockpit.

She reminded herself that he'd been thoughtful enough to bring her a hot lunch, and felt ashamed of herself.

Seong Su pointed at a hatch in the back, between the bunks. "The bathroom's back there, Hwa Young, along with the shower. Good clean water."

"It's called the head, and the ship is a closed system," Eun muttered, as if Hwa Young didn't know that. "It's recycled piss."

"Aww, don't be like that," Seong Su pleaded.

"It's fine," Hwa Young assured him, and to Eun: "I'm coming through. You may want to hold your nose."

Hwa Young was relieved to find that the shower already had soap, a shampoo bar, and a set of towels. Even if they had almost certainly been used by Eun and Seong Su, she wasn't going to allow squeamishness to stand in the way of cleanliness.

After the shower, she examined the navy blue uniform before putting it on. It fit better than she had hoped, although fastening the lancer pin made her feel like an impostor.

I'll be the best, she promised herself. *Better than the best.*

She heard voices indistinctly through the bulkheads.

Hwa Young emerged, ready to salute, in case it was a surprise inspection.

"I figured I'd find you here, Hwa Young," said an all-too-familiar voice.

It was Bae.

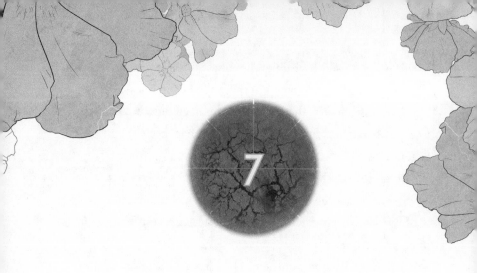

7

Hwa Young shook her head, chiding herself for not anticipating this. Bae *was* head of the class. It made a perverse
sense that she'd also qualify as a pilot candidate.

"Congratulations," Hwa Young said stiffly, even though she
resented having her triumph—such as it was—marred by the continued presence of Bae in her life.

Bae tossed her head. "Like there was ever any doubt."

Hwa Young's fingers twitched, but she kept herself from
balling her hands into fists. She'd just have to work harder to
outcompete Bae—the story of her life.

"I guess we're never going to see Forsythia City again, huh?"
Seong Su said, glancing between Hwa Young and Bae. "The
school, that one restaurant with the really tasty naengmyeon
noodles . . ."

Hwa Young shrugged uncomfortably, reminding herself that

the other two might have family members or friends they were worried about. For her part, it wasn't as though she had any sentimental attachment to the place—and she knew that her one friend, Geum, was on the ship with her. If leaving Serpentine was the price she had to pay to be a lancer, so be it.

Bae's lip curled. "It figures your ambitions are limited to a backwater city, Seong Su."

Despite her own lack of nostalgia, Hwa Young was shocked by Bae's heartlessness. "A lot of people were killed," she fired back at the other girl. An image of their instructor, her neck broken, flashed in her mind's eye.

Hwa Young expected Bae to sneer. Instead, Bae looked her straight in the eye and said, "The best revenge is to go on the attack—with lancers."

Maybe we're not so different after all, Hwa Young thought, too disquieted to make a retort.

"I'm taking the top bunk," Bae announced. "Now it's *my* turn to use the shower." She swept past them and slammed the hatch behind her.

Eun didn't make any snide comments about *her* stink. He did, however, lean back in his chair and purse his lips at Hwa Young. "So that's the last one for this bunkroom. You three know each other?"

"We're classmates." She didn't feel the need to elaborate further. Then his words sank in. "For this bunkroom? Who else is there?"

"We've got twenty candidates," Eun said. "Scraping the bottom of the barrel if you ask me"—his gaze raked over her—"but desperate times call for desperate measures."

Hwa Young digested this. She couldn't help glancing at Seong Su. In what universe was *he* more suitable to pilot a lancer than she was?

Don't get cocky. You're only a candidate, same as him.

"Are there other candidates from our class?" she asked Seong Su.

"Dunno." He squirmed under her stare. "They separated us early on."

Since Bae had stuck her with the bottom bunk, Hwa Young sat there and unearthed the flare pistol from underneath the fold of cloth where she'd stashed it, making sure not to point it at anyone.

Eun inhaled sharply. "Where'd you get that?"

"The quartermaster."

He let out a slow whistle. "You might be good for something if you managed to charm *him*. Usually he tries to make me go away by shoving paperwork at me. Guess you're in charge of resupplying us."

I can't imagine why, with your winning personality, she thought, but then reconsidered. Eun might be prickly, but at least she always knew where she stood with him. "Where do I stow this? I assume you don't want me keeping it under my pillow." Which was where she planned on hiding her knife, but he didn't need to know that.

Eun waved toward the bunks. "There are lockers under the bunks. You can store whatever you can fit in them. They're keyed to your badge. Left one's for the bottom bunk."

He still sounded grumpy, but at least he had given her the information she needed. By the time Hwa Young had checked the weapon over and stowed it, Bae had emerged from the shower, her shorn hair perfectly combed.

"Bae," Hwa Young said, since Seong Su had been useless, "do *you* know what happened to everyone else?" Maybe she'd have further word on Geum.

The other girl sneered at her. "Yeah, thanks for abandoning us dirtside while you swanned up to the Eleventh Fleet in your boyfriend's sweet ride."

"That's not what happened and you know it."

Eun wrinkled his nose. "Menace Girl is *not* my girlfriend. I don't fraternize with earthworms."

Bae's eyes narrowed. "I thought you were Geum's friend, but did you even check on zir? Zie was asking for you when the medics took zir into surgery, you know."

Guilt stopped Hwa Young in her tracks. Bae had always, sniperlike, been able to hit bull's-eye with her remarks. "I asked after Geum," she said, painfully aware that it sounded like an excuse. "They wouldn't let me see zir."

"Hey now." It was Seong Su, his eyes sympathetic. "Maybe the commander knows something."

Eun shook his head. "Zie has better things to do than play babysitter with some rando civ—"

The hatch opened. Commander Ye Jun regarded Eun with bemusement. "Which civilian would that be, Hellion?"

It took Hwa Young a moment to recall that Hellion was Eun's callsign. She seized the opportunity to say, "Commander, I'm concerned about my friend that I mentioned earlier, Geum." On the off chance it would help—"Zie's an expert hacker. If that's something the fleet could use."

Commander Ye Jun's gaze sharpened as it moved to her. "First things first, Candidate."

Eun was already saluting. Seong Su and Bae had followed suit. Flushing, Hwa Young did the same.

"At ease," Commander Ye Jun said after letting them hold the salutes long enough to make the point. "It's good that your friends are important to you. You'll see zir soon enough."

Hwa Young wanted to see Geum *now*, but pushing her commanding officer would do no good. She gnawed her lip in frustration, wishing the commander had given her some more definite information.

"I still can't believe you selected the menace who tried to blow up my lancer," Eun growled.

"It was a very strong recommendation." Commander Ye Jun left Eun sputtering and regarded the other three. "Don't mind him. On the battlefield he will be"—zir smile twisted—"your strong right hand."

Eun muttered something about what Ye Jun could do with zir right hand.

"Careful, Hellion," the commander murmured. "If I heard what you said, which of course I didn't, I'd have to write you up for insubordination. Especially now that I have my pick of candidates to replace you."

"*Baby* candidates, *sir*."

"I learn fast," Hwa Young said.

Bae's mouth opened, but Commander Ye Jun forestalled whatever her rejoinder would have been by saying mildly, "You all do, or you wouldn't be here."

"What did you need from us, sir?" Seong Su asked, transparently eager to squash any conflict.

"You'll be sworn in with the rest of the pilot candidates on New Year's," Ye Jun said. "A private ceremony."

Hwa Young frowned. The newscasts had always shown bright-faced new lancer pilot candidates, heroes, saviors-to-be. They never mentioned what happened to the ones who didn't make the cut.

She racked her brain, trying to remember whether she'd heard anything about Eleventh Fleet and its lancers specifically. Only that they were known as the Bountiful Fleet. Either the moniker was ironic or circumstances had changed. "Is there a reason for the secrecy, sir?"

"You like asking awkward questions," zie said with a hint of reproof. "Admiral Chin has her ways."

"Not like we want to broadcast our diminished numbers to the enemy," Eun added.

"Back on Serpentine," Seong Su said, hushed, "I heard the rebels had ways of listening in. Even that there were dissenters in the fleets."

"If there are, they wouldn't be able to hide it for long," Bae said dismissively.

Hwa Young stayed silent.

"Out in the Moonstorm, our gravity isn't entirely reliable." Commander Ye Jun sighed, and zir good humor receded to reveal worry. "Eun will train all the candidates. Eun, keep the smart-ass remarks to yourself. You can save them for me." That last sounded like the most genial of threats.

Eun smiled sourly. "Of course, *sir.*"

Eun's prickliness, which bordered on open disrespect, distressed Hwa Young. Despite some of the instructors' admonishments, she knew it was outward adherence to the forms and courtesies that reinforced Imperial gravity, rather than any thoughts beneath the surface. A lifetime of bowing to her superiors, however, made Hwa Young suspicious of any defiance that wasn't her own.

Commander Ye Jun laid out the training schedule, which would be interrupted during the journey only for the New Year's ceremony to celebrate the Empress's birthday. Hwa Young memorized the schedule without complaint, although zie told them they could access the information through their neural implants as well. Reveille at 0600. Meals together, classes to orient them to shipboard life, hand-to-hand combat training, firearms.

Last of all, after a couple months of this, would be the coveted introduction to the lancers themselves, when some of them would emerge as pilots . . . and some wouldn't.

The first class, according to the schedule, consisted of an overview on faster-than-light travel and communications. Most of the twenty candidates had arrived early the next morning and were already seated. Hwa Young only recognized a few of them. That made sense. There was no reason they would only have selected candidates from her class, out of all the refugees.

Bae was chatting with Ha Yoon as though they'd never been separated. *Her too?* Hwa Young thought, trying not to stare—or scowl. Maybe Dr. Jin, with her fixation on good breeding rather than actual aptitude, had approved Ha Yoon.

She was trudging to a seat in the front, preoccupied with

thoughts of how to win Eun over, when someone hugged her from behind. She yelped and flailed.

The attacker let go immediately. "Hwa Young! It's me!"

"Geum?" She whirled, blinking back tears of relief and gratitude as she beheld her friend.

Geum had showed up in the same candidate uniform. Someone had shaved part of zir scalp, which sported a bandage. "Hey there." Zie grinned brightly. "They shoved some of that regenerative gel into me and gave me painkillers. I'm good as new."

Hwa Young threw her arms around her friend, and they hugged fiercely, heedless of the other candidates gawking at them. "You're safe," Hwa Young whispered over and over. "You're safe."

Which was how Eun found them when he entered. He cleared his throat. "*Excuse* me, no fraternizing. You're soldiers now, not schoolkids."

Geum blinked owlishly at him.

Eun shook his head. "Sit down, everyone. Class is starting."

Eun's lecture opened with a hair-raising overview on the unreliability of communications in the Moonstorm, where aetheric currents could cause transmissions to go astray. Within New Joseon proper, relay towers ensured the dependability of comms. Staying in contact with Fleet HQ was one of the never-ending problems with operations in clanner space.

Hwa Young spent the entire lecture taking notes on the slate she'd been provided. But no matter how hard she tried to concentrate, her gaze swept over the other candidates.

From her class: herself, Geum, Bae, Ha Yoon, and Seong Su. That made five of them and fifteen unknowns. Was the thin, intense person a threat to her? The elegant girl whose hair was almost as perfect as Bae's? What criteria would they use to determine who would be elevated to the rank of pilot, and who would be reassigned to another military occupational specialty?

Afterward, Eun led them to a designated training room. "If it were up to me, this would have come first," he announced, "but I suppose this is soon enough."

The lockers in the room were numbered. Eun read out numbers and names. Hwa Young found hers, number six. To her displeasure, Bae had number five, and Geum was across the room.

"Open up the lockers. They'll respond to your fingerprint."

Inside the locker was a spacesuit. Hwa Young eyed it with trepidation. She couldn't help but think that if she'd had one on Carnelian, maybe she wouldn't have had to lie to the Imperials in exchange for their protection. As it stood, she'd never handled one before.

Eun went over how to check the spacesuits and read the oxygen gauges. How to put them on and take them off. Hwa Young watched Bae and Seong Su, even Geum, in between struggling with her suit, which seemed to have a mind of its own. Were they faster at donning the suits? Nimbler at moving in them?

"Not bad," Eun said grudgingly—to Seong Su. "Usually the big ones are clumsy, but you're a quick study."

Seong Su scratched the back of his neck, embarrassed at having been singled out for praise. "One of my parents is an engineer," he mumbled. "Used to bring suits home, show us how they worked."

Of course. Something no mere ward of the state would have had an opportunity to practice. Hwa Young swore to redouble her efforts so that no one would be able to tell she was at a disadvantage.

"Hwa Young, Bae," Eun said. "Let's see you put them on again."

As Hwa Young divested herself of the suit so she could comply, she asked, "Where's the commander?"

Eun grimaced. "An officer's not going to do the dirty work of teaching Spacer 101, so get that idea out of your head. Besides, zie's attending a staff meeting with the admiral."

It didn't help that Eun was only sporadically good at teaching. He was *knowledgeable,* but he tended to skip around from step to step rather than going in order, which made his directions difficult to follow. Hwa Young reminded herself that it didn't matter that she'd have preferred a better teacher. She had to make do with the one she had.

Eun also kept Hwa Young separated from Geum, which couldn't be a coincidence. *It was one hug,* she thought resentfully. Surely it wasn't a bad thing to greet a friend she'd been so worried about. *Not like we're dating.* But protesting would only make things worse. Besides, it galled her that Geum didn't seem to notice the separation at all, chattering enthusiastically to the candidates next to zir about the suits' special features.

After they practiced putting the suits on and taking them off, and activating the magnets in the boots in case of gravity failure, they learned how to make emergency repairs to suit breaches and activate the first aid systems. "It works better if you have a buddy," Eun said with the air of someone who knew, "but sometimes you're shit out of luck."

"Like if the breach is somewhere you're not flexible enough to reach," Bae said before Hwa Young could speak.

"I can see you're an optimist," Eun said.

Bae bowed her head, not disagreeing—at least not out loud.

Hwa Young waited until the end of the training session to ask the question that had been bothering her. "How *are* pilots chosen? Would it make sense to tell us the criteria so we can strive harder?" She hoped he would accept her sincerity.

"Maybe figuring it out is part of the process," Bae said cuttingly.

"That's not entirely wrong," Eun muttered. "The version of the adaptive interface used by the lancers is cutting-edge. Each unit has its own preferences. Even Commander Ye Jun doesn't decide who's suitable, although zie makes an educated guess as to promising candidates. The lancers themselves pick their pilots."

Hwa Young's heart plummeted. In other words, she could impress Eun and it still wouldn't matter. The lancer might pick someone else based on some arbitrary standard of its own.

The lancer might glimpse her secret and reject her for not being a true Imperial.

No. I can't give up.

"Why are there so few pilots anyway?" Hwa Young pressed.

Geum was mouthing *No, don't* frantically from the other side of the room, but Hwa Young needed to know. They all did.

Eun's eyes darted around the room. Then he heaved a sigh and set his own spacesuit back in its locker with the care of someone who knew his life might depend on it in the near future. He leaned against the nearest bulkhead. "You're gonna find out anyway."

"Find out *what?*" one of the other recruits demanded.

Eun huffed, kicking the deck like a frustrated horse, then squared his shoulders. "It's not just that the lancers pick compatible pilots," he said harshly. "Whatever you've experienced as a link between yourself and, say, a hovercar you're driving, the bond is that much more intense with a lancer. You move the lancer like a part of yourself—but that means when you take damage, there's a feedback loop."

All twenty of the candidates had fallen silent. Hwa Young held herself still, not wanting to miss a word.

"The last battle at Spinel was bad. Real bad." Eun's voice came out low and tense and unhappy. "We were still a full company of twelve pilots then. At Spinel, we lost four in the first wave."

For the first time, Hwa Young looked at Eun as a potential comrade, however grumpy, rather than an obstacle. She hadn't considered what he'd gone through, the battles he'd endured before she met him. And she'd never apologized for lobbing a shuttle at his lancer, either. Especially if he'd *felt* the explosion through the neural link.

"You've seen Commander Ye Jun's left arm. The one that doesn't work anymore." Eun smiled humorlessly. "Zie used to direct us from a sniper unit. Took a hit to zir lancer defending *me*. The battle got chaotic fast, and the rest of the company perished—Admiral Chin blames zir for the losses. Because I didn't dodge the missile fast enough. The technicians repaired the lancer, but it's no use. Normally they'd outfit zir with a prosthesis . . . but prostheses won't work with lancer feedback injuries. Zie can't move zir own arm *or* the lancer's. And zir lancer is relegated to the rear as a command-and-control unit, since it's no good for combat anymore."

Hwa Young had barely breathed as Eun was speaking. She

doubted the other trainees had, either; it was so quiet in the room, you could hear a pin drop.

Eun looked around at the candidates and seemed satisfied by their dismay. "All right, baby candidates. Get out of my hair. You have one hour of rec time before the next training session."

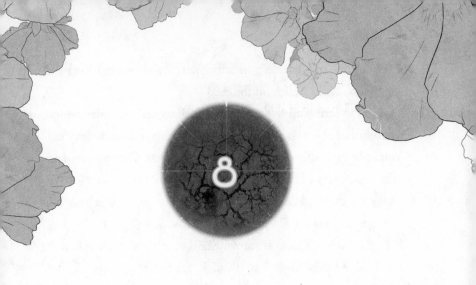

8

Two weeks into training, Hwa Young fought to stay awake in a class that a less diligent student might have classified as stultifying and she chose to categorize as *thorough*. She would have preferred Commander Ye Jun as an instructor, but if she'd learned one thing during her time shipboard, it was that warrant officers and noncoms like Eun did the less prestigious work of drilling the candidates, while actual officers busied themselves with loftier affairs.

Eun was lecturing them about the effects of aether poisoning, something she'd already lived through. Hwa Young knew it wasn't the aether itself that killed you but the delusional thinking that it induced, which caused you to do something stupid and fatal.

If the Imperials hadn't rescued me before the aether fried my brain—

But that had been six years ago, and she was no longer a frightened child hiding in the reeds.

As she scribbled telegraphic notes into her slate, she peered at the other students. Bae, right ahead of her, showed every appearance of being engrossed by the material. Geum, who had taken the seat to Hwa Young's right, was doodling what looked like—she craned her head to verify that her friend was drawing dragons and swords. Well, if zie didn't want to take the opportunity seriously, that was on zir. She'd much rather have Geum for a fellow pilot than Bae, though. As for Seong Su, his lips moved as he took notes, as though he were repeating everything to himself to commit it to memory.

Hwa Young had spent the classes studying the candidates as much as she did the material that Eun or the other instructors presented. Ho Sook, a thin, studious girl who never met anyone's eyes. Chin Hae, who sneered at everyone who dared to talk to zir. Hwa Young didn't consider either of them serious threats to her own candidacy.

Of the others, Hwa Young was most worried about Dong Yul, whose brashness Eun favored, and Hak Kun, a narrow-faced person who answered questions almost as quickly as Bae or Hwa Young herself. Dong Yul had been homeschooled, some kind of special dispensation from the planetary governor; Hwa Young hadn't even realized that was possible. Hak Kun had attended a school in a city to the south of Forsythia. Both of them were eighteen, two years older than everyone from her class. An icicle spike of resentment stabbed Hwa Young's heart every time one of them outperformed her.

It doesn't matter. I'm not going to let anything stand between me and a lancer.

"All right," Eun announced after a gruesome anecdote about someone who had injured herself with a welding tool under the influence of aether sickness. "I'm tired of hearing myself talking about this stuff. I'm sure you are too." He grinned toothily, daring them to share in the joke. No one responded except Seong Su, who did so with his usual sunny smile. "Closing prayer, and then hand-to-hand."

Seong Su had a question for once. "Sir, isn't it unlikely we're gonna end up pummeling clanners with our fists? If we're in lancers?"

Eun heaved a sigh. "For the last time, Candidate, I'm not 'sir.' That's for officers." Notably, he failed to answer the question.

"Yes, sir." Seong Su's expression was bland but friendly and didn't reveal whether he was being obtuse on purpose.

Hwa Young sometimes wondered how much in the way of brains lurked behind that easygoing exterior. Of all the candidates, he was the only one everyone got along with. Surely *that* couldn't be the deciding criterion—except she reminded herself that all the pilots would ultimately have to work together. Maybe she would do better to emulate Seong Su after all.

Eun turned his attention to the closing prayer. It was the same as the one they'd observed at the boarding school: several lines of archaic Hangeul that Hwa Young didn't understand, followed by the Imperial credo—*Trust the Empress. Move at her will. Act as her hands.* Then a bow to the head of the room, which stood in for the direction of the crownworld from which the Empress reigned.

She remembered her second day in the orphanage where the Imperials had dumped her, and where she had worked so hard to escape via scholarship. Hwa Young had made the mistake of asking why they recited meaningless words, instead of translating the prayer into modern Hangeul. Words that people could understand without studying linguistics. The orphanage director had told her to have more respect for history—apparently the ancient words were an oath of fealty from Old Hangeul—and locked her in isolation for a full week for her insolence. Hwa Young hadn't made *that* mistake again, and she wasn't about to repeat it now.

As much as she chafed at the customs, Hwa Young's shoulders sagged in relief as an aura of rightness—if not exactly *peace*—spread through the classroom. She luxuriated in the definite downward pull of gravity.

Geum lingered after Eun dismissed them. The class had a ten-minute break before hand-to-hand, which Hwa Young now recognized as a luxury. "Hey," Geum whispered. "I got something to show you."

Hwa Young didn't want to be late to class, but she owed Geum. Every time she spotted the livid scar that disfigured the shaved portion of zir head, guilt stabbed her. "Coming."

To her surprise, Geum only took her around the corner, not far from where they were supposed to go for training. Zie called up a screen on zir slate with a few expert gestures. "It required some skullduggery, but I found out where they took all the adults."

Hwa Young's eyebrows rose. "Your fathers." A knot in her stomach loosened.

Geum's voice became even more hushed. Hwa Young had to lean close to discern zir words. "This stuff is all encrypted, high-end stuff. They really want to keep it secret. The authorities evacuated about four thousand refugees from Serpentine.

Everyone over twenty got hustled aboard the *Sonamu*." *Pine tree.* "It's a Chollima-class colony ship accompanying the Eleventh Fleet."

Hwa Young frowned. "Lack of space in the rest of the fleet?" That didn't make sense. She didn't know what the *Maehwa*'s carrying capacity was, but families could have fit into the empty conference rooms and unused cabins.

"I tried asking what they did with all the adults. No one's talking. I said I wanted to send a message to my fathers and they shooed me away like I was a fly. I assume if they have a colony ship, it has to do with repopulation or something. So why all the secrecy?"

"I don't know," Hwa Young admitted. "Younger people make better pilot candidates, but surely there are other jobs that adults would do better. Engineering and that kind of thing."

"I'll keep digging, but I think I've already raised some red flags. I don't want them to cut off my access to the ship's computers." Geum straightened. "Come on, let's get to class."

Hwa Young's days dissolved into a blur of lectures and exercises. She became so intimately familiar with her assigned spacesuit and its quirks that she could have put it on in her sleep. That was probably the point.

I will be fighting clanners, she thought blankly in the stark cold moments before reveille, while Seong Su snored like a hibernating bear and Eun tossed and turned, calling out incoherent names. She told herself it didn't matter. That life belonged to a girl who had died amid Carnelian's broken reeds.

She cocooned herself in meditations in which a lancer's cockpit welcomed her, the soothing white and blue and silver lights of her cherished fantasy.

Besides, her family had died. It wasn't as though she'd be facing off against someone she knew.

Died at the hands of the lancers came the whisper again and again, until she learned to harden herself against it. Hwa Young prayed more diligently for the Empress's favor. It was the first thing she did upon waking, and the last thing she did at night. She fixed in her memory the image of Captain Ga Ram's face, the kindness zie had shown an orphan six years ago.

The Empress keeps all her children safe. You are one of her children now.

Even Bae remarked on her piety. Granted, the remarks weren't *kind*—"Who does she think she's fooling?" were Bae's exact words, spoken in passing to Ha Yoon—but Hwa Young was cynically amused to have made an impression.

The one place Hwa Young felt at home, amid the tumult of training and the cold discomfort of the *Maehwa*, was the firing range. Here she excelled, beating the others to emerge as the most accurate shot among the candidates. If it had been up to her, she would have spent all her rec time here, perfecting her aim. Surely, she reasoned, it was preferable to be the undisputed best at one specialty rather than middling-good at a number of them.

The only thing that prevented Hwa Young from focusing obsessively on marksmanship, whether with flare pistols or laser rifles, was Geum. Time and again she bit back her guilty resentment when zie invited her to play video games with zir, or watch the fantasy holo shows zie enjoyed so much. She felt even guiltier when Geum hung out with some of the technicians instead, or made contact with the shadowy black market in pursuit of zir favorite snacks, freeing her to do what she wanted—to be alone.

When they did hang out, Geum was always showing off zir latest hack, like tunneling past the *Maehwa*'s cybersecurity defenses. Zie even offered to show her the file that Eun kept on her, but Hwa Young was alarmed at the risk of getting caught and demurred. The only computer systems Geum couldn't penetrate, ironically, were the lancers'.

They'd snatched a few moments together in a corner of the rec room, where Seong Su was patiently wrestling everyone who challenged him and looking sheepish every time he won. (Hwa Young had known better than to challenge him.) Geum looked up from zir slate with its animated prancing dragons, lips pursed. "Hey, you look stressed," zie said. "Anything you want to talk about?"

I don't know what I'll do if I fail, Hwa Young almost said. She couldn't bear the thought of being dismissed as useless. Unworthy the way Bae implied, just because she didn't come from a prestigious family. If she didn't secure a position as a pilot, she had nothing to look forward to but a dreary life as a refugee, toiling at whatever menial chores the authorities needed warm bodies for.

Hwa Young couldn't bring herself to voice any of this, but Geum, always sensitive to others' moods, patted her shoulder. "The stress is getting to all of us."

Except you, she thought, envious. Still, wasn't it good that someone she cared about had avoided becoming a nervous wreck? "You seem like you're doing all right?"

"There's so much to learn aboard this ship," Geum said, eyes rapturously bright. "I would *never* have gotten close to military security systems before. Not in Forsythia City. Every time I dive into the computers, I find something new. Like the fact that one of the commodores keeps a file of dirty jokes, or that Admiral Chin is on the leaderboard for *Starfighter Shoutout Extravaganza 2* under a pseudonym. One of these days I'm going to knock her off."

The corners of Hwa Young's mouth twitched. "I have no idea how you have time for video games." Or how the admiral did, for that matter. She lowered her voice. "Aren't you afraid of what will happen if you . . ."

"If a lancer doesn't choose me?" Geum shrugged. "They might pick me as a technician or engineer. The techs are a friendly bunch. They say the best ones are former lancer candidates, you know."

Huh. "But you'd rather be a pilot, wouldn't you?"

"Sure." Geum patted her shoulder again. "We'll both make it. Bae will be sorry when she's stuck crawling through ventilation ducts to do maintenance or greasing the gun mounts." Strangely, Geum sounded wistful about the prospect.

Hwa Young checked the time. "We'd better get moving. Come on."

It would be *nice* if she could be top of the class at everything, Hwa Young thought when Bae scored highest yet again on the next drill, a painstaking memory game. Everyone was given the same view of a starscape to study for one minute. Then Eun blasted terrible music videos at them for five minutes—at least, Hwa Young was convinced that he picked the ones with caterwauling and flashing lights specifically to torture them—before projecting a nearly identical starscape and challenging them to spot the differences.

Hwa Young came in fourth on this exercise, behind Bae, Hak Kun, and Geum. Resentment bit her heart anew, and she scolded herself for it. Didn't she want Geum to become a pilot, too? Besides, while she had spent her childhood on Carnelian, learning to read the spoor of moon-rabbits in the grasses, to hear her prey's wanderings in the wind's cryptic utterances, Geum had excellent visual memory and focus honed by years of playing zir beloved games. She should be happy for her friend.

Three more classes followed, including a grueling session of hand-to-hand for which they wore padded armor. Hwa Young was paired with Bae again, since they had the same approximate height and build—though Bae was a half head taller, because of course she was.

As the two of them squared off on the training mat, Bae eyed Hwa Young as though she posed a threat, which was absurd. What did Bae, of all people, have to fear? "It's touching to see you try so hard," Bae said, her voice quiet enough that Eun, on the other side of the room correcting Ha Yoon's awkward stance, couldn't overhear her.

Hwa Young had learned the hard way that shooting back retorts never paid off. Bae had a knack for snappy comebacks. Moreover, all the other candidates deferred to her, whether out of habit or because they'd quickly determined that she was the dominant contender. Hwa Young kept her face as blank as winter ice.

This only infuriated Bae. "Have it your way," she sniffed.

The moment Eun signaled that they should begin, Bae struck. She moved like wind and thunder, unpredictable yet precise. Hwa Young was hard pressed to keep up with her. Blows landed again and again on the pressure points that Eun had drilled into them. Only the armor saved Hwa Young from being disabled.

I have faced worse, Hwa Young thought as she spun and dodged, returning blow for blow. *I have survived worse.* Bae might have a fighter's reflexes and instincts, but the inner core of her was soft. Cosseted. Hwa Young wasn't going to lose to some rich kid who'd had every advantage handed to her.

Hwa Young glimpsed an opening. Committed to it. No room for hesitation, no time for doubt.

Geum, who'd already finished zir sparring match, called out encouragement. *A rich kid like Geum,* murmured a discontented voice in the hollows of Hwa Young's mind. Except she didn't want to think of *Geum* like that. Not when zie was such a loyal friend.

It was a fatal distraction.

Bae kicked Hwa Young on the chin. Hwa Young's head snapped back and she staggered. Normally she'd have seen a high kick like that coming. She'd let herself lose her concentration. Not just because of Geum, but because Bae had *allowed* her to see that opening. A feint that had turned into a real attack.

Within a second it was over. Bae flipped Hwa Young over. Hwa Young landed hard, air whooshing out of her. Bae knelt over her, pinning her arms. She leaned in close and whispered into Hwa Young's ear, her breath hot and vicious: "You'll never be good enough."

Hwa Young's eyes stung as she stared up at the other girl, a single thought echoing over and over in her head: *What if she's right?*

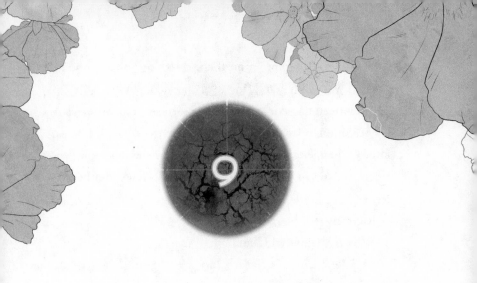

9

Eight days later, when Hwa Young was starting to think she would spend the rest of her life on the *Maehwa* enduring classes and watching Bae pull ahead of her, Commander Ye Jun interrupted the physical training session. She almost didn't notice zir at first, so intent was she on performing her planks without showing any sign of strain. Never mind that every muscle in her body screamed and that she was desperate for a drink of water.

"Commander!" Eun snapped to. "Candidates."

Everyone stopped their planks, staggered upright, and saluted properly. Well, more or less properly. Seong Su was constitutionally incapable of getting the angle right no matter how many times Eun corrected him. Eun did so again, to little apparent effect.

"Sorry to come ahead of schedule," Commander Ye Jun said,

as though zie had come in on them throwing food at one another and was politely refusing to acknowledge it.

Eun looked pained. "Sir, you're the officer here. So *officiate*."

The commander's mouth moved up at the corners. It wasn't a smile. "Change of plans. We induct the candidates today."

Eun sucked in his breath. "They should have another two weeks—"

"Right now."

"Why—?" ventured Geum.

"Because," Commander Ye Jun said, "it has been decided that pilots now are better than pilots later, despite the risk." Before anyone could follow up with the obvious question, zie added, "The lancers have complex and powerful mental presences. With underprepared candidates, there's always a risk of neural trauma." Slight pause. "It's sometimes fatal."

Ha Yoon wrung her hands. "They didn't mention that when they recruited us, sir."

Hwa Young winced at the girl's words. Even Bae looked like she wished she could distance herself from Ha Yoon.

"You can withdraw your candidacy." The commander's tone was impersonal.

Ha Yoon snuck a glance at Bae's face, imperious, and shook her head quickly. "No, sir."

I don't think she's much competition, Hwa Young couldn't help thinking. Ha Yoon performed competently enough when it came to memorizing material, but she lacked a fighter's instincts.

"Come with me, then," Commander Ye Jun said.

They'd learned to walk single file shipboard just as at the boarding school. Hwa Young was last in line. Right behind Ha

Yoon, who had hung back, her fear and reluctance clear. Even Geum was two spots ahead of Ha Yoon. The others had subtly crowded Hwa Young out of an earlier spot in such a way that she'd look petty if she complained to Eun or, Empress forbid, the commander.

Twenty candidates. Thirteen lancers—the twelve regular ones and the commander's control unit—of which two already had pilots. Maybe everyone would luck out and become a pilot or copilot.

Hwa Young had no intention of playing second fiddle as someone's *copilot*.

She was hyperaware of her surroundings all the way to the docking bay. Every footstep in cadence, a perfect drummer's counterpoint to the unsteady staccato of her heart. The way the flagship's regular crew avoided meeting their eyes, as though the candidates bore a contagion. The dry whoosh of air, smelling faintly of metal, antiseptic, and exhaustion. The trickle of sweat between her shoulder blades, which, thankfully, no one could witness.

They emerged at last at an upper level in the docking bay, which had been cleared of other personnel. Here, from a balcony with a suspiciously flimsy railing, they had a clear view of the eleven unclaimed lancers' inert heads. Commander Ye Jun's unit, with the upside-down antler crown emblem, and Eun's, with the orange flame, stood to the side. Catwalks led to the cockpits of the other nine units, standing open like eager maws. She wondered which would be the first to transmute from base gray to colors reflecting the lancer's own capabilities—and the personality of its chosen pilot.

No one waited for them but a technician and a medic. The former was the older man who had greeted Eun when Hwa Young first came to the *Maehwa* aboard his lancer. The other she didn't recognize, a rotund person with incongruously long, nimble fingers clutching a medical kit. Zir presence set Hwa Young's nerves alight, and she took a deep breath to steady herself.

"Line up," Commander Ye Jun said, still solemn.

All the candidates did so. *I'm going to be last,* Hwa Young thought over and over again, fighting not to reveal her rising dismay. What would happen if all the lancers claimed pilots before she had a chance to prove herself?

Maybe queueing up had been a test, too. She cursed herself for not shoving past the others to the front of the line.

Commander Ye Jun stood before them with one arm folded behind zir back. The other dangled as limply as always, a reminder of the risks involved in bonding with a lancer. Zie smiled crookedly. Surely zie was aware that Hwa Young was staring— that they were all staring.

"You have trained long and hard for the privilege of being presented to the lancers," the commander said. "Some of you will emerge pilots or copilots. Some of you will not." Zir gaze swept along the line, lingering on no one. If zie had opinions as to the hottest prospects, zie was good at hiding them.

"If any of you wish to withdraw your candidacy, leave now. A soldier will escort you to your new assignment."

Ha Yoon twitched, but a glance from Bae steadied her.

No one else moved.

"Very well. Best wishes, Candidates. Dong Yul, you're first. You will sit in each of the cockpits for one minute until a lancer responds to you—or doesn't."

That's it? Hwa Young thought incredulously. *We just sit in the cockpit?* She could already do that in her meditations.

She'd expected something more dramatic. Some form of trial by combat. Being the only one untouched by lancer fire. This was . . . disappointing.

The candidates held still, silent, watching Dong Yul with a raptor's intent as he swaggered down the first catwalk. His footfalls reverberated. The docking bay was filled with a low, unpleasant thrum, the familiar sounds of the *Maehwa*'s engines and air filters turned threatening by the tension of the ritual.

The cockpit door closed behind him. They could have heard a pin drop. Hell, an eyelash.

Hwa Young squinted, seeking the slightest hint of color. Had the gray lightened in shade, or was that a trick of her imagination? She was sure from the stuttering breaths of the others that they, too, sought a sign.

"No response, sir," Eun said after exactly one minute.

A sigh gusted from all the candidates.

"You may come out, Candidate," Commander Ye Jun said, as though zie were doing him a favor and not pronouncing the first opportunity spent.

Dong Yul emerged, still with a swagger, but spots of color stained his cheeks. He'd hoped for better, the way they all did. One of the candidates in line—Hwa Young couldn't tell which one—sucked in their breath in dismay.

"You have ten more opportunities," the commander added, as though Dong Yul needed a reminder of basic arithmetic. Maybe he did. He looked stunned by the lancers, ensorcelled by the dust-drab gray everywhere.

Dong Yul made his way into the second cockpit. Silence

descended again. More sweat trickled down Hwa Young's spine. *That won't be me,* she promised herself, knowing all the while that it wasn't up to her.

She hated that. She'd worked hard, just as they all had worked hard, yet the choice was ultimately out of her hands.

Dong Yul entered and exited, entered and exited. Each time, the lancers remained gray, dormant, unmoved by the force of his desire. Hwa Young's vision was starting to dim at the edges from the sheer tension. She could only imagine what was happening to *his.*

At last it came to the eleventh and final lancer. Pain spiked in Hwa Young's palms as Dong Yul strode into its cockpit, his back stiff and his face white with dread. She realized her fingernails had pierced skin, drawn blood; she relaxed her fingers one by one, surreptitiously wiping her hands against her pants. She'd deal with the stains later.

Ten seconds. Nine.

Three. Two. One.

Eun said, exactly on schedule, "No response, sir." Except this time, unlike the first ten, his voice was heavy with disappointment.

Dong Yul came out, pale and shaking, all the swagger gone out of him. "Let me try again," he blurted out. "Give me more time. I thought I felt—"

"Former candidate." Commander Ye Jun's voice cracked out, sharper than Hwa Young had ever heard it before. "Stand aside."

Dong Yul stumbled to the end of the line, not far from Hwa Young. He scrubbed at his eyes. Hwa Young quelled the urge to flinch from his presence, as though his bad luck were contagious. She didn't like him, but there was no need for her to rub it in.

The next candidate tried. Failed. This one was a quiet, hardworking boy completely unlike Dong Yul. Hwa Young had never paid attention to him, sensing he wasn't a true rival. Nevertheless, her heart made a painful lump in her throat when he, too, proved unsuitable. At least, unlike Dong Yul, he didn't embarrass everyone by kicking up a fuss.

What if we all wash out? Hwa Young hadn't seriously given the prospect thought. Now, as she regarded Eun's pale, grim visage, Commander Ye Jun's forbidding expression, she realized the possibility had existed all along. *We candidates aren't the only ones who are stressed.* She couldn't decide whether she resented the commander and Eun for never mentioning it, or whether she was grateful they hadn't added to the candidates' anxiety.

The mood on the balcony, originally anticipatory despite the undercurrent of dread, became strained. Hwa Young suspected everyone was thinking the same thing: *What if I don't make it? What if none of us do?*

Commander Ye Jun didn't give them more time to brood about the risk of failure. "Bae."

Bae didn't have to be told what to do. She didn't quite march toward that first cockpit with Dong Yul's arrogance, but she projected an air of assurance that made Hwa Young dislike her more than ever. If only Bae would show some human emotion, some sign of vulnerability.

Uncomfortably, Hwa Young wondered if her bitterness would affect the lancers' choice. As much as she wanted to shove Bae's superiority back in her face, she didn't like the thought of sabotaging Bae's chances, either. Eun would have told them if the candidates' attitudes had an effect . . . wouldn't he? Despite his brusque manner, he was always looking out for them, and she realized how much she'd come to depend on that.

Hwa Young stared as the hatch of the first lancer cockpit closed behind Bae, swallowing her. *I don't know any such thing.* She was beginning to understand that Eun left a lot of things unsaid, and Commander Ye Jun even more so.

So preoccupied was Hwa Young with her own thoughts that it took a moment for the candidates' gasps to register. Forty-three seconds had elapsed. *What is it?* she wondered, refocusing on the lancer that Bae had entered.

Then she saw it. Leaned forward, desperate to be sure. The color had brightened to the mirror-sheen of silver, with scroll-work embellishments in deep violet. It should have looked similar to the original matte gray, but it was as different as the stars from the dirt.

The lancer itself began to transform with a low, almost musical metallic humming. Eun's lancer in its synchronized form was all angles and armor, like a statue of a warrior of old. Bae's was sleek and graceful, with the aspect of a bird of prey. Eyes—sensor arrays—opened all around the head, crowning it in eerie fashion. Its left arm re-formed into a railgun.

"Well done, Bae," Commander Ye Jun said, and Hwa Young didn't think she had imagined the newfound warmth in zir voice. "You've synchronized with *Farseer One.* That will be your new callsign. And on your first try, too. A good omen."

The lancers have names? Hwa Young thought, too wrung out to be properly outraged. She studied the other ten lancers anew, scrutinizing them for any hints of their inner nature. *Farseer.* That implied it had advanced scan capability.

"You may come out now, Bae," Eun said. To the candidates, he added, "The railgun is a useful weapon to have access to, although not, of course, the most powerful one."

At least that was one thing Bae *hadn't* achieved. "What's the most powerful one, then?" Hwa Young couldn't help asking. Another thing the briefings and lessons hadn't covered.

Eun waited for a nod from Ye Jun before answering. "All lancers can use their gravitic reserves to fire gravity lances. It's where they got their name. But the most powerful known weapon is a singularity lance, which can single-handedly take out a capital ship. The Eleventh Fleet hasn't had that capability in years. It takes a strong bond for even the most talented pilot to unlock the weapon's full ability."

Whatever else Eun might have added was interrupted by Bae's emergence. She held her head high, triumph in every line of her body. The first candidate to be claimed by a lancer.

Bae's eyes glowed with an exalted light. That wasn't just her high spirits, Hwa Young realized after a closer look. Her eyes sheened silver-violet. As Hwa Young gaped, their color slowly darkened to their regular brown. Hwa Young didn't know whether to be awed or chilled by the effect.

Eun nodded at Bae, equal to equal. Hwa Young's heart seized in envy and apprehension.

I can't let her outdo me—except Bae already had, by synchronizing first, and on her first attempt.

The next candidate, Ho Sook, didn't just fail; she came out of the last lancer after only nine seconds, her face drained of color. The medic hurried to her side, shooting Commander Ye Jun reproving looks, as though zie had caused the situation. Zie ignored them both.

More failures. Just like Ho Sook, all of them refused to stay in the last lancer for the full allotted minute. Hwa Young was starting to wonder what was so scary about it. After all, Dong Yul had gone the full minute and survived, right? But there was no way to ask.

More candidates shaken and subdued, taking their place at the end of the line now that they were no longer relevant. Hwa Young's trepidation grew, as well as her determination not to end up like them.

Then came Seong Su's turn. *Surely not him,* Hwa Young thought, aware of how catty she would have sounded if she'd spoken out loud. It wasn't that she wished him ill. He was friendly and well-liked by everyone, and ever since they'd found themselves both candidates, he'd treated her kindly. Despite his strength and adeptness with a spacesuit, though, he'd never struck her as pilot material.

The first lancer had, of course, already claimed Bae, although upon her exit it had resumed its ordinary bland appearance. The ritual still started with the first lancer, although Hwa Young imagined Seong Su was an unlikely copilot for Bae. Hwa Young forced herself to breathe deeply and evenly as Seong Su vanished into the cockpit.

Nothing.

The second lancer.

Hwa Young watched attentively, torn between boredom and anxiety.

Nothing.

The third lancer.

Hwa Young caught herself tapping her fingers against the side of her leg and made herself stop. Bae couldn't see her from her coveted position next to Commander Ye Jun as a newly minted pilot, but it was the principle of the thing.

Nothing.

The fourth lancer.

Fifty-two seconds passed. Hwa Young expected another disappointment.

Suddenly, the fourth lancer expanded in all directions, almost knocking over the ones to either side. Someone must have calculated the spacing precisely, because after it had completed its transformation into a bulky monstrosity, its chest and limbs protected by ridged plates, mere centimeters separated it from its fellows.

Seong Su's lancer was an uninspiring earthen brown with only a hint of coppery highlights where the light struck its armor. Still, for sheer size it was impressive, even if Hwa Young tried and failed to locate its weapons. Eun had mentioned that all lancers had gravity lances, but surely it should have *something* else?

"Commander," Eun said, adhering to the forms even if Hwa Young was sure zie knew all of this already, "Seong Su has been claimed by *Avalanche Four.*"

"Of course it had to be Four." It must have been her imagination, but the commander sounded sad. "It can't be helped."

Why doesn't zie sound happier? Hwa Young wondered. Was the *Avalanche* a less powerful lancer type?

Seong Su emerged flushed and bashful. Hwa Young remembered his sheepishness when winning over and over at arm wrestling. It was much the same expression. She found she couldn't hate him for his success.

Next, Chin Hae washed out. Hak Kun, too, although zie had the most interesting reaction of all the candidates. Zie looked *relieved* to have failed. Had zie been swept away from some other vocation?

Then it was Geum's turn. Zie entered each of the eleven lancers one by one, zir smile never faltering despite the fact that they remained gray, unmoved.

At last Geum tried the eleventh lancer. This time Hwa Young saw what she had failed to notice earlier: Commander Ye Jun and Eun tensed every time it came to the final lancer. As though they'd put it last in the lineup due to some secret fear. Paired with the fact that almost everyone exited it early, it made Hwa Young's dread increase.

Geum only spent twenty-eight seconds in the eleventh lancer. It didn't respond to zir either. When zie came out, zir smile was gone. Whether because of the lancer itself, or because of zir failure, Hwa Young wasn't sure.

"Stand aside, former candidate," Commander Ye Jun said. Then, a reassurance zie hadn't offered the others: "The best engineers are often close friends to lancer pilots. The *Maehwa* has a use for you yet."

Finally it was Ha Yoon's turn. The second-to-last candidate. She stumbled forward, her face pinched and ghastly, as though she faced an execution. Her naked dread made Hwa Young's stomach twist in revulsion. Hwa Young never intended to be that weak.

One by one the lancers rejected Ha Yoon by their silence,

their failure to transform. She came at last to the eleventh lancer. Vanished inside the cockpit.

Maybe she's braver than I thought, Hwa Young thought as the seconds ticked by and Ha Yoon didn't emerge.

One minute passed. "No response, sir," Eun said, right on schedule.

Ha Yoon did not come out.

One more minute elapsed.

Two.

"I'm engaging emergency override," Commander Ye Jun announced, as though zie owed an explanation to anyone standing on the balcony. Zir eyes glowed gold-green as zie linked with zir own lancer. Unlike the other units, it retained its disturbing, almost featureless humanoid form even when it turned gold with green jeweled details, but there was no sign of weapons or extra armor. Hwa Young wondered if this was some side effect of the damage that had injured the commander's left arm.

The gold lancer's eyes flared brightly. Hwa Young felt rather than heard a furious scream in her mind as the eleventh lancer turned a wan, sickly version of the commander's gold. Then the eleventh lancer's cockpit stood open, and it faded back to gray.

Eun and the medic rushed in. Emerged carrying Ha Yoon's limp form together. They laid her down on the balcony. The medic knelt next to her and took her pulse.

The medic looked up, zir face bleak. "She's dead."

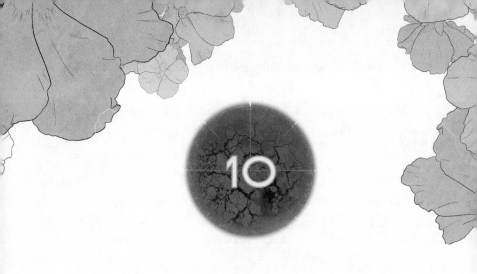

10

wa Young heard screams, prayers, even a thud as one ex-candidate fainted. Geum rushed to the girl's side. People milled about, no longer disciplined, as the medic argued with Commander Ye Jun. The former still crouched over Ha Yoon's corpse.

"You've got to abort this," the medic said, zir voice high and sharp. "Maybe you don't care how many lives you throw away obtaining replacement pilots, but—"

The commander raised an eyebrow, and the medic flinched at Ye Jun's sudden aura of menace. "I wouldn't do this," Commander Ye Jun said, "if we had another choice. But we don't."

The medic waved a hand at Hwa Young. "She's the last one, right? At least you can prevent *her* from becoming a second casualty of this Empress-forsaken ritual."

"Excuse me," Hwa Young cut in. "I get a say in this."

"Indeed," the commander said. "Do you want to—"

"You haven't been straight with any of them," the medic snapped, "so it shouldn't surprise me that you're not being straight with them now."

Eun growled, "You have no right to—"

The medic had overcome zir initial intimidation, or maybe didn't like Eun to begin with. Zie waved at the milling candidates and ex-candidates. "Saving lives is my duty," zie hissed back. "Even if you and the bastard over there have forgotten it." Zie closed the dead girl's eyes, a tender gesture at odds with zir fierce words.

Bae approached and knelt wordlessly next to Ha Yoon. At the medic's glare, Bae said in a rasp, "She was my friend."

The medic nodded and made space for her.

Bae cradled the limp body, stroking Ha Yoon's hair. Her face was blank, her eyes abysmally dark. Hwa Young took back every catty thought she'd had about the two. Bae's stark, controlled grief, dignified in its way, hit Hwa Young harder than shrieking and sobbing would have.

"It's hard on everyone to lose someone so young," Commander Ye Jun said with a quelling glance at Eun. "Nevertheless: it is indeed up to Hwa Young. Candidate, will you make the attempt?"

"At least *tell* her!" the medic cried.

"Tell her what?" Bae demanded before Hwa Young could ask the same question.

"Get back in line," Eun said, his tone harsh.

Bae cast an anguished look down at Ha Yoon's unmoving face, then returned to her spot by Eun.

Dong Yul muttered, "If you hadn't pushed her to stay in the program, *Farseer,* maybe she'd still be with us."

Bae's face hardened into a cold mask. She didn't deign to respond, and she looked away from Ha Yoon.

After everyone else had shuffled back into their proper places, Hwa Young stood alone between two groups. Commander Ye Jun, Eun, and the two newly minted pilots, Bae and Seong Su, were to her left. The rejected candidates, headed by Dong Yul, occupied her right.

"I prefer my pilots and copilots not to come into the bonding ritual with too many preconceptions," Commander Ye Jun said quietly. "The lancers always know. Owing to the circumstances, however"—zie gave an ironic nod in the medic's direction— "I will tell you this much.

"This specific lancer, as Eun let slip earlier, has not been piloted in twelve years because it killed four candidates presented to it." The commander ignored Dong Yul's gasp and addressed himself directly to Hwa Young. "At that time, my predecessor decided to mothball the lancer because of its temperamental nature, despite its extraordinary combat potential. In its place, we were using a different lancer unit that was destroyed at Spinel."

Combat potential. "The singularity lance," Hwa Young breathed.

The commander nodded. "It's the only lancer in the Eleventh Fleet with that capability. Even the admiral agrees that its power would increase our chances of defeating the clanners in this sector. It was my decision to present all of you to it, in the hopes that someone would bond with it."

"And they all failed," the medic said.

"Not yet," Commander Ye Jun said. Zie met Hwa Young's eyes. "Are you willing?"

To Hwa Young's surprise, Seong Su spoke up. "Maybe she

could have the option of skipping the eleventh?" he asked. "As a compromise?"

"I did not ask for your input," Commander Ye Jun said with deceptive softness. "My question was for Hwa Young. It is her answer that matters."

Hwa Young felt everyone's eyes on her. "I'll do it. I'll try all of them."

Eun's mouth twisted. "It's true you can quit in the middle."

"If an earlier lancer in the lineup accepts her, it's moot anyway," Commander Ye Jun said. "Enough. Are you ready?"

Hwa Young tipped her chin up. "Always."

The commander gestured toward the first lancer's cockpit: *There's no time like the present.*

Hwa Young hated the thought of being *Bae's* copilot, but she couldn't in good conscience refuse to make the attempt. Straight-backed, she took step after measured step until she reached the cockpit. It stood open like the mouth of a tomb, or an invitation to the other side of midnight.

She reminded herself that she had faced death and worse than death. That every day she lived among the Imperials, she risked someone unearthing her origins and casting her out. She had given everything up, including her family and people and culture, for this opportunity.

Only the scantest of light inside guided her to the pilot's seat. No one had told her what to do once she was ensconced within. On the other hand, she'd been in a cockpit before, even if it had belonged to Eun's lancer. By touch she located the straps and belted herself in, waiting for light, noise, a shining in her soul. Any indication the lancer had chosen her—even as a copilot.

125

In her meditations, she'd always imagined an immediate connection. The lancer glowing triumphantly as it accepted her. Not this dismal sense of foreboding.

Instead, after an interminable wait in the darkness, while the belt dug into her shoulder, she heard Eun announcing the dreaded words: "No response, sir," and Commander Ye Jun answering, "You may come out, Candidate."

Hwa Young's uniform was already sweat-soaked. It clung unpleasantly to her back as she exited with the same measured steps. Maddeningly, her ankle started to itch, but she wasn't going to stoop to scratch it, or let it distract her.

Next was the second lancer. Hwa Young endured the ritual again, seated herself in the pilot's seat, stared into the darkness while afterimages ghosted around her like the phantasms of other people's futures. She thought she spotted Bae's haughty face among them, complete with the silver-violet eyes that would forever mark her a pilot; seethed that she herself hadn't bonded with a lancer on her first attempt. Refused to acknowledge the possibility that, like Geum, she would have to pursue some other specialty.

Eun: "No response, sir."

Commander Ye Jun: "You may come out, Candidate."

The third lancer didn't respond to her either, nor the fourth. Curiously, she felt an antipathy toward the fourth one, *Avalanche Four*, despite its now-bland exterior. She told herself it was her imagination, or else a natural reaction to a lancer that had claimed someone who wasn't her.

Hwa Young's jaw ached as she entered the fifth lancer's cockpit. She hadn't realized she'd been clenching it to keep anyone from reading her expression. In the darkness she forced herself to relax, sheathed herself in the cherished visualization of her very own cockpit. But relaxation wasn't possible, not when the stakes were this high.

Eun and Commander Ye Jun's refrain had already become familiar. Hwa Young was shocked at herself. *I won't simply accept this,* she vowed even as she remembered Dong Yul's outburst and how much she had disliked him for it.

Next came number six. When she walked out of its cockpit, still unclaimed, the others' stares, ranging from judgy (Bae) to skeptical (the medic), weighed on her like a physical pressure against her skin. They'd already given up on her. She could tell.

Their opinions don't matter. The lancers did the choosing. Not the people. Especially not those who had already failed. Even if one of them was Geum. Even if success meant she would be separated from Geum again.

The force of her conviction shocked her. Seven. Hwa Young breathed in and out, in and out, counting each cycle of exhalations. She already knew this wouldn't be the one, that it had no affinity for her. It didn't matter that *Farseer One* and *Avalanche Four* had taken some time to reveal their choices. She was certain it would be an all-or-nothing choice, rather than a slow appraisal.

Eun and Commander Ye Jun told her to come out once more, so she did.

Hwa Young swept her gaze over the other candidates. Most of them wore pitying expressions. A few kept glancing fearfully at Ha Yoon's still form. At least Geum gave her a shaky thumbs-up.

I haven't failed yet.

Still, Hwa Young would have been lying if she said she was confident.

Maybe it will be the next one.

The eighth lancer enfolded her. The sense of *wrongness* redoubled, stronger than ever. As though her bones wanted to turn inside out rather than remain encased by flesh.

She refused to leave before the full minute had elapsed. But if Ha Yoon had aborted her attempt to bond with the eleventh lancer, would she still be alive?

Hwa Young shuddered and closed her eyes, resuming her breathing exercises and visualization to steady herself. Still, she knew. The lancer that wanted her—that *chose* her—wouldn't present itself as an ordeal to be tolerated, but as a perfect congruence, human intelligence meeting an artificial one in synchrony.

What if I'm wrong? What if she had misunderstood the fundamental nature of the human-lancer bond, and it prevented her from achieving one for herself?

Before she could digest the implications of this unpleasant new thought, Hwa Young heard Eun pronouncing the dreary refrain: "No response, sir."

Hwa Young exited the cockpit while Commander Ye Jun was midway through zir sentence: "You may come out, Candidate."

It was the same with the ninth and the tenth. Hwa Young strove to keep desperation from showing on her face. She was sure the others smelled it on her anyway.

Only the eleventh lancer remained.

"Last chance, Hwa Young." Commander Ye Jun met her eyes, held them. "You can say no."

Hwa Young hesitated and hated herself for it. She didn't want to end up like Ha Yoon, a casualty of the selection process. Couldn't bear the thought of Geum grieving over her the way Bae had for Ha Yoon.

But this was her last chance. Her only chance. And she'd come so far.

"I'll do it," she said, biting off each syllable. She didn't look at Geum, afraid of the expression she'd find in zir eyes.

She approached the eleventh lancer, whose name, if any, Commander Ye Jun had not given. At least she knew that, as with the rest of the information zie had withheld, was deliberate. Zie had only mentioned the four it had killed. It wouldn't surprise her if its history included more deaths.

Since this was her last chance, Hwa Young did her best to savor the experience and notice any details she'd missed earlier. Maybe "savor" wasn't the right word. Her heart was pounding so hard she could feel it knocking against her rib cage. After all, this lancer had killed Ha Yoon. She might not have *liked* Ha Yoon, but the other girl hadn't deserved to die.

Her eyes adjusted to the darkness yet again. The same haze of afterimages enveloped her. In the variegated shadows she saw herself, or perhaps Mother Aera, from a lifetime ago, long-haired. Instructor Kim, her face stern as ever despite the broken neck, the blood. Fire and the aftermath of fire. Perhaps the images, despite their grim aspect, were a promising omen, a sign of a budding mental link with the lancer.

Shit. She'd lost track of time. Her neural implant included a basic chronometer, but she couldn't remember when she'd entered. How much of the single minute did she have left?

And if the eleventh lancer hadn't claimed her, was it ever

129

going to? What if she'd already failed, and it was only a matter of waiting out the choke hold of seconds?

Outside, she could hear a rising murmuration of voices. One of them carried clearly, as though sniper-aimed: "It's been fifty-two seconds. There's no hope."

Hwa Young closed her eyes and wished Bae would shut up, or better yet, that the deck would open up and swallow her.

Numbness cocooned her from head to toe. She'd failed. All that hard work, all that *effort* attempting to outdo Bae, and—

At that point, Hwa Young realized, from the red glow against the inside of her eyelids, that the interior of the cockpit had lit up.

She opened her eyes. Frost-colored fractal patterns had formed in every direction, like the labyrinthine heart of winter, more beautiful than even the most optimistic of her imaginings. Light dazzled her: first white, then storm-blue, then the brilliant silver of ice beneath starlight.

Hwa Young looked down. The same mazy patterns glowed *beneath* her skin, turning it an uncanny arctic white. It was hard to connect what she saw with herself, with her small and frail human body.

She'd never thought of herself in those terms before, but she understood now that her real body wasn't a construct of meat and bone and nervous impulses. She inhabited something greater, something grander, a frame of metal many times larger than a human. She had bones of alloy and armor for skin, and the singularity lance she carried had destroyed starships single-handedly in battles past, and would again in battles future.

Now and forever, she was a weapon, and she would never

again have to cower in the reeds, unable to retaliate against those who had hurt her and her family.

We are winter, said a chilly voice in her mind—or perhaps it was her own voice, grown dark and strange and commanding. *We are the death that waits in the dark. We are the beginning of the end, and the silence beyond the end. We are one, always.*

"—shouldn't have let her!" As though from a hall of infinity mirrors, Hwa Young heard the medic's shrill voice. "If there's a *second casualty*, I'm going straight to the admiral, and I swear by the Empress's consorts you're getting drummed out of the Imperial Army."

Hwa Young landed back in her own skin, breathless and disoriented.

"Hwa Young." It was Commander Ye Jun. "Come out now."

It took her another moment to remember how to puppet the machinery of her body. In passing she noted that the shoulder strap was no longer digging into her shoulder but had molded itself perfectly to her body so it caused her no discomfort. It fell away before she had touched it, as though the lancer itself had sensed her desire to exit.

Hwa Young's eyes readjusted to the light outside, dimmer though it was than the icy glory of the glow within the cockpit. She saw everything through a lens of winter clarity, every detail available for her contemplation. The hot envy in Dong Yul's eyes, Geum gaping as though she'd grown a second head, even the rage in Bae's face.

Commander Ye Jun was the only one who didn't recoil from her regard. Zie inclined zir head to her, like one monarch to another.

"Hwa Young," the commander said, "you have bonded with *Winter's Axiom*. Your callsign will be Winter. Well done."

"Your *hair*," Geum burst out. "Your *eyes*."

My hair and eyes what? Hwa Young wondered, but no one had a mirror. If Bae had come out with violet-silver eyes, what had happened to her own?

But she didn't really care. She had found the other half of herself, the missing part of her soul that she had yearned for all these years. That was all that mattered.

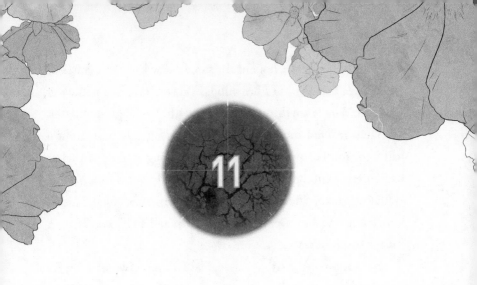

11

In the aftermath of the ceremony, Eun led the three success-
ful pilots—Bae, Seong Su, and Hwa Young herself—back to
the barracks, while the commander headed off to take care
of tasks of zir own. "Seems like a coincidence we're all from the
same class and bunking together," Seong Su remarked with a
glance back at the docking bay as they left their former peers
behind.

"Not as much as you'd think," Eun said. "The commander
felt it would ease your transition to shipboard life to have familiar faces around. And the lancers often pick people with a
shared history, if they get along." He glanced cynically at Bae,
then Hwa Young. "It could as easily have been Ho Sook, Chin
Hae, and Hak Kun, if the dice had rolled otherwise."

Once Hwa Young would have been pricked with shame at
the realization that she hadn't bothered to find out more about
the other students' backgrounds. She hadn't known those three

came from the same school or the same city, whatever it was. For now, she put them out of her mind. Eun would let them know if they would have anything more to do with the failed candidates.

They entered the bunkroom. Bae had already pulled out a mirror from her personal effects, examining herself with her customary hauteur. It figured she'd saved one. Hwa Young, watching surreptitiously, could have sworn that some of that violet tinge to her eyes remained when the light hit them, a mirror sheen like a cat's.

For a moment, staring at Bae, Hwa Young saw not a stuck-up, glamorous girl, slim of figure, but a slender and haughty boy. *It's the haircut,* she told herself uneasily, rather than some unwanted insight. Hwa Young had thought she'd adjusted to the fashion, which no one in the Eleventh Fleet had gainsaid. At times like this, however, it ran counter to the associations she had learned in her early years among the clanners. Associations that Bae could never be allowed to guess, and for which Bae would mock her even if she failed to guess their significance.

"Pass that around," Eun said gruffly. "Might as well get this part out of the way." So of course Bae had to share, which she did without a word, kind or cutting.

The mirror passed first to Seong Su, who squinted into it with an air of bemusement. "Doesn't look much different," he remarked. "Maybe a bit of copper in the eyes, at certain angles."

"It's more subtle for some," Eun agreed, slanting a glance at Hwa Young for no reason she could determine. She hoped he got over his antipathy toward her sooner rather than later because otherwise working with him would get tiresome.

Then Seong Su handed the mirror to her, with unusual care, and she understood why Eun had reacted so strangely, and

Geum as well. When the light hit *her* eyes, they turned wintry blue with ice-silver flecks in them. Unsettling to be sure.

More obvious, however, was her hair. Like Mother Aera, Hwa Young had black hair. Most people did, whether clanner or Imperial, although some of the clanners from the more far-flung clone lines had hair in varying shades of brown or even blond.

Now, however, the deep black was interrupted by a wide white streak through the right side of her hair. Combined with the eyes, it gave Hwa Young a feral aspect she thought she could get to like, even as ambivalence bit her heart at the fact that, between the haircut and the white streak, she looked less like Mother Aera than ever. It almost made her unrecognizable. No one from her old family would have identified her as a fellow clanner.

"People who know what to look for will clock you as pilots even if you aren't linked," Eun said. "Try not to be captured by the enemy, because playing stupid won't work. And if you're linked—well. You'll stand out like a peacock among pigeons."

Seong Su was gawking at Hwa Young. "How come the rest of us didn't get hair streaks?"

Eun rolled his eyes, but he was grinning. "If you care that much about *fashion*, you can find some hair dye on the black market. You didn't hear that from me, by the way."

Hwa Young sensed he was holding something more back, but she could unearth it later.

"Your official status as pilots will be confirmed," Eun said, "once you've been sworn in at New Year's. Your training will continue in the interim. Try not to get yourselves killed by engine radiation or mutant centipedes before then."

Hwa Young woke half an hour early on New Year's Day, exhausted from the past weeks of exercises and drills. She'd had a nightmare about the deck fraying into jagged pieces, each one a mirror containing the trapped visage of Mother Aera and the rest of her family. She woke with her shirt clinging damply to her back and sweat fouling her scalp. Strangely, however, a chilly sense of calm enfolded her, as though the dream had lost its old power over her.

We are winter, came the lancer's voice again. *We are one, always.*

Did the others hear their lancers speaking to them? And how could she find out without sounding like she was hallucinating? If Hwa Young was certain of anything, it was that the voice really did belong to *Winter's Axiom.* The grandeur of its presence filled her with mixed glee and awe.

Hwa Young could hear the other pilots' breathing and Seong Su's uninhibited snore. Eun groaned and mumbled gibberish in his sleep, with the occasional comprehensible nugget of military slang. The word "cabbage" was uttered more than once. She wondered if that had been some unlucky late comrade's callsign, and what the story was behind it.

As for Bae . . . Hwa Young thought of Bae, who didn't snore, or toss and turn the way she herself did. Would she start having nightmares of her own about Ha Yoon's death? Not like Bae would accept sympathy from Hwa Young of all people.

After her shower, Hwa Young emerged to meet Bae's hostile eyes. *Farseer.* How much did she see? "You're up earlier than you have to be," Bae said challengingly.

Hwa Young made a gesture: *So are you.*

"Hope you didn't use up more than your water ration," Bae added before shouldering past her.

Bae knew as well as Hwa Young did that the shower cut off after a set period of time. Nobody got to luxuriate in the water. At least it was adequately warm.

I should give her space. She's mourning Ha Yoon. But if Hwa Young was honest with herself, she couldn't tell the difference between Bae in mourning and Bae being Bae.

By the time everyone was awake and dressed, Hwa Young had run through the meditation, except this time it was based on the real thing. In fact, it had the opposite effect of making her heart race with eagerness to sit in the cockpit again . . . and pilot *Winter's Axiom* for real.

"All right, gentlefolk," Eun announced in response to an inaudible cue, "line up for inspection."

Hwa Young and Bae did so immediately. They'd had practice at school as well as the past weeks of training. Hwa Young didn't like Bae, but better her than one of their more slapdash former schoolmates.

Seong Su was third and last, and he shuffled into place with all the grace of a wounded boar.

"Don't slouch," Eun snapped. "Look at Bae and Menace Girl if you're not sure what good posture looks like. Were you raised by bears or something?"

"Didn't have bears in the city," Seong Su said cheerfully, as though Eun hadn't insulted his family. "Do they taste good?"

Eun growled under his breath. He pronounced Bae "adequate" and groused about a nonexistent spot on Hwa Young's right boot. Weirdly, she found his fussing reassuring, like that of an overprotective older brother.

They stopped by Commander Ye Jun's office on the way out. Zie stood outside it, waiting for them with no evidence of impatience. "You make an excellent mother hen, Hellion," zie observed as Eun corrected Seong Su's salute, not for the first time.

Eun harrumphed. "Don't you start, sir."

Commander Ye Jun's smile faded. "Admiral Chin has high standards, and she has not been kindly disposed toward the lancer squad since Spinel. Look sharp and don't speak unless you're spoken to."

"Yes, sir," Hwa Young and Bae said in unison, followed by Seong Su half a beat later.

The commander led them single file along the starboard side. Hwa Young visualized the route: they would take a lift to the command deck, located in one of the two best-shielded areas. (The other was Engineering.) She'd memorized as much of the ship's layout as she could coax out of her ID badge in her precious free time, and had almost messaged Geum asking if zie could find her a more complete map, except Geum would accede and they'd both land in the brig.

Some of the sailors and marines who passed them sported unkempt uniforms. Hwa Young, just behind Bae, could feel the weight of the other girl's judgy stare. *They're busy with work,* Hwa Young told herself, but even she wondered why one private's arm was covered with orange slime up to the elbow. Sealant? Grease? Something worse? She caught a whiff of the sharp chemical stench and was glad it wasn't her.

Both Commander Ye Jun and Eun remained dauntingly quiet, as though they thought someone was watching them. Hwa Young surveyed the ceiling. She assumed the ship was riddled with cameras for security reasons, even if she couldn't spot them. Something else Geum would know about.

Then the lift doors opened, and Hwa Young gaped. Bae stifled a gasp.

"I bet you could pawn those decorations for a fortune," Seong Su said reverently.

"What are you, a *merchant*?" Bae said under her breath.

The hall here gave the impression of vastness, although Hwa Young was convinced this was an optical illusion. Impossibly long silk scrolls hung to either side, depicting an endless range of mountains piercing a sky suffused with rose and gold. Vines grew up the bulkheads and dangled white-pink maehwa blossoms, each five-petaled and fragrant with the promise of plums. While ordinarily a tree, the vine variant must have been genetically engineered for displays like this.

Hwa Young's eyes pricked at the sight and smell of living plants. The sterility of the shipboard environment had affected her more than she'd realized. The only thing missing was a sky, and the earthy smell of decaying leaves, and the wind, and . . .

It's not like walking on a planet at all. And yet.

Besides, her home now was the cold depths of space, and the black winter of the aether-swept void.

"Come on, Pilots," Commander Ye Jun said, not unkindly. The roughness of zir voice made her wonder where zie came from, and if zie had spent any part of zir childhood planetside. "We don't want to be late."

Even without the commander to guide them, Hwa Young could have told when they reached Admiral Chin's office. More maehwa vines surrounded it, carefully trained and trimmed so they didn't overgrow the hatch. Privately, Hwa Young thought it a great indicator for any assassins who sneaked aboard.

"Form up," Commander Ye Jun said, and they did. "Admiral Chin, Commander Ye Jun reporting with the new lancer platoon. Request permission to enter."

The hatch opened. "Enter," a stony voice said. Hwa Young would have liked to observe the interior before entering, but the commander had already crossed the threshold.

The admiral had an immense office, because of course she did. Transparent protective cases contained curios like celadon vases painted with lucky patterns of crane or bat. A ceremonial sword held pride of place on a mount above the desk, its blade gleaming silver-gold.

Above the sword, a banner displayed the military's symbol: the Starry Taegeuk and Sword. The taegeuk symbol showed the opposing and complementary forces of yin and yang in Imperial red and blue, with a white four-pointed star in each.

The admiral herself drew the eye. She was an elongated woman, fine-boned, almost delicate despite the harsh voice. Hwa Young had heard that people who grew up on the poorer, unrulier space stations had builds like that, due to the weaker gravity. Her eyes were light brown, afire with the intentness of a hunting falcon. Hwa Young didn't know what all the medals on her uniform meant individually, but the intent was clear: *Don't cross me.*

Commander Ye Jun waited until the entire platoon, such as it was, had entered, and the hatch had closed behind them. Zie saluted sharply. Hwa Young and the others did likewise.

For several moments, the admiral didn't speak, instead raking each individual—including the commander and Eun—with her stare. A chill went through Hwa Young's blood as the admiral's gaze captured hers. Hwa Young automatically lowered her eyes in respect to an authority figure or elder, the way she'd learned as a child. That was one thing the clanners and Imperials had in common.

"At ease." Admiral Chin rose to address them, straight-backed. "Hwa Young. Bae. Seong Su." She caught and held each pilot's gaze as she pronounced their names. "Whatever life you had before the Eleventh Fleet, leave it behind you. It has shaped you but no longer owns you. Your service belongs now to the New Joseon military."

She nodded toward Commander Ye Jun, her mouth twisting in contempt. "Commander, show them your hand."

The commander did so, zir face impassive.

"You must be prepared to lose everything." The admiral's mouth curved in a smile more severe than reassuring. "It is only through the willingness to sacrifice everything that you can be worthy to defend the Empire of New Joseon."

Eun's breath hitched. Hwa Young didn't look in his direction. She knew he'd criticized the way the Empire had used the Eleventh Fleet. Here, however, he kept his grievances to himself.

I should have listened to him more closely, Hwa Young thought, acutely uncomfortable beneath the admiral's regard. Still, this was her one opportunity to learn what manner of person the admiral was, and to judge her character. Hwa Young wanted to know that she could trust the admiral's leadership.

I don't trust her. The words pierced her thoughts, clear and sharp as an icicle. Part of her wanted to respond to the admiral's bracing sentiments and air of authority. Another, larger part of her, the part that was inextricably connected to *Winter's Axiom,* was suspicious of that impulse; wanted to know what the admiral *wasn't* saying.

Stop being unreasonable, Hwa Young told that inner voice. This was a swearing-in ceremony in desperate circumstances. The admiral wasn't about to treat new recruits as confidants. Hwa Young wouldn't have, had their positions been reversed.

The admiral's sharp voice intensified; it could have sheared through metal. "There are only five of you now, and upon you rest the hopes of the Eleventh Fleet." Her grimace suggested she wished this was not so. "Strive to excel so we can drive back the clanners and the Empire can be safe again."

Admiral Chin reached behind her and removed the ceremonial sword from its mount, resting the naked blade upon her wiry hands. Up close, Hwa Young saw fine engravings on the gleaming metal, words of courage balanced against words of death. "Swear on blood and bone to the Empire of New Joseon: I am the fist of the Empire. *Trust the Empress. Move at her will. Act as her hands.*"

The admiral removed the blade, leaving them to clasp one another's hands. Hwa Young was surprised by the clamminess of Seong Su's palm, the smooth dry texture of Bae's skin.

The admiral placed her own hand atop all three of theirs. "You belong to us now." She nodded at Commander Ye Jun. "Train them better than the last set, Commander. Dismissed."

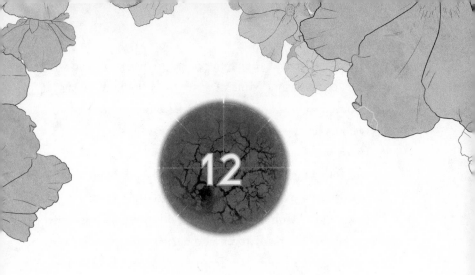

12

For the New Year's Feast on the *Maehwa*, Commander Ye Jun accompanied them to mess. Someone had gone to the trouble of decorating the hall with banners in the five traditional colors: black, red, yellow, green, and blue. If anyone from the Empress's line haunted the *Maehwa*, ready to receive or give blessings, Hwa Young discerned no sign of them.

The commander smiled benevolently at no one in particular, which Hwa Young was beginning to recognize as one way zie hid what zie was thinking. Eun, on the other hand, drummed his fingers on the table, as if his discontent weren't already obvious. "I suspect First Fleet gets real rice wine instead of the nonalcoholic plum wine they foist on us," he said.

Hwa Young bet that wasn't the last of the luxuries First Fleet, which guarded the crownworld, enjoyed.

Seong Su screwed up his face. "Now that's no fun."

"What, tea isn't strong enough for you?" Bae asked, lip curling.

"My parents served all manner of stuff," Seong Su said with suspicious enthusiasm. "Mineral water from the holy spring on Nacre bottled right proper, or citron tea from Citrine, even ginseng tea on a lucky—er. Good times, anyway."

"Merchants," Bae declared with a sniff.

Hwa Young's interest had been piqued by a different matter. "The traditions are different from fleet to fleet?"

"That's right," Commander Ye Jun said, eyes focusing on her as zie came back from whatever zie'd been contemplating. "First Fleet uses teaware from the Imperial treasury. Fourth Fleet makes offerings to the flagship's resident ghost, although they don't, as is rumored, involve human sacrifice. Eighteenth Fleet holds a martial arts contest, and it's bad luck if the admiral loses, so people connive to make sure he wins. I'm sure we'll hear all about his 'victories' once Eighteenth Fleet catches up to us with those reinforcements. And I've never gotten a straight answer as to what Ninth Fleet does, but it involves worship of fox spirits."

"You'd think they'd enforce the same traditions in every fleet, all the same," Hwa Young pressed.

The commander laughed. "First Fleet is unlikely to give up its privileges. Most of its officers are related to the Empress herself. It's not our concern."

Hwa Young knew zie had deflected her, and zie knew she knew. She wasn't in a position to push further, so she filed away the question for later pondering.

"And us?" Bae asked, nodding toward the ensign who was passing around the threatened bottle of nonalcoholic plum wine.

"Beyond the choice of beverage?" The commander's eyes crinkled. "What *we* do, in the lancer squad, is toast each other.

We go around the table, senior to junior, and we tell each other something we've never told anyone else."

Hwa Young could tell she wasn't the only one who hated this idea.

"Don't overthink it," zie added kindly.

The wine arrived. It looked innocent, and it smelled like overripe plums. Respecting this particular tradition, assuming the commander wasn't pulling one over on them, would have been easier if she could have gotten drunk in truth. Even drunk, Hwa Young was sure she could avoid speaking the unspeakable.

I'm not one of you, yet here I am.

Commander Ye Jun lifted zir cup. It looked the same as the others', jade-colored porcelain embellished with a motif of stars and clouds. "To the Eleventh Fleet."

They echoed the toast, cups clinking.

"Me first, I suppose." The commander tossed the drink back as though it would anesthetize zir misgivings. "I joined the military because I'd broken up with my boyfriend on the crownworld. He's probably an Imperial advisor by now."

Eun stirred. "You told the unit that last year, sir. Or did you think I was too drunk to remember?"

"Too drunk?" Bae demanded. "On nonalcoholic wine?"

The commander's grin was slow and unexpectedly wicked. "*That* year, Copilot Ji Soo got us some contraband. Cherry liqueur from some forsaken world far from New Joseon. I don't think even the brigands we 'liberated' it from knew where it came from originally."

Eun shook his head at the reminiscence. "It was best straight from the bottle," he said, "but Ji Soo insisted on watering it down with this nonalcoholic junk to 'disguise' it from the other tables. Impossible, of course. Plum wine is amber and once you added the slightest quantity of liqueur, the whole thing turned bright red."

"You wouldn't have gotten drunk if you hadn't snatched the bottle and insisted on finishing it," Commander Ye Jun said.

Hwa Young blinked. The commander had almost sounded . . . catty?

"Well, if you're going to be *that* way about it," Eun shot back, "*why* did you break up with your boyfriend?"

Hwa Young wondered if that was getting too personal, but the commander only nodded, a glint in zir eye.

"My boyfriend," the commander said, "who I won't name, wanted to get physical for the first time."

"Do I really want to hear this, sir?" Bae asked, eyebrows shooting up, while Seong Su squirmed.

"Oh, nothing happened," Commander Ye Jun assured them. "Because you see, He Who Will Remain Nameless wanted to lose his virginity in the Empress's bedroom."

Hwa Young almost spat out her mouthful of ersatz plum wine. Seong Su pounded on her back, which only made matters worse.

"Her *bedroom*?" Eun wanted to know, with entirely too much interest for Hwa Young's taste.

"The Empress has five palaces on the crownworld, and each palace has a bedroom reserved for her use. My boyfriend said it would be 'safe' if we picked one at the Autumn Palace, which was under renovation. Said no one would catch us." The commander shook zir head, mouth twisting wryly.

"So you dumped him," Bae guessed.

The commander spread zir hands. "Let's just say I knew who'd be blamed if we got caught, and it wasn't going to be my ex." Zie eyed Eun. "Your turn."

"Sure, make us get personal," Eun grumbled. He stared into his cup. "I like the spinach here."

Seong Su picked up a giant glob of sautéed spinach and deposited it on top of Eun's bowl of rice. "You can have my share, then, sir."

Eun fidgeted with his chopsticks, then nodded to himself as if he'd come to a decision. "No, that's not really what I meant to say. I bribed someone to get this assignment."

Seong Su's eyes went round. "Shouldn't you maybe not be confessing that, sir?"

"It's the Empress's birthday," Commander Ye Jun said, "and we've toasted each other. These are secrets we'll keep among ourselves. Go on, Eun."

"I come from a family that deals in salvage." Eun's voice was unemotional, but spots of color formed on Bae's cheeks at the reminder of her often-voiced contempt toward merchants of any type. "When I enlisted as a lancer candidate, I did well on all the tests except the one on hand-eye coordination. The examiner even told me it was an outdated requirement, that modern equipment can correct for a small hand tremor."

Hwa Young regarded him with renewed respect. She hadn't imagined the hand tremor when he ferried her from Serpentine to the *Maehwa* after all. And it certainly didn't seem to slow him down.

Eun looked at the banners at the other side of the mess hall, his eyes unfocused. "Salvage is dirty, dangerous work, especially near the Moonstorm border, but it pays well. My mothers and auncle knew my dream. They wanted me to have a shot at piloting a lancer. And the examination board . . . well, let's just say that certain Imperial bureaucrats aren't averse to having their palms greased."

Bae looked appalled, which Hwa Young thought was hypocritical of her, given that she coasted through life on the strength of her mom's connections. All the same, Hwa Young didn't know how she felt about this revelation, either. Would she be so sanguine about this bribe if she'd been denied a place with the candidates, and someone else had taken her spot?

"*Hellion* chose you," Commander Ye Jun said. It took a moment for Hwa Young to realize that zie was referring to the lancer, not Eun's callsign. "That's all we need to know."

Seong Su and Hwa Young nodded. Bae, too, after a split second of hesitation.

Bae tossed her head when everyone looked at her. "I'm happier here than I was back home."

Hwa Young blinked. She wouldn't have guessed that. She'd always assumed that Bae enjoyed lording it over everyone else.

Bae glanced down—barely a flicker of her eyes—then added, "I hate my mom." It came out as a fierce whisper. "It didn't matter how hard I worked, how much I achieved. Nothing was ever enough. Nothing was *going* to be enough unless I married an Imperial heir."

The bottom dropped out of Hwa Young's stomach. She couldn't help saying, "So it wasn't personal. Our rivalry." All that time she'd been trying to overcome Bae's superiority at everything—and Hwa Young hadn't even been the *reason*.

"Personal?" Bae scoffed, but there was an undertone of rue—even humor—in her voice. "You were in the wrong place at the wrong time. 'Work harder on your sharpshooting,' Mom would say. 'She's just a ward of the state, how can you let her outdo you?'" Bae shook her head. "Not everything is about you, you know."

The words stung, yet Hwa Young felt light-headed with relief. *She doesn't hate you. It's not personal.* Then she wondered why Bae's opinion mattered so much to her.

Seong Su jumped in before Hwa Young had worked out what to say. "I used to disassemble my cousin's game controllers then play innocent when zie looked for who did it. No one figured it out."

"*That's* your great crime?" Eun demanded, but he was smiling. "Well, if anyone disassembles my lancer, I'll know who to blame."

"Don't be like that," Seong Su protested. "I wouldn't know where to begin."

"That's what you *say*."

The others were looking at Hwa Young now. She sipped the plum wine. It tasted better than it looked, lushly sweet. She thought of all the things she could admit to, if she wanted to give up her future. "I sleep with a knife."

She watched Bae's face, dreading the other girl's reaction. Bae merely nodded, as though to say *No surprise there.*

"Good for killing nightmares, I expect," Eun said, teasing.

"Leave her alone," Commander Ye Jun returned, a note of warning in zir voice. "We all have them."

The somber mood that descended over the table at those words didn't last long. Soon the food arrived. Judging from the others' eager smiles, Hwa Young wasn't the only hungry one.

Back on Carnelian, the clanners had celebrated New Year's

by gathering together at the house of the Eldest and devouring cinnamon punch, rice cakes decorated with succulent edible flowers, roast boar if the hunters had been lucky. In Forsythia City, Hwa Young had visited Geum to give zir the year's gift—a lancer model kit, a laser multitool, whatever she could afford—then share in the boarding school's feast: soup with coin-shaped rice cakes to attract prosperity, zucchini fried in seasoned egg batter, rice yaksik made rich and sweet with honey and dried jujubes and pine nuts. They'd dressed in traditional hanbok for the occasion, an embroidered silken jacket with pants or skirt according to preference, and made offerings to the Empress and her line.

Hwa Young couldn't have borne it if the galley had served the same foods she'd eaten with Mother Aera and the rest of her family back on Carnelian. To her relief, tonight's meal was better than their usual cardboard ("Low bar," Bae sniffed): egg pancakes stuffed with some unnamed protein whose chewy texture suggested it had been vat-grown, plus the obligatory rice cakes and vegetables fresh from hydroponics rather than the reconstituted fare she had acclimated to.

She was beginning to relax into the meal when the admiral entered with several people in tow. "The admiral has some civilian advisors in her circle," Commander Ye Jun said by way of explanation.

Hwa Young told herself not to stare, even if everyone else was. The civilians in their florid clothes stuck out like hoopoes with their fanciful plumage. Some of them wore *jewelry*, pearls and abalone shell and diamonds amid glittering chains of gold and silver, all of which glinted gaudily amid the more drab uniforms.

Bae said cynically, "So much for Mom's ambitions. She would have loved to worm her way here. But she never made it off Serpentine, so she probably perished there along with her dreams."

Hwa Young blinked, taken aback by Bae's open callousness. "How'd you discover that?" she blurted out.

Bae shrugged with one shoulder. "One of her associates got a message through to me. Wanted me to deal with our holdings on Serpentine, as if *that* matters anymore."

Eun looked at her, his lips pursed. "It's not good to speak ill of the dead."

"I'm sure the proper rites were performed for her," Bae said as though speaking of a stranger.

Hwa Young forestalled a spill of pitying words. Bae clearly didn't regret her mother's death.

Bae looked neither to the left nor right, and downed the rest of her plum wine, nonalcoholic though it was, in a single long draught.

After the repast, Hwa Young had a rare hour's liberty. Eun and Seong Su headed for the rec room, citing table tennis, which Eun was good at and Seong Su was almost good at. Bae retired to the bunkroom with an air of *don't follow me.*

Hwa Young admitted in her deepest heart of hearts that she wondered what Bae planned to do, but that wasn't a good enough reason to foist her presence on the other girl. Besides, Bae would merely poison the room with thinly disguised contempt and a side of exasperation. So Hwa Young queried the ship's computer as to Geum's location.

She found Geum down in one of the clanking rooms that surrounded the greater chamber that housed the engine proper. The atmosphere could not have been more different from the grim stateliness of the admiral's quarters, or the gaudy cheer of the mess hall she'd just left behind. Here some genius had festooned every spare surface, and some that weren't, with origami models of improbable spaceships.

The genius was Geum. Hwa Young could have fingered zir origami design sense in an unlit room. Zie liked certain combinations of mountain and valley folds, and the way zie scorned to use a single cut of the scissors in place of complex and frankly eldritch topologies of creases was also pure Geum. The only thing that would have impressed Hwa Young more would have been if zie had figured out some way of constructing the origami figures from sheet metal.

The genius zirself was folding a three-headed crane when Hwa Young entered the room; zie sat between two other people who were probably engineers or engineers twice removed. One of them was singing a song that would have made Hwa Young blush if she'd understood the references, some of which had to do with the Empress's proclivities. The other was diagramming a circuit, or a labyrinth, or the intestinal crenellations of a dog, in a gelatinous substance with a piece of disreputable wire.

"Yo, your pilot friend's here," the first said, breaking off from her song.

Guilt washed over Hwa Young. She had scarcely spared a thought for Geum after forming her connection with *Winter's Axiom*. It occurred to her now that zie might resent her for becoming a pilot where zie had failed.

"Hwa Young!" zie cried out, waving so vigorously zie almost upended the other engineer's gelatinous sculpture-thing. "Finally had a moment for us techs, huh?"

She winced at the reproof in her friend's voice.

"You can't just use her *name*," the diagrammer hissed. "She's a pilot!"

"We know each other," Hwa Young said, awkward with the implications. What, exactly, did protocol require of them? She'd never considered how their relationship would change if she became a pilot and Geum didn't, yet that was exactly what had happened.

"I expect you pilot types are too busy for mere mortals," Geum said.

"Later I will be. But not now." Geum's passive-aggressiveness stung. Hwa Young attempted a smile. Her face felt stiff. She didn't want Geum to be mad at her. "I hear there's a black market, but I didn't manage to find you a gift."

"Nonsense." Abruptly, Geum stood, and the diagrammer scrambled away, scoring a deep, wobbling gouge into her gelatin. "All the flagship's computers are mine to explore! That's gift enough for me—"

The two other engineers tackled Geum. The first one clapped a hand over zir mouth, which occasioned a great deal of muffled squawking. "Don't *say* things like that!" the first one explained in a hushed voice. "Admiral Chin has as much of a sense of humor as a broken faucet."

Geum mumbled something that might have been *Broken faucets are fun-loving creatures.*

Hwa Young bowed politely to the engineers, distracted from

her guilt over the fact that access to the flagship's computers wasn't something *she* had arranged for Geum's benefit. "I'm Pilot Hwa Young." More like a pilot in training, but they knew that already. "Who are you?"

"Trainee Geum's new best friend," the singer said belligerently. It was not an accident, Hwa Young gathered, that she neglected to state her name, although squinting revealed that her badge said *ENGINEER HYO SU*. "You better have some respect for those of us who fix up lancers after you pilots blow them to hell and gone like what happened at Spinel."

"Actually," Hwa Young said, seizing the opportunity to gather some intelligence, "why did the old squad do so badly at the Battle of Spinel? Were they outnumbered?"

She realized as the words left her mouth that, in her eagerness to uncover what had happened, she'd hurt Geum's feelings. Her heart sank. Geum sat hunched and sullen, zir face averted from her, no trace of zir usual smile.

"Given your *busy schedule*," Geum muttered, confirming her fears, "I was hoping we could do something fun together. Not talk about lancers."

Hyo Su ignored the comment, incidentally letting go of Geum, in favor of answering Hwa Young's question. "Not outnumbered. Ambushed. The clanners were at a disadvantage in numbers, but they fought smart."

Geum wriggled out from the other engineer's grasp—this one was *ENGINEER CHAE WON*. "Eh, let's do something fun instead—" Geum began to say.

Chae Won locked eyes with Hwa Young and laughed nastily. The gelatin picked up the vibrations and jiggled in response, which Hwa Young would have preferred not to witness. "*Your* lancer might have made a difference. Too bad *Winter's Axiom* was in mothballs at the time. Admiral Chin may be a hardass, but she doesn't like taking unnecessary risks. Unlike the bastard."

Ah, yes. For whatever reason, people called Commander Ye Jun that. Hwa Young wondered if zie had only picked up the nickname after the disastrous Battle of Spinel.

"Tell me more about Spinel," Hwa Young urged the engineers, unable to help herself.

Geum's expression fell.

Hyo Su's voice dropped theatrically as she warmed to her subject. "Battle of Spinel. The last planet we visited before Serpentine. Supposed to be where we finally gave the clanners the what-for. Admiral Chin had it all planned out.

"But the bastard screwed it up. Instead of following the admiral's orders, zie pulled the entire lancer company out of position. Trying to carry out a raid to win some glory for zirself. The lancers got ambushed for their trouble. Four of them down in the initial ambush, the rest dead covering the retreat. And now the bastard and Hellion are the only ones left from the old company, and we're down to a bunch of baby pilots. No offense."

"That's not what I heard from Eun," Geum said reluctantly. "He says Commander Ye Jun anticipated a sneak attack. If it hadn't been for the commander disobeying Admiral Chin's stupid orders and sacrificing the lancers, the entire Eleventh Fleet would have been wiped out."

Chae Won jeered and plunged her hands into the gelatin down to the elbows in search of—what? "Everyone in the fleet knows that the senior warrant officer"—her voice dipped mockingly—"has the hots for zir real bad. Please. Like *he's* reliable. No, the admiral has the right of it. The commander's lucky zie hasn't been cashiered."

Hwa Young searched her memories and couldn't make up her mind as to whether this was scurrilous gossip, or scurrilous gossip rooted in cold hard evidence.

"Besides," Chae Won added, "even if he's oh so scrupulous about fraternization regs, the commander saved his life that battle. So he's *really* not objective."

"Huh" was all Geum had to say to that, with a slow nod.

Hwa Young looked askance at Geum, unsure of what to make of it herself.

"We were telling Geum here," Hyo Su said, gesturing expansively around the auxiliary engine room, "that it was the Empress's blessing that zie ended up with us engineers, instead of you poor doomed lancer jockeys."

Hwa Young narrowed her eyes at Hyo Su. Waited for some protestation from Geum that the pilots were hardly "doomed." But zie seemed happy to side with zir new technician friends.

"Mark my words, it's only a matter of time before the bastard gets you killed while trying to prove that—"

Hwa Young swallowed intense frustration when someone banged on the hatch outside. "You in there," a low voice growled, "quit gossiping and get back to work!"

"It's New Year's," Hyo Su yelled back, and told whoever-it-was what they could do with their suggestion.

"I wouldn't have thought," Hwa Young said, "that New Year's was an excuse for lack of discipline."

"See?" Hyo Su said to Geum with the air of someone producing a trigonometry theorem out of thin air. "She's got that high-and-mighty lancer pilot attitude already. No wonder she came out with weirdo hair. She'll fit right in."

Instead of defending her, Geum only laughed.

Hwa Young bristled. "I'd better be going," she said coolly. "I'm sure we'll see each other later." But she was starting to have her doubts.

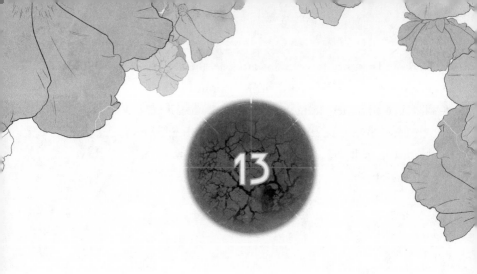

13

The next day began with a briefing, or what Commander Ye Jun claimed was a briefing. Before she headed to the conference room, Hwa Young stifled the urge to look at her feet and check for telltale floating, given her snooping around after gossip about the commander. She'd already prayed to the Empress this morning, but maybe there was time to sneak in an extra prayer?

On the other hand, Eun, Bae, and Seong Su had already lined up at the bunkroom's open hatch. Eun looked impatiently at her. "You coming or not?"

The extra prayer would have to take place another time. *Sorry,* Hwa Young thought in the Empress's general direction. *An extra prayer this evening.* And then she was ashamed of herself for attempting to bargain with the Empress of all people, even as an abstract.

Commander Ye Jun awaited them at the conference room, a

glass of water in hand and a pitcher before zir, along with something that looked suspiciously like a decorating bag full of pink frosting, complete with a nozzle.

Hwa Young scarcely noticed those, however, due to the candy model of . . . the fleet? At least, Hwa Young thought it was the fleet. It took up the center of the table and had been constructed from spun sugar whose smell filled the room with nauseating sweetness. She spotted the five active lancers in the vanguard, including an extremely stylized representation of *Winter's Axiom* in blue sugar embellished with delicate white frosting and edible (she assumed) silver sprinkles.

We do not look like that, Winter's Axiom said in her head, with an offended dignity like a cat's.

Hush, Hwa Young told the lancer, stilling her face so the others wouldn't detect her startlement. She wasn't used to her lancer talking to her, especially since it was often taciturn. Were the others being confronted by similar statements? *I need to pay attention.*

Most interestingly, the candy ships and lancers were all connected to one another by struts of yet more spun sugar, as though the fleet were a single entity. Hwa Young studied the sculpture, trying to determine what parts of it were structural and what parts were, well, eye candy.

Eun cussed under his breath, then said, "I didn't realize it was arts and crafts day. I left the glue sticks at home."

Bae side-eyed the whole display. "I . . . thought we were here for a briefing?"

The commander smiled narrowly. "This *is* the briefing. We're using this to simulate our next mission. It's gimmicky, but people find gimmicks easier to remember."

"I hate it when you say that," Eun grumbled. "At least this time you didn't sculpt the ships out of rice."

"We don't have the rice to spare," Commander Ye Jun said. "Sugar, on the other hand . . . Everyone, sit down." Zie sipped sparingly from the glass of water.

They all did, spacing themselves evenly around the table.

"Did you really waste good rice, sir?" Seong Su asked plaintively. "Next time just ask me and I'll eat it for you."

Eun cleared his throat before Commander Ye Jun could answer. "Get to the point, sir."

Commander Ye Jun walked around the table and handed each pilot a printed card and a set of dice. The backs of the cards were blank, and Hwa Young instinctively angled hers so the others couldn't read it. Bae and Eun did the same. Seong Su, who sat across from her, did not. She bet he forgot to hide his hand when playing card games, too.

"Wouldn't it be more stable if you laid the 'fleet' down on its side?" Bae asked. "It looks like an ersatz rocket the way you have it."

"Good observation." Commander Ye Jun's eyes glinted. "Read your card. It explains the rules of the game, and the roles you'll play."

A game? Hwa Young thought in vexation. *Why couldn't we have a regular briefing like normal people?*

Nevertheless, she read the card. The first words: *You are a clanner.*

She froze, unfroze. Took long, unsteady breaths in an attempt to calm herself. *It's just a game. The commander doesn't know . . . or did zie?*

"Bae, Hwa Young, Eun, Seong Su," the commander said,

"you're the clanners. You will be working together to destroy the fleet. I'll play the Imperials." Zie waved a fifth card, which zie had retained. Zie was careful not to reveal the side facing zir.

The commander began pacing back and forth, back and forth, at the head of the table. "As Eleventh Fleet, my goal is to reach Carnelian and establish a base. As the clanners, *your* goal is either to prevent Eleventh Fleet from reaching Carnelian, or to stop the establishment of that base."

Hwa Young froze. Unfroze. A staticky roaring started up in her ears. "Carnelian?" she asked, fighting to keep her voice steady.

Zie misconstrued her question, luckily for her. "You probably haven't heard of it. It's a clanner moon that's been lingering at the edge of the Moonstorm. We razed it six years ago, but there are signs that the clanners have revitalized it . . . and that it's the home of their new forward base of operations."

Hwa Young reread the rules card to cover her reaction. *"Probably haven't heard of it."* She'd never expected to see her old home again, let alone as a lancer pilot pledged to the other side. Was this the Empress's idea of a cruel joke? Could Carnelian truly be operational again?

Were they truly heading to Carnelian for their first mission?

Hwa Young couldn't keep her emotions from churning inside her, though she kept her face still as ice. The commander's words echoed in her mind. *Reach Carnelian and establish a base.* Such dry, clinical words to express the idea that she would be fighting against her former people. It was like her nightmares had splintered into real life, plunging her into a pit of horror.

With an effort, she forced herself to focus on the card's text, even as her stomach roiled. By repeating the words to herself, she could distract herself from the news the commander had just delivered. After all, they had a sugar-spun mission at hand.

According to the permitted actions on the card, she could select maneuvers to attack or disable parts of the fleet. Each time she succeeded—that was determined by dice rolls—she could break part of the sculpture. This simulated damage. Parts of the sculpture that fell off were considered destroyed and were no longer available for the commander's use.

"Sir, why are *we* playing as the clanners?" Bae demanded. "Shouldn't we be planning ways to *beat* the clanners?"

"How do you propose to do that without knowing how to think like a clanner?" Commander Ye Jun countered. "It's only by stepping into their shoes that you can learn to fight them more effectively."

Hwa Young tangled herself up trying to figure out what the least suspicious reaction to this statement was and how to implement it. Staring straight ahead like a statue wasn't it. Nor was fidgeting. She settled for reading the rules yet again, as though engrossed, even though she had already committed them to memory.

"Any other questions?" the commander asked.

Seong Su raised his hand. "Could I have a glass of water, too, sir?"

Bae rolled her eyes, but the commander wordlessly retrieved a glass from one of the cabinets in the back and poured for Seong Su.

The game began. Eun attempted to take charge, but Bae kept arguing with him. Seong Su squirmed every time Bae made a counterproposal to Eun's plans. For her part, Hwa Young was so distracted by the revelation that they were going to Carnelian coupled with the simple statement on the card—*You are a clanner*—that it was all she could do to focus on the game and the rattling of dice rolls.

The one time she did successfully destroy a battle cruiser's engine with a clanner suicide run, her hands shook so badly that she broke off the wrong part of the sculpture. The commander didn't get to repair that bit, either, because Seong Su had already pounced on it and was nomming happily on the candy, despite the serious side-eye Bae was giving him.

Hwa Young's stomach turned at the thought of suicide missions, even if she needed to think of the clanners as the enemy. At least none of the others seemed to divine the reason for her nerves.

It turned out that for every move they had, Commander Ye Jun had a counter, which zie narrated at length. Sometimes it involved transferring engineers from one ship to another for emergency repairs. Sometimes it involved fancy maneuvers with monofilament net to slice up intruders, which Hwa Young hadn't realized the fleet carried. Hwa Young was starting to be vexed by the sheer number of actions zie had access to. Maybe zir card was printed in a smaller font than her own?

In one notable instance, Commander Ye Jun rolled a critical success and blew away an entire clanner fleet with the singularity lance controlled by *Winter's Axiom*.

Winter's Axiom was pleased. *We did that.*

Whose side are you on? Hwa Young demanded, but the lancer didn't answer.

And every time Commander Ye Jun pulled out another trick, out came zir decorating bag. The commander's successes were simulated by shoring up the sculpture with frosting. Zie repaired the spun-sugar sculpture with understated glee, even though the "fleet" increasingly resembled a shambling monster holding court over the table.

Then the commander's badge beeped. Zir expression went blank. "Excuse me," zie said. "I have to take this call privately."

Hwa Young was secretly grateful for the reprieve. The commander had just responded to what they'd thought was a cleverly coordinated, multipronged attack by a devastatingly effective use of chaff particles that confused the sensors. It was hard to *stay* coordinated when none of your sensors could see the targets.

When the hatch had closed after zir, Bae scowled at Eun. "If we'd followed my plan—"

"If we'd followed your plan," Eun said with the air of someone who'd heard it all before, "we would have been filleted by the game's 'lancer squad.' I'm telling you, *Farseer*'s sensor suite at full capability can see things coming from the next system over and—"

While they quarreled, Hwa Young rose and stretched, vertebrae cracking. *Just how small* is *the text on zir card?* she wondered. Did zie have yet more nasty tricks in store for them? She walked over to the commander's seat and picked up zir card.

The blank side stared back at her.

Seong Su noticed. "Whoa, you can't just—"

Hwa Young turned the card over.

The other side was *also* blank.

"Hey," Hwa Young said over Seong Su's protestations, Eun and Bae's arguments. "The commander's cheating. Zie's just been making up all zir moves, while we're stuck with what's printed on our cards."

Eun was diverted from declaiming a scathing list of reasons why Bae's *Farseer* should never get into melee combat. (Thin armor and its status as the platoon's warning-and-control system were at the top of the list.) "Did zie really?" Eun came around the table to verify that Commander Ye Jun's card was, indeed, blank.

This only upset Seong Su further. "Sir, we shouldn't be doing this."

"No, if the commander's cheating, we have the right to know." Bae nodded to herself. "Check the dice."

Bae was right. The commander had a special set of dice, unlike any of theirs, that skewed zir chances of rolling successes. For example, the six-sided dice had sixes on three faces.

"We were never going to win," Hwa Young said, fuming. "Not with the odds stacked against us like this. What exactly was zie trying to tell us? What the hell kind of briefing is this?"

She should have held on to her temper, but the unfairness of the entire exercise had gotten to her. First the news that they were going to *Carnelian* of all places, and now this. Damned if she was going to put up with this fake "exercise" any longer. Before anyone could stop her, she grabbed the pitcher and dumped its contents over the "fleet." She took a moment's vicious satisfaction in Seong Su's appalled expression and Eun's muttered "Now you've done it."

"Thanks so much!" Bae snarled. "Because of you, we're going to be scrubbing toilets for the rest of this journey!"

Hwa Young wasn't paying attention to the others' raised

voices. Instead, she was studying the sculpture, which was dissolving at an alarming rate. She thought she glimpsed something hidden within the flagship's translucent engine room. Another card?

This time, when she reached for the sculpture, Bae grabbed her wrist. "Oh no you don't."

Hwa Young hissed in indignation. "Look at it! There's something inside the flagship."

"Let go of her," Eun said sternly.

Bae snatched back her hand so quickly Hwa Young was almost offended.

Eun delivered a calculated chop to the sculpture, which caused it to dissolve into fragments. One of them landed on Hwa Young's cheek, sticky and sharp. Seong Su grabbed another fragment and popped it into his mouth before anyone could stop him. Eun pulled out the hidden item, which was indeed a card. He showed it around.

YOU WIN, it said.

"Come out, sir," Eun said in a very loud voice. "I assume this was the point of the exercise."

The hatch swished open. Hwa Young turned to stare at zir, gaping. Even the "call" had been part of the exercise.

"Very good," Commander Ye Jun said. "You passed."

Bae's eyes sparked with anger. "Sir, you could have given us a *real briefing* instead of this . . . this . . ."

"If there's one thing I've learned about warfare," the commander said, calm in the face of Bae's wrath, "it's that cheating is the *point*."

This silenced Bae.

"The clanners are not going to broadcast their plans—or if

they do, it will be to trick us, or to fake us out. The clanners are not going to go easy on you because you're novices and there's a learning curve and you haven't learned to coordinate effectively. The clanners think they've destroyed all of Eleventh Fleet's lancers, but once they realize some of us survived, and once they realize some of us are *new,* they will exploit that. The clanners are fighting for their survival."

Hwa Young shivered. For a moment she was a child in the reeds again, a child who had lost her entire family.

The Empress keeps all her children safe. She repeated the words in her mind until her breathing steadied.

"So we snatch every advantage we can, and fight to win," Hwa Young said, willing herself to sound certain. "But sir, what you said about the mission—was that fake too?"

Commander Ye Jun's smile was genuine. "No, that part's real. Eleventh Fleet means to establish a forward base on Carnelian. We don't know how the clanners restored an entire moon that quickly after we destroyed it six years ago, but we can't afford to let them control a territory so close to the Imperial border.

"Assuming the moon's trajectory doesn't change, we will arrive in a matter of weeks. That's not a lot of time for training. And the closer we get, the greater the risk of clanner attacks. We may have to scramble to repel ambushes on the way in.

"As for *our* role," zie continued, "we will act as a forward patrol. Eleventh Fleet can dodge, but a base *can't.* Our job will be to identify incoming threats and eliminate them, especially since we can evade detection more easily than a detachment from the fleet proper. Once the base is fully operational, of course, it will have defenses of its own. But before it's completely established, it will be vulnerable. That's where we come in. We *have* to be a fighting machine—the Empress's fist—or the clanners will defeat us, and the mission will fail. Understood?"

"Understood, sir," Hwa Young and Bae said, while Seong Su saluted (sloppily) and Eun nodded.

Commander Ye Jun eyed the table and the soggy, sticky remnants of the sculpture. "In that case, I leave the four of you to clean up this mess. Dismissed."

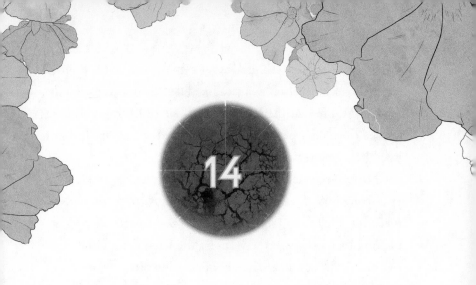

14

Their days blurred into routine—again. Reveille at 0600 ship's time. Showers and breakfast. Exercise, which Hwa Young didn't mind, although Seong Su complained as though he couldn't bench-press more than the marines already. Geum would have slacked off. Zie had always gotten by with the least effort possible, saving zir energy for technological pastimes. At least Geum had zir wish now.

I wonder where everyone else ended up, she thought sometimes. Ordinarily she would have messaged Geum, but the spat they'd had on New Year's still smarted. She thought about sending a conciliatory note, then didn't.

Hwa Young had more and more trouble sleeping, anticipating a clanner attack at any moment. Today they were only two days' flight from Carnelian. The ominous quiet troubled her.

They had piled into their lancers, ready for the latest training mission. Hwa Young loved and hated these sessions. Loved them because they enabled her to commune with *Winter's Axiom,* to armor herself in icy calm. Hated them because Commander Ye Jun had them practicing basic drills over and over, until she could have done them blindfolded and asleep. It didn't help that she knew that was the *point.*

The commander instructed them in coordinating their lancers. Seong Su's *Avalanche* took point, because of its immensely powerful shields. Its job was to attract and fix the enemy's attention. Its most powerful weapons, the burst guns, were effective practically at melee range, as opposed to precise, long-range weapons like railguns. "Think of yourself as a shotgun, not a rifle," the commander told him. "If they make the mistake of letting you get close, the enemy is in for a world of hurt."

The other lancer that operated far forward was Bae's *Farseer.* Unlike Seong Su, Bae's job was to *avoid* being seen, due to her lancer's thin armor. Ideally, *Avalanche* fixed the enemy's attention while *Farseer,* with its stealth capabilities, nimbleness, and advanced sensor suite, sent recon data back to the rest of the unit, and perhaps also to the rest of Eleventh Fleet.

Eun's lancer, *Hellion,* controlled the artillery. With *Avalanche* acting as shield and *Farseer* as spotter, he bombarded the enemy with missiles from a distance. Because they were easier to track back to the source, *Hellion's* attacks meant that he had to be aware of counter-battery fire, and the lancer had shields as protection, although not as powerful as *Avalanche's.*

As for Hwa Young, her lancer, *Winter's Axiom,* acted as a sniper unit. *Hellion* assaulted the enemy with powerful but indiscriminate barrages, while her role involved precision shooting. Hwa Young, unlike Eun, was meant to attack from cover:

strike and move, strike and move. Like *Farseer*, *Winter's Axiom* was lightly armored, the trade-off for greater mobility.

The final lancer had no overt combat capability, something that Commander Ye Jun was up front about. "It's strictly a C2 unit. Command and control. It enables me to give orders from the battlefield, and is capable of certain cryptology and analysis functions." The commander's smile had twisted. "Besides, who needs *two* snipers in a platoon?"

Hwa Young also learned that the commander's callsign really *was* Bastard, although no one would give her a straight answer as to whether that was the name of zir *lancer*. Surely not?

Pay attention, she told herself. She was determined not to mess up *this* time. Especially since *this* time, they were drilling with the fleet's fighters.

Had her hero Mi Cha ever made rookie mistakes? Hwa Young had a hard time imagining it. Yet surely everyone went through a learning curve of some sort. Maybe someday, if she proved herself, she'd have an opportunity to ask.

Previous live training scenarios had ended in various disasters. Like the time Seong Su rammed a local asteroid and sent it careening toward the flagship, necessitating a course correction. Or one of Bae's rare errors, when she overdrew her batteries and her lancer went unresponsive so the fleet had to delay to retrieve her, a grueling operation that extended the scenario by another hour. Most embarrassing was the time Hwa Young broadcast in the clear instead of using the dedicated line, which was encrypted to prevent the enemy from listening in. She'd accidentally switched the setting because Geum had sent her an unauthorized virtual greeting card in the middle of training—

a sign that zie had forgiven her after their quarrel, perhaps—and she was trying to delete it without giving zir away.

This training mission, at least, was more exciting than the previous ones had been because it was their first time coordinating with a fighter squadron. The fighters screened their advance, harrying a computer-simulated enemy while the lancer platoon got into position. That was the easy part; determining valid targets was harder. Hwa Young accidentally ended the exercise early by firing a blank that would have hit the lead fighter. In the hair-trigger excitement of the moment, she'd gotten it confused with the real target, a simulated enemy fighter.

"This is where your tendency to fire at anything that twitches is a disadvantage," Commander Ye Jun told Hwa Young dryly over the comms. "While it's true that IFF"—Identification Friend or Foe—"is not one hundred percent reliable, you should *generally* refrain from shooting at friendlies."

Our aim is excellent, Winter's Axiom said while heat rushed to her face.

Yes, Hwa Young thought back at it, *but we have to aim at the right thing.*

Winter's Axiom disdained to respond to that.

"You're lucky, Winter," Eun said. While he continued to call her "Menace Girl" on the ship itself, he was scrupulous about using her callsign during training. "At least you're not patched into the fighter pilots' comms. You don't want to hear the things they're saying about you there."

"We might as well debrief," Commander Ye Jun said. "Bastard to *Maehwa* CIC, request permission for the platoon to dock."

"Request granted" came the distinctly grumpy response.

Hwa Young wanted to sink into the deck already, but she had

to focus on the docking maneuver. It would suck if she fouled that up too. Especially since the very first things they'd drilled, over and over until the repetition became mind-numbing, were how to launch and how to dock. As Eun pointed out, a lancer that couldn't get off the ship (or back on it, for that matter) was of limited use.

Debriefing was just as humiliating as Hwa Young had expected it to be. Commander Ye Jun assigned her remedial training with the simulator, working with the targeting system and increasingly complex scenarios in which she had to identify hostiles and fire at them *without* committing friendly fire.

After she'd finished the session, Hwa Young returned to the bunkroom. Bae was combing her hair, the line of her back blade-straight. "I don't know how you do it," Hwa Young admitted to her.

Bae stiffened. "What do you mean?"

"You make everything look so easy." She didn't know how Bae would react. Accept her backhanded admiration? Throw it in her face?

Bae tossed her head as if she still had long hair, then resumed combing. "Some of us are willing to do what it takes to look good, Ice Princess."

Ah, yes. Bae's new nickname for her. Too bad she knew it wasn't a compliment.

Hwa Young shrugged. No point wasting time trying to get on Bae's good side. "Catch you later." She heard no response as she exited.

Back in Forsythia City, she'd wished for more hours in her day. Life aboard the *Maehwa* made it clear she hadn't been efficient enough. She rarely had any leisure, and the few hours she scratched out were spent studying the lancers' systems or on the treadmill so she could improve her endurance for the grueling training sessions.

What the hell. She headed to the rec room after all, wishing Bae would thaw just a little, and wondering why she kept making overtures to someone who needed no company but her own ego.

On the way, Hwa Young stopped by the flagship's commissary. Lancer pilots, like the rest of the crew, received pay keyed to their badges. But the black market within the fleet operated on a parallel system of unofficial currency, namely the loathed and loved chocolate marshmallow pies of which everyone received one a day, sealed against the ravages of time in a plastic wrapper. She'd asked why the black market had settled on this of all things, and Eun had explained to her that chocolate pies didn't go bad, ever.

Hwa Young had learned more through accident than cunning or observation that Eun had a minor addiction to the citron-flavored sports drink that the commissary doled out in woefully inadequate quantities. The stuff was rarely available from the commissary proper and went for a fortune on the black market. Hwa Young couldn't imagine why, given that it was called the attractive name of Radioactive Sweat. Still, she performed the now-familiar dance of buying choco pies so she could hunt down Mi Sun, the shady black market person, to procure three bottles of the drink as an apology. After all, when she screwed up, it reflected badly on Eun, who had trained her.

The rec room was sparsely inhabited at this hour, mostly by—Hwa Young's heart sank—a knot of four fighter pilots, who were clustered around a manhwa. As far as she could tell from a glimpse, it featured . . . fashion duels? With any luck, they'd stay so engrossed in the manhwa that they wouldn't remember that she was the one who had "shot" their leader in the simulation.

The rest of her squad was here, too. Bae must have beaten her here while she detoured to the commissary, and she looked regal in her uniform. Seong Su was perennially sloppy, and today Eun's collar had slipped sideways, but they were in the midst of ping-pong, so that made sense.

"I'm beat," Eun announced after bouncing a trick shot off the *edge* of the table to win the match, something he did with distressing regularity.

Hwa Young set the bottles of Radioactive Sweat down next to him.

"You're the best," Eun added appreciatively. "You want the next match?"

One of the pilots, a tall, rakish woman, lifted her head. "Hey," she said, eyes narrowing, "you're Winter, aren't you? The one who *shot* me? Hard to mistake the hair."

Great. Hwa Young should have known she wouldn't get lucky today.

Eun interposed himself between Hwa Young and the fighter pilots. "Hold up, Falcon One. It was training. I promise she'll sweat for it."

Hwa Young was taken off guard by the idea that Eun would go to bat for *her.* Especially since she'd screwed up. His sudden formality—addressing the pilot by her callsign rather than her name or "space jockey"—also alarmed her. Did he think there was a real possibility of a fight?

Seong Su belatedly shambled over next to her, looking sheepish. Hwa Young glanced at him, startled again by the idea that her fellow lancer pilots would close ranks around *her*. Even Bae took position to Hwa Young's other side, despite her haughty, bored expression.

Falcon One sneered. "I think it's up to *me* to make sure your rookie doesn't make the same mistake twice. Because next time it might be a live round, not a blank." She handed the manhwa nonchalantly to the fighter pilot next to her, a burly person who rivaled Seong Su in size, and rolled back her sleeves.

Eun understood the signal. They all did.

The fighter pilots might not have the impressive physiques of the *Maehwa*'s marines, but they weren't stupid, either. They spread out in a semicircular formation, readying themselves for the fight. Only then did Falcon One throw her punch.

The punch failed to land by virtue of Eun dodging, or more accurately, attempting to dodge and running into Seong Su, who bulled forward at exactly the wrong moment. Hwa Young rapidly revised their chances of emerging unscathed—

An alarm howled through the rec room. "This is Admiral Chin." Chin's stern voice came over the PA system, echoing oddly. "All hands to battle stations. I repeat, all hands to battle stations. We are under attack by the clanners."

Hwa Young choked back an incredulous laugh at the timing, even as gooseflesh erupted on her arms.

This is it. Time to face her past.

"We'll finish this later," Falcon One promised.

Eun scowled in her direction. "Come on," he said to Hwa Young, Bae, and Seong Su. "We'll school these dumbass space jockeys later. Right now, we've got some clanners to obliterate."

15

Having hastily suited up, Eun, Hwa Young, Bae, and Seong Su burst into the docking bay to a scene of modest pandemonium. As she sprinted for her lancer, Hwa Young caught fleeting glances of technicians making last-minute adjustments to the machinery. The deck officer shouted hoarsely, fighting to be overheard above the tumult.

I was just here, Hwa Young thought, marveling at the change in atmosphere. Her lancer's presence pulled at her like a great magnet. It was their first battle.

Their first battle against clanners.

My old family is dead, she told herself. *I serve as the fist of the Empress now.*

She repeated the words to herself as she entered the cockpit and sat. The straps fastened themselves, and the slight pressure steadied her further. She couldn't afford to be weak. Not in her first real battle.

The lancer powered up, wintry lights of white and blue and silver pulsing in time with her heartbeat, then dimmed to standby mode. After weeks of drills, going into standby was second nature. It scarcely required conscious thought. Distantly, through the lancer's hypervigilant senses, she heard the mechanics and deckhands calling to one another, the jargon of the fighter pilots as they scrambled.

Later, Eun had said, they would train live-fire exercises in tandem with the fighter squads, who offered support, screened their advances, and harried the enemy fighters in turn. But time had run out, and "later" had never come.

Hwa Young checked over the status screens, which Eun had explained to them as a redundancy in case something interfered with the pilot-lancer bond. They showed her gravitic reserves, her supply of ammunition for the kinetic sniper rifle, the charge levels of the radiant cannons and the singularity lance. She ached to use the last one, although Eun, the killjoy, had warned her that the lancers' most powerful weapons only unlocked when the pilots' bonds with them deepened, and not before. In the meantime, she could contribute via long-range precision shooting with the rifle.

She would have been bubbling over with mixed nerves and dread, but *Winter's Axiom* steadied her. *We are the death waiting in the dark,* it reminded her, with the predator's patient expectation. Anticipation, not a precipitate knock-kneed rush into action.

This is it. This is what I trained for. The anxiety she'd felt earlier receded beneath a shell of ice. She leaned into the cold, focused calm that *Winter's Axiom* offered her, and which was almost addictive in itself. She'd pay for it after the battle as the backwash of adrenaline hit her all at once—if she survived—but that was something she could worry about later.

She waited, and waited, and waited. Objectively, she knew not much time had passed. Subjectively, the seconds pressed against her awareness.

Finally the comm chimed. Hwa Young expelled her breath and toggled the channel open. "Winter on standby."

Eun's voice came over the line. "Hellion to Bastard. Bastard, do you read?"

That's odd, Hwa Young thought in the awkward moments that followed. Shouldn't the commander be faster to respond than this?

A new voice interrupted. "Deck officer here. You lancers ready or not?"

"We're waiting on Bastard," Eun growled. Over the lancers' private channel, he added, "Zie'd better haul ass or we're going to be ejected, ready or not. Winter, Farseer, Avalanche, you all ready?"

"Ready," Hwa Young confirmed, followed by the other two.

Yet another voice interjected. "This is CIC"—Combat Information Center, where all the highest-level decisions were made—"to Lancer Control. Lancer Control, are you ready to launch?"

Eun sighed. "CIC, this is Hellion. Bastard's running behind schedule." Eun's sour tone suggested that he regretted everyone's life choices. "Give us five minutes."

CIC cursed. "You were supposed to be out there yesterday. The fighter squadrons are already out there risking their asses. What good are you if you're not out there with them?"

Hwa Young would have liked to know that herself.

"Scorch the Bastard," CIC snarled. "Lancer Platoon One, prepare to launch without Bastard, since zie's busy picking zir nose. On my mark. Five, four, three, two—"

"Belay that."

Hwa Young sagged in relief at the interjection of Commander Ye Jun's voice, then corrected her posture. *I have to be ready to launch the moment the order is given.*

"Bastard," CIC said, "we are sixteen minutes into live combat and the clanners are breathing up our noses." (Hwa Young wondered what it was about this particular officer and noses.) "You are going to launch *now* or—"

"The lancers," Commander Ye Jun said in that deceptively amiable tone zie liked so much, "answer to me. If the admiral has opinions as to the lancers' proper deployment, she can start by *talking to me.* Until then, I will deploy them as I see fit."

A pissing match, Hwa Young thought with disgust. *I'm going to die in the docking bay without seeing action because my leaders are engaged in a pissing match over who orders whom.*

Finally, CIC spoke again, with stony politesse. "You are clear to continue, Bastard. *Good* hunting."

Hwa Young couldn't imagine a more hostile or pissed-off farewell.

"Sir," Bae's voice cut in, "I don't know about the rest of you"— Hwa Young imagined that was directed at her in particular— "but I would like to know what the *plan* is. Sir."

"It must be desperate times to drive you to a sir sandwich," Commander Ye Jun remarked, as though that mattered. "You're all patched in to CIC's recon reports?"

"Yes, sir," Bae said.

Hwa Young's tactical display projected a schematic directly

over her field of vision. It centered the flagship, with the fleet outflung and lighting up the sky with point-defense fire against incoming missiles. Eleventh Fleet showed up in lambent blue, the clanners in hostile ghost-trails of dead gray, like clotted moths. They were already nearby, weaving in and out of Eleventh Fleet's halo of fighters. Hwa Young wondered how they had gotten so close without the outriders catching wind of them.

Hwa Young wasn't the only one with that question. "Sir," Seong Su said, "how did the clanners advance without us spotting anything?"

"They may have improved on the old stealth systems," Commander Ye Jun said, as though this weren't a tremendously dismaying piece of intelligence. "Still, the clanners almost certainly believe that Eleventh Fleet is without lancer defenses. This gives us a unique opportunity to surprise them, even if the admiral doesn't realize it. I'm not going to let the hotheads in CIC blow it for us."

Hwa Young blinked. "Unique opportunity" wasn't how she would have described their circumstances. More like "completely screwed." Still, since orders were orders . . . "Tell us what to do," she urged.

It is a season for death. Winter's Axiom's voice echoed in her mind again.

She had the feeling her lancer liked prey very much. Before bonding with it, she would have had reservations about its naked bloodthirstiness. Now she felt a bone-deep echo of its hunter's nature. *Wait for the plan,* she counseled it, or herself.

I have waited twelve years. I expect excellent *prey,* it added as an afterthought.

"A quick lesson for you," Commander Ye Jun said. "Gravity

lances act as powerful and focused gravitational waves—which pass through matter. They can go *through* the *Maehwa*'s hull. One lance by itself won't damage the hull so badly that it can't be repaired. However, four lances, intersecting at a common target, will amplify the effect to a lethal degree. We have a single opportunity to make a strike on the clanner flagship from *within* the *Maehwa*."

For a minute, Hwa Young wasn't sure she was hearing the commander correctly.

It was a lunatic plan. Like any good Imperial citizen, Hwa Young had grown up watching bulletins that depicted lancers slaughtering enemy fleets and driving back battalions of tanks. She had assumed that most of them were computer-generated fantasias even as her heart longed for them to be pixel-by-pixel truth. In all that time, though, it had never occurred to her that lancers might attack while still cocooned *inside* their carrier.

There's probably a good reason this isn't done more often, she thought uneasily. After all, the commander had acknowledged that the maneuver would affect the *Maehwa*'s hull.

"This is only possible," Commander Ye Jun went on, "because we're at such close range. Gravity lances become weaker at greater distances. Ordinarily we'd have to take the fight to the enemy."

A gray moth-smudge lit up in red as the commander painted the target. "That's a probability cloud representing the likeliest locations of the alleged clanner flagship. It's a big target, but the longer we wait, the hazier our chances of hitting it. We're going to aim our lances so they intersect inside its engine. Do you understand?"

One by one the confirmations came in.

Commander Ye Jun had the world's steadiest voice, even if Hwa Young couldn't keep herself from noticing the flickering of Eleventh Fleet fighters dodging, flying, dying on her tactical display. "All units power up."

Hwa Young's awareness flowed out of her body and into the great armor chassis of *Winter's Axiom*. Elation flared in every corner of her mind before settling into a predatory intentness. She *was* her lancer, aware through its senses of every vibration in the deck and every electromagnetic chirrup, aware of the battle-field entire.

Hwa Young's enhanced senses told her that, to her right, Seong Su's *Avalanche Four* had taken an eager step forward.

A grating noise cut through the sounds of engines whirring to life. "Deck Control to Bastard, what the scorch is your lancer unit doing? You are not cleared to stomp around here willy-nilly!"

Hwa Young was tempted to point out that CIC had been begging them to power up and fight moments ago. Ten years from now they were going to find her shriveled remains mummified inside the lancer because they never had an opportunity to *fight*.

To fight people you would once have called kin, that persistent, unwanted whisper reminded her.

The commander was unfazed. "I've got this, Deck Control." To the squad, zie said, "Aim for the target I've marked. The enemy flagship's engine room should be there. Ignite gravity lances on my mark."

Hwa Young glared at the red sphere, imagined it exploding. Focused the entirety of her being so that the targeting reticule projected onto her field of vision centered itself correctly.

"Mark."

Hwa Young exhaled in a puff, fingers twitching with the memory of a rifle's trigger. For a second she saw nothing. Then the clot on her tactical display collapsed into the shape of a clanner ship, a vast triangular mass with protrusions signifying gun turrets and missile ports and scan arrays. It blossomed outward in an explosion.

Eleventh Fleet protected its fighters behind belatedly activated shields. Two unlucky fighters, caught by the shell boundary, were cut in half and met similar fates as the enemy.

No, Hwa Young thought, *what if one of them was Falcon One?*

She didn't like Falcon One. She'd almost gotten in a *brawl* with the woman and her cronies. All the same, she wanted Falcon One to have survived, even if she knew, rationally, that either way, two fighter pilots had died.

"All right," Commander Ye Jun said, as controlled as ever, over Seong Su's whoop of triumph and Eun's terse congratulations. "Their flagship's down, but the clanners aren't disengaging," zie told them tersely. "There must be a second capital ship. Time to go out there and inflict some more punishment."

In the dreams of her early childhood, after the destruction of Carnelian but before being remanded to the Imperial orphanage, Hwa Young had often imagined herself inside a lancer's cockpit—the same imagery that comforted her in her meditations. She hadn't known what the interior would really look like other than magnificent: glowing panels, glowing buttons, glowing lights everywhere. The first thing she'd learned about life in New Joseon was its surfeit of light, so she envisioned that carrying over to the lancers' interiors.

There was a snub-nosed kid at the orphanage who liked to steal her lunch and dump the contents in the recycler. She imagined that she'd use her lancer to smash zir lunch and leave globs of rice on zir shirt. Or the dreary woman who never bothered to remember her name. A smash for the woman, too, and maybe mess up her stupid hairdo. Or the official who'd stopped by to inspect the orphanage and looked down his nose at all the orphans, referring to them as "ratlings." A smash for his shiny bald head.

These fantasies dwindled as Hwa Young applied herself to becoming the best possible Imperial citizen so she would prove worthy of a lancer of her own. She memorized all the prayers and praises, and recited them diligently at the appointed hours. Even as a child, she knew that fantasies of revenge, while satisfying, would only get her in trouble if she acted on them. She was too smart for that.

One thing Hwa Young had never questioned before the past weeks' training, however, was the idea that lancer combat involved a lot of smashing. She had always envisioned herself close to the locus of action. She'd imagined the enemy blinking out between one beep and the next, and that she'd be close enough to see it. Hell, in this case "close enough" made no difference given that *she* couldn't see through the *Maehwa*'s hull, instead relying on the lancer's awareness of scan fed through the flagship's CIC.

As she prepared to launch, Hwa Young wondered how much of the corpsed clanner flagship's debris she'd be able to spot. Whether any part of it had survived the conflagration.

Whether anyone aboard had been someone she'd known, or could have known, in a mirror life.

We are together now, Winter's Axiom reminded her. *We share our kills.*

The flutter-burn sensation that washed over her skin told her that the *Maehwa* had performed a shield blink—shutting the shields off for a second, then restoring them in a tighter radius to exclude the fragments.

"That was some spectacle," Seong Su said.

"You're not here as a sightseer," Bae snapped.

Commander Ye Jun disregarded them both. "CIC, Bastard requesting launch clearance for Lancer Platoon One."

Finally, Hwa Young thought, perking up. *Real fighting.* She shivered with excitement, vowing to herself that she wouldn't mess up like she had in training. Not when it mattered.

"Admiral Chin wants to have words with you, Bastard."

"She can have words with me *after the battle,*" Commander Ye Jun said, implacable. "I say again, requesting launch clearance for Lancer Pla—"

"Clearance granted," CIC said. "Enjoy your five minutes of glory while it lasts."

The commander said, "Launch on my mark—mark."

They launched in formation. The five lancers flew simultaneously through the open bay and to the launch chutes. The less time they wasted, the less precious atmosphere would bleed off into the aether. While humans could breathe aether for short periods of time, too much of it caused symptoms similar to drunkenness. Hwa Young remembered the weeks she'd spent recuperating after the attack on Carnelian, drifting through hallucinations and suffering from vertigo. The orphanage director had told her with particular glee that if she'd gulped any more aether, she would have rendered herself permanently delirious.

Hwa Young allowed herself a moment—only a moment—to glory in the sensation of acceleration, as *Winter's Axiom* and the other lancers flew away from the *Maehwa*. The faint light of local stars and more ominous flares of explosions illuminated the lancers' humanoid forms as they spread out so they wouldn't risk colliding into one another. Currents of aether swirled around them, which she felt like the distant tickling of a breeze against the lancer's armor.

I'm flying, she thought, elated beneath the unnatural shell of calm. *I'm flying!*

The fleet spread out in every direction around them. Imperial fighters swooped daringly in and out of their flight corridors, sometimes caught up in hellspark dogfights with opposing fighters. Hwa Young assumed there was a logic to the ships' positions and maneuvers, but that was Admiral Chin's concern and not hers.

And beyond that—beyond that was Carnelian.

Hwa Young had always imagined Carnelian beautiful and intact in her waking moments, had always dreamed of it fragmented, like a kaleidoscope of ruined futures. She hadn't expected the clanners to be able to restore it in her lifetime, or at best, within a couple of decades.

But here it was, a ruddy disc in the distance, like a copper coin smeared with purple-gray wisps of cloud. It was hard to connect that vision with the hills and starbloom winds of her childhood. The hills, the mountains, the valleys, even the courses of rivers—all those would be different, if she walked the moon again.

The clanners had caught them two days' flight from Carnelian's last reported location, but apparently the reports were not entirely up-to-date. Carnelian had an "orbit" in Imperial parlance, really a glorified name for its wandering trajectory. Like many moons that were not under Imperial control, its path through the Moonstorm varied depending on the vagaries of its inhabitants.

Commander Ye Jun had made it clear that the moon had been restored. But Hwa Young hadn't believed it, not in her marrow, until she saw that red disc, beautiful and whole and intact.

And it wasn't just whole and intact, it was an active clanner base. Hwa Young wondered how this had come about. Had the Empire grown lax on account of Carnelian's initial disintegration, allowing the clanners to sneak back in? Had the clanners discovered ways to accelerate the painstaking process of moon formation? All questions that the commander hadn't possessed answers for.

The lancers left the flagship behind them. Ahead, the *Maehwa*'s shields glimmered like a layer of first frost over the darkness of deep aether. Hwa Young spotted Seong Su's lancer in the lead. Her tactical system overlaid it with a copper-brown circle: *Avalanche*.

Tactical informed her that the clanners had gone dark. Eleventh Fleet's fighters were sweeping the area for other hostiles. The *Maehwa*, if not the rest of the fleet, was out of immediate danger.

"Shields will go down in a few moments," Commander Ye Jun said without telling them how zie knew. "When that happens, accelerate to waypoint one. There's one more clanner capital ship, and we've got to take it down before it can scream for help or report to its masters."

The commander had marked a series of waypoints in the navigation interface to guide them through the chaos of the battlefield. Waypoint one showed up on tactical, blinking brightly orange at the outskirts of the battlefield. Once the shields were down, they'd be free to fire without danger of hitting their own ships. At the same time, with the fighters busy, they would be on their own if the enemy counterattacked.

The ice-flicker vanished. The commander snapped, "Now!"

Hwa Young willed herself forward, and the lancer sprang ahead like a hawk eager for the hunt.

Suddenly they came across the remnants of the clanner flagship. The haze of shards had an inexplicable void at its heart. As though something there had shoved aside the various fragments and pieces. Or was it a natural consequence of the explosion's outward force?

"The bastards," Eun breathed, and then said inexplicably, "'Scuse. I bet the second capital ship hid *inside* the shrapnel. Nothing else in their fleet would take up that much space. How'd you see it, sir?"

Hwa Young squinted at the void. No one would think to look in the middle of all that destruction for a *second* capital ship. She imagined that it had been dangerous for the clanner ship to linger that close to their flagship's destruction, that they had risked being pummeled by high-speed debris in order to secure their hiding spot.

"Old trick," the commander said without elaborating. "Our job now is to destroy the second ship *before* it can call for help or report on this battle. We will only have the narrowest window of opportunity. If the clanners call for reinforcements—well. Let's just say the complications are not in our favor.

"Avalanche, take point. Farseer, use him as a shield—that's what he's for—and scout for us. Hellion, bombard the area with everything you have. Winter"—zie sent her a holo schematic—"the instant Farseer paints the target for you, take out the ship's comm tower."

"Time to pummel something!" Seong Su exclaimed with ridiculous enthusiasm.

"It's not a video game," Bae said cuttingly.

Hwa Young thought privately that she didn't care how Seong Su envisioned the battle, as long as he did his job.

The clanners saw them coming and reacted. Hwa Young's tactical display had updated with the second clanner capital ship, now revealed, and tracked its movements. After the spectacular demise of their flagship, the clanners would have been fools not to expect lancers.

Hwa Young was frustrated that the ships themselves appeared as distant specks, distinguished from the stars only by their rapid movements. Now she understood why Eun had emphasized the need to rely on the tactical display in order to understand what was happening in the battlefield. Space was too big, the distances too great, the maneuvers too quick, for a pilot to rely on the naked eye.

Close your eyes, Winter's Axiom advised suddenly.

It was madness. But she did so, gripped by a compulsion she couldn't name.

And this time she *did* see—through the lancer's senses, which were receiving data from Farseer's panopticon-like scan arrays. It was like a map projected into her mind, centered on *Winter's Axiom* itself. Now she *saw* a full clanner squadron of twenty fighters disengaging from an Imperial squadron in the distance and rolling in order to arrow toward *Avalanche* instead. *Winter's Axiom* remained well to the rear, as befitted its role as a sniper.

"That confirms we're getting close to their family jewels," Commander Ye Jun remarked. "Evade at will."

Hwa Young's pulse went into overdrive. *This is it. This is real.*

Her stomach rebelled as missiles sprayed toward them. Through her link with *Winter's Axiom,* she perceived them as trails of lightning. She wondered what she'd eaten earlier to cause the nausea, then remembered: the clanners were the enemy. Their very presence disrupted local gravity, two antithetical systems battling each other. She grabbed a dose of antiemetics and jabbed them into the side of her neck, wincing at the pain.

This has to work, and fast. She was positive she'd gone green from her eyeballs to the inside of her mouth, and she couldn't afford to be distracted from her job by mere *nausea.* The stabbing pain in her neck grounded her, brought her back to the hot immediate hellscape of battle.

Bae reacted first to the torrent of fire. Her lancer swerved and ducked behind one of the large chunks of the luckless clanner flagship. She timed the maneuver perfectly, matching her vector to the fragment so she stayed in its shadow.

Hwa Young had lost track of Eun. Seong Su lingered, slow to react, either because he was distracted or because he had frozen in panic. "Avalanche, fighter's on your nine," Commander Ye Jun called out.

"Ouch, that's gonna sting," Seong Su complained before sucking in his breath. Because of his slower lancer, he wouldn't be able to dodge in time. The fighter was too close.

"Hang tight." Eun.

Hwa Young could pick it off, maybe—but she had her orders. Her job was to ensure that the enemy capital ship didn't call for help.

Seong Su would have to rely on his shields, and perhaps reinforcing fire from *Hellion*. She couldn't do anything for him.

Hwa Young drifted into the inner stillness that she had cultivated for the past six years. It was up to her now. If her aim strayed by five meters in any direction, she would miss, and the remaining capital ship would be able to bleat its predicament to any listening reinforcements. The less information the clanners had about the fate of their fleet—and the disposition of the Imperial forces that opposed them—the better.

Scan only showed her target as a blur. She needed better eyes on the target.

Then the blur resolved into a precise point as Hwa Young's lancer received close-up scan data from *Farseer*. "I've done my part, Winter," Bae's haughty voice informed her. "Don't mess up."

"Just watch me," Hwa Young shot back.

Before, she'd worked with the other lancers to take out the clanner flagship. This time, it was just her and her aim. No one to blame but herself if she messed up.

As though in a trance, she focused her will on the lancer's long-range radiant cannon—and fired.

16

The clanner capital ship's comm tower exploded in a haze of glowing particles. *Winter's Axiom* had the longest range of all the active units, even without the singularity lance, but its radiant cannon required a steady hand and pinpoint targeting with the aid of computer stabilization. She hadn't been absolutely sure she'd hit the target in live combat, but she'd carried off the feat after all.

Hwa Young expelled her breath all at once, unsteady with relief for a moment, then steady again. The battle wasn't over.

She didn't get to luxuriate in her accomplishment for long. Between one blink and the next, a tremendous impact *pierced* her in the head—no. It had pierced *Winter's Axiom,* and she felt the pain through the link.

The next thing she knew, Eun was screaming in her ear, Bae raised her voice in that waspish tone Hwa Young had endured for six years, and even Commander Ye Jun sounded worried. All their words shattered around her like fragments of ice.

Ice. Or snow? Hwa Young stared in abstracted fascination as crystals of ice wafted through the cockpit. More crystals formed when she exhaled. Then she came back into her body enough to mark the creeping cold. Her connection to *Winter's Axiom* wavered. She was no longer vast and unconquerable, just a halfway corpse huddled in the freezing dark.

Not just cold, but a breach from somewhere above her. She could *feel* the hole as though it gaped in her own skull. The projectile had clipped the visor of her helmet. It must have taken a downward trajectory from the top of the lancer. If it had come any closer to her, it would have punctured her head.

"Hwa Young!" Bae's voice snapped her out of her shocked musings.

That's not just water, Hwa Young thought, staring at the snow. The deafening alarms made it difficult to concentrate. In the cockpit's tidal washes of blue and red light, alternating erratically, some—most—of the ice fragments gleamed red-black. Frozen blood.

Her blood.

"Never transmit names," Commander Ye Jun snapped at Bae. "Even if you're sure the channel's secure." To Hwa Young: "Winter, we can keep the incoming enemy fighters off you for another five minutes, but you've got to return to base."

Hwa Young's vision swam in and out of focus the way it had six years ago when she'd started to suffer aether sickness while watching the lancers mop up the crashed remnants of her old home. She cursed herself for her weakness. "Understood, Bastard." She had to say it twice before the words came out audibly.

Cognizant of the storm of frozen blood motes, Hwa Young refocused on the targeting system. Took a potshot at one of the darting mosquito clanner fighters and clipped it, not bad. Her real motivation, however, was the warmth that summered through the cockpit as the radiant cannon vented waste heat. She could have lingered in that warmth, clutching it to her for comfort.

I'm not thinking clearly, am I, Hwa Young noted. Hysteria was setting in now that the battle-calm had ebbed, leaving her shaking with the aftereffects of adrenaline. She reached out for the serene chilly presence of her lancer and met only a staticky emptiness. That worried her more than the physical damage.

The heat wave melted the crystals. Blood rained down on her in a gruesome splatter.

Priorities. She had to seal the cockpit breach *now.* Wouldn't it be terrible if she became so delirious with aether sickness that she flew into enemy fire?

The cockpit's alerts screeched so loudly that Hwa Young considered silencing them so she could think clearly. The only reason she didn't drift off into bemused contemplation of the starlight and explosions was the cacophony. No, better leave them on, especially since she bet her bad luck wasn't over.

Hwa Young spent two precious seconds with her eyes squeezed shut, fingers pressed to her temples, to plan. The lancer came with automated repair systems, but automation depended on her now-disrupted bond, which she had no idea how to reestablish. The snowdrift of frozen vapor told her that something was awry and she would have to effect repairs herself.

"Winter," Commander Ye Jun said, so dead-level calm that she could taste zir concern, "your vitals are erratic. Do you require assistance?"

She bristled, even though the commander hadn't intended it as a slight. Zie was asking if she wanted to cede control of her lancer to zir, something she knew was a theoretical possibility. They had not yet drilled it because, as Eun had remarked caustically, a rebellious lancer was apt to fry an interloper's brains. Besides that not-inconsiderable risk, the attempt would distract the commander from the battlefield when the others most needed zir attention.

"I'm fine, sir." She wondered if she was lying.

Her heartbeat had gone thready. All the more reason to deal with this quickly so she could receive medical attention. For once she appreciated Eun jamming thirty hours of training into every twenty-four-hour period. She discovered that if she relaxed, her body slipped into the lifesaving patterns inculcated by the drills. A few weeks of drills could start a habit, when the learner practiced diligently—and Hwa Young had always been diligent.

Hwa Young overrode the automated repair subsystem, since it wasn't working anyway, to prevent it from engaging at an unexpected moment and fouling her up. (Eun had told them, with none of his usual sourness, a hair-raising anecdote of a fellow pilot whose face had been burned off by an ill-timed encounter with a laser's internal optics. Hwa Young was no great beauty, but she liked her face the way it was.)

Still seated, she set up a series of waypoints—not ideal, but better than vectoring straight into an unknown situation now that she no longer had an overview of the battlefield's status through her lancer. Having to do this manually was the pits, but she was glad Eun had insisted that they learn how, instead of relying on the *thought becomes motion* immediacy of the normal pilot-lancer bond. The backup navigation computer beeped, warning her that the path would take her perilously close to what it identified as a chunk of engine block. Hwa Young didn't give a damn what it used to be as long as it didn't collide with her.

Then, having memorized the path, she reached forward and unfastened her safety harness.

The lancer's interior maintained half-standard gravity unless the pilot specified otherwise. This saved its gravitic reserves for more interesting things, like combat. Hwa Young had not yet had cause to fiddle with this setting. The accompanying inner hum assured her of Eleventh Fleet's united will as a buttress. She would not have surrendered that for any trivial reason.

We are winter. She remembered the lancer's voice, and longed for it with a heart-deep ache that shocked her.

Hwa Young climbed up, glad of the hand- and footholds, and assessed the crack. It looked bad, but even a partial seal would help her, and then she could risk the backup air supply. The repair diagnostics indicated that the projectile, whatever it was, had lodged itself in the armor.

She toggled the lancers' channel from her suit. "Commander," she said. "For the next five minutes, I'm going to be unable to adjust my trajectory." She sent the waypoints to the C2 unit. "I'm attempting repairs."

"Understood, Winter. We've got your back."

Why am I disappointed? Hwa Young thought when Bae didn't chime in with some cutting remark.

Shaking her head, Hwa Young retrieved the tool kit. She clipped it to her belt, keeping a tight grip on the handle. It would suck to get caught off guard by some sudden motion or collision and end up knocked out by a wayward wrench. She could imagine Eun's scorn, or Bae's, if she allowed that to happen.

This close to the hole, the aetheric currents swirled through the crack in her helmet and over her skin like a corpse's breath. Hwa Young opened the kit. She unfolded a sheet of flexible foil with adhesive backing. It crackled and clung unpleasantly to her gloved hands. She removed the backing and pressed it into place long enough for the adhesive to set. Messy and impermanent, but it only had to last until she docked and a technician could carry out proper repairs.

"Completed," she reported thirty seconds later, having made the journey back to her seat. She strapped herself in safely despite the jarring change of vector she'd programmed the lancer to execute.

Hwa Young replaced the tool kit, then fished for the medical kit under her seat. She sprayed skinseal over the wound. It stung, and then a blessed numbness spread through it. The skinseal included stimulants, antibiotics, and analgesics, all of it to stabilize her until she could reach safety or rescue.

Safety. A laughable illusion, when she was surrounded by the fragmented carcass of one ship and the baleful wraith of another. Hwa Young had wished to see her targets up close. Would she live long enough to regret her bloodthirstiness?

Hwa Young checked the tactical display again. Seong Su and Bae operated far forward, the former dodging incoming fire with a boxer's steadiness. Bae shadowed his moves, allowing him to take the brunt of the fire while she acted as a forward observation platform. She broadcast her scan suite's data to the rest of the fleet. On tactical, the two seemed impossibly distant, consummately choreographed: the steady copper-brown light of *Avalanche*, the mercurial silver-violet of *Farseer*.

Gathering her concentration felt like stitching windblown threads with cold-numbed fingers. Nevertheless, Hwa Young refused to give up and leave the battle. Imagined Bae's mockery, although her more reasonable inner heart argued that Bae had graduated from such pettiness.

Hwa Young corrected the spin imparted to *Winter's Axiom* by the earlier impact. The world gyred around her. No matter how often they'd rehearsed the maneuver in training, she'd grown up first on a moon, then on a planet, places where *up* and *down* had fixed meanings. Out here, where the orientation of ships and lancers changed from moment to moment, her inner ear rebelled.

Whether the antiemetic remained effective or the pain overwhelmed any last traitorous urge to puke, Hwa Young overcame her nausea enough to take advantage of the tenuous cover offered by the clanner ship's remnants. The seeping cold made her miserable, her fingers stiff and clumsy to respond. A juvenile corner of her mind wished for someone to tuck her into bed with an extra-thick quilt and hot citron tea.

That's odd, Hwa Young thought dreamily as she chased the retreating bulk of the *Maehwa. Why is there so much more of that black snow?* She gazed at it, entranced by the flurrying patterns it made.

"Winter." It was Commander Ye Jun. "Your vitals look atrocious. I'm executing command override on *Winter's Axiom.* The ride's gonna get bumpy. Acknowledge."

"I can handle it." Her head throbbed with the intense pain of a migraine. Why hadn't she noticed that before?

Still, it had been a long— She consulted the clock function in her neural implant. Less than thirty minutes had elapsed since they launched. That couldn't be correct. They must have battled for hours.

"Sorry to be so high-handed," Commander Ye Jun said, as though they were lingering over nonalcoholic plum wine and dismal fried snacks. "I must not have made myself clear, Winter. They call it an *override* for a reason. You hang tight and we'll fly you in as sweetly as a bee to the hive. You don't have a choice in the matter. I can tell you from long years of practice that choice is overrated, anyway."

What does this have to do with anything? Hwa Young was in the middle of not-saying when she learned what zie meant by *override for a reason.*

She had thought her connection to *Winter's Axiom* had withered earlier, when the headshot hit it from above and clipped her as well. But there remained a thin murmuration of icicle thought and intent, which she had taken for granted, and which she discovered only when the commander ripped it away with all the gentleness of a power drill to the optic nerve.

Hwa Young screamed, and then stopped screaming. The first was bad enough, that reflexive loss of control. The second was worse, because as bad as screaming was, it was *her* scream. The not-screaming was the commander's doing.

A vision flashed into her mind of a middle-aged woman with her long hair half pinned up, a woman with a face very like Commander Ye Jun's, save for the exhaustion in the wrinkles around her eyes. *The Empress?* Hwa Young thought in a shock of recognition, but it was hard to think clearly.

The Empress sat at an outdoor table in an autumn garden,

brilliant with the red leaves of maple and the golden leaves of gingko. Before her rested a baduk board with a game in progress.

"Listen," she was saying in a voice like smoke and honey, a voice that made Hwa Young want to trust her, "if *I* have to spend four hours of this damn ceremony in a hanbok that weighs more than I do, to say nothing of the damn *shoes*, the *least* you can do is trim your damn bangs."

The woman placed a single white stone, and suddenly several amorphous groups of stones coalesced into an overwhelming advantage for white.

The vision ebbed, leaving her scrabbling for any thread of connection—to *Winter's Axiom*, to the commander, to anyone. The commander had severed her from her lancer. Had lodged zirself in the crenellations of her soul. The will that moved her hand was not hers.

Commander Ye Jun hadn't overridden her *lancer*; zie had overridden *her*.

Zie's saving my life, Hwa Young told herself as her body, controlled by the commander, performed actions that she had not chosen, because she was too blurry with shock and pain to understand them.

"I do apologize," zie said, and this time zie wasn't speaking over the comm link but directly into her head. "This is the surest way, and we can't afford to lose you and your unit."

Hwa Young tried to formulate a response, and fell instead into an infinite echoing darkness.

17

O nly the long habit of discretion saved Hwa Young when she regained consciousness.

Instinctively, she reached through the haze of waking for her connection to *Winter's Axiom*. The lancer responded to her with only the faintest of presences, like an echo in a vast cavern. Fear gripped her: what if she wouldn't be able to reestablish the close bond that she had already come to rely on?

She was in a crowded tent with a definite downward gravitational pull, extraordinary and pleasing. If she knew one thing, even muddled by pain and blood loss and worry about her lancer, it was that she must never take gravity for granted. The steadiness of the pull reassured her that Imperial rituals were being observed here.

Her head pounded, but it was a distant pounding, with a strange lack of pain. They must have given her painkillers. She couldn't think in straight lines; couldn't *focus*. For a time she concentrated on breathing in and out as though each exhalation were a test.

Someone had bundled her not in a quilt but in a military-issue blanket like the ones that covered their bunks on the *Maehwa*. For several stuttering moments, Hwa Young ran her fingers disbelievingly over the rough, unlovely fibers: warm, though not comforting. She could have sworn she'd been sleeping under one of Mother Aera's quilts, the jasu embroidery of satin-stitched flowers lovingly handsewn. She'd almost called for Mother Aera as though she were ten years old and the past six years had evaporated.

No one here, in this makeshift sick bay, would recognize Mother Aera's name. No one would understand the significance and shout that she was a filthy clanner. No one would hustle her to the brig or stuff her into a gimchi jar.

Besides, she thought wretchedly, she'd just participated in the destruction of clanner ships.

But anxiety still gripped her heart.

Hwa Young sat up, grimacing at the renewed throbbing in her temples. She reached up: someone had bandaged her head. Thirst scratched at her throat, sudden and unwelcome.

She looked around. The tent accommodated about twenty people on pallets. A single impressively muscled medic attended the wounded. Zie was cursing in an unbroken venomous stream as zie manhandled a thrashing patient as though they were an uncooperative dumbbell.

Hwa Young thought about offering assistance, then reconsidered. The medic jabbed the luckless patient with a syringe that looked like it wanted to be a sword when it grew up. The patient went limp.

Hwa Young looked away and steadied her breathing. Something was wrong, and not just the forced severing of her connection.

Then it came to her: the air. The air throughout the tent smelled of late-season starblooms, a fragrance Hwa Young had experienced only in dreams since Carnelian's earlier destruction.

She sucked her breath in, made herself exhale slowly, trying to quell a rising tide of panic. Had her comrades abandoned her? And why was she on Carnelian, her old home, and not on the *Maehwa*?

The medic caught sight of her. "You," zie said in the same tone zie might have reserved for a cat who had vomited on a favorite carpet. "You should still be out cold."

Hwa Young admitted inwardly that being out cold sounded like a great option, if only she could afford to sit idle. "Water," she croaked. It came out before her real question, which was *Where are the other lancer pilots?*

The medic didn't look mollified, but zie brought her the desired water in a flimsy paper cup. "Damn lancer pilots. One of these days you lot will realize you're not immortal and stop banging yourselves up with scorching death-defying stunts. Healing matrix can only do so much."

This struck Hwa Young as unfair. How could she have predicted that the clanner capital ship would return fire so accurately? But she held back her retort. It was a bad idea to offend someone who could single-handedly grapple a thrashing person, to say nothing of the giant syringe.

"The *Maehwa*," she said. "Commander Ye Jun. Where's the rest of my unit?"

The medic's answering grunt was unpromising. "As far as I

know, Pilot, they off-loaded you while the flagship undergoes repairs. That stuck-up girl with the violet eyes checked on you a couple times while you were unconscious. Seemed to think you would expire. I told her it's not like I let my patients die and shooed her out."

Bae? Hwa Young thought incredulously. *Bae was worried about me?*

"The rest of the squad is out patrolling," the medic went on. "We've set up temporary bases here on Carnelian. I shouldn't be surprised if the clanners sneak back to blow us all up."

The bases are set up already? How long had she been out? She began to ask, but the medic had turned away. Hwa Young raised her voice: "Who do I report to now?"

The medic sniffed without looking back at her. "You're staying in bed until I clear you for duty. Do you know how much synthetic blood I pumped into your system? You could have died!"

Hwa Young thought it likelier she'd expire of aggravation or anxiety. No use confronting zir, especially when the world was tilting and blurring around her. "Wait a moment—" she began to say, and did not remember lying back down.

The next time Hwa Young woke, Geum sat at her side. Zie had scrunched zirself up cross-legged next to Hwa Young's pallet. To all appearances, Geum was playing a popular game on zir slate that involved dragon breeding. Hwa Young assumed it was actually a back door into someone's top-secret computer network.

"Geum?" Hwa Young said, touched that her friend had come

for her, even if she didn't know why. "We *are* on the moon, aren't we?" She was starting to question her understanding of the situation. "What are *you* doing here?"

"You look like ass," Geum informed her instead of answering the question. "According to the medic, whatever projectile punctured your head left toxins in your bloodstream. No wonder you look like you belong in a tomb."

Hwa Young digested this. She didn't feel like she'd almost died. She'd suffered worse. But she didn't want to reveal that. She tried again. "We're on Carnelian?"

Geum considered the genetic characteristics of a particularly fetching dragonling with antlered horns and dappled blue-violet scales on zir slate. "They dropped some of us off here, yeah," zie said in a hushed voice. "The fleet's in orbit to scare off the clanners. The marines set up this base and hustled us out here like sheep. We've been doing the rituals more often than usual to counter the clanners' influence." Zie mimed the attitude of prayer.

Geum added, after a pause, "You're worried about the other pilots, I expect? As far as I know, you're the only one who was injured."

Hwa Young opened her mouth, closed it. She remembered the Imperial fighters who'd gone up in smoke. *Empress guard their souls.* Then she realized Geum meant the only *lancer pilot* who'd taken harm. "How many people are in the base down here?"

Geum shrugged. "Lots?" Zie typed in a query that looked like NUMBER OF DRAGON EGGS, COLOR SORT. An answer flashed on the screen. "An entire marine division," zie interpreted, "and—" Zir mouth tightened as zie reconsidered whatever zie'd been about to say.

Hwa Young's throat closed up for a moment. Then she said, "I'm sorry I was such a brat earlier."

Geum patted her arm. "It was stupid to fight." But zir gentle tone told her she'd been right to apologize. "Let's get you out of here."

Hwa Young took the hint, wondering if the authorities knew that Geum was using the dragon game as a front for zir hacking activities. "I could use a meal," she admitted. She glanced at the medic to confirm zie was otherwise occupied. There was probably some formal sign-out procedure, but the red tape was bound to be a mess after a battle. Better to get out of here and worry about paperwork later.

Surreptitiously, Geum helped Hwa Young to her feet. She wobbled, both glad of her friend's help—and the fact that they were on speaking terms—and mad at herself for needing assistance. Together, they made their way out of the tent.

Outside, it was day, or night, or something partaking of both. In the Moonstorm, the paths of the moons varied, and so too did the positions of the stars. Hwa Young had been born beneath the Moonstorm's unchancy half-light, rather than the steady day-night cycles of a normed and calibrated Imperial planet, so she was used to this, but she assumed Geum and the others were feeling unsettled.

A sick yearning started up at the pit of her stomach. If she could have bitten into the honey core of Carnelian and filled her belly with its essence, she would have done so without shame or hesitation.

Then she saw the discomfort on Geum's face, and shame and hesitation struck her like twinned fists.

Geum had started chattering, the way zie did when zie felt awkward. Hwa Young had been too wonderstruck by nostalgia to mark it earlier. "—don't know how the clanners stay sane out here," Geum was saying. "The stars moving every night, like they're laughing at you, no constellations you can rely on . . ."

"If you travel by starship from system to system, the constellations change anyway," Hwa Young pointed out.

"Yeah, I guess."

Busy feet had tramped down the gold-russet grasses. Everywhere the sweet, floating fragrance of starblooms perfumed the cool air. Hwa Young met every new vista with mixed trepidation and joy. Eldest Paik had told her and her siblings stories of seedsilk traveling unimaginable distances to sprout on newly birthed moons. Had something like that happened here, in the years she'd been away?

Considerately, Geum took her to a latrine and waited for her to relieve herself. They continued to the larger tents where the marines in their green uniforms had set up a makeshift mess.

Geum hadn't been kidding about the marine presence. Soldiers stood on watch at carefully selected checkpoints, patrolled the encampment, exchanged messages about supply trucks or beacons or recipes for choco pies. Hwa Young had scarcely interacted with the marines during her training. Eun's only comment had been "Stay out of their way. If you annoy them, you deserve the butt-kicking."

Hwa Young could tell they'd reached the mess by the smell of the gimchi stew. Her mouth watered. *I'd better not be drooling,* she thought even as her steps quickened.

Geum laughed. "You can't be that badly off if you're attracted to the horrible food in camp."

"Whose food you calling horrible, you uncivilized brat?" the cook, a bald and bulky man, demanded as they entered the mess. He must have overheard Geum's comment. "This gimchi has come all the way from the fabled chefs of the crownworld to grace your table." He broke into a guffaw.

"Don't mind Cook," said the not-much-older guard on duty. "He has a story for every dreadful thing he tries to stuff down our gullets. Lies, all of it."

"Nonsense." Cook winked at Geum. "I'll win you over yet."

Hwa Young didn't know how to react to Cook's easy manner. Geum, more socially adroit, laughed at every one of his jokes, even when he speculated outrageously on the Empress's taste in consorts. Between the two of them, they set Hwa Young up with a heaping tray of gimchi stew, rice, and banchan dishes like salted mung bean sprouts and marinated anchovies.

"I know how hungry pilots of any kind are after a battle," Cook added, his voice softening. "Eat up, and don't hesitate to ask for more. We're well-provisioned for now."

Hwa Young located a corner of the tent where she could watch the others and brood over the ominous *for now*. She fell upon the food, not caring that the stew burned her mouth. It was deeply mediocre gimchi stew, with cursory strips of vat protein for flavor. Even the orphanage had served better, and the boarding school's offerings had been vastly superior. But she couldn't deny the paradoxical deliciousness of a meal that filled her belly when she was ravenous.

"How long *was* I out?" she finally asked Geum, dreading the answer.

Geum, who'd snagged a less overburdened tray for zirself, finished chewing a mouthful of rice. Swallowed. "A week."

Hwa Young almost choked on her stew. "That's not—" She checked her implant, which she could have done earlier if she'd been thinking clearly. Geum was correct.

Geum patted her hand. "Your friends have been worried. Seong Su checked on you twice, and Eun came by once on the commander's behalf, he said."

"*You're* my friend." But she was touched in spite of herself. Especially since she knew that Bae had stopped by, too.

Geum's eyes softened. "Eat up. I don't care what Cook says about how well-supplied we are, I always wonder. So we might as well take advantage now."

Hwa Young wolfed down some sautéed spinach seasoned with sesame oil and soy sauce, then asked, "Don't you have things to do?" *Like pal around with the unpleasant engineers Hyo Su and Chae Won*—but she wouldn't say that.

Geum looked shifty. "Not so loud!"

Hwa Young shook her head, but she wasn't going to rat out her one friend if zie was skipping out on a shift. Especially her one friend who presumably knew more about how the encampment worked than she did after being unconscious for a week. She'd hate to have Bae gloat at her funeral because one of the guards shot her for getting some fine point of protocol wrong.

Hwa Young had downed most of her meal when a mechanic shuffled into the mess. He waved nonchalantly at Cook, then performed a double take so flawless that Hwa Young wondered if it was a joke.

"Geum, you spider," the mechanic growled, "so that's where you've been skulking. You're not in Eleventh Fleet to eat more than your share, you know."

Hwa Young set down her tray and rose. "I requested the

technician's aid." It felt weird to call Geum that, but she couldn't refer to zir as *my friend*. Not in this context.

She didn't outrank the mechanic, who was a warrant officer and whose expertise was valuable in its own right. All the same, if he respected the lancers . . .

The mechanic shook his head. "Can't imagine why," he said pointedly, "since it's *your* lancer zie's supposed to be repairing, Winter."

Geum crimsoned.

Still, it wasn't as if Hwa Young could pilot her lancer while she was out cold, so she didn't see the rush. She just hoped that her bond with it could be repaired sooner rather than later.

"I'll take it from here," she said to the older mechanic, doing her best to summon the hauteur that came so easily to people like Bae. "Come on, Technician."

She and Geum hastily dumped the meal's remnants in the recycler, put away the trays, and strode out of the tent with their heads high. When they'd put sufficient distance between themselves and the mess, Geum began to giggle. "'Technician'! You look like you were born in that uniform."

Geum had meant it as a compliment, but the statement speared her at the pit of her stomach. She might have earned a place among the lancers, even participated in a battle, but she still carried an ugly secret. It weighted her down like lead.

Hwa Young shoved her ambivalent feelings into a box at the back of her head and felt an incipient ache at her temples. "Thanks, I think. You're going by Spider, really?"

Geum giggled again. "Chief's always going on about how my fingers are as nimble as spiders."

Hwa Young didn't agree that spiders made for a flattering

comparison, but she kept the thought to herself. They were still walking, headed for the camp's outskirts. "Where are we going?" Hwa Young asked, prodding the space in her mind where the bond with her lancer should have been as they strolled. Its absence hurt like the gap left by a pulled tooth.

"Shh."

Then Hwa Young spotted an indistinct shape, hazed by the dust and pollen in the air, above the crest of a hill. *Winter's Axiom.* She could feel it, even if she couldn't fully see it. Yet its presence was only a faint, chilly shadow in her mind, and she wondered if Commander Ye Jun had damaged her bond with it beyond repair.

Geum saw her look and said, "Your lancer's down in a valley. Something about avoiding reconnaissance. They didn't want the clanners finding out we have an active singularity lancer, even if it hasn't developed that capability yet. They threw tarps over it."

"Tarps?" Hwa Young said incredulously.

"Yeah, it's half-assed."

She thought furiously. "Patch me in to Commander Ye Jun." She didn't *want* to talk to the commander, but she didn't want to offend zir, either. Not after the command override. But she did need to know what her orders were.

"Sure." Geum closed the dragon-breeding game and brought up the comms app. Hwa Young noted in passing that all of zir sacrificial hatchlings, sold for in-game cash, were named Bae. Geum handed the slate to her.

After several seconds, Hwa Young reached the commander. "Let me guess" was zir first remark, as though things were *normal* between them. As if zie hadn't taken control of her body, and she hadn't seen zir memory of the *Empress herself* in zir past—an image that Hwa Young still couldn't shake. Why *had* she seen the Empress? But that was a question for another time. "You're with that hacker friend of yours."

Geum opened zir mouth to say something witty. Hwa Young discreetly kicked zir in the shin. "Sir, my connection with *Winter's Axiom* seems staticky." She didn't like admitting it, but it seemed important for her commanding officer to know.

"That's not uncommon after the type of injury you sustained." Commander Ye Jun's voice was kind.

Relief washed over her, partly because of the reassurance, partly at the realization that she trusted it—and the commander zirself. Command override had frightened her, but ultimately she knew it had saved her life. "Where and when should I report in, sir?"

Static, then: "We'll be returning to base in four hours. I'll expect you at your lancer then."

"Understood, sir."

Commander Ye Jun signed off without another word. Hwa Young didn't take it personally. She didn't know zir mission or its risks. And she had the information she wanted.

Hwa Young and Geum kept walking. They reached another hill, beyond which soldiers stood guard. "We can talk more here," Geum said, abruptly subdued. "You know, this isn't the only camp on Carnelian."

That was right; someone had mentioned a second base.

Geum worried at zir lower lip with zir teeth, then looked away. "You remember the colony ship *Sonamu*? The one they shuffled the other refugees aboard?"

Hwa Young wished, not for the first time, that Geum were better at getting to the point. "What about it?"

Words spilled out of Geum in a rush. "This is the military encampment. But there's another one in our shadow—south of us, according to local notions of 'south.' That one's all civilians. They landed the *Sonamu* and they're disassembling it. I didn't understand the significance before, but I get it now. They're using it as the basis for a colony to drive out the clanners."

Hwa Young blinked at this information. "Why are they using refugees for settlers?"

The stories of Imperial colonization were cleaner and more glorious in the history classes. Carefully screened and selected volunteers: the flower of New Joseon's yangban scholar-elites to govern, the best and brightest workers and scientists and geomancers to give the colony the means to flourish. She'd never heard of colonies scraping up dregs from a battle.

Just because she'd never heard of something didn't mean it didn't happen, though. Especially with the government's choke hold on the news services.

"There's something you could help me with," Geum said, dimpling at her.

Hwa Young knew it had to be a big favor if zie was resorting to *dimples.* "Name it," she said recklessly.

"I've been hacking into the personnel rosters. I found out that my fathers are at the other base."

Hwa Young inhaled sharply, light-headed with gratitude at the unexpected good news. She enfolded Geum in a hug, and the two of them clung to each other for a long moment.

Fresh purpose blazed before her. Geum's family had made it after all. "Did you send them a message?"

"I tried messaging them through the official service, but

everything's censored. Then I hacked into the message system and sent a note. Nothing."

"Then we'll have to go in person. How far away is the base?" she asked.

Geum's face brightened. "An hour away by rover."

"We'll go together," Hwa Young said. "Driving a military rover can't be that different from driving a regular vehicle."

Geum pulled up a map of the encampment that zie had embellished with doodles of dragons. "We can't stray from this route," zie warned her. "I keep hearing about the clanners leaving mines and explosives around. The road, at least, is swept regularly."

"Gotcha. Geum, can you forge orders from Commander Ye Jun authorizing me to sign out a rover?"

Geum whistled. "Sneaky. I didn't know you had it in you."

"Will the rover itself tattle on us?"

"It doesn't record its path. No one can track us that way. They're afraid the clanners will steal one and download our movements."

Hwa Young grinned. "Then let's go."

In theory, Hwa Young approved of the fact that the vehicle pool was well-guarded. In practice, it made absconding with a rover tricky. The marines—two of them, both tall and solidly built—eyed her and Geum curiously as they approached and Geum gave the passcode. Geum looked like zie was seriously considering flirting with them—zie had a type—so Hwa Young stepped on zir toe to remind zir to stick to business.

The marine on the left, two centimeters taller than her compatriot, lifted her chin in challenge and resettled her rifle. "Your business, Pilot?" Her nose wrinkled, and Hwa Young was suddenly aware that she reeked of sweat and blood. Geum hadn't reacted to the stink at all, a measure of either the strength of zir friendship or zir obliviousness to anything that wasn't a machine (or dragon).

"I need a rover," Hwa Young said. She displayed the ersatz orders.

The other marine kicked the ground and spat. "Got nothing better to do than take a joyride after busting up your own lancer? Real smooth. Hopefully Eighteenth Fleet will bring us better pilots along with food and equipment—if they ever get here."

Huh, Hwa Young thought, unease coiling within her. She'd heard vague rumors about reinforcements, but training had occupied so much of her attention that she hadn't thought much about the details. Too bad mere pilots were rarely privy to the plans of the top brass.

Left Marine shook her head. "Don't mind zir, Pilot. You two can take the vehicle on the far right."

"Thank you," Hwa Young murmured, and grabbed Geum before zie could get conversational.

18

Hwa Young caught herself relishing the joyride, especially the way the rover's interface lit up in her signature colors of white and blue and silver. She kept waiting for Geum to comment on it, but zie was staring out the window, zir expression pensive.

Of course. Geum might have located zir fathers' records, but zie wouldn't really believe they were okay until zie saw them for zirself. The best thing she could do for zir was to get both of them to the base as quickly as possible.

Despite her attempts to quell the inappropriate swell of emotion warming her heart, Hwa Young gloried in the rover's speed, the way it responded to her handling. She'd always had great reflexes. While she knew better than to let down the window so the wind could whip through her hair, she could still smell the sweetness of starblooms inside.

The last time she'd roamed on Carnelian, she'd been too

young for Eldest Paik to trust her with a real vehicle. Still, she used to sneak out into the faster of the family's two hovercars—why settle for a slow one, even if she couldn't drive it?—and sit in the driver's seat, imagining she, an explorer who would bring home the wealth of galaxies, was driving into the starry sky and through the aetheric currents. Either they never caught her or, more likely, the household adults considered this harmless childhood play. She tried to go for a drive several times but never figured out how to relieve the ever-vigilant Mother Aera of the keys.

Geum was tapping at zir slate.

"Hey," she said to Geum. "Any response yet?"

Geum's head turned. Hwa Young could see the pallor of zir face in her peripheral vision. "Nope."

"I'm sure they're okay," Hwa Young said, aware that it wasn't much of a reassurance.

Geum smiled wanly. "Thanks. We'll find out, won't we?"

"Of course we will."

The sky shifted from red to dusky orange to violet and back again, sometimes in the space of moments. Hwa Young had forgotten how much she'd missed the chameleonic vistas, the gold-tinged clouds that veiled the local suns and stars. As a student in Forsythia City, she'd learned brush painting with everyone else. Imperial art teachers taught stereotyped landscapes based on masterworks by the crownworld's court painters, and everyone had committed a butchery of Kang Man Shik's famed *Sunrise over the Phoenix Mountains,* with its stylized clouds and tame skies. Hwa Young had fought the temptation to paint Carnelian's skies. It would have given away too much.

"It creeps me out," Geum said out of nowhere.

It took Hwa Young a moment to come out of her enraptured contemplation. "What?"

"The sky. I miss the sky back on Serpentine. A real sky, not—not whatever this is."

She couldn't help herself: "I think I could learn to like it."

"Huh," Geum said, looking at her sidelong. Then zie lapsed back into silence.

Hwa Young would have enjoyed driving forever, as though caught in a wheel-shaped dream, until she circumnavigated the entire moon. But halfway to the civilian base, Hwa Young realized she had a problem.

She was sure she was the only person from Eleventh Fleet who had ever lived on Carnelian. Even if it had changed from the welcoming home she remembered, now that the clanners had reconstructed it by means unknown, Hwa Young understood Carnelian like no one else did. Beyond the characteristic singing winds, she was no stranger to the way the shadows shifted and gyred upon the moon's surface. The marines had complained about the way it made them jump at phantom enemies. But Hwa Young knew this enemy was real. And now, she realized, there was something odd about the sound of the wind.

"Someone's following us," she said.

Geum sat straight up and looked around wildly. "I don't see anything." Then zie reconsidered. "Granted, I don't know how you could tell, the way everything shifts. Are you sure you're not imagining things?"

"I'm sure."

She couldn't have anatomized her certainty into words, diagrams, numbers. Didn't need to. During training, Eun sometimes badgered her to explain why she had chosen this tactic or that stratagem. But her choices were *right*, even if she couldn't always explain why.

Sometimes—sometimes Hwa Young reacted on instinct. Ever since she'd survived the disintegration of Carnelian by acting *contrary* to her training, she'd learned to listen to that gut feeling.

Irrationally, she wanted to lower the window, stick her head out, and shout taunts at whoever was following her. Thanks to a lifetime of practice, Hwa Young was (sometimes) good at ignoring irrational impulses. The bullet- and laser-resistant shielding wouldn't do her a lick of good if she made a target of herself.

"What—what should we do?" Geum asked.

"Keep going," Hwa Young said grimly. "You said it yourself. We can't afford to leave the road. And we're halfway there, anyway."

Hwa Young had considered swerving off-road to see if she could trick the stranger into revealing themself. But it was better if she didn't let on that she knew she was being tailed. She hoped the pursuer hadn't spotted Geum's reaction earlier.

As she continued driving, Hwa Young took inventory. She had the rover, although she was going to have to exit it to investigate the base—assuming they arrived safely. She had the knife, not that she expected it to do her any good, and the gun that the quartermaster had issued her. She longed for a proper rifle now that she was groundside, and cursed herself for not thinking to check one out, assuming the military base had any to spare.

Geum remained tense and silent for the rest of the drive. Hwa Young couldn't help but exhale in relief when the civilian base came into view. She decelerated; it would also suck if they got gunned down by their own side because they blazed in un-announced like potential hostiles.

At first glance, as Hwa Young examined the base, it looked as if they'd docked the *Sonamu* for repairs. Then Hwa Young's eye picked out incongruous details: struts and scaffolding, parts of the ship that had been removed, disassembled, rearranged. The end result looked like a mechanical hive sprawling sideways across the landscape, buildings of metal connected by cobwebs of yet more metal.

"I didn't know a ship could come apart that quickly," she remarked in a low voice.

"Chollima-class ships have modular construction," Geum said, visibly relaxing. Zie always liked talking about technical things. "It's so they can be converted into living facilities, research labs, factories, and so on."

The sentries stopped them at the outer perimeter: two marines who could have been brothers, with the same corded necks and bored expressions.

"Window down, please," Left Marine said while the other one sneered at them. "Name and authorization?"

"I'm Pilot Hwa Young with Technician An Geum." She produced the counterfeit order for his inspection.

Left Marine's demeanor became friendlier. "Say, nice shot on that clanner ship. We all heard."

She made herself smile. "Thank you. Have you spotted any clanners out here lately? I could have sworn I saw a shadow on the way in . . ."

"Shadows everywhere in the Moonstorm." Right Marine shook his head, mouth twisting as though he'd drunk rice vinegar.

"There's patrols out there and no one's reported so much as a sparrow's tail feather."

"Got it," Hwa Young said, then refocused on their purpose. "I need directions to the administrative headquarters." She assumed the settlement had one, and that it would be the best place to track down Geum's fathers. One nice thing about Imperial government was its one-size-fits-all devotion to organization and consistency, a boon to miscreants everywhere.

Right Marine told her where in the half-disassembled, half-reassembled maze of twisty little passages she could find HQ. She parked her rover in the indicated area, noting with approval that the other vehicles were arranged in pedantic rows. It was a far cry from the other students' slipshod attitudes in the military preparedness class back on Serpentine.

Geum was hunched over zir tablet, working at who knew what, stirring only when Hwa Young asked zir to move so she could conduct a quick search of the rover. She didn't know what she expected—bugs? A bomb? But nothing turned up.

She didn't make the amateur's mistake of patting her handgun or knife, just in case she was still being watched. That would make their location on her person obvious. A professional would expect her to be armed, but she saw no reason to make their job easy.

"Ready?" she asked Geum.

Geum's head bobbed. "Lead the way."

The smell of starblooms suffused the air, and fallen, silver-withered petals swirled along the ground and clustered at the base of the converted colony ship. Hwa Young hadn't appreciated how enormous the structure was, intended for tens of thousands of people, even if it wasn't at full capacity. Her head was throbbing again. She ignored the pain as she and Geum hurried past the busy groups of workers, doing everything from reinforcing the makeshift walls to machining tools out of deprecated parts of the hull. Geum, who would ordinarily have been inclined to linger and watch, was clearly too worried about zir fathers to do so now.

More guards stopped her and Geum, and checked their credentials, before allowing them into the hulk of the former ship. Hwa Young wondered if they'd cut proper windows, and what they'd use in place of the quartz panes that Carnelian's old households had delighted in. Right now, there were no visible windows. Once they passed the threshold, they might as well have been in a ship in outer space, or possibly a giant refrigerator. Even the viewports had been covered, for no reason she could discern.

The two of them had gotten halfway to Admin HQ when they heard a low whistle.

"Do you have a problem?" Hwa Young demanded, turning on her heel to glare at . . . Min Kyung, one of the less useful students from their boarding school. She'd completely forgotten about zir existence. Hwa Young blushed at her outburst.

"Hey, glad you're alive," Geum said, more tactful.

Min Kyung was cradling a case full of seedlings. Hwa Young remembered zir efforts in the school garden; zie'd had a notorious black thumb, even killing the otherwise immortal green onions.

Min Kyung's gaze went from her hair to the lancers' sun-and-lance insignia. "Damn, you're really a lancer pilot. I'd heard, but . . ."

Hwa Young sighed. "What do you want?"

"What are *you* doing here?"

"We're looking for my dads," Geum said. "What happened to everyone's parents? Are they all here?"

Hwa Young was glad Geum was here to ask the questions. Coming from her, an orphan, it would have sounded weird.

"I think your dads are in Manufacturing," Min Kyung said. "Everyone who was unsuitable for military service got shunted over here and given some shitty job." Min Kyung pursed zir lips. "You probably already know this, but Bae's mom didn't make it off-planet. She's probably, well, you know."

Dead. Hwa Young remembered Bae mentioning this. Still, she felt a pang for the other girl. Hwa Young knew what it was like to lose family, even if it sounded like Bae hadn't gotten along with her mom.

Min Kyung looked ruefully down at the seedlings. "I tried to tell the admins that I'm no good at gardening, but I got assigned to Agriculture anyway. They're hoping to achieve self-sufficiency. Everyone's sick of ration bars so maybe soon we'll have fresh tangerines."

Hwa Young was impressed by how little Min Kyung had retained from the boarding school's classes on terraforming, geomancy, and gardening. Even genetically modified tangerines required a minimum of three years to start bearing fruit. But she politely refrained from correcting zir.

Geum opened zir mouth, presumably to ask how to get to zir fathers, but Hwa Young spoke first. She wanted to squeeze some more information from Min Kyung while they had zir attention. "I'm surprised the people in charge were so selective with the refugees they brought aboard the flagship," she said, choosing her words carefully, "given how short-staffed Eleventh

Fleet seems to be. I wonder why they put you all on the *Sonamu* instead."

Hwa Young remembered how uncomfortable she'd been in the temporary holding space for refugees on the *Maehwa,* and how eerie it had been that no one had been rescued who was very young, or very old, or injured. That still bothered her. She wanted to be assured that those other people hadn't simply been abandoned.

Min Kyung started to fidget, almost dropped the seedling case, and recovered zirself with a sheepish grin. "I mean, Eleventh Fleet needs people who act as the Empress's hands and soldiers and all that. If they're going to keep the fleet's gravitic reserves topped up to fight the clanners with all that ritual, they need the best of the best. Which means Eleventh Fleet took the best prospects for itself, and left the rest of us for . . . this."

"But I suppose," Hwa Young said, more to herself than to Min Kyung, "that they also need the colonists to establish an alternate source of gravity here on Carnelian, which is why they brought the rest of you along at all, even if you're not 'the best of the best.' If they're going to kill off the clanners . . ."

Was that the other reason Eleventh Fleet was chronically short-staffed? Having to resettle populations to establish Imperial norms on the planets that they defended successfully, while maintaining a skeleton crew of so-called elites? (*Have we heard of any successes?* a snide voice asked in the back of Hwa Young's head.)

Geum was shifting zir weight from foot to foot, clearly impatient.

"Something like that," Min Kyung said agreeably. "I don't pay attention to that stuff. I always figured our leaders had it under control." Zie eyed Geum. "Anyway, like I said, I spotted one of Geum's fathers the other day in the Manufacturing sector to the northwest. It's a separate building, big red stripe, can't miss it. One of the noisiest, too."

"Thanks," Geum said with a brave smile. "Uh—keep quiet about seeing us? Just in case the authorities don't approve of us being here."

"Sure thing," Min Kyung said. "Say, Hwa Young, I never got a chance to thank you and Bae for, you know, saving our skins back on Serpentine."

Before Hwa Young could formulate a response, Min Kyung had already sauntered off, swinging the seedling container in a frankly alarming fashion. With their luck, the tangerines would grow upside down or maybe inside out. She was tempted to call after zir to be careful, then decided it was none of her business.

"C'mon," Geum said, practically bouncing on zir toes.

They exited the main body of the settlement and headed northwest. Someone had put up signs, a lot of them, each one in the same stately blue font. The consistency of the font choice steadied Hwa Young, as it was no doubt intended to do.

"Do you feel it?" Hwa Young asked uneasily when she felt the queasy fluttering of nausea for the second time. "Or is it just me?"

Geum nodded soberly. "Yeah. The gravity isn't completely steady. The base must not be as well-regulated as it looks."

The minute fluctuations in local gravity gave Hwa Young flashbacks to Carnelian's destruction. For a moment she crouched in the reeds again and imagined the walls shuddering apart around her. She stopped, squeezed her eyes shut, and recited prayers to the Empress. After a moment, she heard Geum's voice joining her, and that helped more.

They reached the northwest building, which resembled an enormous crate that had fallen off a farm truck and grown fungal masses while waiting for someone to retrieve it. Hwa Young strode through the entrance while borrowing Bae's most haughty expression, hoping to intimidate people into asking fewer questions. Geum came with her, glancing around zir in search of zir fathers. Workers in coveralls saw Hwa Young coming and ducked out of her way.

She didn't have to keep up the imperious act much longer, because she heard Geum crying "DAD!" in a voice that could have raised the dead.

Geum flung zirself at zir older father, who was caught by surprise in the middle of inspecting a table full of tools.

"Geum!" He swung his child up in the air as though zie were a toddler, then enfolded zir in a bear hug. "Your other father should be back any moment—he'll be so glad you're here!"

Hwa Young watched the reunion, envy twisting in her heart like a snake and its venom. *I will never have this,* she thought, hating herself for the shock of six-year grief that threatened to overcome her. In silence she turned away, telling herself it was to give them privacy, and knowing that it was instead her own bitterness.

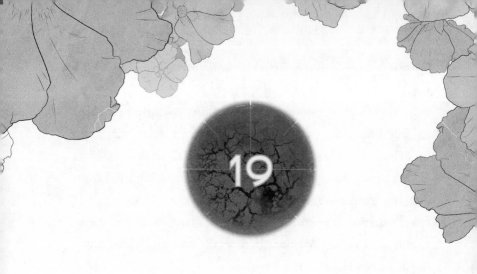

19

"Don't worry about me," Geum said to Hwa Young after what felt like an insufferable wait. "I know you have to get back to base. My dads said they could organize a ride back for me." And zie smiled at her, radiant, from within the circle of zir older dad's arms.

Hwa Young had smiled weakly and made her way back to the vehicle pool, alone and forlorn.

The lancers were her family now. All the same, she couldn't imagine receiving such a warm welcome from, say, Eun or Bae. Especially not prickly Bae. And she didn't really *want* Seong Su to hug her. With his strength, he might crush her.

The guards at the vehicle pool didn't give her any trouble. Hwa Young checked the rover; even with her thoughts swirling, she hadn't forgotten the earlier sensation that someone was following her. Still, she was running low on time; she needed to report back to the commander in an hour. She'd have to chance it.

Hwa Young entered the rover, keenly aware of Geum's absence, and removed her pistol from its hiding place beneath her shirt, then holstered it at her waist so she could reach it more easily. Better to look stupid than be dead.

"Don't hesitate to radio for help if you get waylaid by clanners," one of the guards told her between sneezes. "'Scuse. Damn pollen sets off my allergies."

"I'll keep that in mind," Hwa Young said.

She was grateful for her neural implant's timekeeping function. Out in the Moonstorm, you couldn't rely on the ebb and flow of light in the sky to tell time accurately. Several stars streaked past, brilliant and beautiful. Once upon a time she would have craned her head back to admire them, and thought of the folktales Eldest Paik had told her about aether-riders and far-travelers. But she couldn't afford to get distracted by childhood stories anymore.

The sensation that someone was following her returned fifteen minutes into the journey, not coincidentally when the civilian base had dropped out of sight in the rearview mirror as she dipped into the far side of the hills. Hwa Young hadn't lived this long without trusting her instincts, but it would be nice if said instincts gave her more details. She wanted so badly to turn off the road, to make her trail less predictable, but it would be no use. Whoever was tailing her knew her destination. Everything else was minutiae.

She grew tenser and tenser as the drive progressed, pain radiating from the base of her neck and throughout her shoulders, despite her best efforts to stay relaxed. If this had been one of Geum's racing games, there would have been shitty jangling music to encourage her to accelerate. As it stood, only the jackhammer percussion of her heartbeat accompanied her, and the howling of the wind, which buffeted silvery starbloom petals across her windshield.

The attack came just as she had convinced herself that she was imagining things. She heard a tiny crack above the hum of the engine. Barely kept from losing control of the vehicle in a wild U-turn. Instead, she accelerated.

What the hell had that been? The rover was still handling fine, so it wasn't the levitators or engine—

She punched the button on the radio. "Winter to Base Two—"

The radio didn't turn on. Dead. Not even static. She bet if she stopped the rover and investigated, which she wasn't about to do, she'd find that someone had shot out the radio unit.

Nobody accidentally disabled the radio first. She was being ambushed. Her attacker didn't intend for her to call for help, which meant she was on her own.

Hwa Young didn't know which direction the attack had come from. She had two choices. Disengage the safety protocols and run for base—of course, the attack had come at the midway point, leaving her with two equally bad options. Or stand her ground and fight an enemy she couldn't see.

For the first time, Hwa Young resented Carnelian's hills for the lack of visibility they offered. In the old days, the hills and ravines had been a side effect of the moon's formation. Something to do with the fluctuations in gravity. Even Imperial planets weren't immune to the effect, although her teachers had claimed the mountains and rivers were there by design, according to proper geomantic principles.

The road was clear, but not *safe*. She didn't want to lose

her transportation as well. She was going to have to take her chances off-road.

They better not disable the nav next, Hwa Young thought. Why did she have the worst luck with vehicles? First the school shuttle, then her lancer, and now this rover. Maybe she should have roller-skated.

She veered left, skimming just beneath the crests of the hills so as not to silhouette her vehicle. She had no idea what kinds of weapons her attackers had, but she didn't like the idea of being nailed by a rocket launcher or laser because of her carelessness. Of course, if the clanners had aerial surveillance, they'd call down an artillery strike and she'd be a goner.

I have to return to base. I have to return to base. Empress protect me.

Was she being singled out because she was a lancer pilot? That was the only theory that made any sense. Perhaps, and her blood chilled, the clanners somehow knew she was the lancer with the sniper that had taken out the second capital ship. They might be out for revenge.

She drove farther into the hills, keeping an eye on the terrain in case she ever got an opportunity to return to the road. Out here, dead reckoning was a dead loss. She could already see the constellations flowing and shifting above her, a slow and lethal drift.

The military readiness class had only taught Hwa Young and her classmates the most elementary scouting and navigation skills, most of which assumed the presence of a fixed sun and a fixed north and fixed stars in the sky, a fixed landscape that didn't warp according to the vagaries of local gravity. If she escaped the clanners now, it would be through the skills she'd picked up as a clanner child—memorizing angles and distances and landmarks while always realizing the latter were as treacherous as lake ice.

Hwa Young glanced at her rearview mirror again. This time she spotted her pursuer, an armored vehicle that was steadily gaining on her. Hwa Young cursed her lack of comms, her lack of a rifle, her lack of ability to call in an orbital strike that could take out the hostile, and never mind that she'd be caught in the blast radius too. She'd willingly pay the price.

Her only hope, outrunning the enemy, looked increasingly unlikely. It was only a matter of time before—

She felt rather than heard the percussive bang of the shot a fraction of a second before it took out her rover's levitators. The vehicle skidded wildly, then crashed to a halt, almost turning turtle in the process. Hwa Young had a freezing flashback to the shuttle accident back on Serpentine, Instructor Kim's death. They'd never given her a proper funeral. She imagined she heard the woman's accusing whisper: *Not acceptable.*

The airbag deployed, shoving her roughly back against her seat. Any illusions she had that it would be soft and cushioning were shattered. She lay stunned for an indeterminate period.

I'm not going to let myself be easy meat. It felt impossible to move, even a flicker of her eyelids or a turn of her head. She tested her fingers. They weren't broken. She reached for the knife and dislodged it with an effort, punctured the airbag since it had served its purpose. Damn sure she wasn't going to let it trap her like a lethal mushroom.

The air bag deflated with agonizing slowness. She sheathed the knife, then scrabbled frantically, head throbbing in time with the pounding of her heart, until she had retrieved the gun. Almost managed to stab herself in the thigh in the process.

How much time had elapsed? Seconds? Minutes? She hadn't been paying attention to the implant's clock function. The rover, formerly her hope of escape, had become a death trap. She had to get out of here.

At least Geum's safe at the base, she thought, trying not to get distracted by the idea that she might have seen her friend for the last time.

The rover's door had crumpled in the crash, so there was no way she could get out from the driver's side. She scrambled to the other side and exited that way, agonizingly aware of her forefinger, which she held away from the trigger so she didn't cause an accidental discharge—aware that she might have to react at a moment's notice to fire at her attacker.

She emerged just in time to see the armored vehicle bearing down on her. She raised her arm and fired once, guessing at the driver's location through the dark-tinted windshield. The flare bolt splashed sparks in all directions and had no other effect.

If the driver floors the accelerator, I'm a goner. There wouldn't be anything left of her but a red blotch soaking into the earth, soon to be blanketed by starbloom petals. Her comrades might never find her body before local predators cleaned the bones.

The driver swerved to avoid hitting her. Hwa Young's mood sank. They hoped to capture her alive. Did they intend to torture her? Ransom her? She wasn't used to thinking of herself, a ward of the state, as particularly valuable, but as a lancer pilot . . .

Hwa Young ducked behind the rover's wreckage. Prepared to fire again.

Can I disable their vehicle? If she'd known it would come down to this—herself on foot against someone in an *armored car*—she would have rammed them while she was still in her rover so they'd be on even terms.

To her astonishment, Hwa Young heard a window being lowered. She poked her head around the side of the rover and fired once, twice, barely missing the figure. It returned fire, narrowly missing her hand. That was a bullet that had whizzed by her, not an energy blast. A clanner for sure, then.

Nice try. Hwa Young exchanged fire twice more, then—then nothing. Her finger pulled the trigger fruitlessly. The sound of the click over the rising wind was the loudest thing she'd ever heard. To say nothing of the fizzy whine of the pistol's battery dying.

Where was her backup battery pack? Suddenly Hwa Young remembered she'd shoved it, uncomfortably, into her boot. She withdrew, keeping the rover between herself and the idling car, as she dug into her shoe.

She reloaded. The pain of the crash made her stiff and spoiled her aim. *Don't think about the pain. Think about how much you want to kill the person who did this to you.*

One more try. She heard a cry as she clipped her attacker— well, one of them anyway. There could be more in the vehicle. Then it occurred to her that she couldn't feel her hand, or the weight of the pistol in it. Because the pistol had fallen from her hand.

I would never drop it, she thought at the exact moment she worked out that, whether by skill or chance, the attacker had shot her gun out of her hand. Pain reverberated all the way up to her shoulder, like the knelling of a terrible bell.

Hwa Young drew her knife with her left hand, lamenting her clumsiness and wishing the jangling pain in her right arm would quiet down. She'd done drills with her off hand, but only "to balance the body," as Instructor Kim had liked to say, not with the serious intent of becoming an ambidextrous fighter. Still, if she could close the distance without taking a bullet to the head, she could mess up her attacker.

She gathered herself, then charged toward the armored car, screaming. Maybe her luck was turning, because the driver had opened the door and emerged, rifle raised.

Hwa Young's right arm might be injured, but her legs were fine. Her spring took her to the driver in heartbeats. She jabbed forward only to find the point of her knife deflected by the driver's body armor. Aimed upward for the face.

The face—

She'd seen that face before, six years ago, and all the years before that, and every day in the mirror besides.

Hwa Young froze, her knife one centimeter from the woman's eye. "Mother Aera?"

20

I'm dreaming this.

Mother Aera couldn't be here on Carnelian. Not the Carnelian she'd returned to, where the Imperial occupation was under way. For a crazed moment, Hwa Young saw her heartmother through doubled vision, a lens of refracted possibilities. Past and present collided, shattered.

And left her physically overextended. Mother Aera, no fool, caught her in a joint lock and forced her to the ground with her arm behind her back. Hwa Young's attempts to resist only resulted in screaming pain from the elbow all the way up to her shoulder. She desisted, afraid the pressure would break the joint.

"If you think I'm going to—" Hwa Young snarled.

"Hwajin—"

A name she hadn't heard in six years. She flinched.

"Hwajin! I'm not going to ease up until you give me your word that you'll hear me out. I'm not here to fight."

"If you're going to cut my throat, do it already," Hwa Young gasped, breathless with pain.

It was the gusty sigh more than anything else that convinced Hwa Young this wasn't some late-breaking hallucination. Mother Aera had always sighed like that. "And use that knife you're carrying to do it, too? Don't be stupid. If I'd wanted you dead, you'd be dead. Moons know you gave me enough opportunities. What were you thinking, driving without an escort?"

Great, now she was being lectured about her lack of security precautions by her former mother, the clanner. She glared impotently at the dirt right in front of her nose, resisted the urge to spit out the grit in her mouth on the grounds that the gesture would be misconstrued.

"Hwajin, I'm here to get you out of this mess. Or—all right. Let's just talk, okay?"

"Is that what's passing for diplomacy among the clanners?"

The vibration of Mother Aera's laughter transmitted itself through her arm, and Hwa Young winced at the fractional increase of pain. "Let's not mince words, child," Mother Aera said. "It's not like the Empress is talking to our envoys anyway. And I'm more concerned with *you*." Then, thoughtfully: "Are you a boy these days, or is this a crownworld fashion thing?"

The haircut tangent was so very Mother Aera that Hwa Young, trapped by six-years-dormant habits of obedience, muttered, "Fashion thing." She thought furiously, then added, "How long—" Couldn't finish that either.

How long had Mother Aera been tracking her movements? Only since she arrived at Carnelian? Or—a terrifying thought invaded her mind—had Mother Aera followed her through the six long years of her assimilation, never making contact? The possibility made her sick with suppressed fury.

Or, it occurred to her, had she been trying to make contact, and failing to get through?

That gusty sigh again. "If I'd had any way to retrieve you earlier"—great, now her heart-mother was talking about her like a misplaced bolt of fabric—"I would have done it. We thought you'd died in the aether."

Hwa Young seized on the "we." "Who else—"

"Only myself," Mother Aera said quietly, "from our household. There was a clanner ship in the area, scooping up survivors. We barely snuck out without alerting the Imperials."

Hwa Young's eyes prickled with unwanted tears. She was shocked to discover that the faces of her siblings, of her uncle and aunts, were indistinct blurs in her memory. *I'm done grieving,* she told herself fiercely. It didn't help.

Mother Aera continued talking. "We have—let's say sources of information. The fact that Eleventh Fleet still has operational lancers after the Battle of Spinel was of great interest to us. I wasn't expecting one of the pilots to be—" Her voice roughened, snagged on the word. "To be my heart-daughter."

What could she say? *I'm not your daughter anymore?* She was no one's daughter in New Joseon.

"I'm listening," she said, because she had no other options. Not good ones, anyway. She was stranded halfway between the two Imperial bases and no one expected to see her back for another half hour. "Say what you came to say to me."

Her heart hurt as though someone had driven a knife through it. She'd promised herself to the Empire. She had comrades.

What was she supposed to do with this phantasm from the past she'd amputated?

Mother Aera released her hold. Hwa Young rolled over and rose to her feet, coughing. Just her luck that Mother Aera had grabbed the injured arm.

"You should get medical—"

"Get to the point."

When she was younger, she'd have gotten scolded for the show of disrespect, but Mother Aera didn't press her now. "I have something to show you. Come into the car."

Walking voluntarily into a clanner's armored car struck Hwa Young as either a terrifically bad idea or some form of treason, but she'd given her word. And never mind the question of whether she needed to keep a promise to a clanner, a point of ethics that her classes had neglected to cover. Hwa Young was starting to think boarding schools didn't teach you anything useful about life. "Fine."

Mother Aera ushered her to the shotgun seat, which was either very trusting or very calculated. Hwa Young buckled herself in without comment. Experimentally, she reached out for the reassuring presence of her lancer in her mind. Either it still wasn't talking to her or it was too far away. She schooled her face to stillness to hide her dismay.

The vehicle's dashboard didn't light up or present Mother Aera with an adaptively personalized interface in the manner of Imperial technology. The controls you got were the controls you got, a factoid about clanner tech Hwa Young had forgotten in her six years away.

Now that the shock of the encounter was ebbing, Hwa

Young assessed her surroundings. Mother Aera carried at least two guns and probably more knives. She was the one who'd taught Hwa Young the essentials of firearms and knife fighting, back when.

It didn't escape Hwa Young's notice that the armored car only activated in response to Mother Aera's handprint and a passcode. Mother Aera matter-of-factly covered up her hand as she entered the latter. Geum would have hacked the system; on the other hand, Hwa Young was glad her friend wasn't trapped here with her. Mother Aera had no reason to treat Geum as anything but another Imperial.

"Where are we going?" Hwa Young asked.

"Not far. I don't want to be this close to the road in case your friends show up."

That was what she'd feared, but better to have some freedom of action by keeping her calm in the passenger seat, as opposed to being trussed up like a gimbap seaweed roll and tossed into the trunk.

"Let me guess," Mother Aera remarked as she drove into the hills, through the drifts of dust and petals—a picturesque scene under other circumstances. "You think I'm going to cut your throat anyway and leave your body as bait for the winged tigers."

"It had occurred to me, yes."

"I'm not angry you chose to live among the Imperials."

"I didn't say you were."

This time Mother Aera caught herself before the sigh gusted out. "Only a little farther." She didn't specify beyond that, but Hwa Young saw what she meant once she parked the car beneath an outcropping that shielded it from aerial surveillance.

"You're not going to get much ransom for me." Hwa Young

didn't know if this was true, but she doubted Admiral Chin would go to extreme measures to win back a green pilot.

She hated the fact that she didn't know how badly she wanted to be rescued, no matter how much Mother Aera's survival discomfited her. Another lesson from her traitor heart.

"How do you feel about slideshows, Hwajin?"

Hwa Young suppressed a groan. "You kidnapped me for a *slideshow*?"

Mother Aera inserted a data crystal into the dashboard. It whirred and clicked obstinately until she banged on it with the heel of her hand. "Sorry, the pollen gets into everything."

Hwa Young grimaced in understanding. Fortunately, she didn't have allergies, unlike some of the marines.

The presentation started up with a flicker of static, then a holographic map of the Empire. The latter looked laughably small, presented thus: a confetti-pancake of stars and systems and space stations connected by shipping routes and relay towers, all protected by the Imperial fleets. Hwa Young could have crushed it in her hands if the hologram had possessed any substance.

"You have wonderful intelligence," Hwa Young said dryly, although she didn't know how accurate the map was, just to make Mother Aera twitch. Still, the level of detail, especially regarding the core worlds, dismayed her. *It could be faked*, she told herself uneasily. "I'm proud of your spies."

"There's no need to be snide, Hwajin. I haven't shown you the really classified stuff."

Hwa Young didn't respond to the gibe, nor the fact that Mother Aera was using her old clanner name an awful lot. If Mother Aera had come for her five years ago, six years ago,

Hwa Young would have wept to hear herself called *Hwajin*. Begged for a mother's embrace. Instead, she shook with fury: how dare Mother Aera show up *now*, years after she'd given herself to the Empress's service? The years stood between them as surely as palisades.

"They'll send search parties once they realize I'm missing," Hwa Young said. She hoped this wasn't a bluff. "You should make the most of your time."

Mother Aera's eyes narrowed, but she turned back to the hologram. "This, as you know, is the Empire of New Joseon," she said. She made a gesture, and a full third of the Empire glowed red. "These sectors are on the brink of rebelling or joining the Moonstorm."

She gestured again. The crownworld shone like a white-green star; the core worlds surrounding it glowed golden. "The Empress's hold over the core worlds, on the other hand, is complete. One could even say tyrannical. And she's looking to extend that tyrant's hold not just over the periphery worlds but beyond."

Hwa Young bristled at this description of the Empress's rule. The Empress *protected* her children. That was the *point* of the Empire. And besides, Hwa Young couldn't believe the peripheral worlds were on the brink of rebellion; that had to be a clanner lie.

"We have intel that the Empress has been testing a new weapon," Mother Aera said soberly. "One capable of destroying whole worlds. We have reason to believe that it's already been tested on some uninhabited planetoids. Former planetoids, I should say."

Hwa Young couldn't tell whether the queasy knot of unease in her stomach came from having her past shoved into her face in the form of her heart-mother, or if it was due to this outlandish claim. "If you expect me to betray the Empire for a *rumor*—"

Mother Aera grabbed her hands. Shocked by the contact, Hwa Young let her. She remembered the strength of those fingers, identical to her own, which had corrected her grip on a rifle so many years ago.

"It's more than a rumor." Mother Aera's voice hardened. "You think the Empress is only going to use her new weapon on the clanners? She won't hesitate to turn it on any of her own worlds that challenge her rule."

"No one would rebel." Hwa Young hated how sullen her voice sounded. As she spoke, an idea kindled in her brain. Even though Mother Aera had gone to the trouble of concealing the armored car, projection units like this hologram were no good for camouflage, according to Geum, because the flicker always gave away your position. But if you *wanted* to give away your position to signal for help . . .

"Can I see the map?" Hwa Young asked. Without waiting for a response, she touched the hologram, zooming in on the peripheral worlds.

"Surely you don't *believe* what the Imperial news services tell you," Mother Aera went on, ignoring Hwa Young's interruption. "The propaganda? Her forces put down riots on the worlds of Jasper and Olivine. They wiped out an entire city on the latter. There's nothing left but mice and their shadows."

Hwa Young pretended to listen while feigning clumsiness in zooming in and out, using the holo to send a signal: four long pulses, two short, four long again. *HELP,* in the Imperial military code. She hoped Mother Aera hadn't caught her at it, but if so, Mother Aera was playing it cool.

As she tapped out code, though, Mother Aera's words seeped in. How could the Empress be *vicious* or *tyrannical* when her rule had provided Hwa Young a new home, a friend, comrades? When her prayers to the Empress throughout the six months at the orphanage and the six long years at the boarding school had given her the wish of her dreams, a bond with a lancer?

Still, a worm of doubt gnawed inside Hwa Young's chest. What if there was an element of truth to Mother Aera's accusations?

That was something she could deal with later. For now, she had to stall for time, keep Mother Aera talking, until rescue came. If it did.

"I don't know," she said, wishing that her hesitation were wholly feigned. "I don't know what to believe anymore."

Mother Aera's eyes softened. "It must be hard for you. But you belong with your people, not the Imperials. You can come with me. Grow your hair out again like a proper clanner woman."

Hwa Young stilled.

She could go back with Mother Aera, find out what had become of the other settlers on Carnelian. Carry the perfume of starblooms with her now and forever, instead of being haunted by the Moonstorm's transfigurations and changeable vistas in her dreams. She'd never again have to worry about being second best because Bae outperformed her.

She could, and it would mean leaving behind Eun, who had trained her despite all his grousing. Geum, who had welcomed her from the beginning. Amiable Seong Su. Even Bae.

It would mean leaving behind her lancer, *Winter's Axiom*, and never hearing that arctic voice joined to hers again.

Hwa Young was searching for something more to say, something to distract Mother Aera with, only to be interrupted by a deep rumble.

The steps of a lancer making landfall.

Mother Aera blanched. "Shit, they've tracked us!"

That was Hwa Young's cue. She yanked the data crystal out of its slot, kicked open the door, and dived out, rolling beneath the cover of the outcropping. The crystal might include useful intel; there might be other stray files on it. She wished she'd been able to grab one of Mother Aera's handguns on the way out, but she'd escaped with the crystal and that was what mattered.

The amber flicker of the shield told her that the lancer belonged to Eun. Running through the hills would be a great way to open herself up to friendly fire. The smart thing to do was to stay put and call for help using her badge. He should be within range.

The clanner car screamed out of hiding and darted into a nearby ravine, which would be perilous for something the size of a lancer to navigate. Hwa Young crouched low and watched it escape.

Hwa Young tapped her badge. "Hellion, this is Winter. Requesting pickup."

Eun's exasperated voice responded, "*There* you are. Stay put. We're going to have words about your adventures, you and I."

I bet, Hwa Young thought grimly.

21

Hwa Young sat in a "waiting room" (in actuality, it was a drafty tent) while Commander Ye Jun had yet another meeting with the brass, alternately fuming and wondering if she should have taken up Mother Aera on her offer of a relaxing vacation retreat with the clanners. She was more than tempted to slip out and get herself a proper dinner. The single, awful ration bar the commander had provided her was long gone; too bad she couldn't say the same about the aftertaste.

"Any intel has to go straight to the top," Commander Ye Jun had said after receiving her carefully edited report of the ambush. Zie made her repeat everything from the beginning, although zie was at least kind enough to offer her a glass of water. And then zie stuck her in this waiting room in case the authorities wanted to question her directly, although that hadn't happened yet.

Hwa Young had mostly told the commander the truth, omitting only the awkward relationship between herself and Mother Aera, and the fact that she knew Mother Aera's name. Commander Ye Jun hadn't pressed too hard as to why "the clanner" hadn't killed her outright, especially when Hwa Young offered the dubious alternative explanation that maybe "the clanner" wanted a captive for torture or questioning.

It's not an important detail, she told herself fretfully. She was loyal to the Empire. She'd escaped with the data crystal and handed it over to her commanding officer. Nobody needed to know the inconvenient truth about her heritage.

Still, part of her wondered . . . and worried.

Eventually Hwa Young dozed. The backwash of adrenaline had left her exhausted, wrung out like a rag. She didn't dream, or if she did, she remembered nothing but an amorphous dread, a hanging darkness whose consequences she glimpsed but dimly.

Hwa Young woke some time later to the smell of . . . chocolate? She blinked and saw Seong Su looming over her, a chocolate bar in hand. Next to him were Bae, her expression aloof, and Eun with his hands jammed in his pockets.

"Nice to see you awake, Menace Girl," Eun said, glowering at her. "Do you plan on getting kidnapped by clanners on a regular basis?"

Despite the heat that rose to her face, she was gratified by the note of concern in his voice.

"She doesn't look all that banged up." That was Bae, talking about her as though she weren't right there.

Nevertheless, Hwa Young looked sidelong at the other girl, alerted by the undercurrents in her voice. For once Bae didn't look like she'd stepped out of a fashion magazine. Dark smudges shadowed her eyes. Had she been *worried*? Bae had already lost Ha Yoon, Hwa Young recalled guiltily.

On the other hand, Ha Yoon had been Bae's *friend*. Not someone she held in scorn. It wasn't the same.

"That must've been a real scare," Seong Su said, interrupting Hwa Young's musings. He held out a half-eaten chocolate bar. "Um. This was supposed to be for you, but I forgot and chowed down on it because I was hungry. Sorry."

Hwa Young couldn't help laughing. "It's fine." She took a bite, mostly to show him she was grateful.

"So what was it like, seeing a clanner face to face?" Bae asked.

The distance between them slammed down on Hwa Young's conscience like a leaden weight. While they were all lancer pilots, the secret of her clanner heritage would always separate her from them. Hwa Young struggled to keep her voice calm as she gave an edited account of the way Mother Aera had ambushed her.

"Look at you," Bae said after Hwa Young had finished. "You're barely able to sit upright." There was the faintest hint of worry in her tone.

"You do look like hell," Eun agreed, eyeing her critically. "C'mon, folks, let's clear out so she can get some more rest."

After they were gone, Hwa Young napped again; woke later at the sound of a throat being cleared. Lashed out.

Commander Ye Jun was standing over her at a discreet distance, zir expression quizzical.

Hwa Young flushed and lowered her arm, then rose and performed a belated salute.

"At ease. The data crystal's been passed to Cryptology to see if they can decipher what's on it," Commander Ye Jun said. "You're free to resume your normal duty roster. Which I realize no one has told you yet."

The commander ran her through her new schedule, which mostly involved instructions to recuperate. "When Medical clears you for duty—really clears you, not you sneaking out when their backs are turned—you can join us on patrol. For now, go to sick bay."

Hwa Young grimaced. "Understood, sir."

The commander departed, and she watched zir go, forlorn. She knew zie wasn't excluding her from the rest of the platoon, but she still felt the other pilots' absences as though the chambers of her heart had been hollowed out.

Maybe Geum will have time for me, she thought, and set out to find zir instead. She could always go to sick bay afterward.

Hwa Young finally found Geum playing *Elite Operative Strike Force 7* with a small circle of five off-duty marines in the lee of a temporary shack, all of them yelling and laughing and pounding one another on the back whenever someone failed at stealth. She tried to envision having enough time back on the flagship for video games. She'd played some with Geum back on Serpentine; she had a narrow talent for first-person shooters.

"Hwa Young!" Geum said, face brightening gratifyingly once zie noticed her. "Uh, you wanna play? Someone's got to have a spare console . . ."

"No, I was going to ask you about something else." She was dying to know about the data crystal, and Geum would be discreet.

"Is it urgent? I *just* made it to second place"—one of the marines called back a friendly taunt—"and I want to see if I can show these meatheads some *real* gameplay."

A different marine squinted at Hwa Young. "Wait a sec. Is it true you ran into clanners outside of base?"

Clearly scuttlebutt had run ahead of her, but she didn't know how much she should reveal to people outside her unit. Still, a clenching in her heart eased when she realized that it wasn't that Geum didn't care. Zie simply might not have heard the rumor.

Geum sat bolt upright and studied Hwa Young, frowning. "Whoa, I didn't know that. You okay?"

Hwa Young hesitated. "Yeah. It's fine. I'm headed to sick bay—Commander Ye Jun's orders." She liked seeing Geum carefree and happy, even if the happiness didn't include her. "Come get me when you have a free moment tomorrow, then."

"Will do." And Geum returned to the circle of gamers.

Hwa Young lingered over her breakfast tray in sick bay, wondering if Geum had forgotten zir promise to find her or, more likely, was hard at work. *Zie might even be fixing up my lancer,* she thought optimistically, fiddling with the data slate she had liberated from the medic.

I'm not that *injured,* Hwa Young thought grumpily. Were the fleet's medics inclined to be overcautious? She'd secured a modest supply of painkillers from the medical tent for her headaches; that was all. Sitting around uselessly in a tent for the sick and wounded galled her, especially when she was dying to know what else was on that data crystal she'd filched from Mother

Aera. If its contents were encrypted, there had to be a reason. When she messaged Commander Ye Jun, zie said that so far Cryptology hadn't cracked the encryption. Maybe Geum would have better luck.

She had made up her mind to slip out and stroll around the perimeter of the camp—the exercise, and the fragrant air, would do her good—when Geum burst into the tent. "There you are!" zie said.

Hwa Young looked up and grinned, wishing she could hug her friend. Not in front of all the other invalids, though. "Let's go for a walk," she suggested. She didn't want her proposal to be overheard. "Uh—you've eaten?"

Geum looked innocent. "Long ago. C'mon."

The problem with the base was there were marines everywhere, either on mysterious errands or patrolling the place or hanging out off-duty. Geum settled the matter by talking one of the off-duty groups into giving up their spot behind a temporary shack. Zie sweetened the deal by bribing them with stimulant chewing gum.

"Where do you *get* all this stuff?" Hwa Young demanded in a whisper after the marines had gone away.

"Trade secret." Geum winked. "Besides, you're not here to ask about the black market, or are you? I traded shifts with one of the other technicians, so I have a little time, but I owe her a big favor."

Hwa Young sobered. "I don't know if you heard this, but I stole a data crystal from the clanner who tried to kidnap me."

Geum whistled. "Did it have any useful info?"

"Commander Ye Jun made off with it. But I need to know what's on that crystal." Would Geum ask her for a reason? Tell her to wait until the brass figured it out? "As of yesterday they hadn't broken the encryption on it, but if anyone could do it . . ."

Flattery had the desired effect. Geum puffed out zir chest, beaming. "I'd *love* to have a crack at it. Let me see what I can do."

They sat side by side in the shack's shadow. Hwa Young craned her head to look over Geum's shoulder as zie opened up the fake dragon-breeding game. "Do you ever play that game for real?"

"Maybe?" Geum shrugged. "I yanked the graphics from the game because I can't draw and dragons are cute, but the code is mine. Nobody ever thinks that it's secretly a hacking interface."

"Aren't you afraid someone's going to open up the app on your tablet thinking they're going to play a game and find out about this?" Hwa Young asked, mildly appalled.

Geum's grin was feral. "Shows what you know. None of the marines would be caught dead playing a 'little kids' game' like *Dragon Hatchery Hijinks.*"

Geum typed and typed, dragon animations alternating with cryptic lines of text scrolling past. Hwa Young wanted to know if the animations somehow facilitated the hacking, but she was afraid of the answer.

"I'm in!" Geum crowed, zir eyes scanning the screen. "They haven't cracked the crypto, but they've copied the data in its encrypted form without causing the crystal to erase its contents, which is something."

"That's good, right?"

"Yeah. It means *I* can make a copy and work on it without alerting the powers that be."

Time ticked by. Hwa Young clenched and unclenched her hands. She didn't consider herself useless by any means, and she was good at the kind of math they'd taught in math class, but cryptology was something else entirely. In this matter, she was painfully dependent on her friend's expertise.

At last, Geum straightened. "I couldn't decrypt the whole file, but I found some clues. Tried some tricks the official cryptologers hadn't thought of. Let me send you a copy of what I got. I have to return to work now."

Hwa Young opened her slate, which blinked once to indicate it had successfully received the file. Hwa Young wondered if she could get Geum to switch hers over to dragons too. Maybe another time.

They both stood up. "Thanks," she said. "I really appreciate it." And this time, because no one was watching, she enfolded Geum in a clumsy hug.

Geum patted her back. "I'm just glad you're okay."

Hwa Young smiled with her eyes. "Thanks. Hey—I'm sorry I didn't manage to get you anything for New Year's. We've . . . we've never missed a year before." Maybe she needed to investigate the black market's offerings. Surely there would be something that Geum would enjoy. After all, what else was she going to blow her credits on?

Geum blushed. "Aww, don't worry about it. Things have been kinda hectic. You can make it up to me next year." Zie winked, then headed off.

Hwa Young set out as well and found a nook in which she could read the contents of the file near the perimeter of the camp. The winds blew gold and silver out of the distance, stirring up dust and pollen; the skies above performed their chameleonic dance of color and shadow. Part of her wanted to put the slate aside and breathe, dreaming of running through the grasses and over the crests of the hills. Part of her knew she had more urgent things to do.

Hwa Young studied the contents of the file. Geum had decrypted portions of it, but the only part that made sense was a detailed set of plans for an attack on an . . . Imperial gravitational observatory?

Hwa Young's opinion of the clanners plummeted. While she didn't believe *all* the Imperial propaganda about the clanners and their barbarism, attacking a bunch of *harmless scientists* was kind of low.

On second thought, maybe the clanners had some sneaky goal. Perhaps the observatory was located in a strategically valuable area, or they were working on classified research. She couldn't imagine that Imperial forces would build a scientific facility in a strategic location; the latter made more sense.

We can't afford to sit on this intel. Who knew if the brass would crack the cipher in time? Her instincts insisted that she should pass on Geum's work, even if she didn't know the data's full significance yet. She had to tell someone. Tell Commander Ye Jun, since zie was her CO. This would also mean ratting out Geum, but she would take responsibility. With any luck, the commander wouldn't hold the hacking shenanigans against the two of them. Not when they had an opportunity to prevent a clanner attack.

She looked around, suddenly paranoid that she was being watched. A thread of insect song reached her, high-pitched and eerie, over the hubbub of tramping feet, voices, the skittering sound of dead leaves against the buildings' walls.

Here goes nothing. First Hwa Young tried calling the commander using her badge. No such luck; the messaging system informed her that zie was not available. She didn't like the idea of confessing to *hacking zir file system* in writing, but this might be time-sensitive and she didn't want to wait.

She flagged her message *URGENT* and explained how she'd found out about the planned attack as delicately as she could. (What was a good euphemism for *My friend and I hacked your files,* anyway? *Was* there one?) She ended up settling for: *At my request, Technician An Geum cracked the encryption* . . . , eliding the whole question of what they'd been doing snooping in the first place. The commander was too smart *not* to call her on it, but she'd deal with that when it happened.

After hitting *SEND,* Hwa Young walked around the camp to burn off her nerves, ignoring the side-eye that all the guards gave her. *Shouldn't you be paying attention to actual dangers instead of a wandering invalid?* she wanted to ask them. At this point she had to concede that she was, in fact, an invalid. She tired quickly and had to pause several times to get her breath back. When she'd picked up the painkillers, the medic had told her something about the body needing time to integrate synthetic blood. She was certainly feeling the effects now.

Midway through her fourth circuit, Commander Ye Jun got back to her. "Bastard to Winter, please respond."

Hwa Young couldn't read zir tone. Was that the cool reserve of *I have other things on my mind,* or the cool reserve of *You are in deep shit?* "Winter here. Did you receive my message?"

"I did."

Definitely the cool reserve of *You are in deep shit.* She only hoped that she hadn't gotten Geum in trouble as well. Maybe she should have taken credit for breaking the cipher, even if it was outside her skill set.

"Winter, how do I put this . . . when Admiral Chin wants us to go off on a wild dragon chase, she'll send us on a wild dragon chase. Put the matter out of your mind and focus on physical therapy or whatever the medics want you to do. Am I clear?"

"Perfectly clear, sir," Hwa Young lied, all the while thinking *Wild* dragon *chase? How much does zie know about Geum's hobbies?*

The commander signed off.

22

The medics finally cleared Hwa Young for duty. "Go," said the medic she had first seen with the giant syringe, "bother someone else so I can work with people who need me."

It wasn't long before the commander summoned her, and the rest of the platoon, to a meeting, which took place in an office in a temporary building. The space was all bureaucratic lines and angles, matching the block-shaped exterior. Very different from the graceful swallow's-path curves of traditional roofs and the flower-stamped roof tiles that Forsythia City, in keeping with New Joseon tradition, featured in its architecture. This building had a single narrow corridor from which obdurate doors faced left and right, right and left. If you fired down the corridor you'd massacre anyone unfortunate enough to be trapped in it.

Commander Ye Jun stood at the head of the room, examining a document on zir slate. A holographic tactical map filled the room. Glowing blue triangle icons, labeled *ELEVENTH*

FLEET, intersected zir torso. Another blue fleet, labeled *EIGHTEENTH FLEET,* was on an intercept course, its trajectory shining in a curve the color of phantom skies; these must be the incoming reinforcements that she'd heard people mention in passing. Carnelian itself was a globe of alternating red and blue, indicating its contested status.

Bae was already seated, with a cryptic red notation floating over her head. Eun was bent over his own slate. Hwa Young and Seong Su saluted, then took their seats. An unaccustomed warmth started up inside her now that she was with the squad again. Though she'd been grateful for their visit while she was recovering from the ambush, being a *functioning* member of the team felt even better.

Out of reflex, she reached for her connection to *Winter's Axiom.* As Commander Ye Jun had reassured her, the link had strengthened after her initial scare. Now its presence sheathed her mind in a reassuring icy armor. She fiercely hoped that the lancer would respond to her every thought when they entered combat again.

"New mission," Commander Ye Jun said. Zir gaze settled on Hwa Young for a moment. "Due to intelligence that we have *fortunately* been able to recover from the clanner kidnapper's data crystal, we know the clanners are planning a raid on this facility." Zie pointed at an otherwise nondescript speck labeled *GRAV OBS.* "A gravitational observatory. Our job is to head there and stop them. Our platoon *should* be sufficient to get that done."

Eun scoffed. "It's got to be a trick. They're separating us from Eleventh Fleet so they can wipe us out."

"It may be so," the commander said in a carefully neutral tone, "but we have orders direct from Admiral Chin."

"And if there's nothing there?"

"That won't happen." Hwa Young spoke before she could think better of it. Mother Aera wouldn't have *planned* to have her precious data crystal liberated. She'd been counting on persuading Hwa Young to desert. "If it were a feint, they would have chosen a more convincing target, like a military base. We have to find out why the clanners care about some scientists."

Bae stirred. "Too bad we can't call HQ and ask if there's any top-secret research taking place there."

The commander smiled grimly. "Even if it weren't for the unreliability of communications, HQ wouldn't release that information to us anyway. What matters is that we know our mission."

Hwa Young had learned even in her brief time as a lancer pilot that HQ was known for its inscrutability. Still, *she* cared about finding out whether Mother Aera's wild talk about a New Joseon superweapon had any truth to it. Maybe events at the observatory would shed some light on the issue.

Zie spent the rest of the briefing detailing the route, then: "We're to leave at 0400 hours, when the transport arrives. Make your preparations. Dismissed—Oh, Hwa Young, you stay."

Hwa Young watched the others file out, stomach sinking. *It's about hacking.*

"This is about hacking your superior officer's files," Commander Ye Jun confirmed once the door had shut behind the others. Zie was no longer smiling.

Hwa Young gulped, then made herself face zir squarely. "I'm prepared for the consequences, sir."

"I realize that the circumstances under which you were recruited were unusual, even traumatic. But I need to know that

I can rely on my pilots *and their friends* to respect the chain of command."

She couldn't look away from zir face, zir merciless eyes. "Understood, sir."

The commander exhaled slowly. "Do you? Screw up again, and I will sever you from *Winter's Axiom.* I can find another pilot if I have to."

Hwa Young's heart froze. She didn't think zie was bluffing. Zie had once entered her mind in a forced communion; what were the limits of zir powers?

Her connection with *Winter's Axiom* had only recently returned. She couldn't bear the thought of losing it again. And not just losing it, but her position as a lancer pilot—a part of the squad.

"I— It won't come to that. Sir."

"Good." The commander stood up. "You may go."

She fled.

Hwa Young could tell from her room in the temporary barracks when the transport arrived, hours later. A high-pitched whine penetrated the walls, and then the entire building shook. Something had landed, something big. Maybe not the size of a carrier like the *Maehwa,* but still sizable—as it would have to be to accommodate five lancers.

Eun rounded everyone up. "Rise and shine," he announced with obnoxious cheer. He could have roused bones from their sleep. "It's time."

They assembled in front of the barracks, where Commander Ye Jun was already waiting. Zie looked them all over as though zie could divine the contents of their duffel bags. Perhaps zie could. The attack transport awaited them in the shadow of a hill. Hwa Young smelled the extravagant fragrance of smashed starblooms and saw that the grasses and weeds around the transport had been blown sideways. It was bigger than Hwa Young had anticipated. It must be capable of holding a full company of twenty-five lancers, not just a single platoon as she'd assumed.

"Attack transport *Chamsae*," Commander Ye Jun said. *Sparrow*. There was no name painted on the vessel's hull, only a cross and a horizontal line, the character for *eleven*. "The lancers have already been loaded. Most of its cargo capacity accommodates the lancers and batteries. Fortunately, there will be plenty of space. Still, we'll take quarters as befits a platoon, rather than spreading out throughout the ship."

Hwa Young didn't like this. She should have felt it when her lancer was moved, and she hadn't. Another consequence of command override? But the lancers had been quiescent, offline, for the process. Maybe there was an innocent explanation. As for the crowding, she could live with that.

She checked the connection again, just in case.

We are hunting, Winter's Axiom said, with such chilly satisfaction that her concerns eased.

The boarding ramp already extended to the moon's surface and had gouged a line into the dirt. *The Empire leaves its mark everywhere*, Hwa Young thought. She was third to ascend into the transport, after the commander and Bae. The stiff line of Bae's back concerned her. She hadn't been paying attention to the other pilots after Commander Ye Jun's reprimand, and it hadn't occurred to her that the others had their own worries. Was Bae still remembering Ha Yoon's fate?

No officer of the deck greeted them; the *Chamsae* had only a skeleton crew, most of them otherwise occupied. Hwa Young stopped from hunching her shoulders as they passed the first set of bunks reserved for the pilots' use, separate, according to Eun, from the ship's crew quarters. She missed Carnelian already: the flowers, the open sky, the wind. The thought of the voyage to come already made her tired.

"Welcome to the *Chamsae*, Commander," a hoarse voice came over the PA—the ship's captain. "This is Captain Ga Ram. As soon as you're strapped in for takeoff, we can get going. Expect to feel some jolts so we can conserve gravitic reserves for your use."

"I understand. Thank you," the commander responded.

In silence they found their couches and strapped in. Hwa Young was selfish enough to claim a seat across from a viewport, next to Bae. Bae eyed her with pursed lips, then looked away.

The transport's engines rumbled, higher-pitched than the *Maehwa*'s—tenor to its bass. Hwa Young clung to her armrests as the *Chamsae* lofted skyward, into the depths of the Moonstorm. She looked sideways at Bae, whose face might as well have been a hollow mask, unreadable.

In the viewport, Carnelian resembled a child's misshapen skull, an afterthought of mirages and uneasy moments. Hwa Young longed to reach toward the viewport and catch the receding moon in her fingers, impossible though it was.

She'd meant to ask Bae what was wrong, although the odds of Bae giving her the time of day, let alone an honest answer, were dim. Instead, the person who spoke to her was Commander Ye Jun. "Homesick?" zie asked.

A spear of anxiety shot through Hwa Young's heart, until she came to her senses and realized the commander meant Serpentine, not Carnelian—of course. Instead of answering, though, she asked, "Do *you* miss home, sir?"

The commander's mouth quirked upward at one corner. "My mother and I quarreled the day I left the crownworld. She said the military was a great waste of my potential. That I should be focusing on politics. I disagreed, obviously."

Was that cryptic memory of the woman in the garden the commander's mother? Hwa Young had thought it was the Empress at the time, but the thought seemed silly now—she must have been mistaken. "She's good at baduk, right?" Hwa Young asked.

Eun was mouthing something at Hwa Young that was probably *shut up,* but she was too curious to let it go. It was just a board game. What was the big deal?

Commander Ye Jun eyed Eun with open amusement. "It's one of her hobbies, yes. Perhaps someday I'll introduce you to her. She'd *love* your 'drop a box on the board and call it a win' maneuver."

"That's because Hwa Young always loses otherwise," Bae said without looking in their direction.

I only ever lost to you, Hwa Young thought.

By now the transport had cleared Carnelian's thin haze of atmosphere and was well into the dark embrace of the Moonstorm.

"You should get rest while you can," the commander added over Seong Su's exuberant snore. "It's going to be a long trip."

The next days passed in a haze of worry. Commander Ye Jun's threat haunted Hwa Young: *Screw up again, and I will sever you from* Winter's Axiom. No matter how civil zie was to her during the journey, she couldn't forget those words.

I uncovered important information, Hwa Young thought reproachfully, but the commander was right. She shouldn't have snooped in zir files.

At least her dreams had shifted, sometimes in embarrassing directions. One night she drifted off, wrapped in an unaccountably pleasant dream of shopping for ducks with Bae. In the dream she and Bae walked arm in arm, except Bae wore a spiked gauntlet like something out of a poorly researched historical drama, and the spikes kept poking Hwa Young's flesh.

She was in the middle of explaining to Bae that gauntlets were out of fashion and the hot new trend involved wearing cicadas in your hair for the music when she realized someone was prodding her in real life.

"Ice Princess," Bae was saying with increasing exasperation, "you can't possibly still be asleep. Are you hoping I'll slap you?"

"I'm sure you'd enjoy that," Hwa Young shot back before she realized she was awake. The commander would take a dim view of zir pilots getting into a fistfight over reveille.

Her glance snagged on the glow of the clock on the bulkhead. Reveille? Hardly. Four hours remained. She double-checked with her neural implant, which confirmed the time.

"Hurry up and get kitted out," Bae said. "Scan spotted a clanner ship on the approach to the observatory."

Seong Su popped up behind Bae. Hwa Young didn't know

how she had missed him, given his size. "Commander says we have five minutes to prep for a raid."

Hwa Young banged her head against the top of the upper bunk in her haste to scramble out. She was already dressed, but she needed to put on her suit. Conscious of Bae's perennially judgy stare, she fished out her knife from under the pillow and shoved it in the top of her left boot.

Bae sneered. "Expecting to get into one-on-one combat? I bet you'd be a *great* duelist." Her voice dripped sarcasm.

Hwa Young averted her eyes rather than shooting back a retort, and wished Bae's words didn't sting so much. *What did you expect? Just because you were friends in a stupid dream doesn't mean you get along in real life.*

Eun stomped in. "Scorch it!" he shouted with more vitriol than usual. "Good thing you're up." He spoke rapidly, as though by sheer willpower he could induce time to flow backward. "How the scorch did they find us? They can't have stealthed spotters parked behind every piece of debris in the Moonstorm."

"Eun," Hwa Young said, blood going cold as the pieces quickly fell into place. She wanted to shake herself for not anticipating this.

He kept talking.

"Eun!"

He stared at her. "What. Is. It."

"Did the commander bring the data crystal that I stole off the clanner?"

"How did you—yes." He understood. "You think she *meant* for you to make off with it. That it's been transmitting our location this entire scorching time."

23

"Captain to Bastard." The captain's voice came over the PA. "We're under attack. The clanners are here in force. Like ten times the numbers that we were led to expect. Repeat, we're under attack."

Hwa Young shook her head, distracted. She hesitated as she finished pulling on her spacesuit, stomach knotting in guilt. Her attempt at bringing home intel had instead put her squad in danger. If only she'd figured it out earlier—

"Check your damn oxygen," Eun shouted in her face. "I'm not having you expire because you get another hole punched in your scorching lancer and you run out of air."

She swallowed a retort. He was correct. She'd skipped two steps of her suit check, a sign of how flustered she was. Bae wouldn't have forgotten. Hwa Young waited for Bae's inevitable condescending remark, which never came, and that stung more.

While Hwa Young restarted the check, because she didn't

trust her memory, Eun called Commander Ye Jun. "Commander, we need updated orders. It's urgent," he said into the comm link. "Dammit, pick up. Did zie beat us to the docking bay?"

"Commander Ye Jun is not receiving messages right now," the autoresponder said in a politeness level that was higher than Eun rated.

Eun made the kind of tormented growl that Hwa Young associated with poorly trained dogs. "Why does zie never pick up when I need zir to." He glared at Hwa Young, Bae, and Seong Su. "Let's hoof it."

Eun settled for messaging Commander Ye Jun while they headed toward the docking bay. It was almost comical, except Hwa Young knew from experience that mere seconds could make all the difference.

The commander was present, and Hwa Young felt herself breathe a sigh of relief. Zie stood next to zir lancer, an enormous tactical holo occupying the entire bay. The only reason Hwa Young didn't perform a double take at the realistic squadron of clanner fighters hovering in midair was that each ship was the size of her fist.

"I got your warning that the crystal is bugged," Commander Ye Jun said to Eun first thing. Zir serene expression contrasted with Eun's scowling face and the boiling aggravation in his eyes.

"You could have—"

"Not now, Hellion." Commander Ye Jun held out the data crystal. "Winter, you take the bug."

Was this an oblique punishment for the draconic hacking shenanigans? "Sir."

The commander raised zir voice. "The rest of you, deploy behind this asteroid cluster—" Zie indicated it on the tactical map. "We'll counterattack, but from cover. Launch as soon as you're cleared. We'll be with you shortly."

Bae and Seong Su sprinted for their lancers. Eun lingered a moment, giving the commander a searching look, then headed off.

Hwa Young wanted to ask why the commander had sent the others away first. Then the transport veered sharply to port, and she almost lost her balance.

"I'll make this quick," Commander Ye Jun said, scarcely flinching at the movement. "You're going to load your lancer with a tracer round. Don't fire at whatever random target crosses your sights, no matter the provocation." Zie removed the data crystal from zir pocket and passed it to her.

Aha. "So you want me to remove the tracer inside the round and replace it with the data crystal"—and its bug. "But why go to the trouble, sir?"

The transport captain's voice interrupted them. "Commander Ye Jun, our point defenses are holding, but they won't last much longer." Swear words, then: "It's like they know exactly where we're going to be!"

"Not wrong," the commander murmured. To Hwa Young, zie said, "I'm gambling the clanners got lazy and they've tied the guidance systems of their missiles directly into the signal that bug is transmitting. This gives us an opportunity, a short-lived one. We're only going to get one chance."

She understood now. "I wait for your signal, then fire the bug into your chosen target." Until she fired, *she* would be the missiles' target. It would take all her cunning to survive.

"Correct. They'll figure it out, but maybe we can take out their carrier this way. Go."

It was Hwa Young's turn to sprint for her lancer, although she was mindful that the attack transport's sudden maneuvers could send her sprawling. She almost smashed into the deck when the ship flipped abruptly, saved only by her magnetic boots. While the transport had artificial gravity, the captain had turned it off when evasive maneuvers began to save reserves for the lancer units.

She shivered as she lowered herself into the cockpit of *Winter's Axiom*—not with dread, but anticipation. *You're back,* breathed a voice through the halls of her soul. *Winter. The white hunt, the stopped breath, the hollow death. Together we will shatter everything that opposes us.*

The voice thrilled her. Even though she had sensed their bond repairing over time, she had still been afraid that command override would separate her from the voice forever, and relief gusted through her now that they were together again. Part of her, the part that was inextricably connected to *Winter's Axiom,* wanted to be master of the battlefield, the one meting out destruction. She loved having her need for wartime power understood—and welcomed.

Once she had entered her lancer and its glow of wintry whites and blues and grays, her job had only just begun. Vibrations traveled up from the deck to the cockpit as the others launched. One, two, three, four—that last one must be Commander Ye Jun in zir command-and-control unit.

She heard the others' comm chatter as they flew out into battle:

"Farseer to Avalanche. Hostile on your six." Bae, sounding simultaneously crisp *and* judgy.

"I've got you covered, Avalanche." Eun.

Commander Ye Jun interjected, "Farseer, don't let them draw you too far out."

Hwa Young returned her focus to her task. *Launch first. Then surgery on the ammo.* Hwa Young could do it here, but that would continue to endanger the transport, and she refused to do that. She wished there were some automated way to attach the unwanted bug to the tracer round. But the lancer wasn't equipped for such work. Once she had launched and found herself a suitable respite, she would have to handle the task manually.

Hwa Young strapped in, trying not to hyperventilate as she remembered the last time she was in this position. Trying not to imagine there was something wrong with the wintry air inside the lancer. Her readouts assured her that everything was fine. She sank further into her connection with the lancer, into the chill of its mental embrace.

The consoles pulsed around her in time with her heartbeat. *Don't waste time, don't waste time.* "Winter to *Chamsae*. Request clearance to launch."

"Go, for the love of the Empress and all her consorts," came the reply.

The bay opened up again. Hwa Young was lucky she had her flight computer patched into the attack transport's fire control, or she would have flown into the hell-scatter of antimissile fire. She spotted the other lancers only as minute glowing specks, already distant, leaving occluded trails in the aether and its clouds of stellate dust.

The comm chimed. Hwa Young toggled it on as she hugged the trajectory of the attack transport. "Winter here."

"This is Bastard," Commander Ye Jun said. "Continue shadowing the transport. We want the clanners to think their bug is still aboard until we've lured them into range."

"They're hoping to blow up our legs and leave us stranded here?"

"Yes. If anything gets by us, it will be tempting to take it out. But you are to rely on the point defenses. Do not, I repeat, do not shoot until I mark the target for you. Clear?"

"Clear, sir."

"I knew I could count on you. Bastard out."

Hwa Young set *Winter's Axiom* to autopilot. She mouthed a prayer to the Empress and her crown—futile, considering she was in the midst of battle—and unbuckled herself.

I am winter's hand and winter's shield. No one will harm you.

The world tilted dizzyingly around her. She focused on the lancer's interior, the reassuring solidity of its structure, her connection to its heart of ice. Her weeks of training couldn't overcome the instinctive desire for a fixed *up* and *down*, something even natives of the Moonstorm struggled with.

Think about your feet. Think about your feet. Her feet were *down*. The rest of her was *up*. That was all that mattered. Fighting nausea that she hoped wasn't a sign of an imminent gravitic failure, Hwa Young made her way through the narrow passages to the back of the lancer, where the specialty ammunition was stored.

When she got there, she stared in bewilderment at the unfamiliar box in front of the magazine. *What in the world . . . ?* Not a small box, either. It could have contained an eight-year-old. Webbing held it in place.

The box had a label: *SURPRISE! HAPPY BELATED NEW YEAR!* it said in Geum's cheerful, rounded handwriting. In neon pink.

"Geum," Hwa Young said aloud, "I am going to *kill* you."

She removed the webbing, mindful that she might have to reuse it, and tried to shove the box aside. It rattled alarmingly as she shifted it. Unfortunately, there was no space back here, just enough for her and the box. She couldn't open the magazine with the box in her way.

Hwa Young cursed Geum, not very creatively, because creativity was for people who didn't have combat emergencies or friends. What had Geum been thinking? Except she knew what Geum had been thinking. Zie had wanted to leave her a nice care package where she wouldn't find it until . . . well.

The comm crackled. Hwa Young opened the line. "Voice only," she added. She didn't want Commander Ye Jun to witness her dilemma. She'd get a whole new callsign, like *Box Girl* or maybe *Outboxed.*

"Bastard to Winter. Are you in position yet?"

"Yo, Winter," Seong Su said, "is there a reason your video's off?"

Hwa Young ground her teeth and didn't answer.

"Avalanche, *focus.*" Eun's voice cracked like a whip.

Bae almost spoke over him. "Hellion, I'm painting a target for you."

"Acknowledged, Farseer. Get out of there before you're bombarded too."

"There's a complication," Hwa Young panted as she maneuvered the scorching box out of the back area and into the copilot's seat.

A slight pause. "Dare I ask for details?"

"I'll handle it. I'll notify you when the data crystal is ready."

"See that you do." Commander Ye Jun cut the connection.

By then Hwa Young had successfully wedged the box into the copilot's seat, taking the additional precaution of securing it with the harness so it didn't come loose and knock her out. The way her luck was going, she wasn't ruling anything out. Besides, she'd internalized the spacer's rule that you never left items floating around. It took only one bad move in low gravity for them to become deadly projectiles.

"We're going to have a talk, Geum," Hwa Young snarled as she wrenched the magazine open and located the tracer rounds, each slotted into its own place in a complicated feed mechanism. The bugged data crystal in her pocket felt as though it were driving spikes into her skin. "How do I—"

A cool sense of certainty took over. Her hands moved, and the round opened—*Winter's Axiom.* It was guiding her. In the back of her mind, she wondered if this signified some new evolution of her connection to the lancer. What else would it show her?

Guided by autopilot, the lancer swerved from a rogue missile. Hwa Young yelped and closed her fist around the circuitry she'd just pried loose. Moments later, beads of blood, almost perfectly spherical, floated free. She'd punctured skin.

She didn't think the blood would interfere with the bug's ability to transmit, though, so she retrieved the crystal and jammed it into the round's hollow interior, then closed it up and replaced the whole affair.

"Weapons system, load tracer one followed by regular bullets," she said. Then she called in to the commander.

"Winter to Bastard. I'm in position. Repeat, in position."

Now that she had taken care of the preliminaries, she had time to be scared again, if in a distant way, beneath the numbing cold of her lancer's presence. She reacquainted herself with the battle before her.

Clanner ships swarmed the area. The pilots looked to be outnumbered four to one, terrible odds even for a lancer platoon. Bae flitted far forward, nimbly dodging barrages of missile fire as she acted as a spotter for Eun. Seong Su maneuvered even closer to the frontal wave of the assault, covering Bae with his robust shields. Eun lurked behind the shadow of an asteroid, using his artillery to attack enemy ships with indirect fire from long range. For zir part, Commander Ye Jun had parked zir lancer in the scan shadow of another asteroid, lurking off to the side, not in danger—yet.

Hwa Young saw, too, what she'd missed while she was wrangling the wretched care package and the doctored tracer round. Through the lancer's senses, she picked up a haze of fragments and heated dust, the remnants of the missiles that the *Chamsae*'s point defenses had, so far, successfully shot down. More missiles were incoming from all directions. The aether was thick with them, like a migration of deadly birds.

"*Chamsae* to Bastard," the attack transport's captain said over the comms. "We are down to twenty-seven percent point defense ammunition. Repeat, down to twenty-seven percent of ammo. We can't keep this up much longer. One of the missiles got through and took out a starboard thruster. Whatever you're going to do, do it soon."

There they are. In her mind's eye she saw the clanner task force as a flock of red motes. There was a swarm of twenty-two unstealthed to attack. One hung far back. She guessed Seong Su had disabled it.

That's odd. The last time she'd been in battle, her lancer hadn't had scan range out this far. Had she misunderstood the capabilities of their platoon? Or had their scan *improved*?

A cold wind blew through the cockpit. It should have frightened her, but what she felt was a wintry exultation.

"Bastard, this is Winter. Your instructions?"

Hwa Young didn't know what other matter had the commander's attention. She could only trust that zie hadn't forgotten her.

"I have your target, Winter," Commander Ye Jun replied. "Fire at the following coordinates."

Hwa Young double-checked the coordinates against tactical. "Sir, there's nothing there, unless it's stealthed."

"I'm aware. Signal analysis suggests there's something hiding there. Do it."

She emerged from behind the shadow of the *Chamsae*. Lined up her sights, cross-checked against the tactical display once more. It pained her to fire at an apparently empty region of space based on the commander's say-so.

Trust the Empress. Move at her will. Act as her hands.

The commander wasn't the Empress, but zie was her CO. That would have to do.

She fired into empty space.

The recoil on the lancer was minimal given the comparative masses, but she felt a slight shudder despite the shock absorbers.

One second, two seconds, three seconds . . . nothing.

She could tell when the bullet met its target because the

latest salvo of missiles swerved, made a U-turn, and headed *back* toward the coordinates Commander Ye Jun had given her. Moments later, a tremendous explosion bloomed outward, swallowing twelve of the twenty-two clanner units.

Ten clanners left against five of them. Two to one, much better odds. Hwa Young wanted to cheer, pump her fist, but she kept her emotions in check as she radioed the commander.

"Winter to Bastard, new orders, sir?"

The delay was longer this time. She saw the commander's face in the holo; saw zir unaccustomed paleness, and that zie had bitten through zir lip. Blood floated in front of zir face.

"Sir, are you all right?"

"Keep your mind on the battle, Winter. Your new task is to defend the *Chamsae*. Maneuver and fire at will."

This she could get behind. "Understood, sir."

"You need any help back there, Winter?" Seong Su asked. He and Bae had withdrawn some distance from the front. He maneuvered his lancer clumsily to avoid smashing into a nearby asteroid.

"I'm clear, Avalanche," Hwa Young replied.

"Nice to see you do something right," Bae remarked.

Even the backhanded acknowledgment warmed Hwa Young. Bae was Bae, after all.

The surviving clanners had pulled back to regroup. Hwa Young entertained herself shooting down stray missiles that got too close. There were fewer of them now, but everything she could do to help improved the attack transport's odds of survival. She suspected another thruster had gone belly-up; the *Chamsae*'s movements were increasingly erratic.

Then Hwa Young heard it.

"Distress call incoming," the computer said.

Play it, she thought to *Winter's Axiom.* It could be a trick, but she felt obliged to hear it out.

The recorded call began playing. "This is Head Researcher Chung Chi Ja of Abalone Gravitational Observatory. We have spotted a fleet of clanners." The scientist gave the vector of approach. "We have important information for the authorities. If there is an Imperial fleet in the area, we request your assistance. I repeat, this is Head Researcher Chung Chi Ja . . ."

Hwa Young felt frozen. That desperation in the head researcher's voice—it sounded just the way she'd felt all those years ago when her home was under attack.

"Bastard," Hwa Young said, "this is Winter. I'm forwarding a distress call from the observatory. Your orders?"

The minutes ticked by with no response. Had the others heard it, too? Or were they too preoccupied by their pursuit of the remaining clanners?

Minutes might make all the difference to the researchers— and their intel might be vital to the Empire. A lancer and its pilot had saved her when she was a child, after all. It was her duty to repay that now.

"Bastard, this is Winter. Absent orders otherwise, I'm responding to the distress call."

Still no response.

She couldn't wait any longer. While the others battled ahead of her, Hwa Young slipped away alone.

24

What does a gravitational observatory look like anyway?
Hwa Young wondered as she sped through the aether,
hoping she would arrive in time to rescue the people
calling for help—and that she hadn't fallen prey to a trap.

Here, amid the dust-shirred aether currents, she could imagine herself as an adventurer from the days of old, searching for a destiny written in stars and silver, rather than someone haring off on a reckless mission without her CO's knowledge. But she wasn't an adventurer. As much as she'd loved the old stories that her parents had told her, those tales wouldn't help her now. She needed to rely on her training as a lancer pilot, and the iceberg presence of *Winter's Axiom* and its experience.

She slowed her approach, wishing she had *Farseer*'s scan data to guide her. So far she saw nothing but the shadows of her own misgivings, mysterious dust motes floating in hazy clouds and stirred by the aetheric currents.

The border world of Abalone came into view at first as a pearlescent disc of pale greens and murky blues and luminous violets. Its sun shone in the distance, red-orange like an overripe fruit. The gravitational observatory should have hung in orbit around Abalone. Hwa Young didn't know why it had to be in space rather than being anchored safely around a planet or moon. What she did know, looking through *Winter's Axiom*'s senses at the hell-cloud of debris, was that someone had shattered it like thin ceramic.

Was she too late? Were there any survivors? Her heart thumped painfully against the walls of her chest. If only she'd gotten the message earlier . . . if only she hadn't waited for the commander's response, which had never come anyway . . .

She forced herself to concentrate as she stared dry-eyed at the floating wreckage. The clanners must have attacked the place while the lancers were distracted by the battle with their secondary forces. But the wreckage didn't mean the enemy had departed. She had to proceed carefully.

She guided *Winter's Axiom* closer to the debris, careful to avoid any fast-moving fragments. One glanced off its armor; she felt it like a sting on her own skin. There weren't as many fragments as she had feared, though. Without a strong gravitational pull to keep them in orbit, they had either drifted elsewhere or disintegrated.

What am I looking for? Hwa Young thought as she surveyed the catastrophe. Human figures, some scrap of evidence that had survived against the—

Wait.

On first glance, the wreckage had appeared as an overwhelming mass of splinters and dust and irregular debris. It was

hard to discern any pattern other than the pattern of oblitera-
tion. It would have taken a forensic specialist to put together
the clues, unwreck the jigsaw pieces, and figure out what the
observatory's final moments looked like.

Except.

Look.

Hwa Young wasn't sure whether *Winter's Axiom* or she herself saw it first: a series of glints among the debris. Someone, or
something, was signaling with their suit light.

Her heartbeat quickened. There it came again. Long flashes
and short, in the pattern that said *EMERGENCY. REQUEST
RESCUE.* Over and over, without further detail.

Who knew how long the victim had been out here, hoping—
and despairing?

It could still be a trap, but she couldn't *not* respond.

Hwa Young took a winding route toward the distress signal.
If the individual who'd sent the signal still lived, and wasn't delusional with aether poisoning, the only way to evacuate them
would be to put them in the copilot's seat. Which meant opening the cockpit and losing some of her precious air, of which she
had a limited supply.

She unharnessed herself and wrestled Geum's care package *back* to its original position so that the copilot's seat would
be free, cursing her friend yet again. Even if there was no way
Geum could have anticipated the situation.

As she moved closer, she saw that it was in fact a person, or
something shaped like a person, in a standard Imperial spacesuit almost identical to the one she was wearing. Alive or dead,
she couldn't tell. Hwa Young imagined she saw the convulsive

movements of their hand as they flicked the light on and off, on and off.

No attack came.

Of course not, Hwa Young thought grimly. If she were setting an ambush, she would wait until the foolhardy pilot exited the lancer before springing the trap. She would be stupid to fall for it.

At the same time, the survivor—assuming that was what they were—needed rescue. Hwa Young remembered what it was like to be a survivor, what it was like to be powerless and to hope to be saved. She could no more have turned back from the survivor than she could have cut out her own heart.

What options did she have that minimized her odds of being sieved?

She had two assets, herself and *Winter's Axiom*. Three if she counted the care package.

What if Geum left me something I could use? After all, zie didn't consider life worth living without video games. There might be some tech toy that could help her.

Hardly daring to hope, she squeezed into the back where she'd stuffed the box. She used her knife to cut the tape holding the box closed, almost slicing herself in the process because of the cramped space. She suppressed a growl; she was usually better coordinated, but her desperation, and the aftermath of the earlier fight, was making her clumsy.

"Scorch it!" At the bang that came from the box, she flattened herself to the side of the pilot's seat, not that it offered much cover. She hadn't thought it was going to be rigged to blow, but that had been unforgivably careless of her. Someone could have blackmailed Geum or forged zir handwriting or—

Hwa Young blinked. Glitter floated in the air. Pastel rainbow glitter. And festive shreds of rainbow crepe paper. All over everything.

The box hadn't contained a bomb. Good thing, because she would be splattered all over the cockpit if that had been the case. Geum had rigged it with glitter and confetti.

"I don't have time for this nonsense!" Hwa Young growled. She became aware that blood flowed and beaded oddly in the half gravity in the cockpit. In her haste to reach cover, she'd slashed her thigh through her spacesuit. Which meant she had to seal the hole.

The absurdity of the situation hit Hwa Young. Here she was, trying to rescue someone who might have critical information, and she was thwarted by a cockpit full of the world's most colorful glitter because . . . because her friend had wanted to give her a nice surprise. It could be worse. She started to laugh, wheezed, made herself stop.

She quickly sealed the hole in her suit with the repair kit, then returned to the box and brushed aside more glitter to reveal its contents. Taped to the inside lid of the box was an envelope. *For my favorite friend,* it said, this time in a cheerful orange.

Hwa Young's eyes misted inconveniently. *I don't deserve you. Even if you have the most rotten timing.* She shoved the letter into a pocket to read later. It deserved a moment to itself.

Then she hastily inventoried the box's contents: a handheld game console, a spare set of batteries, cartridges for several shooter games. (Geum knew her tastes.) The rest of the box was taken up by prepackaged snacks.

"I might forgive you after all," Hwa Young told her absent friend. That is, if zie could forgive her for what she was about to do to the game console. Hwa Young lacked Geum's genius for electronics, but zie had shown her the basics. And Eun had made sure everyone knew how to use their computer systems.

She retrieved the tool kit and dug out the console's guts. She didn't need to do anything fancy to it, only program the holographic projector to magnify the game graphics. It might not be completely convincing, but any distraction while she was out of her lancer was a good one.

Then Hwa Young fed the gaming console into another altered tracer round and returned to her seat to load it into its kinetic rifle. She could already see the game graphics cycling through demo mode, and—for love of the Empress's rib cage, why was it playing a collision between an armored personnel carrier and a school bus on loop?

Too late now, Hwa Young thought as a fake explosion flickered at the edge of her vision and a holographic shard of windscreen flew through her arm. Her own recent head injury throbbed sympathetically. She aimed away and triggered the rifle, shooting the console and its holographic projections into space, away from her and her lancer.

Hwa Young opened the cockpit. The air swooshed outward, which she saw rather than heard. Working quickly while her magnetic boots anchored her to the lancer's outer carapace, she clipped her tether to a clamp. Heart hammering, she unlocked the magnetism on the boots and drifted free, her tether the only thing connecting her to *Winter's Axiom.*

She would never enjoy floating through the aether, but it didn't frighten her. Nothing would be as terrifying as ricocheting between moon-fragments had been as a ten-year-old.

In the distance, she glimpsed the flicker-static of the game console's hologram as it glanced off a shard and flew in a new direction. She barely had time to register the glowing colors before it blossomed in an effusion of fire. Hwa Young threw her hands in front of her face, shielding herself from the blast, as her heart pounded out of her chest.

Someone had attacked it.

Shit. She had to go dark and pray she could recover the victim before the hostiles lit her and the lancer up. It was only a matter of time before the clanners traced the luckless game console back to her position. Unlike the clanners, she didn't have stealth.

Hwa Young remotely piloted the lancer to the lee of a particularly large observatory segment that looked like it had belonged to a hydroponics unit. Glittering sprays of ice and disarrayed leaves spun in the aether like necklaces of thwarted spring. Trying to navigate for the lancer and herself at the same time was so disorienting that she overshot and almost slammed into a metal spike.

Sweat slicked her palms and made the entire suit cling unpleasantly to her.

If anything hits me, I'm dead. It didn't have to be a bullet or a missile. A sufficiently fast particle, too small even for *Winter's Axiom* to spot, could penetrate her suit and puncture her heart.

She finally reached the floating—body? Person? *Not corpse, not yet,* she chanted inwardly, as if saying it would make it true. Hwa Young pressed her helmet against the other person's so sound would transmit itself to them. "Rescue is here."

The hands on the flashlight didn't stop.

"Help is here," she added, redundantly. She grabbed their waist.

They didn't kick or struggle. The tinted faceplate made it impossible to see their head.

"I'm here to rescue you!" Hwa Young yelled fruitlessly, pressing her helmet against theirs even harder. They must be afflicted by panic or aether sickness.

The world lit up around them. Not fireworks, but missiles hitting the lancer's reflexively ignited shields, which wouldn't hold up to the barrage for long. And as long as the shields were up, she couldn't return to the cockpit, either.

She was trapped out here.

25

Before despair had a chance to sink its roots into her, Hwa Young flinched and shielded her eyes from the sudden barrage of explosions in the distance. Another attacker? No—they were exploding *beyond* her. A counterattack against *her* attacker. She'd witnessed that fire-flower pattern before, hectic oranges and reds like the summer heart of fire.

Eun. Eun came to my rescue again.

"Hellion to Winter, are you in the area after haring off or did you get yourself killed? Answer or I'll kill you myself."

Hwa Young toggled the suit's comm, praying to the Empress that she wasn't about to attract every predator in the area. Good thing she couldn't *hear* the explosions in the aether's smothering embrace or calling him back would have been futile. "Winter here," she rasped. "I've recovered a survivor of the attack on the Abalone Gravitational Observatory. They may need medical attention."

It bothered her that the suited figure struggled so little. She considered murmuring some reassurances to the person, but they'd yet to respond to anything she'd said.

"Can you get back into your lancer?" Eun asked.

"Only if I lower my shields." Hwa Young didn't elaborate. He knew better than she did that doing so would make her vulnerable to any incoming fire.

A new voice cut in: Commander Ye Jun. "We'll cover you. Be ready to move, Winter. We won't be able to buy you much time. And we're going to need your assistance as soon as you're back in the cockpit. We'll discuss your decision-making later."

"Understood, Bastard."

For a second, Hwa Young couldn't see past the curtain of tears in her eyes, couldn't think past the hard lump in her throat. The other pilots had come for her. She hadn't been entirely sure they would. They had her back after all.

Focus. She could be grateful later. Right now, what mattered was dragging the surviving researcher to the safety of her lancer's cockpit.

She heard the chatter over the comms as she applied a second's thrust to readjust her vector. She'd save the rest for the sprint to the cockpit.

"Farseer here, you're never getting a better opportunity. You should be receiving surveillance data now. Looks like a single destroyer lying in wait."

"Copy that, Farseer," Commander Ye Jun said. "Hellion, on my mark—mark."

Hwa Young didn't wait for the explosions to resume. She powered down her lancer's shields, then burned hard for the cockpit, which stood open.

She didn't have time to decelerate, instead smashing into the cockpit's interior like a demented comet. Without letting go of the hapless figure—it would suck to go through all this only to *lose* the survivor—Hwa Young hooked one ankle around the base of the chair, yelped, refocused on her bond with *Winter's Axiom* through the pain of the collision. The cockpit closed.

The whoosh as breathable atmosphere filtered back into the cockpit from the reserves was the most beautiful sound Hwa Young had ever heard. As tempted as she was to pop her helmet off and inhale, she waited for the lancer's assurance of safety and for the atmosphere gauge to glow blue.

"Bastard to Winter, do you read? Secure your passenger and get back into the fight. You're easy meat."

"Acknowledged," Hwa Young said through clenched teeth.

She disliked the body's weird combination of floppiness and stiffness. *Don't be dead don't be dead don't be dead.* The suit *claimed* the person within was alive, but the readings looked bizarre. She didn't have time to administer first aid. It wouldn't do either of them good if the lancer blew up.

As she strapped the survivor into the copilot's seat, her ankle throbbed miserably. Hwa Young hoped it was only a sprain and that she hadn't broken it. At least she didn't strictly need it to work the pedals, which existed as a backup manual control system; *Winter's Axiom* responded to her every thought.

Hwa Young resumed control of the lancer and jetted toward a larger chunk of the unfortunate observatory, matching its velocity for several seconds before peeling off to shelter behind a different one. She didn't want to stay in one place too long, didn't want to be *predictable*. At the same time, a sniper did her best work from cover, rather than while dashing from one location to the next.

"Farseer, patch Winter into your updated surveillance data," Commander Ye Jun said.

"I mark your position, Winter." Bae was as prim and precise as ever. "I've highlighted the target for you. Over."

Hwa Young locked onto the target. Breathed in, breathed out, attentive as ever to technique, despite knowing that the lancer's computer-aided targeting system would compensate for any small deviations.

Out of the corner of her eye she saw her comrades' positions on the tactical holo, repeated in the halls of her mind through her connection to *Winter's Axiom* and its senses. Bae and Seong Su were far forward, with the latter stoically accepting enemy fire so as to shield Bae's more lightly armored unit. Still, even Seong Su's lancer couldn't withstand that level of punishment indefinitely. He'd been hit several times, and she detected the telltale flicker of shields about to go belly-up.

I'm not going to let my comrades be smeared into particles. Hwa Young loaded a tracer, an undoctored one this time. Aimed for the destroyer's CIC. Fired. Their CIC would be shielded, but her bullet should penetrate deeply enough to mark the target, and Eun's artillery would do the rest.

A tremor passed through *Winter's Axiom,* or had she imagined it?

"This is Bastard. They'd clocked you, Winter. Withdraw."

"Withdraw *where?*"

The rebel destroyer wasn't out of tricks, although it was badly damaged and sparks flew from it like swarms of hornets.

Hwa Young didn't understand what it was doing at first; she thought it was having difficulties steering, or that it had sustained damage to its thrusters. Then it flipped so it pointed straight at Seong Su, instead of firing at it with broadsides.

It's going to ram *a lancer?* Hwa Young thought incredulously. She opened a call to Seong Su, but Bae beat her to it, as always.

"Avalanche, get the hell out of there!" Bae yelled. Her lancer, more nimble, had already sprinted out of the way. It didn't have much in the way of weapons, but she had jammed the destroyer's attempts to call for help. "No way your shields will withstand—"

"I'm doing what I—"

The destroyer exploded, catching Seong Su's lancer within the blast radius.

Vaporizing it.

Hwa Young almost broke out of cover to race toward him, *toward* the explosion. She tasted blood. She'd bitten through her lip. Blood splattered against the inside of her helmet, obscuring her vision. The pain in her ankle didn't trouble her anymore. It felt like it belonged to someone else.

Silence held them all in suspension for one moment, two. Then—

"Bastard to all units."

As if that meant something other than *the pathetic four of us who remain.* Hwa Young felt a hot rush behind her eyes.

"We're withdrawing to the *Chamsae,*" the commander went on. "That includes you, Winter."

Talking hurt. Everything hurt. She reached for the chilly numbness of the lancer's presence, but even that didn't dampen the pain. The only real thing was the star-field of glitter that she glimpsed through the blood, the reminder of Geum's whimsy.

"Winter." The commander's tone gentled. "Hellion will escort you out. Follow him. You don't have to think. Just come back to the *Chamsae*."

Hwa Young didn't remember anything between Commander Ye Jun's order to retreat to the *Chamsae* and winding up in the docking bay, staring blankly into space. The glitter that had seemed so festive and cheerful only hours ago now reminded her that they'd just lost Seong Su. Her mouth was dry and tasted of blood.

"Bastard to Winter. Winter, you can disembark now."

Hwa Young continued staring at the cockpit's dimmed lights. She didn't want to move; couldn't think of any reason to leave her lancer and face reality. If she pretended she hadn't heard the order—*had* it been an order? She lost herself contemplating the line between suggestion and command.

"Hwa Young!" It was Bae this time. Then, to the commander: "Is she—is she dead too?"

Commander Ye Jun said, "Her vitals are fine. I'm more concerned about the person she risked herself to rescue. Medic's on standby. Bae, coax her out of there."

Hwa Young's head seemed to be disconnected from the rest of her body, from the rest of the world. She'd been thinking about someone, and they were gone, or she was gone.

The cockpit whooshed open. Normally she would have startled, because she didn't remember anyone warning her about an override. She didn't want the commander in her head *again*.

"Hwa Young," Bae said, this time from in front of her. "I'm

going to retrieve your passenger first, make sure they get the medical attention they need. You read me?" Her voice was low and harsh. "If Seong Su died to save you, you better make it worth it."

Even in her grief and outrage, she was beautiful. Her short hair was mussed, but perfectly so. She turned her head, and for a moment Hwa Young was distracted by her flawless profile. Only tear streaks marred her face, and those were right and proper.

"Come on," Bae said without warmth.

Numbly, Hwa Young helped Bae maneuver the survivor out of the copilot's seat. This time Hwa Young marked what she had not while she was out in the battlefield, buffeted by the aetheric currents, although she should have noticed it then. Her heart stuttered.

The suit weighed too little. *Massed* too little, even in the absence of a steady source of gravity. Weight aside, she should have observed that it had too little inertia for an ordinary adult. Unless someone had fit a child into it, grotesquely.

Bae and Hwa Young eased the suit to the deck. The medic pounced on it. Removed the helmet.

All of them stared at empty space where there should have been a head.

"Well, *that* was a waste," Bae said, her face twisting. She wasn't looking at Hwa Young, but Hwa Young knew herself to be the target of the other girl's anger.

"Someone *rigged* the vitals," the medic said in bafflement. "You're never supposed to do that!"

"Not like there's anyone alive to blame for it," Eun remarked. He had come up next to Hwa Young and was looking down at the suit, its fingers still making hand signs in a parody of life. "Someone must have wasted valuable time programming the suit to attract rescuers, instead of evacuating themselves. I wonder why."

The medic peeled the rest of the suit open. It had been crammed, inefficiently, with data crystals and machinery that looked like it had been ripped out, wires and all, from the now-destroyed facility.

Hwa Young spoke without thinking. "*This* is what Seong Su died for?" Her throat hurt. Water leaked hotly out of her eyes.

No one corrected her. She felt better. She felt worse.

Commander Ye Jun's shadow fell over the hoard of crystals. Hwa Young looked up, prepared for the reprimand. In her peripheral vision, Bae tensed. She hadn't known Bae cared one way or the other.

"The clanners worked hard to destroy this information," the commander said, "and someone at the observatory sacrificed themselves to save it. There must have been a reason." Zir good hand flexed. Zie knelt and hit a switch that Hwa Young hadn't noticed earlier. The suit's fingers stopped moving. "A clever ploy, and one I wish hadn't been necessary."

"Do we . . ." Eun's voice softened. "Do we know the names of the people who perished in the attack?"

"We'll find out."

"And . . ." Eun jerked his thumb in Hwa Young's direction, glowering at her. "She ran off without waiting for permission."

"She and I will talk." Commander Ye Jun rose. "Medic, thank you for your attentiveness. Bae, you and Eun go clean up."

Bae started to say something cutting, but Eun shook his head and she desisted.

Hwa Young watched the other two pilots move off, their heads bowed. She choked back a sob. Two other pilots, not three. Even the bond to her lancer, which ordinarily calmed her, could not entirely anesthetize her grief, or make it bearable. Perhaps it wasn't meant to be bearable.

The commander's voice brought her back to reality. "Bring the suit with you. Data crystals included. At least the person we couldn't rescue was creative with their choice of container."

Hwa Young resented the commander's ghoulish levity. Then she realized zie had counted on that, because zie had mapped every angle and U-turn of her soul. The emotion, however trivial, gave her something to think about that wasn't the loss of Seong Su.

Death, Hwa Young thought. She wasn't going to hide from the enormity of what had happened. *His death*.

She wanted to ask if there would be a ceremony for the fallen, for Seong Su and the person who had saved the data crystals instead of themselves, for the rest of the observatory's staff. She almost did. But the commander's expression was hard, and she held her tongue. Zie would make arrangements and let everyone know in due course.

Hwa Young was puzzled when the commander didn't lead her to zir office but to zir own lancer in its cradle. Cold sweat burst on her skin at the prospect of an interrogation. Still, she followed zir into the lift with her burden. It was a tight fit, the two of them and the human-shaped bundle.

The C2 unit powered up. Its lights shone luminous jade green, flecked with gold, like the painting of the inverted crown on its exterior. More lights flickered in a matrix of queries. A dizzying array of holo readouts crowded the cockpit; she had no idea how the commander kept from getting fatally distracted.

"A clever job," Commander Ye Jun said. "Too bad this individual didn't survive. I bet they were a tremendous asset to the observatory. Hand it over."

Hwa Young handed the suit over, stomach aching in dread and confusion. She'd expected zir to launch into accusations, not . . . whatever this was. Unless, despite her screwups, this was a gesture of *trust*? Her heartbeat quickened.

The commander rummaged through the data crystals. Each one lit up as zie touched it, the lancer's lights flickering in response, as though it was talking to the crystals. Probably it was.

"We're using my lancer for its cryptanalysis functions," Commander Ye Jun said. "It's our best hope of deciphering whatever information is on these crystals."

Hwa Young nodded, wondering what else zie was capable of.

"There could be a worm or a trap," the commander added casually. "If a virus gets into my implant, I might convulse or attack you. If that happens, cut my throat. I assume you have that knife still."

Hwa Young's mouth went dry. "Sir, I couldn't. You really think the clanners set up such an elaborate trap?"

"Unlikely but possible. It's good to stay alert." Zie continued sorting the data crystals.

The commander means it. As much as the thought of attacking zir horrified her, she clung to zir faith in her. She meant to repay it with her loyalty.

No attack came. Columns of data spilled into the cockpit and beyond, filling it up like miniature constellations. Commander

Ye Jun moved on to the next data crystal, then the next. She couldn't tell what zie was looking for.

The commander straightened in triumph. "Found it!" And then zie blanched.

Hwa Young didn't see it. There were only numbers, columns and columns of them, shimmering and floating in the air like the glitter still in *Winter's Axiom*'s cockpit. She was good at math, but even she couldn't process galaxies of numbers in a font size that tiny.

"Let me play it in video format, slowed down. It's a record of something the observatory saw two weeks ago—which means it happened even longer ago, given the time it takes light to travel."

The numbers condensed before Hwa Young's dazzled eyes into a video overlaid by a map of the local Imperial systems. As she watched, she saw an Imperial star and its world—*Topaz*, said the label, one of the nearby systems—collapse into each other. They shrank smaller and smaller until they winked out entirely. The star's light was replaced by utter darkness fringed by the bright haze of a young accretion disc, formed from trapped gases being heated until they glowed.

For a second, on the map, the entangled fleets of both Imperials and clanners, dozens of ships, lingered at the event horizon—the boundary beyond which not even light could escape the black hole's pull—before fading away in a redshift smear.

Hwa Young's mouth went dry.

"The birth of a black hole," Hwa Young breathed. "But how?" She had only learned about black hole formation in her boarding school classes—had never expected to witness one being born, even in a recording. But all her instructors had claimed that none of New Joseon's worlds orbited a star massive enough to meet such a fate. Had the gravitational devotion of Topaz's citizens been so strong that its smaller star collapsed anyway?

"In the past," Commander Ye Jun said hollowly, "New Joseon's unity has been an asset. Our worlds are bigger than the clanners' moons. We control more reserves of gravity. But *too much gravity*, and a world collapses into a black hole.

"The observatory recorded this observation of Topaz's destruction. They saw this because they were explicitly looking for it, and because the observatory is close enough to Topaz to have seen it. The image of the collapse lasted the merest fraction of a second. The *Maehwa*'s sensors aren't this sensitive, and the other worlds are too far away to have seen the event yet. Even if they already know, the Empire must have covered it up."

Hwa Young shivered. She'd never thought the government's control of communications and news services could be put to such use. "We can't let the rest of the Empire fall like this." An awful thought occurred to her: "Could that happen to *us*? If we—if we are *too* loyal to the Empress?"

"It appears so. Certain worlds, like Topaz, have always been known for their devotion. The Empress has spent her reign encouraging extreme displays of faith, cracking down on dissenters, and shutting down independent news services. On Topaz, at least, they must have passed the critical threshold, and the resulting excess of ritually generated gravity from well-meaning loyalists caused the system's collapse." The commander was grim. "We have to get this information to authorities willing to do something about it—before it's too late."

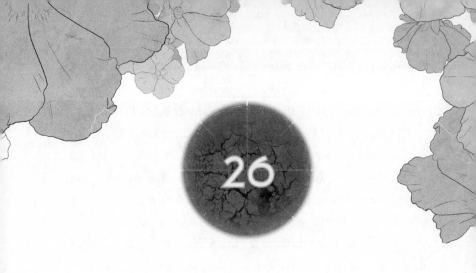

26

"What next?" Hwa Young asked, impatient for action. Commander Ye Jun held zir hand up. "Not so fast— let me run communications analysis on the rest of this data to see if there are any other surprises."

Hwa Young schooled herself to stillness, reciting prayers inwardly and wishing she were of more use.

The commander sucked zir breath in. "I wasn't expecting *that*."

"That what, sir?"

"The observatory was in the habit of logging, saving, and relaying any messages that reached it, whether or not they could read the content. Standard operating procedure. Most of it isn't any interest to us, freighter manifests and personal mail and the like. Except I've identified a decrypted communiqué—from First Fleet. It's addressed to Admiral Chin."

Hwa Young had almost forgotten about the other fleets. In

her time with Eleventh Fleet, they had grown so accustomed to handling everything alone that the possibility of reinforcements, intermittently promised, seemed increasingly like a mirage.

But it was Eighteenth Fleet that was supposed to reinforce them, due to their reduced numbers. Not First Fleet, whose sworn duty was the defense of the crownworld. What could First Fleet be doing at the border, far from their usual stomping grounds?

"Sir, do you want me here for this?" Hwa Young felt obliged to ask.

The commander examined the message's routing information. "This is addressed to Eleventh Fleet. Properly, Admiral Chin should hear this first, but if there's a chance that *First Fleet* has new orders for us . . . no, we'd better hear them out."

Her eyes narrowed. "Wait, it was already decrypted? But how?"

Zir expression flickered as zie checked the data again. "It looks like one of the scientists got curious and applied a *lot* of unauthorized computer time to the problem of decoding the message. A whole series of messages, now that I know what to look for."

Hwa Young hissed. "Isn't that treasonous?"

Commander Ye Jun looked at her sidelong. "It is, but since the culprit's almost certainly dead . . ." Zie pressed a button.

A blurred holo image fizzed into existence, then sharpened into the visage of a stern, gray-haired man whose left eye had been replaced by a coruscating lens. "This is Admiral Hong of First Fleet with an update for Admiral Chin of Eleventh Fleet," he said in a crisp baritone. "With the aid of Chollima-class colony ships, we have evacuated the major cities of the Topaz system for future use."

Hwa Young recognized the name. They'd *just now* watched a recording of Topaz condensing into a black hole, swallowed by the gluttonous singularity two weeks ago. But what did he mean, *"for future use"*?

A scenario coalesced in her head. Some researcher had gone in for a hobby in codebreaking, turned up messages that made them suspicious or curious, and convinced the observatory staff to peek at Topaz. The same person, or one of their colleagues, had risked everything to get the information—including this communiqué—out.

"Per the Empress's direct order," Admiral Hong continued, "the experiment at Topaz was a success. The gravitic generators work as planned. We were able to wipe out a major clanner offensive through the deliberate formation of a black hole. I have attached a detailed operational report for your perusal."

Deliberate formation of a black hole.

The world swam before Hwa Young. The singularity collapse hadn't been an accident. It had been *on purpose*. It had been *planned*.

The Empress, whose protection and benevolence she had trusted in for the past six years, had wiped out *her own people* so she could experiment with a new weapon.

Hwa Young recalled Mother Aera's desperate words now. *Testing a new weapon . . . Capable of destroying whole worlds . . .* She blanched as the truth of her heart-mother's claims hit her now with full force.

"Steady," Commander Ye Jun murmured. Zie paused the recorded message.

"Th-the Empress," Hwa Young stammered, her stomach

queasy. She couldn't tell whether it was with the implications of what she'd just learned, or her shaken faith. "She would never—"

"She absolutely would. She once told me that when it comes to war, do whatever it takes to win. No matter how awful."

Hwa Young blinked stupidly. "You've talked to the Empress, sir?" She remembered the image she'd seen in zir memories during command override, with the game of baduk. She'd thought she'd only imagined the image of the Empress's face in the commander's vision. Had it truly been her?

The commander looked off to the side, an uncharacteristic deflection. Zir expression was as blank as uncarved stone. "I thought you'd figured it out earlier. The Empress is my mother. I am one of her illegitimate children."

Of course. Zir childhood on the crownworld. The upside-down crown on zir lancer. Zir callsign: Bastard. The New Year's story zie had told about zir ex-boyfriend and the Empress's bedrooms. The clues had been in front of her the entire time.

"And you're *here?*" Hwa Young blurted out. As opposed to lounging in some pavilion on the crownworld while servants fed zir bonbons, or training tame cranes to do tricks, or whatever it was that illegitimate children of the Empress did.

"I didn't want a life of silk robes and court dances and writing poetry. I wanted a lancer." Zir voice was somber. "Surely that's something you understand."

Hwa Young had nothing to say to that.

Commander Ye Jun resumed playing back the message.

Admiral Hong said, "While First Fleet is at full strength as of this communiqué, we are being pursued by a second clanner fleet as we head for Carnelian. We cannot allow them to compromise the colony ships traveling with our fleet, which serve as the gravity source for the new weapon. I repeat, they cannot compromise the colony ships. They may represent our last hope of securing Imperial influence on this area—in particular, winning Carnelian as a stronghold for the Empire. I will be assuming operational command and require immediate assistance from Eleventh Fleet."

Hwa Young digested this. No one was ever going to give *her*, an individual lancer pilot, a strategic map of the war between the Empire and the clanners. But she gathered that the Empress was desperate to secure the area around Carnelian, and that Admiral Hong hoped to win Carnelian by creating and weaponizing yet another black hole—this one fueled by the devotion of the Topaz refugees on the colony ships.

Silence. Then Commander Ye Jun said, "Did you mark the numbers, Hwa Young?"

She leaned forward, eyes narrowing as she reviewed the databurst Admiral Hong had sent. "They evacuated over *two thousand* citizens from Topaz? To generate gravity for their—for their—"

"Yes. I'm guessing they don't know about their true purpose. That they think they're performing the usual prayers and rituals as part of their daily routines."

Hwa Young's nausea redoubled.

"It fits the information we have." Nice of zir to say *we*. The commander straightened. "I'll inform the others of this discovery. We're heading back to Carnelian. Perhaps, if we reach First Fleet early enough, we can persuade Admiral Hong to conquer Carnelian *without* using the black hole weapon."

Captain Ba Ram and zir crew had patched the attack transport back together after their clash with the clanners, although Hwa Young wasn't sure how. As the transport sped toward its destination, Hwa Young helped out with ordinary maintenance tasks as an outlet for her guilt and frustration.

Commander Ye Jun had taken the news of the Empress's new weapon with surprising equanimity. Hwa Young had trouble doing the same. The prayers and meditations that had comforted her growing up brought her no solace. When she visualized the Empress's face, she could only think of the people who hadn't escaped the collapse of Topaz. The face that had once struck her as welcoming and protective now appeared serenely cruel.

They'd sent tight-beam transmissions to the *Maehwa* to pass on Admiral Hong's message, but so far they hadn't received any acknowledgment of receipt, a worrying sign. Hwa Young was on the fence as to whether the clanners had somehow blown up First Fleet in their absence, the clanners had a new and unusually effective jamming system, or Admiral Chin was so preoccupied that she wasn't replying.

Commander Ye Jun called a meeting to share the revelation about Topaz and discuss Admiral Hong's message with the other pilots. Eun swore viciously for five minutes and would still have kept on going, except the commander finally told him to pipe down. Bae was uncharacteristically quiet. When Hwa Young asked her what she thought, Bae said only, "It figures that there would be a way to weaponize our very faith."

Hwa Young laughed bitterly in response. She'd always thought of her prayers and the comforting pull of gravity as an unalloyed good. It would never have occurred to her to find a way to turn gravity into a weapon of mass destruction.

Who am I kidding? This disquieting thought occurred to her. After all, the lancers possessed *gravity* lances. Was the difference only one of scale?

"People are why we can't have nice things," Bae added.

"You can say that again," Eun agreed.

Hwa Young remembered the slow-motion holo image of Topaz and its star collapsing, the two battling fleets sucked into the new singularity. For all that First Fleet claimed to have evacuated two thousand people, what had the population of Topaz been? Surely more than that—much more. How many people *hadn't* made it out?

She'd thought the conquest of a world was bad enough, like Serpentine's loss to the clanners. But a conquered world could be *re*conquered. Its citizens could, in theory, resist. They weren't consigned to the terrible undeath of a singularity's maw, unable to escape its event horizon. Hwa Young wasn't a physicist, but she remembered that much from her classes.

No wonder the rebels were desperate to overthrow the Empire. What defense could they possibly have against the singularity weapon?

What felt like an eternity later but was only a matter of hours, Hwa Young spotted First Fleet through the viewport. *Those aren't moons,* she thought blearily as the wedge shapes of the vanguard destroyers came into view. If she squinted, she could see on each one the single golden stripe, the character for *one,* that indicated First Fleet.

"There they are," Eun said from next to her. "Captain Ba Ram said we'd be within visual distance soon. Eleventh Fleet is just beyond them."

"No sign of the clanners?" Hwa Young asked. She could almost say the word without stumbling now.

"What, scared they'll put another hole in your lancer?" Bae said. "Maybe you can practice your dodging skills."

"Maybe," Hwa Young agreed, hearing the undertone of remembered worry.

Eun checked his slate. "Nothing that the *Chamsae* could detect. We'll know more once we're patched back into Eleventh Fleet's recon network."

Hwa Young listened as Captain Ba Ram called Eleventh Fleet's flagship. "*Maehwa*, this is attack transport *Chamsae*. Requesting permission to dock."

"Better freshen up, Winter," Eun added to Hwa Young. He didn't say anything to Bae, who looked pristine as a newly minted crescent moon in her uniform. Not a strand of her hair was out of place.

"Of course," Hwa Young said, resisting the urge to add *sir* in Seong Su's memory. Especially since Eun would remember that *her* actions had led to Seong Su's death. She ducked into the head to use the mirror and straightened her collar.

The *Chamsae* adroitly maneuvered past the ships in the vanguard and approached the much larger *Maehwa*. It docked; a shudder went through the deck. "Sorry about that," Captain Ba Ram said through the intercom. "Welcome home, everyone."

Some welcome, Hwa Young thought. She expected they would go straight into battle once the clanners showed up.

They had to adjust to full gravity now, generated and

maintained by the *Maehwa's* much larger crew. Hwa Young wished she could say she'd miss the transport, but everything about it reminded her of Seong Su.

"Ready?" Commander Ye Jun said.

If only she'd performed some small ritual of her own in acknowledgment of Seong Su's death. Now it was too late. After she and the other pilots disembarked from the *Chamsae*, no trace would remain of their presence.

"Ready," Bae said first, because she was always prepared. Hwa Young echoed the word, less enthusiastically, and then Eun.

Hwa Young almost stumbled into Bae as she emerged onto the deck. Bae didn't sidestep to avoid her, but she didn't offer a steadying arm, either.

Then she saw who had come to greet them: Admiral Chin herself. Her arm was in a sling. Hwa Young was curious about the story behind the injury, and the admiral's escort of two marines.

"Commander Ye Jun," Admiral Chin said—but quietly, so her voice didn't carry, and Hwa Young had a moment to puzzle over why. "Your diligence is appreciated." She said "diligence" with no particular respect or affection. "Marines, escort former pilot Hwa Young to the brig."

27

"Hwa Young's being arrested? What for?" Commander Ye Jun asked.

Admiral Chin smiled thinly at zir. "We received and verified intel that 'Hwa Young' is a clanner."

The world tilted around her. *I was so careful. I was* loyal. How had they found out?

She'd served hard and well, only for her heritage to betray her when she least expected it.

For a second, Hwa Young was the feral child in the orphanage again, thrashing and kicking anyone who threatened her. How could she achieve her dream of piloting her lancer—even fighting in battles alongside her squad—only to have it snatched away like this? A shout of protest started up in her throat. It took all her self-control to swallow it down like slow poison.

As the marines came for her, she heard, as though from a great distance, the other pilots' voices.

"You're out of your minds—" Eun bellowed. Nice to know he believed in her, even if it was a lie.

At the same time, Bae's grudging voice: "She's always been loyal. Who cares where she comes from?"

Commander Ye Jun was speaking to the admiral, low and intense. Hwa Young couldn't discern zir words.

Wrapped in shock, Hwa Young didn't resist the marines as they took her to the brig. She did note that they closed ranks around her, as if trying to hide her between their bulky forms. Were they trying to arrest her *quietly*? Maybe it would screw with morale if it became known that a clanner had become a lancer pilot.

Not twenty paces before they reached the first empty cell, alarms went off. "Are we under attack?" Hwa Young demanded.

The marines exchanged worried glances. "None of your business," the latter said.

Hwa Young considered pressing the issue, or provoking them. She was fast, and she was good with a rifle. But she didn't *have* a rifle, and she hadn't trained as intensively in hand-to-hand as a marine. Best not to risk it. Besides, the long-long-short pattern of the red lights told her what she needed to know: the clanners were attacking.

They deactivated the commlink on her badge and relieved her of her gun, then herded her into the cell, clearly in a hurry to be off. She didn't resist that, either.

The brig had stark gray bulkheads, and a toilet bolted to the deck, and the smallest sink Hwa Young had ever seen, as though it had been constructed for the use of a magpie. You could maybe wash one hand at a time, and Empress help you if you had beefy hands like—Hwa Young shut down that line of thought as her stomach twisted.

This is it, Hwa Young thought blankly, staring at the bulkheads and their scratchwork of graffiti. She might be stuck in the brig for the rest of her life, interrogated by Admiral Chin's lackeys. Worse, she wasn't a lancer pilot anymore.

Stifling a sob, Hwa Young curled up in a corner and allowed despair to wash over her.

Ironically, it was the need to pee, some time later, that propelled her out of her funk. After attending to that, Hwa Young began to sit down again—then felt a prodding in her boot.

Her knife. She still had her knife. Conveniently, the alarms had distracted the marines from searching her too thoroughly. While they'd removed the very obvious pistol, they hadn't removed the knife, probably because it wasn't standard issue.

Maybe Commander Ye Jun still trusts me after all. She clung to the hope that zie had been trying to get her out of this. Too bad Admiral Chin was unlikely to listen to zir.

Still—she remembered the way the other pilots had spoken in her defense. *They* still considered her one of them. And what had Bae meant, *Who cares where she comes from?*

She couldn't afford to huddle in the "safety" of the brig. Not when her comrades might need her. She had to escape and rejoin them.

Hwa Young peered through the bars of her cell down the hall. There was a single guard. Another marine, judging by the green uniform. Hwa Young thought she might have a chance to escape if she could catch the woman by surprise.

She slunk back into a corner of the cell and retrieved her knife, wondering at the marines' laxness. They probably expected well-behaved prisoners—one disadvantage of Imperial forces, with their deference to authority—rather than former clanners who were paranoid enough to carry extra weapons.

An *ordinary* knife wouldn't have done her any good against the metal bars. But this was the knife she had taken from Mother Aera, with an edge that could cut anything short of neutronium. It was worth a try.

Hwa Young examined the door with its electronic lock. She wished she'd paid more attention to Geum's chatter about circuits and, more usefully, lock picking. Her best guess was that cutting out the lock would enable her to shove the door open.

She held the knife in such a way that she shielded its presence partially from the cameras—though, especially during combat alert, she doubted anyone was paying *her* close attention—and started sawing at the lock.

"Hey, you," the guard called without looking up from—of course. She was monitoring the cameras. "Stop whatever you're doing. There are sensors on the locks and, if you keep at it, you're going to make me cranky. And you don't want to see me when I'm cranky. Crank*ier*, I should say. This isn't the kind of job that does your mood any good, if you know what I mean."

Hwa Young's hand stilled. Okay, so her first approach had failed, but she had valuable new information: the guard was bored and really, really liked to talk. Rather than wasting time pondering other approaches, Hwa Young discreetly covered the knife with her body and decided to take advantage of the guard's garrulity.

Hwa Young called back, "I thought *my* job was boring"—not much of a conversational gambit—in an effort to keep the guard talking while she switched her attention to the door's hinges. The guard had said there were sensors on the *locks*—not necessarily on the *hinges*. Especially if the things Geum had told her about military contractors cutting corners were true. She bet the *hinges* didn't have sensors attached to them.

The guard hooted incredulously. "*You?* Boring job? A high-and-mighty lancer pilot?" Malice colored her voice as she added, "Must suck to have your lancer locked up, just like yourself, when there's action to be had."

This alarmed Hwa Young. Though she hadn't totally thought through her escape plan, she had definitely counted on being able to make off with her lancer. Since she didn't have the faintest idea how to pilot a spacegoing transport or shuttle, something she needed to remedy, she was going to have to either bribe someone to get *Winter's Axiom* or crowd into the copilot's seat of a lancer with a fellow pilot. Or free her own lancer. A problem she could deal with *after* she got out of this forsaken cell.

"It sucks, okay?" Hwa Young shot back, imitating Bae's late friend Ha Yoon at her most petulant and feeling like an enormous heel. "At least people respect *you*." She hadn't thought about Ha Yoon since her death, and that made her feel like a *giant* heel.

More laughter. "Respect? *That's* a joke. I only have this duty post because I lost a bet."

"You're kidding." Hwa Young didn't care, but anything to

keep what's-her-face talking. "What kind of bet?" She finished cutting around the first hinge and moved on to the second of three, working carefully.

The guard cracked her knuckles and yawned hugely, then fell silent.

Hwa Young's heart almost seized. *Does she suspect . . . ?* She hastily finished with the second hinge and pried it free with her fingers. The sharp edges tore into her skin and left streaks of blood. Oh well, it wasn't as if she expected to leave no evidence of her presence.

"Well, it's an embarrassing story," the guard began, "but since neither of us is going anywhere . . ."

You *might not be going anywhere*, Hwa Young thought uncharitably while making vague, encouraging noises. I *have places to be.*

The guard stopped partway through describing what even Hwa Young, who'd never played many games, recognized as an extremely bad hand of flower cards. "Wait a sec," she said in a comical tone of dawning realization, eyes still on the monitor, "you're—"

Hwa Young didn't allow her to finish the sentence. She sheathed her knife, ignoring the blood dripping from the gash in her hand she'd given herself as she carved away the hinges, and kicked. For a second she thought her weak left ankle was going to give way, but she kept her balance.

The door screamed as it exploded outward in response. Hwa Young caught a glimpse of the guard's *oh shit* expression. Hwa Young wasn't done; she was still in motion. She scooped up the door, an awkward proposition, and charged the guard, brandishing the door as a makeshift battering ram.

"What the—*oof!*" the guard cried as the door's edge hit her squarely in the abdomen. She doubled over, retching. Hwa Young slammed her again. The guard fell.

Hwa Young only had time to spare the briefest glance for the guard before moving on. The guard lay still. At the least she was unconscious—or wisely faking it.

"I'm sorry," Hwa Young whispered as she progressed through the *Maehwa*'s corridors, seeking the nearest hallway terminal. Hwa Young made a point of wiping off her hand against her uniform, aware she was still dripping blood. The crew members she passed didn't give her a second glance. Which suggested the guard hadn't put out an alert before Hwa Young knocked her out. Time was on her side—for the moment. Meanwhile, she needed to find a way to contact Geum, who might be able to locate and unlock her lancer.

The first terminal she reached was out of order. Hwa Young cursed her fortune. However, one of the offices she'd passed two doors earlier had a malfunctioning door. Maybe there was something useful inside.

Hwa Young backtracked to the office and ducked in. It belonged to some petty officer who had conscientiously locked their desk—but she still had her knife. It only took a moment's work to slash the lock into pieces and pull out . . . a stash of hawthorn candies and crunchy sesame-honey cookies.

"Seriously?" Hwa Young demanded. Her mouth watered, but she wasn't here to purloin snacks, even tasty snacks that had been stashed away against regulations. She tried the next drawer down. It wasn't locked—and it contained what she needed, a couple of battered data slates.

She grabbed the one on top. It powered on after a moment's

stutter. Its owner had hacked the splash screen so it displayed a blue-eyed tortoiseshell cat sitting on a grinning carp, as opposed to the official Starry Taegeuk and Sword of the military. Perfect—it would attract Geum's attention, assuming zie wasn't preoccupied with some urgent engineering matter.

Geum to Geum, Hwa Young typed, on the grounds that she didn't want to make it *too* obvious who she was.

A mere two seconds later, Geum called her back. "You better be Hwa Young," zie began hotly.

"Keep your voice down," Hwa Young said, doing the same herself. "I need your help."

"Things are hectic over here," Geum said. In the background Hwa Young heard clanging, the screeching of the alerts, swearing. "I'll do what I can."

Because she wasn't completely lacking in manners, Hwa Young said, "I got the care package. Thank you. But right now I need to know where the other pilots are and how to get to my lancer."

"What's going on? Where *are* you?"

She gave her location, then added, "I got separated from the others." She didn't elaborate. Maybe Geum hadn't heard about the arrest after all.

Maybe Geum didn't realize she was a clanner.

"My lancer, Geum. Please."

Zie whistled. "You don't ask for much."

"Please," she repeated. *There's no one else.* But she didn't want to guilt Geum on top of everything else. Either Geum was willing to help or zie wasn't.

More cursing in the background. "Give me a few minutes," Geum said, raising zir voice so she could hear zir clearly. "I *can* tell you your lancer got unloaded to the usual spot, so head there and I'll call you back."

Of course: they wouldn't have had time to haul the lancer into storage in some obscure corner. She should have gone to the docking bay from the beginning. "I appreciate it, Geum. You're the best friend a pilot could ask for."

"You mean I'm the best friend *anyone* could ask for."

She could tell she'd pleased zir.

"Go!"

Hwa Young shoved the slate under her arm and went, doing her best impression of a harried private. As she passed people, she looked straight ahead and avoided meeting anyone's gaze. This worked until she reached the final corridor opening into the docking bay.

A technician did a double take when he recognized her. "Winter! Why aren't you—"

"I'm urgently needed by Commander Ye Jun," Hwa Young said, this time emulating Bae's breezy hauteur. "*I* for one don't want to disappoint zir."

The technician glanced over his shoulder, paling as though he was afraid the commander would materialize and challenge him to a baduk match with no handicap.

"Thank you very much," Hwa Young said, and swept past him.

That could have gone worse.

She spotted *Winter's Axiom* straight off. Every part of her yearned toward it, powered-down gray hulk that it was. They hadn't bothered locking it down beyond the standard magnetic clamps. Who had time for that in the middle of the battle? Perhaps they'd counted on her being safely stashed in the brig and unable to hijack her own lancer.

As if her thought was the trigger, Hwa Young almost lost what little was in her stomach when the *Maehwa* executed a roll. No time to waste. She hastened toward her lancer.

Winter's Axiom. She called to it with every fiber of her soul, but it did not answer. She felt hollow and alone. Scorch it—they must have deactivated the connection.

She messaged Geum and explained the situation. Waited tensely for a response. *I'm at my lancer,* she added. *It's going to look weird if I hang around trying to hack it myself.*

She yelped when the connection finally reestablished itself: a winter wind blowing through her soul. The lancer lit up in its familiar white, blue, silver, shining like arctic stars.

We have lives to reap, Winter's Axiom informed her with a predator's anticipation. *You are back.*

Hwa Young's heart contracted painfully at the wistful hint of query in the second statement. *Of course I am.*

"Geum, was that you?" she asked through the slate.

"Sure was," Geum said, justifiably smug. "I've linked you to CIC and Bastard, so you'll be able to find the other lancers on nav and raise comms to your people. I may also have messed with the IFF so they don't shoot you down as a hostile."

That hadn't occurred to her. "I owe you *all* the choco pies."

"And then some." It was a joke, and they both knew it. "Go. Kill the clanners, save the Empire."

One of these, anyway, Hwa Young amended as she climbed into the cockpit. *It's time.*

28

Hwa Young almost sobbed in relief as she entered her lancer and was embraced by its lights, tranquil and coolly welcoming. *I will never be separated from you again,* she thought. It wasn't entirely clear, even to herself, whether she meant *Winter's Axiom* or the comrades who were fighting out there *without her.*

She didn't dare ask CIC to clear her for launch. Even if the crew wasn't generally aware of her arrest, CIC—and Admiral Chin—would be. Instead, she called Geum again.

Geum's face, lit ghoulishly by red lights, appeared. "What now?"

"I need a launch override."

Geum winced. "You're right, you waltzing out there without clearance won't work. Let me—" Zie dropped silent, and the holo fizzed out. Hwa Young thought she'd lost the connection. Then the image came back. "I've faked credentials for you, but go fast."

"Thank you," Hwa Young said breathlessly. "Later."

She wondered, with a stab of guilt, how much trouble the bay's crew would get into for letting her escape. How much trouble Geum would get into, if the admiral caught zir.

Act now. Deal with consequences later.

Hwa Young wasn't sure whether that was the lancer or her own thought. Was this blurring of identities a normal side effect of the bond? She hoped she'd get to ask Eun one of these days.

The launch rattled her teeth, shook her all the way down to the marrow. Hwa Young didn't have time to make it smoother. Her injured ankle throbbed. She choked back a macabre laugh. At least she didn't need to walk on it.

As she emerged from the bay, it took several moments to realize she'd entered a battle. Initially, all she saw was the Moonstorm's veiled darkness, and sheaves of luminous dust blown this way and that by the aether's unchancy currents, the pinprick eyes of stars staring through the embrace of night, the ruddy coin of Carnelian some distance below them.

As she acclimated to the cockpit's shelter and sank deeper into her connection to the lancer, she saw lasers, and the fiery hell-blossoms of missiles exploding, and light reflecting off the hulls of Eleventh Fleet's ships, the darting daring shapes of the clanner fighters harrying Imperial fighters. Several of the clanner fighters spotted her and peeled off to harass her instead.

Hwa Young mapped a course to the other lancers, who were fighting a tightly coordinated defensive action leading the enemy fighters away from the less maneuverable *Maehwa*. "Winter to Bastard," she said, praying the commander would accept her call. A clanner's call. "Do you read me? I'm here to help."

"Winter, this is Hellion," came Eun's irascible voice. "Get

out from under the *Maehwa*'s shadow so I can swat your mosquitoes."

"Hold on. I have a better idea."

The fighters' guns narrowly missed her.

"Bastard would disapprove," Eun said tightly, "if I stood by and let you get shot down."

Hwa Young dodged through the fighters' ever-varying formations. She almost lost herself in the lace woven by the maneuvers, where a twitch too far in one direction or another would have resulted in a collision. Bae was too far forward to do anything but patch her into the fleet's recon data. Eun was the only one close enough to help her, especially with his long-range weaponry.

"Bastard, this is Winter. Where's First Fleet?"

The commander answered her at last. "They're lurking behind Carnelian's scan shadow. According to CIC, they're pummeling the clanner outpost on the far side of the moon. Needless to say, the clanner reinforcements are doing their best to stop First Fleet."

"Gonna be an interesting fight if Admiral Chin notices Winter out here" was Eun's cynical comment.

"She's an admiral," Bae returned. "With everything flying around the battlefield, she's not going to notice one more dot on a tactical display full of moving dots."

The transmission arrived without warning, interrupting whatever Hwa Young might have said in response. She recognized the one-eyed visage of First Fleet's admiral.

"This is Admiral Hong of First Fleet. As senior commander in this salient, I will be incorporating Eleventh Fleet into my command. We will be eliminating the clanner threat in

Carnelian by drawing in their fleet, then destroying this moon and thus denying it as a base to the enemy."

Hwa Young's mind went blank as she struggled with the implications. While she'd only encountered one clanner on Carnelian, that clanner was Mother Aera—and, like it or not, this had once been her home. To say nothing of Geum's parents and the refugees on the secondary Imperial base, and all the marines, and even the cook. Could Admiral Hong really wipe all those people out so callously—all to score points against the clanners?

If Admiral Hong really created a black hole here, First Fleet and Eleventh Fleet could save themselves by staying outside its event horizon—the singularity's point of no return. But people trapped on Carnelian wouldn't be able to escape so easily.

"The gall," Eun breathed. "After asking for Eleventh Fleet's 'assistance.' I don't think Admiral Chin is going to take kindly to becoming Hong's lackey."

"He's the senior admiral in all of New Joseon," Commander Ye Jun said somberly. "He can get away with a lot."

"As such," Admiral Hong continued via transmission, "all lancer units are to report to the following rendezvous point." He also gave instructions to the rest of Eleventh Fleet, but Hwa Young had difficulty focusing on him. She was too busy dodging clanner fire.

The one advantage, from Hwa Young's standpoint, was that the two fleets were sharing their recon information—for now. Which meant she and the other pilots had a clear view of the power source for First Fleet's secret weapon: the Chollima-class colony ships.

"Oh no," Hwa Young said involuntarily.

Through Bae's scan suite and her lancer's senses, she could *see* the distorted images of objects and distant moons, too close to the colony ships. It was gravitational lensing—an effect that meant meteors and moons appeared double, and ships and stars showed as distorted caricatures of themselves.

Gravitational lensing was only that noticeable if the gravitation levels were rising to the point of an imminent collapse.

"We've got to get the colony ships out of there before they implode," Commander Ye Jun confirmed. "They have no idea what they're doing. They'll be praying to the Empress, generating gravity no matter what the consequences."

"Can you call Admiral Hong?" Hwa Young asked. "Talk him out of this?"

She lost track of the conversation for a few moments as a fighter darted across her field of view. She fired. It exploded.

"—not directly," Commander Ye Jun was saying. "But I can make a plea to Admiral Chin." Several seconds later: "Or not. Her autoresponder says she's not available, or not available to *me*. Ten to one she's exchanging sharp words with Admiral Hong about his usurping her command."

"Then I'll make him listen," Hwa Young said. Before anyone could stop her, she initiated a broadcast in the clear. Anyone would be able to listen in, including the clanners. *Especially* the clanners. *That* would get everyone's attention.

"This is Lancer Pilot Hwajin—" The name hurt like an icicle going through her throat.

"Empress's *underpants*, Winter—" Eun.

She ignored him. The one she had to worry about was Bae, because Bae had jamming capability. Would Bae trust her enough to let her complete the transmission?

"You're really doing this, Winter?" Bae's voice was quiet, but Hwa Young knew its every nuance, could hear the tension thrumming beneath the surface.

Hwa Young toggled the channel back to pilots-only. "We've fought together," she said, willing Bae to believe in her. "We're both lancer pilots. *Trust me.*"

A pause. "Make it count," Bae snapped. She was not, in fact, jamming Hwa Young's transmissions.

She's giving me enough rope to hang myself.

"I am Lancer Pilot Hwajin," Hwa Young resumed, "heart-daughter of Aera. I have important information for clanner leadership."

Hwa Young still had access to the information from the gravitational observatory. She transmitted all the data she had about Topaz and its collapse, about Admiral Hong's weapon, about his plans to destroy Carnelian. How much time did she have to speak before Admiral Hong was no longer distracted by, presumably, his dispute with Admiral Chin?

She could hear the byplay on the pilots' channel as Commander Ye Jun and Eun argued.

"I know we were supposed to stop Hong, but she's *selling us out to the clanners,* Bastard—"

"Have faith." The commander sounded bored, which Hwa Young recognized as a lie. The more calm zie sounded, the busier zie was calculating zir next move. *Everyone's* next move. "The real threat is to Carnelian. We can't allow Admiral Hong to carry out his plan. There are limits to what I'm willing to condone, even in war."

Hwa Young realized that the clanner fighters who had been

shooting at her had disengaged. Her heart lifted. Maybe they were going to hear her out after all.

The comms chimed. She accepted the calls. Two new faces showed up: a person Hwa Young didn't recognize, although zie had blunt features, and Mother Aera. The unfamiliar person spoke first. "This is Admiral Mae of the Moonstorm. Speak."

How much should she spell out? She wanted to make sure the clanners understood the danger. "First Fleet is about to trigger a gravitational collapse with the secret weapon that Mother Aera warned me about. They lured you in so you'd be ensnared. You've got to get out of there."

"It's very generous of you to warn us," Admiral Mae said dryly. "What's in it for you?"

Hwa Young's hands shook. Then she leaned into the embrace of *Winter's Axiom*, and its chilly, reassuring calm descended over her. "You don't have lancers of your own. I bet you could build them if you could obtain units to reverse-engineer. Take us in and you'll have those units."

It was an audacious offer. A *treasonous* offer. No one in New Joseon would ever trust her again.

But she couldn't stand by and let an Imperial admiral destroy an entire moon and its population, either. It didn't matter if Admiral Hong was acting as the Empress's will. His plan was too monstrous to be allowed to come to fruition.

Admiral Hong finally caught on. "Admiral Hong to Bastard," he said in a growl. He must have obtained the callsign from Eleventh Fleet. "You're harboring a traitor."

That's me, Hwa Young thought with a giddy sense of unreality.

"I order you to eliminate her," Admiral Hong continued.

"I find it interesting," Admiral Mae said at the same time, "that your heart-daughter is making her offer on an open channel. Does she have a death wish, Commander Aera?"

Inanely, all Hwa Young could think was *My heart-mother is a* commander?

"You can shoot me down," Commander Ye Jun was saying to Admiral Hong. "You can shoot down Winter. But Winter is under my protection."

"I don't care if you're one of the Empress's spawn," Admiral Hong retorted, with vicious precision, "even *you* can't pardon *high treason.*"

"High treason," Commander Ye Jun said, "or a change in our diplomatic posture? Because if you carry out this—"

"It's already begun," Bae interrupted, quite unlike her; but the situation was unlike any other they'd been in.

Hwa Young's mouth was dry. She could see it. They all could.

The gravitational lensing effect near the four Chollima-class ships had intensified. Stars and moons, formerly visible as points, now manifested as smeared discs. Light itself created spectral bursts—rainbows, if rainbows heralded ruin.

As Hwa Young watched, several clanner fighters *and* Imperial fighters, entangled in a dogfight, swerved too close to the gravity well of the Chollima-class ships and were sucked closer, closer, until they collided into the first of them.

"Admiral Hong," Commander Ye Jun said, "I cannot allow you to condemn an entire moon to destruction. You must order the Chollima-class ships to stand down."

The admiral's lip curled in a snarl. "I'm afraid that's not possible anymore. The collapse has already started."

A text message appeared from Commander Ye Jun. *I'm buying time. DESTROY THE COLONY SHIPS.*

Hwa Young hesitated. There were *two thousand people* on those ships.

But they were two thousand people who were the burgeoning heart of a singularity. And once the singularity formed, it would swallow not only those two thousand, but Carnelian, First Fleet, Eleventh Fleet, and any clanners who hadn't gotten out of the radius of collapse.

Killing two thousand people was monstrous.

Allowing those two thousand people *and everyone else* to die was unthinkable.

"We can't hold this base against the clanners," Admiral Hong said flatly. "HQ ran the calculations. The only thing left is to deny it to the clanners by demolishing *their* forward base on Carnelian. The Empress herself gave the order. If that means I give my life in her service, too, so be it."

"So you agreed to this," Commander Ye Jun said, equally flatly.

"She's the *Empress*. Of course I agreed. But she's right."

Dimly, Hwa Young understood that she should have sprung into action when Commander Ye Jun sent the order. But the monstrosity of the act had transfixed her: a planetary population, evacuated and existing under the most stringent of Imperial law, used for the sole purpose of weaponizing gravity.

It wasn't any different from what she did as a lancer pilot, except in scale. Maybe scale mattered. The difference between a ship, or an intact moon, or a singularity was all the difference in the world.

The difference between a battle and a war; the difference between a murder and a massacre.

"Hellion," Hwa Young said, "your instructions?" Normally she would have asked Commander Ye Jun, but zie was occupied distracting Admiral Hong from his genocidal strike against Carnelian.

A genocidal strike that, if the admiral was to be believed, the Empress herself had authorized.

I never met you, Hwa Young thought, grieving, *but I prayed to you. I believed in you.*

"Do it." Eun's words came as though dragged out of him. "It's the only way left."

A phantom scent of starblooms filled the cockpit. She knew it for her imagination, or some ghost summoned by the lancer itself. There was no way the air filtration systems would have permitted a moment's perfume.

It didn't matter. People lived on Carnelian, and had resettled it after rebuilding it. People, clanner or Imperial, who didn't deserve to die the nowhere death of a singularity's hunger.

This is the threat. We are the answer to the threat.

"It's up to us now," Hwa Young said.

"Understood, Winter." Bae sounded calm—too calm, Hwa Young understood now. Eun echoed Bae a moment later.

"Hellion to Admiral Mae," Eun said a moment later in a voice scraped clear of feeling, as they all turned to face down the First Fleet fighters. "We are in position to make an attack run against the colony ships. We request covering fire."

29

Admiral Hong's defenses were swarmed by clanners on every side, up and down and around, a whirlwind of insects. Hwa Young had misgivings about trusting clanners, even clanners that included her heart-mother, but everything advanced too quickly for her to do anything but move and fire, move and fire, in response to Eun's staccato instructions guiding them through the battlefield moment by moment.

She had almost reached the burgeoning event horizon, the boundary beyond which nothing, not even light, could escape, when Bae's shouted warning jolted her out of her combat reverie. "Winter, you're too close! Take this vector out—"

Hwa Young would once have resented Bae's micromanaging. Now it was faster simply to accede. She willed the lancer to move in the indicated direction—because she trusted Bae.

When did I start trusting her?

When did she decide I was worth saving?

"*Winter.*"

"Sir, repeat that?" That had been the commander's voice. Hwa Young had missed zir latest set of orders.

Her tactical display showed a barrage of missiles from First Fleet, as well as fighters swarming to intercept them. Admiral Hong was clearly determined to stop her and her comrades.

"I need you to fire four tracer rounds at the indicated targets," Commander Ye Jun said. They lit up on her display as the commander sent the information over: one for each of the colony ships, specifically their engines. "Hellion will paint them red with his artillery, and then we're hauling ass out of here before we're caught in the blast radius and wiped out when their reactors go critical. Farseer, you're the one in the most danger with no one to shield you, but you must stay on top of the colony ships so Winter has the best chance of accurate fire."

Hwa Young closed her eyes for a moment, heard the threnody of lost souls in the halls of nightmare. "Understood, sir."

She knew the situation, unbearable as it was.

"We're monsters," Eun rasped, "but we're doing this to save lives."

There is a threat. We are the solution to the threat.

Hwa Young remembered, despite the knotted lump in her throat, that she was bonded to the monster that had killed Bae's best friend.

How many similarly terrible decisions had *Winter's Axiom* guided its pilots through?

She wasn't sure whether it was the lancer that directed her now, or her own icy heart, but she knew what she needed to do. She had her orders, and the orders had a purpose.

Winter's Axiom. The season of death. Now she knew the reason for her lancer's name.

And it had chosen *her.*

Her face was wet, but she had no time to wonder why.

Hwa Young's world narrowed to the pinpoint necessity of hitting the targets. There would be no margin for error. There never was.

A flight of clanner fighters burned up intercepting a swarm of missiles converging on her position. She marked them in passing, as though they were a poetry recitation in the language of vectors, and not a sacrifice in the present moment.

She heard Commander Ye Jun and Eun conversing with the ease of long acquaintance, and Bae's voice too, crisply calling out incoming hostiles. *Someone's missing,* she thought as she lined up the first of the targets. A faraway pain started up in her heart when she realized she'd forgotten, even for the span of moments, about Seong Su.

Hwa Young lost awareness of the world around her. Just her and *Winter's Axiom,* together targeting the colony ships. She fired once, twice, thrice. Ground her teeth as the lancer's rifle hiccuped on the reload, but cycling the ammo solved that issue. The fourth shot soared free. The tracers glowed red as they flew to the colony ships: their paths would guide *Hellion's* fire, and any clanner blasts, to their targets. Now that she had marked the prey, the following artillery barrage would destroy their engines, triggering a fatal explosion.

Two thousand souls condemned by her hand, damned to fire and darkness.

"Farseer, withdraw *now,*" Commander Ye Jun said. "Cover her retreat, Winter."

A sniper unit was not optimal for laying down covering fire, to the extent that "covering fire" meant anything in space. But Eun had the more urgent job of battering the Chollima-class ships into submission. And the commander's lancer no longer had attack capability.

Bae soared like a swallow, narrowly dodging debris and missiles both. She was always in motion, refusing to take cover any longer than a second. Hwa Young wished she could take her attention off the piloting and shooting long enough to appreciate Bae's poetry of flight.

Her focus returned to the colony ships. At first she thought Eun's barrage had failed, that nothing had happened despite the fury of red-orange explosions. Amid the tumult of battle, it was difficult to discern whether the gravitational lensing effect had dissipated.

Then she saw the missiles slamming home, for a fractional moment before the cockpit's reactive shielding kicked in to save her from losing her vision. Fireballs exploded outward from the points of impact and swallowed all four ships.

"Well done," Commander Ye Jun said.

Hwa Young saw zir face again on comms, smeared with sweat and dust, bruised around the eyes—too much acceleration dodging a near-hit, perhaps. Was that *blood* leaking from zir eyes?

"Hate me later, if you must," the commander added. "It had to be done. The responsibility is mine."

The responsibility might be yours, Hwa Young thought, *but we worked together to do the job.*

They'd saved Carnelian—but at what price?

"It had to be done," she whispered to herself. She'd taken

lives to save lives. Maybe she didn't say it out loud. Maybe *Winter's Axiom* said it with her mouth.

If she repeated it enough times, maybe she'd believe it.

She glanced at her tactical display. First Fleet, its plan foiled, had reversed course in a well-organized withdrawal.

Hwa Young wanted to join up with Commander Ye Jun's lancer, like a child huddling for warmth, but clustering their units served no good purpose. Flying in tight formation was for parades and displays, not the battlefield. She cast a weary eye over the readings, a hell-scatter of alarms and proximity alerts and enough detritus to jigsaw back together into a couple of dreadnoughts.

The lensing effects had indeed been dispelled. She could see clanner ships without the distorted rainbows that heralded an imminent collapse, and beyond the ships, the sweet shivering tide of dust, the waiting gazes of stars and wandering moons, even the curve of Carnelian beneath them, a red hulk that smelled, in her imagination, like drifts of starbloom.

Admiral Mae's face reappeared.

How did zie—? Had Hwa Young's comms been hacked? Then she saw the note that Commander Ye Jun had forwarded the call, initially addressed to zir, to all the pilots.

"You are very unlikely to be welcome back among your own people," Admiral Mae said, in the understatement of the century. "I offer your lancer squad safe harbor and alliance with the Moonstorm, in recognition of the service you have rendered us."

Service, hell. There had been important selfish reasons for it, too. But Hwa Young wasn't in a position to quibble.

Commander Ye Jun appeared over video, looking much worse for the wear. Zir eyes were still bleeding from the acceleration of the battle, and zir military uniform sported a rumpled collar and sweat stains. Nevertheless, zir gaze was direct and unsmiling.

"I accept," Commander Ye Jun said, "on the condition that you spare Eleventh Fleet from further attack."

"That's quite a demand, given your position."

"Take it or leave it." The commander smiled zir friendliest smile.

"We will spare Eleventh Fleet as long as it refrains from operations against Moonstorm assets."

It was the best offer the commander could expect. Hwa Young willed zir to agree.

We're outcasts now.

"Acceptable," Commander Ye Jun said. "My compliments to your forces, Admiral Mae, and would you let us know where we can dock?"

It's over, Hwa Young thought in disbelief as the clanner admiral—*their* admiral, now—patched Commander Ye Jun into zir flagship's CIC for docking instructions. They were no longer part of Eleventh Fleet.

The Moonstorm fleet was in full retreat now, a show of Admiral Mae's good faith. The two Imperial fleets were likewise withdrawing behind Carnelian's shadow while zigzagging through a morass of wreckage.

The battle was over.

"We can afford to fly in tight formation now," Commander Ye Jun said after zie had finished making arrangements with Admiral Mae. "All units on me."

Hwa Young followed zir instructions. Even in close formation, she saw zir lancer as an elongated speck. An eternity ago she had seen the lancer for the first time; had seen the emblem painted on the side of the cockpit. The upside-down crown. She'd been the last to unriddle its significance.

The clanner flagship rose before them, a huge cylinder bristling with rows of gun turrets and delicate antennae and fighters swarming like bees around their hive. Hwa Young fought a surge of panic. All her nerves screamed that it wasn't safe to be this close to an enemy ship.

But they weren't the enemy anymore, and she would have to adjust to her new circumstances. They all would.

The flagship's docking bay opened to receive them. *Like a mouth.* Like the singularity whose gluttony they had narrowly escaped.

The rebels' bay had not been designed to accommodate lancers. Launch cradles like cocoons held sleek fighters in place. Paintings of winged tigers decorated the bulkheads, strangely festive, in contrast to *Maehwa*'s lack of décor.

The crew signaled frantically as Commander Ye Jun came in low and slow, impossibly controlled. They guided zir to a spot that had been hastily cleared, judging by the number of crates and shuttles shoved to the side. There was a near-mishap when someone inexplicably walked backward into the commander's flight path, but zie managed to avoid smashing them.

Bae came in next. No mishaps for her. Her landing looked as though someone had diagrammed it out of a textbook. The resentment Hwa Young would once have felt was replaced, instead, by admiration.

Eun swept in after that, landing precisely at Commander Ye Jun's side. By then the commander had already climbed out of zir lancer. Hwa Young was afraid that Eun was going to bowl zir over and regret it ever after. But Eun, however worn down by the battle, was a better pilot than that.

Hwa Young landed last. By the time she emerged, the other pilots had drawn together in a tight knot. She joined them, self-conscious.

"Unity is survival," Commander Ye Jun said in ironic greeting as zie opened a spot in the circle for her. The clanner words, not the Imperial ones.

A woman arrived from the other end of the bay. Hwa Young would have recognized her anywhere in a hundred lives, as though she were painted in lines of nova and ember. "Indeed," Mother Aera said. *"Unity is survival*—and now you're one of us."

SELECTED CHARACTERS

CLANNERS

Do as others do. Stay where others are. Unity is survival.

CARNELIAN
Mother Aera (f)
Hwajin, Mother Aera's heart-daughter (f)

THE EMPIRE OF NEW JOSEON

Trust the Empress. Move at her will. Act as her hands.

THE CROWNWORLD
The **Empress** in her All-Wisdom (f)

FIRST FLEET
Admiral **Hong** (m)

CARNELIAN
Hwa Young, formerly Hwajin, known as Winter (f)
Geum, Hwa Young's best friend, a hacker (nb)
Bae, Hwa Young's nemesis, known as Farseer (f)
Ha Yoon, Bae's best friend (f)
Seong Su, the class clown, known as Avalanche (m)

ELEVENTH FLEET

On the *Maehwa*, the flagship:

Admiral **Chin** (f)

Commander **Ye Jun**, known as Bastard (nb)

Senior Warrant Officer **Eun**, known as Hellion (m)

ACKNOWLEDGMENTS

Thanks to my editor, Hannah Hill, and the folks at Delacorte Press, as well as my agent, Seth Fishman.

Thanks to my beta readers: Cyphomandra, Dhampyresa, David Gillon, Helen Keeble, Yune Kyung Lee, niqaeli, Sherwood Smith, Vass, and Ursula Whitcher.

Thanks to my cheerleaders, brainstorming partners, and alpha readers: Joseph Betzwieser, Marie Brennan, Rachel Brown, Chris Chinn, Pamela Dean, Eller, Naomi Kritzer, Layla Lawlor, Jennifer Mace, Ellen Million, and Sonya Taaffe.

Additional thanks to Becca Syme and Terry Schott for their coaching and encouragement. QTP!

I want to call out my beloved husband, Joseph Betzwieser, for getting me addicted to mecha by telling me ALL the BattleTech stories when we were dating in college! Archer and LRM-20s 4eva.

The mechanics of the "game" in Chapter 13 (such as they are) were inspired by Chris Bissette's solo RPG *The Wretched* (https://loottheroom.itch.io/wretched) plus a delicious simulated "physics experiment" on radioactivity and half-life in high school physics involving doomed M&M's (thank you, Mr. Parsons!).

And a special scritch behind the ears for my adorably fiendish catten, Cloud, who did her damndest to sit between me and my keyboard and "help" me write this book. Any typos are her pawlt.

ABOUT THE AUTHOR

YOON HA LEE is a Korean American who was born in Texas, went to high school in South Korea, and received a BA in mathematics from Cornell University. Yoon's previous books include the Hugo Award–nominated Machineries of Empire series and the *New York Times* bestseller *Dragon Pearl*. His hobbies are game design, composing, and destroying readers. He lives in Louisiana with his family and a flopsy catten, and has not yet been eaten by gators.

YOONHALEE.COM

 t